WAR

of the

Sun

BLADE OF THE SUN SERIES BOOK 3

J . L . C R E S

ISBN (ebook): 979-8-9905535-6-9

ISBN (paperback): 979-8-9905535-7-6

https://jlcres.com

BLADE OF THE SUN SERIES

*To all the women (especially mothers) out there—
it's okay to do something that makes you happy.*

AUTHOR'S NOTE

Please be warned this book contains content that may be difficult for some readers including violence, foul language, assault, all forms of abuse, and references to rape. If this is upsetting to you, please spare your mental health and don't read. But if instead, you want to see how a woman can reach her full potential despite all odds, then please continue. For those of you who love spice and multiple love interests (*hell yes*) keep reading, my friend.

DAELARIAS

THE LOST LANDS

Wyvern Cove

Barhold Bay

Marsael

AVARIA

Thaumaden

Niveala

Hidden Fjord

CAVARIL

Elstil

Morgaard

Stillanej

Millaciel

Fael

Tillian

LAEVARIS

Persi

Rivencross

Loch Cavernous

Dolinmar

Sinner Bay

Galeport

Laurealis Sea

JAARN

Darkmoor

Ironhold

Crimsonridge

Sterling Outpost

Kcevi

Avralitoth Caves

Jael

BEAMUS

Harkenforge

GORVA

Markaic

Anchorage Bay

Atismoor

Tempest Cove

Kesserdale

Nixian Sea

N E S W

- Town
- Capital
- City
- Mine

GODS OF DAELARIAS

Valirr: Father of all Gods

Fallia: Goddess of family and fertility

Damiv: God of pain and sadness

Avilt: God of wisdom and knowledge

Faktirnor: God of War and strength

Yasmil: Goddess of beauty and cunning

Patrov: God of patience and self-reflection

GLOSSARY

Solveig (SOHL-vay)

Vidarr (VEE-dar)

Ragnar (Raaj- NAR)

Cadoc (CAD-awk)

Jorah (Jorr-UH)

Kaeden (KAY-den)

Batair (BUH-tair)

Malphas (MAL-fuss)

Aren (AIR-en)

Thaemon (THAY-mon)

Sigurd (SIG-yurd)

Eirik (AIR-ik)

Lochlann (LOCK-lan)

Sindari (SIN-dar-ee)

Tyr (TEAR)

Maseeri (Mahhs-AIR-ee)

Drakoni (Drah-KO-nee)

Dampkir (Damp-KEER)

Jartiq (JAR-teak)

.

CONTENTS

CHAPTER
One

TEMPEST

I've been walking (or flying) around the land of Daelarias for centuries and never had I once thought that immortality was a curse. Or at least … until the past one hundred years during which I've succumbed to grief, isolation, and loneliness.

I was always a popular and social child growing up. Preferring company over solitude. My family was large and we had social gatherings and events nearly every day to bring people together. My mother who was sister to our queen was the quintessential host and nearly everyone in our kingdom would readily accept an invitation to one of her parties. I learned from the best and became a friendly and flirtatious Drakonian boy growing up. The only thing that ever prevented me from forming new relationships was my unpredictable temper. I could be as peaceful as a quiet sunny day before flipping to a raging thunderstorm in mood by the blink of an eye.

Walking into school today, I'm excited about the upcoming Jubilee match tonight. I'm lead point on the team with Ragi as the captain, and we're on a winning streak for the past three games.

1

There's something about Jubilee that thrills my inner dragon. Jubilee matches can quickly become violent, flying in the air and passing the heat retardant disc around, which is probably why I love it.

My mood sours quickly though when I turn a corner and see Ara on the ground with Zake standing over her in a threatening manner. A rumbling sound starts unintentionally in my chest which is strange and new.

I pause trying to overhear what he's saying.

"You can't break up with me, you spoiled princess! I run this school and you're mine. Even though you're pretty for a female, you're still strange and no one else wants that. You're lucky to have me. I mean—who wants their female distracted with books all day? Inventing? You only need to know how to raise hatchlings, that's it." Zake sneers down at her before saying, "Now, stop sniveling. I'll see you after the Jubilee match tonight and we'll forget all about this."

I'm so angry at his words and the possibility he shoved her that I don't remember storming over to him and punching him in the side of the head. Oops! Must have blacked out or something. He drops heavily like a sack of grain. I hear a ringing in my ears and look down at my arms which are covered in blue scales. Unfortunately punching that idiot doesn't calm the rage flowing through me. Thunder starts to shake the ground beneath my feet and when I glance outside a violent storm is developing outside the halls of the school.

A small, graceful hand touches my scaled arm before I hear Ara's voice through the haze of anger, "Temp! Temp! Take deep breaths … I'm fine. He didn't hurt me—see? I won't let that prick corner me again. He simply took me by surprise and I stumbled backwards. Honestly."

Her touch helps me focus and the angry rumble in my chest shuts off. I turn towards her and scan her body for injuries finding none. But I can see dried tear tracks down her cheeks. Fucking dick!

"Are you sure, Ara? Want me to go get Ragnar?"

She shakes her head and loops her arm around mine walking us towards the classroom and leaving Zake unconscious in the hallway. "No, I don't need my big brother to fight all my battles. Or you for that matter. I should have known what I was getting into when Zake started courting me. I think I'll just find a quiet place, hoard all my books, and grow old alone in my own lair."

My mouth turns up at the corner unintentionally at the picture she describes, putting me back in a good mood. It's so … Ara. She loves to sit around reading and inventing in some dark cave somewhere. But she's tougher than she thinks and is rather good in a fight.

"Alright but let me know. I don't mind beating his face in again, and I know Ragnar would too. Since you won't let me right now, I'll just have to injure him more in the Jubilee match tonight. His team is definitely going to lose especially now that you've given me the motivation to kick his ass!"

Ara smiles and blushes before smacking me on the arm. Then we say our goodbyes before she enters her classroom.

I shake off the memory before I get upset… again. I always found it hard to control myself and my growing powers as a teenager with such moods, usually resulting in the destruction of something or in some cases— someone. There used to be only one person who could help control my storm of emotions other than Ara and that was my cousin, Ragnar. Ara and Ragnar are siblings but everyone knew Ara was adopted by the royal Drakoni when she was found as a tiny hatchling.

I miss Ara. Ragnar. My mother. All of them.

Sadly, all the Drakoni are now gone. *Gone.* Within the span of only a few months, my entire family, community, my people were massacred. I've spent years searching, researching, and looking for them without results. Hoping I was wrong and not everyone was killed. I've fallen into a deep depression for the past several years, isolating myself in Avaria near Lake Cavernous, avoiding our northern homelands.

Then one day, I smelled a new scent. Shifter. Not Drakoni like myself but … primal … animal. Wolf.

Intrigued, I started to follow the scent. I remembered learning about wolf shifters and a few other forms of shifters in my studies but hadn't traveled much out of the northern part of

3

Daelarias back when my people were alive. We were content in the mountains and forests of our homeland.

I yearned for some form of contact and socialization at that point, and I was willing to do anything. Many have forgotten my people or were forgetting. Drakoni are a forgotten thing and the King of Laevaris has made sure to remove us from history. Over the years, I've learned the common tongue so I could at least trade and obtain supplies in Avaria. The Drakonian language is just another thing that is lost to time and realizing there is no one left to speak our tongue just adds to my listless thoughts.

The wolf shifter scent I tracked led to an area just south of the city, Thaumaden. I observed from the shadows a large community or pack of them interacting. Envy like I haven't known before flooded me, followed by sadness, at what I was missing. They seemed happy… and open. They didn't hide what they were here in Avaria and they were thriving as a people.

I approached them cautiously allowing them to scent me. Many of the male wolf shifters immediately went on guard shifting into their more primal and aggressive form. That's when I met Nara. She came out of a central cabin and approached me just as cautiously sniffing the air. She was important—or held authority— as far as I could tell since the shifters nearby all deferred to her. She was middle aged, didn't appear too old, however looks can be deceiving in shifters and Drakoni given our long lifespans.

"Might I ask why a male Drakoni is approaching the South Paw Pack?" she asks stopping ten feet in front of me with a large male wolf shifter standing next to her. "I haven't seen one of your kind in many years and many here don't remember."

Pleasantly surprised that she remembers my people, I attempt to form the words I need in the common tongue: "I am one of the only survivors as far as I know …" Struggling to form the words and keep the sadness from entering my voice, I know I failed when she walks forward and rests a hand on my arm. I nearly flinch away at the contact since it has been several decades from my last skin to skin contact with another creature.

"I'm sorry for your loss. As another shifter in this world, we grieved for your people. I remember. Regardless of how the Kingdom of Laevaris tried to rewrite history, here in Avaria, there are still some people who remember. My name is Nara Carvarri and I am the eldest healer in our pack." At her introduction, she wraps an arm around my shoulder folding me into her welcoming embrace as if she knew I needed the touch. Perhaps her wolf can instinctually tell. Then she turns to the other male with her and says, "This is Alpha Hariq, my husband and leader of our pack. You are welcome here and we would enjoy hearing your story. Please join us?"

The alpha nods his head in deference to me which I return and then reply, "I would love some company and appreciate the offer. Forgive my poor speech. I don't practice the common tongue nearly enough."

The alpha laughs walking beside me then says, "None of us speak nearly enough and as a pack we typically prefer speaking to each other through the pack link. Don't worry, Drakoni, you won't offend us with silence or stumbling words." Then once we reach their cabin and he offers me a chair near their fire he asks, "What may we call you?"

"Excuse me for my poor manners. Obviously my lack of socialization is taking its toll. I go by Tempest."

Nara smirks at me and hands me a steaming cup of karaf before sitting down and saying, "Tempest, eh? I'm assuming your mother had a sense of humor and you were an unruly child."

I nearly choke on the laugh that slips out and surprises me. I haven't laughed in years. Then tears enter my eyes at the thought of my mother. "Yes, she had her hands full with me. I obviously had a temper … still do if I'm honest."

We spent that afternoon and evening laughing and talking while I forgot for the first time in many years that I was alone. From that day on, I stayed with the South Paw wolf pack and managed to hold off succumbing to my loneliness and depression. At least … I wasn't quite as alone.

The pack is great and welcomed me with open arms (or paws) once their alpha and his mate accepted me. I help where I can which usually consists of me flying in dragon form to obtain things or trade with other cities in Avaria. It saves them on travel time. I also help with the farming and hunting for their pack.

The females in the pack occasionally show an interest in me but still tend to keep a distance. I can tell they only want a male shifter that is a potential future mate. And since I'm Drakoni, they know we can never have a future together. Drakoni males can only mate with other Drakoni or Elarians. Both of whom were massacred. Gone. End of story.

My life *has* improved and at least I have a sense of community and friendships but I'm still lonely. To know that you will live a long life alone is a hard thing to swallow.

Then everything changed …

CHAPTER
Two

SOLVEIG

I wake up groggily with a splitting headache. *Damn! Did I drink too much wine last night with Jorah and Ragnar?* I contemplate before opening my eyes. *We must have gotten a room since I'm in a nice comfortable bed for once!*

Confused and slowly becoming alarmed as I gather my wits and pieces of my memory, I open my eyes and look at my surroundings. I'm laying in bed in a small plain room. No sign of Jorah or Ragnar.

Then I remember … *Oh fuck!* The fight, the needle piercing my neck, losing consciousness, the man with reptilian eyes. Just like Ragnar's …

Now I'm awake. Looking around, I'm relieved to know I'm alone or at least until I notice I'm in different clothing. Someone has changed me into a clean tunic and nothing else!

The flash of vulnerability is quickly replaced with anger. *Who does he think he is? Stealing mated women and drugging them?* He has to be Drakoni given how his eyes looked. Either that—or I was more affected by that drug than I thought.

A tingling in my hands and a flash of dizziness makes me feel like I'm going to pass out. My thoughts unwillingly drift to a memory of waking up confused and disheveled after Counselor Malphas attacked me. *Fuck. Don't let yourself go there. This is not the time to have a flashback. You are stronger now and you have mates.* I mentally chant, grounding myself by reaching out and attempting to feel for those mate bonds.

Closing my eyes, I try to concentrate with my foggy mind and attempt mind-speak with Ragnar.

Ragnar! Where are you? I try to send to him but it feels like as soon as I talk it slips away and doesn't latch onto his mind. I can't even really grasp his mind at all. Must be that drug that I was injected with. Or I'm too far away. *Where am I?* Focusing on Ragnar more, I can feel the mate bond still, Jorah's newly formed mate bond is also still there so I know they are both alive. But it's all very foggy and hard to grasp. My headache immediately gets worse too. *Great.*

I decide I'm on my own … at least for now. Looking around the room, I don't see any of my weapons or possessions. There's a cup of water near the bed which I hastily drink since my mouth feels like a desert. *I wonder how long I was asleep?*

My thoughts are cut off suddenly when I hear a firm knock at the door. Standing up quickly from the bed and crouching into a defensive position, I stumble a bit trying to gain my balance through the wooziness I suddenly feel.

A middle aged woman with brown hair peeks around the door and seeing me awake smiles before entering. "Good afternoon. I wasn't sure if you'd be awake or not … but I brought some soup if you are hungry?"

Before I can reply, my stomach grumbles loudly making her chuckle. I'm surprised to see someone like her since she seems friendly … too nice to be one of my kidnappers. However, looks can be deceiving as I've learned from my experiences in the past.

"I guess I don't need to answer your question. I would say thank you for the food but—you do have me at a disadvantage, here against my will. I'm hoping you're the one who changed my clothes? Not the man who drugged me?"

She sets the soup down with a clang and a look of alarm on her face turning towards me. "What do you mean he drugged you?" When I continue to stare at her in confusion, she continues. "Ugh! Men! Way to win a woman over … barbarians … all of them!"

She starts to angrily mutter to herself while tidying the room a bit. Then addresses me again: "Yes, of course I changed your clothes. They seemed a bit dirty from traveling so I washed them and thought you'd be more comfortable in a clean tunic. I'll have your clothes back to you soon. No one has touched you since you were in this room but me. I'm Nara by the way, the eldest healer for the South Paw pack and mated to the alpha. I thought when he bought you that you had hit your head or were just exhausted from traveling. But I couldn't find any injuries when I looked you over which now makes sense." She's shaking her head.

"Look—you seem nice, Nara. But can you let me go? I have … friends that I need to get back to. They have to be worried sick. I'll just slip out the door and no one needs to know …" I start to shift towards the door but she shakes her head back and forth blocking my way.

"No, wait. You need your strength back and food. You also need to speak with Tem first. He brought you here and needs to apologize then explain himself. I'll just go get him. It won't take long. Eat and we'll be back …"

Huffing out a frustrated breath I look over at the soup. Which smells good—really good. A girl needs to eat right? I decide I should at least eat something before escaping. Plus—I do feel a bit woozy from whatever he stuck me with so a few minutes to gather my equilibrium won't hurt, right?

Just before she exits the door I remember something. "Wait! Did you say South Paw *pack?* And *alpha?* What did you mean?"

She hesitates, then deciding something in her head, nods before answering. "The South Paw pack—our community. It's made up of wolf shifters. Mostly. We settled here over one hundred years ago."

"Wolf shifters? Wow … okay. That's—interesting. Why am *I* here? Also how long was I asleep? Where are we?" I start panicking a bit at how little I know of the situation I'm in but also a bit amazed. I've never met another shifter … other than Ragnar but he's Drakoni which is a whole different species.

"Yes, wolf shifters. You were asleep for nearly two days, hence why you are so hungry. If you want more food after the soup let me know. As far as the other questions … just wait—I'll get Tem," she says before making a hasty exit and closing the door. I hear a lock click into place. Well, there goes me thinking she's a nice woman.

Slurping down the soup quickly, I then check the window to find it's locked as well—from the outside. There's also several guards outside that I can see in the afternoon sun. The cabin I'm in looks to be near some sort of outer wall or barrier which is where the guards I can see are located.

Oh Goddess Yasmil! There, prowling around the barrier, is a silvery wolf. So beautiful with its shimmering coat. Graceful yet dangerous-looking. It nips at a guard who seems like it's conversing with it. *That must be one of the wolf shifters!* They're big too! Bigger than I would have imagined—coming up to the other man's chest in size. *It's going to be harder than I thought to escape this place.*

Assuming these wolf shifters have as good a sense of smell as Ragnar does, I need to be careful. But first—I need to pry open or somehow unlock this window. *Maybe wait until night?*

The door handle turns before I can attempt my escape and in walks the man I vaguely remember before my drug induced sleep. *Were his eyes like a Drakoni or were they more wolf?* I try to remember rubbing my temples.

He's tall and lean. Not nearly as muscular or bulky in size as Ragnar. He is handsome though with the same perfect and sharp facial features that my mate possesses. In fact, he sort of bares a slight resemblance to him if I squint just right. Maybe? However, they differ in their coloring. Whereas Ragnar is all dark, this man is all light. Light blonde hair falls to his shoulders with a slight wave and half his hair pulled back using a scrap of leather. After closing the door softly, he looks up at me and I see his eyes …

Light blue eyes that quickly turn reptilian when he takes a deep breath in. Like he is … scenting me?

Smirking he says in a teasing voice, "Hello, beautiful. Sorry for the circumstances in how we met but I'm glad I found you." He pauses slightly uncertain but in a friendly and hopeful voice continues: "You have no idea how long I've searched for someone like you … your scent. I—I can almost smell … I mean … you smell so familiar to me. Like home."

What. The. Fuck. I stare at him with a look of incredulity and anger. Who the hell is this guy that thinks he can just drug and kidnap me from the middle of the city. Then he comments on how I smell? *I mean—what the hell?* "You must be insane. Or as that woman, Nara, called you—Tem? I want to know what kind of sick creep drugs a woman and kidnaps her?"

His mood and facial expression instantly change from teasing and friendly to one of anger and coldness. I see him clench his fists by his sides making me again shift my weight to a more defensive position in case this guy tries to attack me. He sounds and seems unstable and I can't let my guard down around him.

"You … you think I'm insane? A—what did you call me— *sick creep?* Is that because of what I am? Are you rejecting me before I even have a chance to court you? You think I'm not good enough for you … is that it?" He paces back and forth breathing heavily.

Okay, now I'm confused … this guy is honestly crazy. What is he talking about? Also why is he so offended? We just met … "Look, you seem … interesting. Nothing against you … but I typically make it a point to not get involved with men that drug and kidnap me. I'm sure you're a *nice* man in another circumstance but—you did in fact drug me. Why? Also where am I?"

He still looks a bit unhinged but pauses his pacing and takes a deep breath. He seems to calm himself before answering. "I apologize. I—I've forgotten proper social etiquette for courting females. You're right—it's not the best way to make a good first impression but back when I was younger … females— I mean women— appreciated a man that displayed dominance and attention towards them. In my culture, this would have been acceptable but I can see it's not now … I'm sorry. I also just—have waited a long time without hope of seeing someone like you. An Elarian."

His mood shifts *again* into one of friendliness and now flirtation. Smiling at me, he approaches and sits on the bed patting the blanket next to him as if we are best friends already. My wide eyed look of incredulity makes him sigh and continue. "I'm Tempest, but my friends call me Tem. Can we start over? I'll explain everything … just sit with me for a moment. I swear no harm shall come to you."

I decide to trust my instincts which tell me I can trust his words at least. They also tell me—this man is dangerous. Caution is advised. So, I sit on the bed an appropriate distance from him and raise an eyebrow crossing my arms.

"And your name is?" he asks politely.

"Solveig. But my *friends* call me Sol," I reply with sass. "Where are my weapons? And my clothes?" He chuckles and then looking down sees my bare legs and feet before blushing. *Blushing*! Almost like he didn't even realize I was half naked. It's amusing to say the least.

"Uhh … well … I'll get your clothes in a minute. Sorry—I forgot." He runs a hand over his face to compose himself. Keeping his eyes firmly on my face he then says my name slowly attempting the pronunciation correctly. "Sol-ve-eig. It's a beautiful name for a stunning woman. As for your weapons, I'll give them back once I know you won't stab me with them or worse—leave me. You are currently in my cabin on South Paw pack lands. We're just south of Thaumaden in the Kingdom of Avaria."

"South of Thaumaden! Fuck! That's farther than I thought … why am I here, Tempest?"

"I traveled with you back here right away. I was only in the city for trade when I scented you. I had to have you … to talk to you. You are the only Elarian I've encountered in over one hundred years. I had thought this past century that everyone was massacred. I could find no trace of the Elarians nor Drakoni. I had no hope of mating. No hope of finding a companion." He seems sad yet hopeful as he stares at me. "I scented you on the wind and watched. Then I saw your features … those beautiful distinctly pointed ears, piercing eyes, and the rune on your wrist and neck. I knew what you were immediately. An Elarian female."

"Wait. Are you—Drakoni?" I ask with amazement, thinking on how Ragnar will react to this. He will be elated to know there is at least one other Drakoni alive! Now, it makes sense that I thought I saw those reptilian-like eyes before I fell unconscious.

"Yes. A Drakonian male. Searching for a potential mate. Please consider me. Give me a chance."

"Uhh … I—I don't think …" I start to say trying to find the right words to let him down softly without triggering his temper. *Tempest, indeed.*

"I will protect you. Care for you. Anything. Just stay—with me," he starts to beg frantically already noticing my expression.

"It's not that, Tempest … well I mean you did drug me … But I was traveling with two friends," I say looking at him directly to impart the seriousness of my words. "Did you scent them? They weren't hurt were they?"

He shakes his head back and forth. "I only saw the one you were with. He was fine as we left. I didn't mean for those mercenaries to hurt you, only distract you and hold you until I could get there. By the way, you are quite the little warrior. I felt a great amount of pride watching you with those swords of yours."

Then rubbing a hand on his stubbled chin, he continues to say, "That man you were with smelled like a human but also smelled like you. Is he a chosen mate of yours? Shit—I'm sorry. I can find him again … Many Elarian females in the past have taken more than one mate. I can discuss courting you with him-- "

Before he can make this more awkward than it already is, I interrupt him. "Good—no—I mean yes. Ugh!" I run a hand through my fluff of unruly and dirty, long hair in frustration. *Must find words, Sol. Explain. Just tell him!* "Yes, he is one of my mates. And—he is human. But the other man I was with is not."

"Okay, we will find him like I said. Now, what do you mean the other man? I didn't see the other one. I scented another male … he smelled like a shifter. Dominant. Releasing many territorial pheromones. And he smelled slightly familiar in scent but I never saw him. His scent was faint so I assumed he wasn't with you when I … *obtained* you? Honestly, his scent was more *on* you than in the area."

"*Obtained*? Reeeaallly? More like captured … kidnapped … Okay, well, moving on. Tempest, there's no easy way to say this. The other man that was with me is a Drakoni."

Silence.

I worry he didn't hear that last part so I look back over at him and see a look of disbelief on his face.

"Did you hear— " I start to repeat myself but he interrupts.

"There's no way. You must be mistaken … I've looked everywhere for years. Decades. A century! There was no one," he says quietly, then standing up suddenly punches a hole straight in the wall with his fist. He angrily turns around and yells, "*He's* your mate too?! Fuck!" His face flushes red with anger and then blue scales start to appear and ripple down his arms. His bloody fist instantly heals.

Well shit! There goes his mood again. And here I thought I struggled with my emotions. I feel instantly bad, realizing the poor man has been alone for a long time and I just dropped two big rev-

14

elations on him. Another Drakoni is alive *and* the lone Elarian female he just found is mated to another.

"Calm down, Tempest. Let me explain …"

"*No!* We will go find this male. He will tell me where the other Drakonians are nesting. Then, I will challenge him for you. I cannot undo the mate bond but we can share it if he deems me a stronger and more formidable dragon. Come. *Now.*" He grabs my arm and pulls me out the door before I can protest. Everything happens so fast I barely get my feet under me. Stumbling a bit with dizziness at being dragged around, I see Nara's shocked expression as we exit the cabin and a small crowd gathers at the commotion. We must look a sight! Me half dressed in a large tunic and a rumpled appearance from two days of bedrest while Tempest drags me around by the arm angrily and half shifted.

He steps away from me once outside and a sudden strong wind blows me over making me fall onto my back. Before I can blink, I see a huge blue shimmering dragon with white iridescence to its scales is standing in Tempest's place. *Wow! So … pretty? But yet—deadly! Oh fuck! Here we go!*

Not really wanting to be near a dragon when it's angry, I start to shuffle backwards on the ground with my arms and legs while keeping my eyes on the unstable dragon before me. My naked rear end and pelvis are probably on display for everyone to see since Nara didn't manage to give me my underwear or clothes back yet. Tempest (the dragon now) roars out a loud sound into the air then swoops his head down and looks at me. Puffing warm air at me, my hair flies up into my face preventing me from seeing anything for a moment. Large talons reach down and scoop me up before taking off.

CHAPTER
Three

SOLVEIG

We only make it past Thaumaden just north of the city and out of view of it before I see a black speck growing in the distant sky.

I'm hit with a sudden tugging and aching sensation in my chest and I know—I know it's my mate come to get me. Ragnar.

I know it's only been two or three days since I saw him last but—*damn, I miss him.*

Just as we took off from the South Paw pack lands, a huge thunderstorm moved in over the city. It was strange in its abrupt appearance as the sky was clear a moment before. Now, thunder and lightning rumble and flash through the sky scaring me a bit but Tempest seems unconcerned and focused on his destination. It's the rain and wind that are a bigger issue for me. Soaking wet and barely dressed in a shirt, I'm shivering from the cold being so high up in the sky. Even with Tempest's dragon being warm I can't shake the chill seeping into my body.

Unfortunately, Tempest seems to be ignoring me and unaware of my discomfort.

A loud roar rattles the sky and I realize that didn't come from Tempest but rather Ragnar. He's closer and is moving fast …

I feel Tempest's body shudder and slow down in shock. He then starts to descend in a field below us. About eight feet or so above the ground, his wings pull back and he drops me to the ground before soaring up again aiming directly for Ragnar.

I don't have time to brace myself for the drop so when I hit the ground my left ankle gives out and rolls under me bursting with pain. I must have cried out a bit because I hear Ragnar roar angrily a moment after.

Laying on my back, I catch my breath and look up to the sky. Ragnar and Tempest are flying at each other so fast that I know they're going to collide. All I can do is wince when they do and shudder at them clawing each other with their talons. I'm now growing more concerned. I thought Ragnar would be elated to find out another Drakoni is alive, but he seems like he's going to kill him instead. Tempest on the other hand appears determined and desperate.

They claw and slash at each other then Tempest tries to bite his large jaws down on Ragnar's wing. He's not prepared for Ragnar's large, spiked tail that swings around and knocks him out of the sky.

The ground shakes as Tempest hits the dirt a quarter of a mile from me. I roll to my side and try to stand but collapse from my injured ankle, instead shifting so I'm sitting.

Ragnar swoops down landing between me and Tempest while the blue dragon recovers quickly and charges at Ragnar.

Are you injured, my mate? I hear Ragnar's voice in my head and sigh in relief and happiness.

I'm fine just a sprained ankle. Ragnar, he—I try to tell him to stop but he roars loudly making me cover my ears.

Mine! You will submit! You have touched what is not yours! Ragnar screams in my head unintentionally but I can tell Tempest hears him by the way he flinches back.

17

Ragnar doesn't wait and seizes the opening created by Tempest's flinch by wrapping his large maw around Tempest's throat. He pins him to the ground with his teeth pressing into his neck dominantly.

Shaking from fright at what's about to happen or perhaps from being cold and wet while rain pours from the sky, I try to crawl forward since I can't put weight on my ankle yet.

Little mate. My Maseeri. Stop. I don't want you hurt anymore. You are mine and he touched what is mine, Ragnar says to me through mind-speak.

Ragnar don't kill him. He didn't hurt me I swear … well … not really! He is one of the last Drakoni and I thought you would be happy! Please—don't hurt him anymore. I am yours. Your mate! Let him go, I beg him. I can see him hesitate a bit through his body language while processing my words. So I then take a different approach that I know my protective and considerate mate will respond to more. *Please come back to me and hold me. I'm cold and wet. My ankle is hurt and I need you to look at it. Please, Ragi?*

I can see his eyes shift to me while I speak and his jaw relaxes some. He releases Tempest from his teeth but keeps a taloned foot pressed against his chest holding him down.

You will submit to me, now! You are lucky my mate is merciful! Shift back! Ragnar's dragon yells at Tempest and allows me to hear through his mind-speak.

Ragnar releases him fully and instantly Tempest changes back in a gust of wind to a man. A man kneeling in the rain with his head bowed in submission and blonde hair dripping wet in his face.

Satisfied, Ragnar starts to turn around to come towards me but pauses in shock when Tempest wipes his wet hair out of his face and looks up into Ragnar's eyes.

"Tem?" He squints in confusion and then amazement overtakes his features. "Oh Valirr! Is it really you? *Fuck*!" Ragnar says reaching down and grasping Tempest's shoulders before embracing him.

18

"Ragi? Thank Fallia! It's been so long … I had lost all hope. I thought– –" Tempest stutters out with tears in his eyes and returns Ragnar's embrace tightly.

They both quietly talk while manly patting each other's back and wiping tears from their eyes.

"Anyway you can stop with the rain? I think my mate is cold and wet enough from your antics …" I hear Ragnar tell Tempest making me confused.

Tempest looks sheepish for a second running his hand over his wet hair and then rubbing the back of his neck looking my way. "Yeah. Sure, sorry."

The rain instantly lets up and the wind dies down. Clouds slowly start to disperse in the sky above making me look up in amazement.

By the time I look back down towards where the guys were, I startle realizing they are standing closer in front of me smiling.

"Okay … so what now … Are you guys best friends now? I swear men are strange! First you try to kill each other and then you hug it out? Also what's with the rain disappearing suddenly?" I ask confused and a bit annoyed. I'm still shivering and wet from the damn rain and now a bit muddy too from my fall into the dirt. Honestly, I'm a mess. Tempest doesn't look much better with a few gashes on his body and blood dripping from teeth marks on his neck.

Of course, Ragnar looks totally put together. The perfect picture of confident, calm, and controlled. Oh and did I forget to say extremely sexy standing in all black clothing with several weapons decorating his body.

Ragnar steps forward and immediately wraps me in his arms holding me and warmth seeps into my skin. My clothes start to dry instantly … *Oh yeah! I forgot he has the elemental power of fire. Nifty trick—drying clothes!* I must make a pleased sigh relaxing into his hold and enjoying being warm because he starts to do that rumbling thing with his chest making me feel sleepy. *Damn, I missed my mate.*

Missed you too, my little mate. I nearly died when I realized he took you. I couldn't talk to you. You are never leaving my side again. Never, Ragnar says to me mentally while running his hand over my hair gently. *And … the next time someone touches you without consent, they're dead.*

"I didn't realize who he was by just his dragon. Honestly, all I could focus on was him touching you, my mate, and the fact that he took you from me. I think instinct was ruling me. My dragon-side felt threatened and wanted blood. It was hard to focus on anything else. If I was calm I probably would have recognized him sooner," Ragnar explains, still holding me. "Solveig. Tempest, or as I used to call him—Tem—is my cousin!"

"I'm so sorry Solveig. I—I never asked you who the other Drakonian male was. I was so focused on the fact that I found an Elarian that I never stopped to consider anything else. *Fuck*! Forgive me?" Tem asks beseechingly to my mate.

"As long as you didn't hurt her or mate with her. We are good, cousin," Ragnar states searching his eyes for answers to which Tempest shakes his head comically back and forth. "Honestly, I'm so relieved and happy to have found another one of us survived."

Clearing my throat to catch their attention again, I sarcastically state. "Well … Tempest didn't harm me. I mean—if you don't count shoving a needle in my neck and drugging me then dropping me suddenly from the sky so he can fight your big black dragon ass."

Tempest's mouth drops open and his eyes get big while nervously looking over at his cousin. Ragnar's face flushes red in anger before he punches Tempest directly in the nose with a loud a snap. Blood gushes from Tem's nose while he moans in pain and tries to cup his face.

Slurring out the words Tempest tries to speak, "I suppose I deserve that."

Ragnar ignores him then picks me up and sets me on the ground running his hands over my body. He meticulously checks me for injuries and holding my swollen left ankle in his warm hands, he closes his eyes and pushes energy into me. My ankle immediately returns to normal, healed. Smiling up at him in thanks, he looks back at me concerned.

"Tem ... why is she practically naked in only a tunic?" Ragnar asks in a chilled voice.

Tempest mumbles back but it's hard to make out the words with his broken nose that's so swollen now. "Let me heal him, Ragi. I'll be quick and then we can get my stuff. Also, where is Jorah?" I ask. And before Ragnar can protest, I reach a hand out to Tempest and make contact. I pull on my healing rune to assist me in pulling Tempest's injuries onto myself for healing. His nose snaps back into place and moment later and his lacerations finish healing up.

Ragnar doesn't let me hold onto Tempest's injuries for long since he helps me heal myself immediately.

"She's only in a tunic because she woke up in my bed a moment before I lost my temper and decided to track you down for rights to court her," Tempest says.

I can see Ragnar's incredulous look and when he goes to pull his fist back and punch Tempest again I quickly say, "Calm down, my mate. His friend Nara changed me and I slept alone. Tempest hasn't touched me in that way. I'm yours remember?" Then to reassure him, I place a palm on his stubbled jaw and kiss him gently on the lips. He relaxes instantly.

"Your other mate, Jorah, is still in Marsael. Or I suppose he could be traveling this direction slowly," Ragnar replies to me from my earlier question. "He is a good mate. You chose well. That one—he's calm and calculated. He helped me see some reason when I couldn't communicate with you or feel the mate bond well. Although, he was in pain being separated from you so soon after forming the mate bond. We both deduced that you were stolen by another magic user and less likely a human with how quickly you disappeared from the city. I suspected Drakoni based on the scent I tracked around the city but couldn't be sure since there was no scent trail and all the Drakoni are gone. Or they were … until now. Jorah pulled out some of his books and saw that there were some shifter communities near Thaumaden so it was our next guess to travel there. Then, luckily you were already traveling to me, and I could feel the mate bond getting stronger."

Ragnar pauses in thought and then looks to Tempest. "I'm assuming you used your elemental air affinity to cover your scent and hers?"

"Yeah. Again—sorry. I didn't want any shifters following me. I use the wind to shift scents away. I should have known your scent … it smells familiar but I assumed it was just another shifter in the area that she had contact with."

"Wait. Your elemental affinity is to air? Wow … that's amazing!" I say to him while he smiles and Ragnar growls at me directing my attention away from him.

"Yes. It is a handy affinity. Much better than fire!" Tempest teases his cousin who slaps the back of his head in retaliation. "I also have a powerful rune for controlling the weather. Hence—the thunderstorm and rain."

"Again *wow*! That's an incredible power," I say smiling. "I definitely like the sun more than the rain though. Ragnar, can you get Jorah? Maybe it's better if we all meet up back at the pack lands since it's in the direction we were going to travel anyways?"

"I'll get him for you. It's the least I can do after everything. I'm pretty good following scents due to my air affinity. Plus, I doubt Ragnar will leave your side now," Temp says looking over at Ragnar who scowls back at him and tightens his hold on me. "You guys can use my cabin there. Just tell Nara and Alpha Hariq that I'll be back tonight."

"Thanks, Tem. See you soon."

"See you soon, cousin. Try not to disappear," Ragnar says pulling me back from Tempest who changes from man to a large blue dragon in an another gust of wind.

The pretty blue dragon looks back at us once before flying off towards Marsael and my other mate. Shortly after, Ragnar changes to his huge black dragon in a swirl of smoke and picks me up.

Soaring back towards the city of Thaumaden we head south, he says, *Come on, little mate. Lets get you cleaned up and fed. I also want to take advantage of Tempest's bed to lay claim to my mate. No one will doubt you're mine again …*

My blush is instant and probably goes unnoticed being held against his chest. *I like that idea. Tempest might not though. But— don't forget you're mine too.*

CHAPTER
four

CADOC

The past week has been hell, and I think Eirik is just enough fed up with my irritable ass to abandon me on the side of the trail.

Eirik is not only head of my personal royal guard but also my best friend and therefore, he has to put up with me moping about missing my mate. He's stuck with me so far by traveling from our Kingdom of Gorva all the way to the neighboring Kingdom of Laevaris only to discover we won't be successful in obtaining an alliance but instead we are going to war.

Last week I left my new and beautiful mate, Solveig, after finding out King Batair is allied with Jaarn. She overheard his dinner conversation that the Jaarnian army will be attacking Stirling Outpost in my kingdom and also that the Laevarian army will attack Gorva along its borders for a potential distraction. Basically, those allied kingdoms declared war.

I left immediately and sent a messenger to my father, King Ignatius, warning him of the impending attacks. Then, I let him know to send any correspondence to Sterling Outpost as me and Eirik will be traveling directly there.

Eirik and I have been racing against time ever since. When we crossed the Laevarian border into Gorva, there were already some small skirmishes and my men nearly killed us on arrival. In fact, I have a very nice scar on my left upper arm from an arrow that pierced the skin. I'm lucky it didn't get deeper into my arm and the man who shot me nearly fainted on sight of my face. I mean—I am the leader and general of the Gorvian army. The most skilled and largest army in all of Daelarias.

We spent way too long at the border organizing our men and preparing them but at least I feel confident they are ready for a larger more planned attack now. Several captains already reported they were suspicious with the rise in skirmishes and growing army on the other side of the border.

Now we are only a day out from Sterling Outpost and tomorrow we should reach it, hopefully in time. Eirik and I have been barely sleeping and haven't left the saddle. My legs feel completely numb. It's time I admit we must stop for rest and sleep tonight. We're starting to get clumsy and careless in our fatigue which is not acceptable for a soldier. Eirik twisted and sprained his ankle earlier when we hunted for our lunch which could cost him in a fight. I know better than to push my body too hard to where it begins to affects my skills and so does he. Plus, we need to be fresh for tomorrow just in case.

After we set up camp and get a fire started to chase the chill away tonight, I plop down next to Eirik.

"I think my ankle has its own pulse … *fuck,* it aches. What a stupid injury!" Eirik complains with his swollen ankle propped up on a nearly log.

"Here let me wrap it. Otherwise, it will only be worse tomorrow," I state moving closer to him while also handing him some of the berries and dried meat we have.

"Thanks, Cad. I'll be glad when we finally get there tomorrow. I'm tired, man. I just hope we make it in time," he says on a heavy sigh. "It was getting intense along the border. Almost like you could feel the tension rising. I felt bad leaving them."

I grunt in response not really feeling like talking but also because my mind is a whole kingdom away. Once I finish wrapping his ankle, I raise a hand to rub my aching chest. *Damn, I miss her.*

"You're thinking about her again, aren't you?" Eirik says shoving me with his foot and then wincing at the pain in his ankle. "*Fuuck.* That was dumb. You've been a grumpy ass since we left her. I don't know if I ever want to get married or in your case have a mate—if it means I'll be a moping around like you all day. I mean it's only been a week or so! You've changed. She's got you so—"

"Shut the fuck up, Eirik. I can't wait to meet the girl that controls that mouth of yours one day. I'm not any different than I was before her … but honestly—I do miss her. It's crazy …" I say running a hand through my short white, blonde hair in an attempt to vocalize my thoughts. "It's like she's here—with me—inside my chest all the time. But it's like an ache I can't cure without her presence. Like she's connected to me, always. It's a blessing and curse."

"What do you mean? You wish you never mated with her?" Eirik asks raising his eyebrows. "I mean—from what I heard … it sounded more like you're a blessed fucker. She's gorgeous, feisty and from what I saw in the sparring ring—agile …" He smiles suggestively.

I can't help but smack him upside the head and growl a bit in irritation of him even thinking about Solveig in bed. "Get your mind off Solveig and out of the gutter. And yes she is beautiful, feisty, *and* insanely fucking agile but a better word to use would be *flexible*," I say teasingly while he mutters *lucky fucking prince* before I continue. "But what I meant by curse was that I feel as though she shouldn't be separated from me. I'm forever going to feel like a piece of me is missing when I'm not with her. She warned me of this but—I'd still do it again. And again …"

"That is a concern. Especially since you *are* the crowned prince of Gorva … Shit. There's going to be many times you two can't be together every second of every day. I don't know how you two are going to make that work. But I guess first—we need to survive this war. I'll watch your back and then make sure I get you back over to *or under* your princess again."

"I pray to Faktirnor you can. I need her and that woman tends to find more trouble than anyone I know. Good thing she has more than one mate to watch her back since I can't be with her now. Get some rest and keep that ankle propped up. We'll leave at dawn."

"She is a bit reckless but she's tough. She'll be fine … if anything I bet she'll save our asses just to prove a point that she's better than us. Night, Cad."

Smiling to myself with thoughts of my wild mate, I finally close my eyes. I can feel the connection between us but she's far. Too far to talk. So all I can do is try to send her feelings of affection and hope it reaches her across the distance. *Soon, Sol. Soon I'll see you again. Stay safe.*

CHAPTER
Five

SOLVEIG

Ragnar and I quickly make it back to the South Paw pack lands just south of Thaumaden without any further issue. In fact, it's a beautiful sunny day and I would have enjoyed the flight if it weren't for how dirty and exhausted I am. Plus—I just want out of this scrap of a tunic I'm wearing and to be clean and warm. Preferably under the covers with my mate.

Nara and her mate, Alpha Hariq, meet us at the gate to their community and after a quick discussion, and male posturing between Hariq and Ragnar, they let us retreat to Tempest's cabin for rest. Bless Nara—she also gives back my clean clothes, weapons and food.

Ragnar cleans every inch of my body in the bath meticulously, inspecting me for injuries with his intense reptilian eyes. I can tell he's rattled by the whole experience of losing me and needs this time to reassure himself that I'm fine. But a girl can only take so much. I swear, if he runs those callused hands over and around my upper thighs one more time ….

Control snapping, I spin around in the bath and straddle Ragnar. And with a sexually frustrated scowl on my face I grip one of his wandering hands, pushing it between my legs to show him what I want. He gives out a raspy chuckle. *Fucking dragon was teasing me! I knew he wasn't just cleaning me! Well two can play that game …*

I grab his other hand and place it over my breast which he eagerly squeezes before I lean in and lick up his mate-marked neck to his ear. Meanwhile my hands find his hard cock below the water and start to pump, making him groan and close his eyes. I whisper in his ear just to add fuel to the fire, "You're being a neglectful dragon … leaving your mate needy, teasing her, and leaving her wanting without satisfying her. Perhaps I'll have to just wait for Tem to come back and join us." I lean back in the bath and let go of his cock.

One. Two. Three …

Ragnar rumbles in his chest and growls loudly. Then, in a nimble and speedy move, grabs me under my legs, sloshing water everywhere while he lifts me and impales me fully on his hard-as-fuck cock. *Yeesss! Finally!* I think to my satisfied self. The fullness and pressure in my pussy is nearly enough to make me pass out.

Ragnar doesn't let me just enjoy it though … no. He stands in another move, quickly speeding over to the large bed in the room and pinning me on my back. He's going to prove a point and likely punish me for my snarky comment. *This is what you wanted, Sol. Don't back out now.*

It's like I triggered his primal, more animalistic side. Scales erupt down his arms in patches of shiny black color while his golden eyes remain reptilian. He's breathing deeply like he's trying to control himself and failing. Instead of telling him to stop, I tilt my hips a bit, pushing his dick further in. It's all the consent he needs before he's thrusting into me harshly, deeply. It's rough, raw, and borderline painful the way he takes me but I love it! I might very well have bruises when he's done but it'll be worth it.

"YOU. ARE. MINE! I AM YOUR MATE. AND. I. WILL. SLAY. YOUR. LUST," Ragnar yells and growls each word out with his thrusting inside of me, before flicking his finger over my clit and forcing me into an abrupt orgasm. One I didn't even know I was ready for and making me yell out his name.

"You will *never* be needy again since I am not leaving your side. EVER." He squeezes my hips and I feel the sharp tips of talons against the skin before he flips me over, pulling out. He puts me on my knees and places my hands on the headboard of the bed. I don't even have a second to adjust to the new position before he impales me from behind making me shout out in pleasure. I'm dripping with my own body fluids so he easily slides in and out.

"*You. Are. My. Mate. My soul's fire. My Maseeri.* Do not mention another male to me!" Ragnar again growls out between gritted teeth and panting breaths.

I can feel my second orgasm building quickly and know that last one was just a precursor. I must not be paying enough attention to him or it's my lack of response because he slaps me on my ass making me squeak out a *YES!* He keeps thrusting in and out of me roughly while I brace myself against the headboard moaning and arching my back.

"You will come with me. *Hard.* Do not forget who makes you feel this way." He spreads my knees farther apart with his legs and thrusts deeply down into me making me scream his name. Then he leans over my back and pinches my nipples making me bow backwards nearly in half and come so hard I hear a ringing in my ears and blackness at the edge of my vision before my upper body collapses down onto the bed. Ragnar growls out and bites down on my shoulder finding his own release. He then cradles me on the bed sucking and licking at the shoulder bite he eagerly gave me.

In a sleepy haze, I feel him pull out and slide down the bed. He grabs my ankles and turns me onto my back. I'm like a rag doll at this point, easily manipulated into position as he spreads my legs wide open for his perusal. He intensely stares at my pussy as I feel cum and body fluids leaking out of me. Reaching down he grabs said fluids before stuffing it back into me.

"Mine. You will keep it. Then he will know … scent it. Just in case my mate marking and bite marks on you aren't enough of a warning for him," Ragnar states matter-of-factly to me in a show of possession which for some insane reason flushes me with heat and arousal. There's something so attractive about a man that claims his woman.

"Ragi, you know I was only teasing you. I wanted you. Correction—*want* you. Not Tempest. He's nice enough but I have my mates. However, I'm not sorry I got you to lose your control like that. It was …" I say struggling to find the right word for how amazing and heated it was.

"Earth shattering?" he states with a chuckle before kissing me on the lips sweetly while I nod my head. "I know, little mate, I feel the same way. You make me crazy. I can't control myself with you. Just—stay with me and don't tease me around other Drakoni. I don't really want to kill my cousin. Now rest …"

I attempt to respond but my eyes droop, and I give him a dopy smile in my post-orgasmic state before succumbing to sleep.

CHAPTER

Six

SOLVEIG

I wake up in the middle of the night sweating. I feel like I'm sleeping in a firepit with how warm I am!

Ragnar rumbles softly next me as I roll over to face away from him and his heat. His hand shifts to lay on my hip and he spoons himself along my backside making me sigh. I guess there's no escaping my hot dragon so I push the sheet further down my naked chest to hopefully give myself some coolness.

Opening my eyes in the darkness, I see a face directly in front of me. Messy blonde hair falling over emerald, green eyes that are focused on me and wide open. Jorah.

I can't help the huge smile that overtakes my face which he returns. He lifts one of his large hands and cups my jaw running his thumb along the arch of my cheek before he leans in and softly kisses me. When he leans back I see his heated gaze take in my nakedness.

Damn, Sol. I missed you. You're a fucking wet dream, he sends to me through mind-speak so as not to wake up Ragnar.

I always forget that the mate bond allows my mind-speak rune to work both ways between me and my mates, whereas other people can only communicate with me through my magical rune if I initiate it. Feelings and emotions travel from Jorah to me rapidly. Love. Lust. Fear. Concern. Jealousy. Acceptance.

It's hard to piece apart what each emotion is linked to but that's what makes it so nice to be able to speak intimately to someone through their minds.

I missed you too. Every moment. I worried you were hurt in the fight after I was taken … I take a deep breath as tears enter my eyes and he must feel my troubled emotions because he leans in and kisses me again. *I'm so glad we're back together. Did you just get back?*

I'm fine, Sol. I missed you too. Only had a few bruises and a cut on my arm. Nara wrapped it up for me good as new when I arrived. Tempest and I got back about two hours or so ago. I didn't want to wake you.

You should have. Thank Valirr you are okay! It was torture not knowing but at least I knew you were alive through the mate bond, I say smiling then attempt to shift a bit closer to Jorah and away from the furnace at my back. *Fuck, my Drakonian mate is hot to sleep next to!*

Jorah chuckles a bit before silencing himself and looks over my shoulder to make sure Ragnar didn't wake up. Then he reaches out to slowly slide my body closer to him shifting me onto my back. He runs his gaze over my body and reaches a hand out to push the sheet all the way down.

There now you can cool down. He whispers huskily in my head staring at my chest and before placing a cool hand over my breast. My nipples instantly harden and strong arousal flows between Jorah and my mate bond. *Fuck, Sol.*

That's the idea Jorah. I say to him through mind-speak but a soft moan slips out of my lips before I can bite my lip. I peek over at Ragnar who appears to still be sleeping and look back at Jorah.

You are dangerous Sol. I swear you're going to kill me with these curves, Jorah says running his large hand over my breast and then down to my hip. He runs that hand over the agility rune on my right thigh before dipping his fingers down in between my legs causing me to gasp a bit. Then with a teasing look on his face and one eyebrow raised he says, *Hmm ... looks like you don't need me to fuck you.* He pulls his fingers out of my wet pussy showing the evidence of Ragnar and I's activities from earlier.

I feel my emotions shift from arousal and heat to ones of uncertainty and vulnerability. *Oh shit. What he must think ... I'm such a disgusting whore. Isn't once enough? You just slept with Ragnar and now you want to spread your legs for another. Maybe my father and Malphas were right. Jorah must hate me ...* My thoughts spiral out of control pulling me into a flashback which I haven't had in a while.

I've just turned seventeen and am meeting up with a cute stableboy named Ritt that Jorah introduced to me to last month. We have been trading glances and spending a few hidden moments together getting to know each other. But—tonight I told Ritt that I want to meet up after everyone went to bed. I just hope he got the message ... or should I say the insinuation in the message.

Being the princess tends to make boys run the other direction or I guess that could be all the guards that are watching. I'm seventeen and I haven't even had my first kiss! At this age, I am starting to discover my body has wants and needs. It's time to see what all the fuss is about kissing boys and "making out".

I meet up with Ritt just outside of the kitchen entrance. He smiles shyly at me and dare I say in excitement—or anticipation? Running over, I grab his hand and pull him just around the corner. There's a small room that's secluded where the servants fold the laundry that I thought I'd sneak a kiss with Ritt and maybe see what happens.

As soon as we make it into the room, Ritt grabs my face and smooshes his lips to mine before pushing his tongue between my teeth. Surprised, I open my mouth further and let him suck on my tongue. It's nice ... interesting. So—I try to reciprocate by kissing back and place my hands on his chest. Stableboys are always well built and in shape due to the chores and long hours they put in. Ritt is no exception. I'm starting to feel turned on which is good. Then Ritt pushes his pelvis against mine and I can tell he's just as aroused. I guess I'm doing it right then!

I moan as his wandering hands grab my chest and he pushes me gently against the wall. He smiles against my lips before crouching down and gathering the hem of my dress. I give him a confused look, then it dawns on me what he's doing. I nod my head curious as to the next step in intimacy.

He pushes my dress up my legs and reaches a hand just over my underwear while he resumes kissing me. I'm squirming in place for something ... anything while his fingers sneak under the fabric and push inside my slit. Gasping, I lean my head back against the wall while he kisses down my neck and fucks me gently with his fingers. I can't believe how quickly this escalates and that he's that interested in me! But I hear him unbuckle his belt at the same time I hear someone else grunt in surprise.

My head swivels over to the doorway which we had forgotten to close fully to see a younger guard watching us with his hand in his pants. Ritt steps back away from me dropping my dress down and looking panicked.

"Well. What have we here? Young love? Quick tryst in the laundry room at night? Don't stop on account of me. I was enjoying the show ..." the guard states looking from Ritt back over to me. Then the guard takes a few steps into the room when he notices we aren't saying anything and look panicked. He squints his leering eyes at me which then widen in sudden shock. "Well I'll be ... Princess Solveig? Holy shit ..."

Ritt takes that moment to slip out the room behind the guard with an apologetic look towards me. Suddenly, I'm alone.

"I need to go. You didn't see anything. Move out of my way," I state with my head held high desperately trying to fake confidence.

The young guard steps into my path smiling. "Now, Princess … you can't leave so soon. We haven't even met, and I didn't get the show I came to see. I'm Victor. Just back up and hold your skirt up for me, and I'll do the rest …"

"Wait. What? I—I'm the princess! You disgusting ass. I'm not doing anything for you. I'll tell Captain Mavin you cornered me and tried to touch me. He'll have you gutted and thrown in the streets. Or better yet—I'll do it myself."

"Wow. I didn't know you had such a mouth on you. But I also didn't know you were such a whore. I don't take commands from Mavin, Princess, I follow Counselor Malphas. Now shut up and let me see that pussy." Victor rushes forward, pushing me back as I punch him in the face just like Mavin has been teaching me. I might have escaped if it wasn't for the pile of laundry on the floor that I trip backwards over. I fall in a pile of clean blankets and Victor stumbles right on top of me, making me give out a rather loud and embarrassing squeak.

Before he can find the edge of my dress in all the blankets, another tall man clears his throat in the doorway. Counselor Malphas.

Shit. Shit. Shit. I'm not sure which is better. Victor who's trying to sexually assault me or Counselor Malphas who is my torturer.

"Victor. Might I ask what you are doing with the Princess in the laundry room near midnight? Lucky for me, I followed a panicked stableboy running from this direction that was telling another guard, one of my guards, that the princess was being attacked. I graciously told them I would handle it. And look what I find. Now … Victor … you wouldn't be taking something that wasn't given to you, would you?"

Victor stands up quickly straightening his clothes while I clumsily attempt to stand myself. "No—no, sir. I mean Counselor. I was trying to catch her to bring to you after I caught her with the stableboy. We fell into the blankets here but I was going to retrieve her for you."

"Ah. I see. Then you were doing me a service, Victor. Good work. I think as reward. I may let you watch Princess Solveig's punish-

ment. But you are not to touch her without my explicit permission in the future. Do I make myself clear? I must have complete loyalty," Malphas states to a shocked and surprised Victor. He nods his head repeatedly before stepping back and away from me.

"Counselor Malphas. This guard is lying. It's late. I—I was simply meeting a friend to give him a token back and he left. Victor was harassing me and I—I should get to bed."

Malphas walks towards me and calmly states looking down at me. "No, Princess. I can tell you are lying to me. You let that stableboy touch you. Or perhaps fuck you? He will get his punishment later. But as for you …we need to address your punishment. Your behavior is unbecoming and promiscuous. Are you a whore, princess? Because that's what you are acting as. Therefore, you will show me what you did since I'm in charge of you."

Shaking like a leaf and glancing at the door, I freeze in terror for a moment. Unsure what I should do, I decide to try to run. I only make it one step before Malphas grabs me and throws me onto the blankets kneeling down in front of me and shoving my dress up to my waist. "Victor, hold her arms," Malphas orders before reaching up and touching my privates. Using his fingers he spreads my slit, touches me inappropriately and inspects me before grunting. "Seems intact. Good. Now turn over onto your stomach for your punishment."

I can't help the utter embarrassment that must be seen all over my face. Feeling like I'm coated in dirt from his touch even though I'm laying in a pile of clean blankets, I don't have time to do anything before Victor flips me over. Malphas slides his belt out of his pants and I start to cry before I struggle in Victor's tight hold.

The first strike of the belt on my ass makes me sob not just in pain but also relief. For a second … I thought—never mind. He strikes me ten times making my ass sore and welted with streaks of blood before releasing me. I collapse down further into the blankets in relief once it's over.

Malphas leans down petting my sweaty hair back from my face and whispers, "Good girl. Now learn from this, Princess. Those *bodily responses you had for that boy and for me … those are signs of a whore. Don't touch another man again or I'll expect you to be ready for me next time."*

That is the first time I realize I have absolutely no control over not just my life but also my body. Not with Malphas looming over everything. Maybe a part of what he is saying is right …

I snap back to reality to the sound of rumbling and Jorah rocking me in his arms.

"Sol. Solveig. Please. I'm so sorry," Jorah's whispering to me. He must have put his shirt on me because I'm covered and he only has pants on now. Ragnar is rumbling in his chest trying to soothe me as his dragon tends to do.

"What is going on with her? Why isn't she responding?" Panicked, Ragnar's speaking in a guttural voice to Jorah.

"She's having a flashback or panic attack of some sort, I would guess. I've seen her have them before. Just give her time. Solveig's been through a lot and it takes time to get over trauma. At least—from what I've read," Jorah calmly states but he sounds sad, almost tearful.

"I'm fine. Sorry, guys. It's been a while since I had one of those. I thought I was getting better. Stop fretting," I say trying to reassure them. Both startle at my words with looks of relief on their faces.

"Mate. What happened? Why are you having these episodes?! You have been keeping this past from me … let me know what's causing this and I will fix it," Ragnar states reaching for my hand and kissing the back of it. It's a cautious gesture for such an affectionate man so I know he didn't want to trigger me by touching me further.

Be calm and know yourself. I mentally repeat the phrase and try to center myself before explaining something that's difficult for me. My past. My trauma.

The only person that I know would partially understand my darkness is Kaeden. He's not my mate yet, but he's been through his own set of trials after the years he spent in that slave camp. I think it's why fate is pushing us together. Every one of my mates compliments a part of me in some way. But … I'm still nervous. I don't want Ragnar to pity me or look at me different after I tell him. Perhaps that's why I haven't told him everything…

Calming myself and slowing my heart rate is difficult but finally I'm able to cross that bridge with him. But I'm not brave enough to look him in the eye while I rehash my past.

"I sometimes get flashbacks and panic attacks. There's no rhyme or reason to them but they are usually triggered by something. Could be a sound, a touch, a smell …" I say taking a deep breath. "Mostly they involve the years after my mother died when I was almost fourteen. My father, King Batair, who I've come to learn isn't truly my real father … he never cared for me or showed any interest in me but things took a turn for the worst after mother died. He felt I was unruly and wild in need of lessons. Punishments. He said he wanted to *fix* me. He always looked at me with disgust for my different appearance and heritage."

Ragnar growls at this but I hold up a hand to silence him. Needing to get this out while I can.

"He started giving me lessons or punishments usually when I displeased him but sometimes for no reason at all that I could find. He—he also invited his most trusted advisor, Counselor Malphas. At first he would watch, but slowly my father trusted Malphas to *handle* my lessons going forward. My father only participated if he deemed I personally insulted him."

"What did these *lessons* entail, little mate?" Ragnar asks through gritted teeth. Jorah is silently staring at the bed but rubbing his thumb on the back of my hand in support. He knows some but not all my history. And definitely no details.

"They usually were done in the dungeon or occasionally his office. I'm coming to realize the older I get that they were actually torture sessions and fulfilled some sort of sick fetish those repulsive men had. I thought I had earned my punishments for a while. Like I was brainwashed into thinking I did something wrong. That I was disgusting—my appearance. Different than everyone else. Too wild, too outspoken … a disappointment. I learned to compartmentalize my feelings and emotions. To handle the pain," I slowly say fisting the sheets of the bed.

"He—they would sometimes cut me with blades, use a whip, their hands, restrain me, starve me, anything to hurt me. It varied on the day. Malphas quickly learned I could heal faster than the average person which he used to his advantage in the frequency of his lessons. They also kept me in that dark dungeon for days since I tend to heal better in the outdoors and light."

Ragnar stands suddenly punching the nearest wall. "*Fuck. That vile disgusting snake! He's dead. Dead.*"

Jorah just looks at me sadly and asks, "There's more?"

Nodding my head, I bite my lip to hold in the nervousness. I mean—if Ragnar is already struggling with hearing I was tortured, I worry he won't handle the rest very well …

"Malphas started to take over my care and *lessons* after that … mostly. He tried to control everything I did while in the castle. I could tell his followers which were mostly guards, watched me … looking for me to mess up just so he could punish me in some way. Luckily, many of the servants in the castle are my friends and helped me escape frequently to the stables, the forest, anywhere."

I look up then and see Ragnar has calmed some but is focused intensely on me now.

"My flashback just now … it was of the first time Malphas—he touched me. Inappropriately. I was seventeen. Things got worse after that. A subtle touch here or there …"

Ragnar's eyes bulge out of his head and an angry flush overtakes his face. "He took what was not given?" I nod my head looking him in the eye before looking down again. Even though I try to suppress it, shame leaks across the mate bond from me to my mates.

A loud roar shakes the cabin making me look up and cover my ears. Ragnar is almost completely covered in black scales and his reptilian eyes a bright golden glow. He's one second from shifting, I can feel it. Smoke starts to curl from his nostrils and fill the room.

"Ragi—" I start to say but he runs out of the room and then I hear another loud roar above. I move to the window and see a large black dragon soaring up into the sky.

Unable to hold in my tears any longer, I cry. It's been a while. *Does he think I'm disgusting now? That I am a whore and slept with Malphas? That I'm corrupted? Dirty?*

Jorah must feel my despair through our mate bond because he suddenly wraps me in his arms and pushes my face into his broad chest. "Shh, Sol. I didn't know it was that bad. I mean—I suspected something like that could have happened but wasn't sure. It doesn't change anything. I *love* you. Always have. You are the one person that gets me. That knows me. I'm honored you trust me enough to share that part of yourself. I want to know all parts of you—even the darkest ones. I just hope you can forgive me."

Trying to soften my crying enough to speak, I ask confused, "Why would I need to forgive you? You've done nothing but care for me and accept me."

"I started this … I touched you and you were pulled into a flashback. I'm sorry. If you never want me that way again, I'll be fine. Just let me stay with you, okay?"

Understanding his remorse, I stop crying and look up at him. He tucks my hair behind my slightly pointed ears and appears to brace himself for a rejection. Instead, I kiss him fully on the lips and wrap my arms around his neck. He kisses me back with some hesitation so I withdraw and say, "It's not your fault, Jorah. It was—it was the fact that I had sex with Ragnar and you pointed it out while we were about to be intimate as well. It made me self-conscious. It reminded me … that I'm acting like a *whore*. Sleeping with one man and allowing another to touch me. Multiple men. Malphas used to call me a whore and maybe he was right—"

41

I sniffle a bit trying to hold the tears back again. *Damn, Sol. You're a blubbering mess now. Get a grip.*

Jorah grips my face between his hands forcefully and looks me in the eyes with anger in their depths. Surprised I can't help but gape at him. I've never really seen Jorah angry, honestly. "You listen to me, Sol. You are *not* a whore. There is nothing, and I mean nothing, wrong with a woman that is intimate with a man. It's her god given right, just like a man. No different than a man. Why this kingdom judges women so harshly I'll never understand. But you … I know you, Sol. You would only willingly give your body to someone you truly care for. You try to hide your feelings so well behind a mask but when you care—it's easy to see."

He softly pecks me on the lips before continuing: "You are Elarian. It's different than human culture. Normal—accepted to have more than one relationship. From what I've read and gathered, it's better if you do because of power distribution with all your runes. The more powerful … the more mates. And even if you weren't Elarian. You are a strong independent woman who can make her own decisions on who she sleeps with."

Oh shit. Here comes the tears again. Damn, this man is too good. He makes me feel like I matter, as a person—a woman—should.

"You're too good for me, Jorah. I love you," I say kissing him deeply which he returns. After a few minutes, we break apart and I ask, "Do you think … that the others, or Ragnar specifically, thinks otherwise? That I'm—"

"*No.* Is that what upset you when he left? Fucker. I don't care if he's a big mean, black scaled Drakonian male, I'll still punch him in his perfect face for hurting you. He should have known better than to run out on you like that. But my best guess is he was angry, not with you, but with himself or others."

Taking a deep breath, I say, "Okay. It's pretty much morning and we should get dressed. I'm sure Ragnar's little display woke everyone up anyways."

We spend the next twenty minutes cleaning ourselves up and dressing in clean clothes that were laid out. It feels good to have my weapons back in place and pants on! Feeling like a weight is lifted from my shoulders after my confession, I stand up a bit straighter ready to face the day. Then thinking of my mother and my past which I survived, I chant my mantra opening the door to my room and heading out. *Be calm and know yourself, Sol. You got this.*

CHAPTER

Seven

KAEDEN

I miss her. *Damn*, I really miss her.

It's been weeks since I last saw Solveig and it's really starting to wear on me. Others have noticed too including her grandfather, Elder Aren.

My energy feels drained like the color seen in this world is fading. I'm also irritable with just about everyone I come across and if I have one more angry outburst I know I'll be sent back to the Elaritian Forest with the rest of my people. I've been staying in the castle with Vidarr to try and help my future mate-brother and demonstrate my usefulness to my potential mate when she returns, but it's no use. I'm meant to be in the forest with my people and I'm *meant to be* connected to my fated mate. Touching her. Talking to her. Strengthening our bond. Things are starting to feel pointless.

When I really think about Solveig and me, I realize we've only had a handful of interactions and it's not enough. I need to see her. I can feel the tether or pull to her weakening as time goes on as we don't solidify the bond.

There are things I need to tell her. That I want to tell her. I don't want to keep any more secrets from her. That last secret between us nearly destroyed what we have. She deserves better. And therefore, she should know about my human lover ... Tivi.

I'd been in that slave camp and beaten to within an inch of my life. My future dim and hopelessness a common feeling for many years. Then one day ten years ago, they brought in Tivi. She was obviously human and scared out of her mind but she always held onto an inner strength that many lacked.

She ended up on kitchen duty and frequently brought me my meals while I worked in the mines. It was a slow, gradual romance but it was real. As real as you can have as a slave. We were together for five years there until she caught the eye of a new and young guard. They brought her back to her cell later that night, and I'll never forget my last moments with her. I couldn't touch or care for her from across the cells spanning between us but I reached for her anyways. Our words echoing through the silence as the other slaves pretended not to hear. Death was a fact there, an eventuality, and many chose not to focus on it lingering over our heads. I still remember her last words. She said, *Don't give up hope, Kae. You still have a long life ahead of you, and Patrov teaches us patience. Wait for the next part of life, it's coming.*

It's been two nights since I had a nightmare about my forced captivity so today I have a bit more energy but I'm still on edge. My thoughts of Tivi only make it worse as I realize I can't let Solveig, my second chance at love, slip through my fingers.

I loved Tivi but at the same time, our connection wasn't as all-consuming as mine with my future mate. Solveig isn't getting rid of me easily and I need to tell her this. Forget the war. Forget our trauma. Forget running a kingdom or gaining a crown. This is about *us*, our developing bond, and the potential for a life together.

My mind races as I pace the castle hallways on how I should proceed. Just as I decide, I notice I'm standing in front of Vidarr's new office. The previous king's office. I knock and enter when he responds.

"What has you up so early, Kaeden? You look … um … restless," Vidarr says inspecting my disheveled appearance.

Running a hand through my tangled, shoulder-length brown hair I reply, "I—I need to see Solveig. Talk to her. I can't believe I didn't follow her. This is insane … she's my fated mate and I just let her go. It's been too long, Vidarr …"

"Okay, okay. Easy. First, you need to sit down. And then, I need to know what's bothering you. Well, other than the fact that you obviously miss her nearly as much as I do." Vidarr runs a tattooed hand over his tired face and looks at me with weary eyes similar to mine.

Seeing that he's suffering nearly as much as me, makes my burden ease a tiny bit and I drop into the nearest chair. "I feel as though our connection or what started to form is weakening. We never solidified the bond or even had much time together. I don't want to lose her. I *can't* lose her. There's things I want to tell her," I say huffing out a frustrated breath. "I think I'm going to leave and find her."

Vidarr sits up in his chair tensely before leaning forward with his elbows on the desk in front of him. "I see. Well, first off that's not the best idea seeing as you don't know where she is right now and don't have a mate bond to follow." I can't help but growl at him angrily knowing he's right. I'm also jealous.

"Secondly, you need to understand Sol. She doesn't like to feel forced into doing something. So charging after her and demanding she bond with you isn't likely to end well." I go to interrupt him and deny his insinuation but he's right. "She'll come back soon and it's smart to wait. But I can't tell you what to do. I'd rather you stay and help. Honestly, it's made a world of difference to know I have a trustworthy brother guarding my back. I need you here. Sol needs you here."

I stand up and pace the small room. My tall muscular body doesn't fit well within these castle walls and maybe Vidarr is right, maybe I should just take a break. Think about it and spend time in the forest.

"Fine. I'll wait but if she's not back within a week. I'm going after her."

"Deal. I may just join you. I miss her too you know. My chest aches like a knife is lodged in it most days. But you know what's worse?" Vidarr asks me.

"No, what?"

"Not knowing what she's doing or where she's at or if she needs me to guard her back. Missing her smile and her touch." Then he smiles softly with a distant gaze that contrasts with his tough, tattooed appearance. "I miss pulling on that thick braid of hers and making her give me that irritated look."

I can't help but smile picturing that and we both chuckle. *Soon, little mate. You have one week before I come and find you.*

CHAPTER
Eight

SOLVEIG

Walking into the kitchen of the small cabin we were staying in, I see a disheveled Tempest standing there making breakfast.

When I walk in, he runs a hand through his light blonde hair and hesitantly smiles at me handing over a cup of steaming karaf.

"Hope you like eggs. Nara should be here in a moment with the bacon."

"Wow. Thanks, Tem. If I'd known you could cook so well, maybe I wouldn't have turned you down on the mate thing," I say in a teasing manner, hoping it's not too soon for the joke. He half smiles and chokes on a laugh, thank goodness.

"Yeah—you really missed out. Too bad for you! My cooking skills are well known around pack lands. But I heard there's plenty of Elarian women for me to meet soon and demonstrate my skills for," he says with his eyebrows bouncing up and down.

Jorah and him sit at the table with me just as Nara walks in the front door with a plate of bacon. *Mmmm.*

"Morning, friends," she states with a small smile, taking a seat. "We need to discuss your next move. Unless you all are staying? Either way—we need to have a talk."

"Have ... have any of you seen Ragnar? Is he back yet?" I hesitantly ask staring at the table and tracing the wood grain with my finger.

Tempest clears his throat uncomfortably before replying, "Not yet. I saw him leave ... abruptly. Lovers spat?" No one responds so he continues. "He's flying off his anger. He'll calm down and be back. Don't worry, Solveig," he says placing a comforting hand on mine resting on the table.

Ragnar takes that moment to burst through the door and his intense gaze zooms in our hands. Then through bared teeth he snarls, "*Get. Your. Hands. Off. My. Mate.*"

I instantly pull my hand back into my lap and look at the table again biting my lip. I hunch my shoulders in trying to make myself more isolated from others, maybe that will make Ragnar calm down. I can feel Jorah's stare taking in my posture and emotions. *Yeah...fuck that! Why am I acting so insecure? I haven't done anything wrong. If he doesn't want me because of my past, then too bad! It's who I am and has made me into the woman I am!* I straighten my back determined to look Ragnar in the eye and withstand his judgmental gaze.

Jorah slowly stands and in a strong firm voice I've never heard him use before says, "*Calm down. Now.* You're upsetting our mate with your anger. You are going to sit down and apologize to her for your actions and your anger. She thinks you are judging her for her past and events that were out of her control. That she's damaged or dirty. And I for one will fucking punch you in your face for making her think that way."

Ragnar freezes just inside the room while the door swings shut and shoots his eyes from Jorah back to me in shock. I see the anger quickly dissolve from his body posture. He goes to respond but Jorah throws a perfect punch right to his cheek. I can tell Ragnar let him get a hit in by the way he was braced for it and didn't retaliate. While Jorah shakes his hand and mutters angrily to himself, Ragnar shuffles over to me and drops to his knees as if he didn't just get hit in the face.

"Little warrior, my Maseeri—I'm sorry. I—I had to leave. I was losing control of my dragon and didn't want to shift in the cabin. Anger comes easily to Drakoni and with what you told me…" He takes a calming breath and locks eyes with me. Eyes that show not one smidge of judgement. "I feel angry that I wasn't there to protect you. Guilty that I failed my mate. And angry that I cannot go and kill them now. I didn't leave because I was disgusted with you or didn't want you. You are mine. Nothing and no one will change that. You are stuck with my grumpy self and for that I'm sorry, little mate. Your other mate was right to reprimand me. Forgive me?"

Smiling I reach forward and run my hand along his black braid that runs down the center of his scalp while the rest of his hair is shaved closely to his head. Then I lean down and kiss his lips. "Thank you, Ragi. Now get some breakfast because I'd rather not deal with a hungry *and* angry dragon."

"I think the word you're looking for is *hangry,* Sol," Tempest states with a smirk and a mouthful of food to which we all chuckle releasing the tension in the room.

Nara clears her throat after finishing her breakfast catching all our attention. "Now, let's get down to planning. What are your next steps?"

Looking around the table, I realize everyone is focused on me. Taking a sip of karaf to clear my throat I say, "Well … we are looking for a coven of witches. There's a curse we are planning to break and we need to persuade them to help us. Jorah read that they may be located somewhere near Nivenla? Have you heard anything like that?"

Nara starts nodding her head as I speak and replies. "Yes. We are well aware of them. Our people have seen them when out on patrol or hunting. The witches are more northwest of the town in their own community like ours. They prefer isolation from others and they like to be close to Loch Cavernous. I've spoken to them over the years since we established here and they are a cautious group but not hostile. Their leader is named Davi. Tell her I sent you and it may help. I'm assuming you are looking to break the curse on the Lost Lands?"

Jorah and I trade surprised looks before he asks, "You know about the curse? How?"

Nara smiles at him and replies, "I'm older than I look. Wolf shifter, remember? I was a young wolf when war broke out in Laevaris and the city of Elaria become no more. I remember. Not many do … but I do. So does Davi for that matter. She used to live in the Kingdom of Laevaris with her sister before magic was outlawed and wiped from history along with the Elarians. *And* the Drakoni."

She says softly with a sad look at Tempest, "I asked Davi about what happened years ago when we met thinking who better to ask than a witch. She muttered something about a curse and then made excuses to leave changing the subject. You guys will have a tough time getting information if I had to guess. Something happened and she knows. My best advice would be to start there."

Feeling excited we have a starting point, I stand saying, "Alright, boys. No time like the present. We have a witch to hunt down and I for one want to get this over with." Everyone nods and stands grabbing things around the room. "Thank you Nara. You've helped us a lot and—if you need anything let me know, but I don't have much right now. One day maybe … either way we owe you and your pack for your kindness."

Nara reaches forward and hugs me gently then patting my cheek says, "Of course, dear. No thanks needed. Just take care of Tempest. He's like a son to me." Then she whispers in my ear, "He may joke around a lot but he's lonely. Sad. He has a temper yes, but it's gotten worse out of desperation I believe. He's lost hope of a connection, of acceptance, and finding a family. The pack tried its best to fill that hole but he needs his own people. You, the Elarians, and Ragnar. Be safe."

Everyone says their goodbyes and just before we leave I turn to Tempest and ask, "Are you sure you want to come with us? Leave all your friends? It's likely going to be dangerous and tiresome."

He stares at me for a moment. Then says, "I love the South Paw pack, they accepted me when I was at my lowest and cared for me as much as they could. But—it's hard to explain. I longed for my people. Longed for a mate or even hope for a mate. That's what I was missing—hope. You've given that back to me, Solveig. And for that thank you. After watching you with my cousin and your other mate, Jorah, I realize—that we I can't force a connection. Either something develops or it doesn't. And now—I have a chance to meet other Elarians. Or maybe there's more Drakoni alive."

He smiles softly and closes his eyes for a second in happiness. "Who knows? I could meet my fated mate, my soulfire. With you and your group, I have that hope. So please let me go with you and have a chance. Plus—I need to keep my irritable cousin in line. Ha! You thought I have a temper! Just wait!"

Smiling I hug him quickly and step back just in case Ragnar gets all territorial again. "Of course, I want you with us. You're family now. Or … friends?"

"Yeah, Sol, friends. And family sounds good. Really good actually," he states, a bit choked up, and slings an arm over my shoulders as we walk towards the rest of our group outside of the pack walls.

CHAPTER
Nine

RAGNAR

Traveling in dragon form, we make good time. It also helps that my cousin, Tem, can carry my mate-brother. Horses would have delayed our journey by several days. It takes only a full day to arrive close to our destination. I land just north of Nivenla in a patch of trees to camp out and rest. It's late and dark since we traveled nonstop except for a small break so my mate could stretch her legs and relieve herself.

Everyone is exhausted from the past few days, but I know Tem and I need to hunt and provide for my mate. She's hungry … I can feel it through the mate bond. Also my dragon needs sustenance, or I won't be able to carry on traveling much further.

Speaking in Drakonian, I let Tem know to get ready to hunt. As I turn to my mate she says, "Jorah and I will set up camp and get a fire going. Go on and find us something to eat. I'll be right here." Then she leans in to kiss my cheek and turns around busying herself. I keep forgetting she knows the Drakonian language with her mind-speak rune. It's damn convenient. *I'm one lucky dragon.* I watch her like a stalker for another minute before shaking my head and shifting in a burst of smoke and shadows to my dragon form.

Tempest and I spend the next hour filling our dragon bellies before I snag a small female dampkir for my mate. After I butcher and gut the four legged, prey-like animal, I carry it back in dragon form to cook. Tempest beat me back to camp and is already half asleep by the fire. Everything is organized around our make shift camp with a large fire going, a jug of water sitting nearby with plenty of fire wood piled up. I start putting the meat over the fire then clean my hands and look for my capable mate. She's already asleep on our blankets set back from the fire with Jorah wrapped cozily around her back. They make my heart squeeze painfully and I'm reminded again how lucky I am to have a mate ... and now the start of a family with my mate-brothers. Although, I haven't met any others yet.

Once the meat is done, I wake them both and make sure they get plenty of food before we all snuggle up together and rest till the morning.

Dawn breaks and I feel myself stirring from sleep, my little mate's hand is resting precariously close to my morning arousal. If I just shift slightly more to the side ...

Solveig's hand lightly slides over the tip of my erection and I push my hips forward a bit wanting more contact. I glance at her face which appears to still be at rest. Her hand suddenly grasps my engorged hardness and slides up and down slowly. I squeeze my eyes shut trying not to make a sound but a low rumble starts up in my chest, and I'm damn close to relieving my morning ache.

When I open my eyes, I see my mate with a teasing look in her eyes and a smirk on her full, luscious lips. *The little minx was awake the whole time! I'll have to return the favor sometime. Payback can be sweet. Ahh ...*

Next thing I know, my pants are undone and Solveig's lips wrap around the tip of my cock under the blanket. She sucks so deeply her cheeks hollow out, making me cum instantly. She swallows almost every drop like it's her favorite meal while I collapse back limply onto the ground.

Petting her hair back affectionately, I whisper, "Damn, little warrior. What a way to wake up … You best be on guard tomorrow morning from my tongue since it now wants to spar with you." She chuckles in response, leaning back and swatting me on the stomach playfully.

A throat clearing can be heard from her other side before Jorah says, "If you get tomorrow morning, then I'm taking advantage of tonight. Fuck. That was …" He doesn't finish his sentence instead standing up quickly and adjusting himself in his pants while I laugh. "I'll start on breakfast …"

"Here let me braid your hair, my Maseeri," I say kneeling behind her on the blankets.

"You know how? Oh—of course you do! Your braids always look so intricate. I love it when you play with my hair."

"Yes, Solveig," I say kissing her neck where I bit her the other night. "The Drakoni have many customs in hair braiding. Some are for battle and others more for significant events. But we only allow our mates to braid our hair as tis right." She moans as my hands start to finger brush her hair before spending the next few minutes braiding her hair into a large single braid containing many smaller ones that make up the whole. I free a few strands to curl around her beautiful petite and pointed ears before finishing. "Beautiful."

She shyly looks over her shoulder at me and softly says, "Thanks, Ragi," before she kisses me on the cheek and stands.

We all wake Tempest who is a late riser and eat breakfast quickly coming up with a plan for the day.

We walk for a bit before Tempest (in dragon form) signals he sees something from above. Returning to the ground, he shifts and describes seeing a small cluster of wooden structures and cabins laid out in a strange circular swirling pattern that has a larger building in the center. Based on Nara's description, this is probably the witches coven location. I sniff the air and smell the nearby lake.

"I think this may be it, Sol," Jorah states looking down at a map and then checking a book. I swear the boy has an entire library in his bag. No wonder he displays some muscles in that lean frame since he must carry at least fifty pounds of literature.

Solveig nods and goes to respond stepping forward towards the path leading to their community, but an older woman appears in the blink of an eye blocking our way. It's like she appeared out of the misty air. Several other men and women cautiously walk up behind her with their hands loosely at their sides.

"What may we do for you, child? I was unaware of any expected guests and we have a strict appointment policy for our coven." The woman immediately zeros in on Solveig while she talks. Almost like she instinctually knows who has the most commanding presence in our group. Solveig is a queen amongst women radiating light and sunshine. She draws the eye of strangers which can be good but usually ends up being bad.

The older woman speaking is beautiful with silvery grey hair cut into a bob above her shoulders. She stands taller than my mate with a straight proud posture and hands held together before her. Her clothing is well tailored but simple with a burgundy dress and boots. It's her dark brown eyes that make my dragon instincts perk up in response. They make me think she's more predator than prey. Dangerous. I don't sense a threat yet but I feel caution is appropriate. She must be their leader.

"I'm sorry for our abrupt arrival. I wasn't aware of a protocol to approach your coven. Honestly—you are the first witch I've ever seen or met for that matter. I have some questions for you and hopefully you can help us by answering," Solveig says quickly but stands strong showing an emotionless mask that I've seen her use in the castle back in Falal. "My name is Solveig and I'm traveling with my two mates and a friend. If you could just give us a moment of your time then we will be on our way. Nara told us to see you."

The coven leader stands in silence for a bit observing each of us but spends the longest simply looking over my mate's appearance. She does give a small eyebrow raise at the mention of Nara but otherwise her expression is one of disinterest. It makes me nervous and I go to step forward putting a hand on Solveig's waist. Needing reassurance that no one will take her from me.

"I see. I think I can spare a few minutes. I have to say my interest is piqued." *Hmm, could have fooled me with that look on her face at first.* The woman steps aside and holds a hand out indicating for us to walk down the path. "My name is Davinia Kortsicov, but most call me Davi. I am the leader of our coven here. We call ourselves Essence Wielders as we use nature and life-forces to wield our powers. Drawing from our group as a whole or the nature surrounding us. The youngest amongst us tend to call us E*ssents* for short. I swear teenagers will be the death of me in my old age. Why do they feel the need to shorten everything?" she huffs out in frustration and shakes her head with a twitch of her lips. "I suppose it is easier. But most of the general population still calls us witches. It's not offensive just … not as pleasant sounding or correct. Please come with me. We can talk further in the central gathering hall."

We make it down the path and enter the largest building placed in the center of the spiral. Davi indicates we sit around some chairs next to a large fireplace at the end of the room. I sit next to my mate on a couch while Jorah and Tempest take the other couch, placing Davi in a single chair facing us and the fireplace.

A younger witch, or should I say Essent, approaches with warm cider that I gladly accept. My mate sips hers and hums in response making me pleased they are treating her with respect. The younger Essent glances curiously at us tilting her red mop of curly hair.

"That will be all, Cassie. Thank you," Davinia states dismissing the younger Essent who startles and scurries away. "You mentioned Nara … I haven't seen her in a few years so the fact she mentioned me is intriguing. We are acquaintances at best but I would say *friendly* acquaintances. Her pack mates treat us with respect and keep our surrounding community north and northeast of us clear of any large predators." Her gaze focuses back on us looking around. "Now, please introduce your friends, Solveig."

Solveig for the most part keeps her emotions locked down tight but does flush a bit at the order. *My little warrior doesn't like to be ordered around.* "This is my mate, Ragnar. And that is Jorah another of my mates. Tempest is next to him and cousin to Ragnar," she explains, nodding to each of us. We all mutter greetings to Davi who sits regally in her chair and nods back respectfully.

"Well met. Please tell me why an Elarian, a human and two Drakoni have unexpectedly arrived on my doorstep? I must say it has been about one hundred and twenty years since I've seen your kind—Elarian—and Drakoni—that is."

CHAPTER
Ten

SOLVEIG

I can't help but be shocked that Davinia, or should I say Davi, immediately can tell what we each are. I tilt my head a bit and sniff myself. *Maybe—I smell different?* Then I lean towards Ragnar subtly and sniff him. *Mmm, damn. He always smells good. Maybe that's a Drakoni thing and she can tell?*

Chuckling echoes in my head before Ragnar mentally says, *You are amusing, little mate. Stop sniffing everyone. You do carry a scent, but only us shifters use scents to identify others. And other Drakonian males had better not smell as good as me. It's a mate thing.*

Damn it, Ragi! Stop listening to my thoughts!

Sorry. Couldn't help it. I enjoy your mindful banter. But you're right. We should put up extra shields around these Essents. I'm not sure if they have any mind-speak ability. Keep me connected to you though mentally.

"How do you know what we are? Is that—one of your abilities? Also you don't seem much older than forty regardless of your grey hair, forgive my forwardness," I tell Davi.

Davi chuckles showing her first sign of amusement since we got here and smiles a bit at me while I flush a bit in embarrassment. *Really, Sol? Why are you commenting on her age!*

"I am older than I appear. Most Essents are, since we age slowly, and as for my grey hair … I've been dealing with this since I was in my twenties! Ha! I blame my parents. And unfortunately no spell can make this head keep a different color. Not from lack of trying though! As for our abilities—no, we can't sense what others are but Essence Wielders are masters of observation. Some of our first training comes in the form of observing nature and our surroundings. Picking up on magic and life forces."

She pauses, looking at me, her gaze flicking up to my delicately pointed ears then over to my slightly almond shaped sapphire blue eyes.

"Your features are a dead giveaway of your Elarian heritage. I've only seen Elarians back in the Lost Lands, specifically in the Elaritian Forest. Your people tend to stick close to nature and the forest. You're not the most sociable of people but neither are we. Then you mentioned Ragnar here is your mate and I can tell from the mate marking on his neck that this is true. I'm a bit unsure what the rune on your neck and temple stand for but I suppose it could be similar to his …."

She pauses raising an eyebrow to which I don't answer. Then she continues her assessment: "Ragnar and even Tempest demonstrate—how do I say this—a predator-like focus on people. Their gazes are intense and unblinking most of the time. At first, I thought he was a wolf shifter like Nara, but then he moved too fluidly for his bulk of a body to be a wolf. For a second, I saw his eyes change—narrow if you will when he looked at you, Solveig. The only species that has those eyes are Drakoni. Then I deduced that since Tempest is his cousin, he is Drakoni as well. Jorah was the easiest of you all. His mannerisms and body habits portray human and he carries an openness in his eyes. Humans are too trusting but are dangerous in their own ways. Safety in numbers and all that. Their population seems to grow exponentially while ours struggle for fertility and are slow in growth."

"Ooo-kay. Wow. That's—a lot," I slowly say. *Real articulate, Solveig!* I'm amazed that she came up with that in the five-ten minutes we arrived.

"If we've established who we all are now, can you please let me know why you are here? I'm actually growing rather curious seeing as all the Elarians and Drakoni are extinct or—they were," Davi states.

"Well, Mistress Davinia … you see—" Jorah respectfully starts to say.

"Just Davi," she interrupts.

Jorah nods and continues. "We are looking for the answer on how to break a curse …"

Davi squints her brown eyes and shifts them over to me then back to Jorah. "A curse? Do you know who placed it?" she asks.

"No, we don't know who placed it. Only that it was done by a witch, sorry, an Essent," Jorah replies.

Throwing caution to the wind and following my instincts, I decide to trust this woman. She's done nothing but be honest with us and Nara trusted her enough to send us here. Also— time is ticking. I need to get back to my other mates. Oh and deal with the whole war thing. You know—small things. "We are trying to break the curse that was placed on the city of Elaria and restore balance to the Lost Lands. The Elarians cannot re- turn home until we can do this. My grandfather told me that a witch placed the curse."

Shocked speechless, she sputters a bit and stands up sudden- ly. Ragnar tenses up beside me expecting an attack of some sort but instead Davi paces next to our chairs in distress. It's such a drastic change in her behavior that even I'm starting to get a bit nervous.

"Look—I'm sorry if we upset you. We just … need answers. Many people are depending on us," I say pleadingly.

Davi takes a deep breath and stops her pacing. "Damn. I always knew her actions would follow us here. I'm sorry but I can't help you with that curse," she says while I start to interrupt. Throwing her hands up she continues, "The curse wasn't done by me or any in my coven. I can assure you of that. Curses must be undone by the creator of them or their descendants. They are powerful and binding which is why many fear us upon the threat of them. They also take a lot of power and life-force to perform which is why many Essents don't do them lightly."

Instantly my hope withers down with her words and I can see Jorah's frustrated expression before pulling out another book. Likely to search for another location of Essents.

"But—I—I know who placed that curse. I've suspected it for some time. Yes … it must be her." Davi softly says.

"Who?" I ask feeling a spark of hope light in my chest.

"Navelia. My twin sister," Davi replies into the silent room.

CHAPTER
Eleven

S ister? What the *fuck*?" Tempest yells out loudly standing up
and fisting his hands at his sides in anger. "You said no one
in this coven did it! Liar! Do you know how many people
died in that massacre a hundred years ago? Do you know how
many people we lost! Then— not only was everyone dead but
we couldn't even step foot in Elaria, the root of our power, part
of our home. Some selfish *bitch*, your sister apparently, placed
an unbreakable curse to help a self-serving egotistical monarch!"

He stands there staring her down while his light blue eyes
become more reptilian and a few blue scales develop on his arms.
Thunder can be heard booming outside the building and a flash
of sudden lightening streaks across the sky that was just clear a
moment ago.

Davi stands still under his predatorial gaze but instead of
fear, I see … awe. Ragnar stands blocking Tempest's line of sight
and mutters something to him in Drakoni that is too soft for me
to hear but slowly calms him. Ragnar pats him on the back while
Tempest stomps over to look out the window.

"Well, I've never … amazing!" Davi says before shaking her head and putting her disinterested expression back on her face. "I'm sorry for the confusion. But yes—my sister must have placed that curse. She's the only other one capable of doing so, the only one powerful enough other than me, and I've suspected for some time. She isn't part of my coven anymore, hasn't been in some time. So, you see … I didn't lie to you. She lives in the city of Dolinmaar. That's in the Kingdom of Cavaril. She started her own coven over there after we had a disagreement …"

Davi grits her teeth angrily before resuming.

"I've heard from my sources that her coven is small but strong. Just—beware. My sister changed just before that curse was placed. She was an exceptional Essence Wielder, strong, confident, focused, and compassionate. We were close at one point as twins usually are … but a man had come between us. I told her she was crazy. The man was married and he would never leave his wife for her but she wouldn't listen. She said he asked her to place a curse and if she could do it then he would leave his wife and instead marry her. We argued and I worried how much he had changed her. It was like he had brainwashed her giving her that ultimatum. She knew curses drained the life force of the essence wielder and some of the nature in the area, but she thought it was worth it, for him!"

Davi wipes her eyes a bit which had teared up.

"She would lose years of her life but told me she didn't care. I told her not to return to our coven especially if she placed such a curse and that was the last time I saw her over a hundred years ago."

I decide to again trust my instincts, and I can tell Davi truly regrets letting her sister go. She's torn and distraught at losing someone so close to her, a twin! Standing and approaching cautiously, I reach out and placed a gentle hand on her forearm in comfort. At first, she flinches in surprise then settles and places a hand over mine.

"Thank you, child. It's been quite a while since someone showed me comfort just because they care."

"I'm sorry for your sadness. You seem to have cared for her but thank you—we now have a place to look next. I know it must have been hard to share that since she is your sister," I say leaning back. "If you need something in the future, let me know. I may be able to help … as a friend someday."

Davi nods her head and smiles down at me in a maternal way. "You're a sweet Elarian. I may just take you up on that offer however who are you to be able to offer favors and where would I find you? I'm assuming you don't live in Avaria or I would have heard of you. Your kind are rather noticeable."

"Well I'm—" I start to say nervously when a new voice interrupts me.

"She's Princess Solveig of the Kingdom of Laevaris! And now—Queen of Laevaris!" The red-headed younger Essent named Cassie runs into the room waving around a letter with a white owl resting on her shoulders. "Davi! I can't believe it! She's queen now!"

My hands instantly become clammy with nerves, and I look over to my mates while Tempest comes over and stands at my back protectively.

Davi raises an eyebrow at me while she grabs the letter and reads it.

Good morning, Princess Solveig. I hear an aristocratic voice in my head and look around in confusion as Davi reads the letter. My mind races with the knowledge that I've been outed as a princess and is confused on who spoke to me through my mind. Then it dawns on me that it wasn't mind-speak with a person but rather…

Over here, Princess. I look over to the white owl perched on Cassie with a focused gaze. *I'm Fiona. Eldest of hatchlings east of Loch Cavernous. Welcome and greetings. I'm the one who brought this correspondence to my lady, Davinia. She tends to me, provides many mice, and in return I transport messages for her. Davinia has many spies and I make sure she is well informed. I've always wanted to speak to someone other than an uneducated bird …*

Wow. I've never "spoken" to an owl before and man are they wordy. I thought Tyr, my goshawk, was talkative but this bird puts him to shame. She keeps spouting out information making it hard to focus on each thing.

Greetings, Fiona. Beautiful name, I project to her thinking she may like flattery similar to my hawk. *You were in my kingdom, Laevaris?*

Yes, Princess. I'm so glad to finally speak! And to royalty! Your kingdom is rather dull though and the city is smoky! Hard to fly by. It was hard to find a smart enough bird to speak with, but I met a friend of yours, a brawny hawk. I could almost see her swoon in my mind, but then she rustles her wings continuing. *Unfortunately, he had a mate. He told me that the King was killed. Some other men took over and your kingdom is a bit chaotic at the moment. He was searching for you and I've no doubt that hawk will eventually find you.*

Smiling hugely at the thought of reuniting with Tyr and his mate Allira, I get my first sense of homesickness. But then I'm confused and alarmed with conflicting feelings on what Fiona just told me … my father is—*dead?*

"Cassie, might I ask how you know this is Princess Solveig? Also what did I tell you about interrupting meetings and also reading my *confidential* messages?" Davi says in a stern voice looking down her nose at the poor girl.

"Ugh—I'm sorry?" Davi clears her throat loudly. "It won't happen again?" Cassie says—or asks, I'm not sure—before she sighs defeatedly. "You know my uncle lives in Falal, the capital city of Laevaris. I haven't been to visit him in two or three years … but the last time I was there, I saw her."

Cassie tilts her head and points a finger at me. "She was in a carriage with some other royalty for the spring festival. My uncle told me who she was and I'd know her anywhere. I mean—she's pretty memorable with her looks and all."

Then Cassie looks at me apologetically holding her hands up before saying, "Not in a bad way … I mean—you're gorgeous! Stunning even! I wanted to introduce myself earlier … I'm Cassie. And I'd *love* to get to know you if you know what I mean." She winks and shrugs her eyebrows up and down comically so I can't help but laugh.

"Thank you and no offense taken. Nice to meet you, Cassie … these two men are my *mates*," I slowly say.

Her nose scrunches up in dismay before she says, "And … you don't swing both ways I take it—since both mates are male?"

I shake my head with a smile while Davi interrupts with a frustrated sound, "If you are quite done, Cassie, I'd like to speak with my guests on more important matters than your relationship preferences."

Cassie winks at me and then giving her elder a properly chastised look leaves the room, but Fiona flaps her wings and soars over to Davi's shoulders to perch there silently.

"Well, is this true? You are *Princess* Solveig? Funny how you left out that small piece of information in your introductions," Davi says with an irritated look.

I run a hand over my braid pulling it over my shoulder nervously. "Yes. I am. I wasn't trying to be secretive, but you can imagine how that could alter how much people would help us. I mean my father didn't have the best reputation."

"Yes, well, based on this message. Your father is gone and *you,* child, are now the future—or uncrowned queen of the Kingdom of Laevaris."

Jorah takes that moment to walk over and asks to look over the correspondence. After reading it, he nods his head and looks over at me. I suck in a sharp breath and realize I don't feel one speck of sadness for the loss of my supposed father. All I feel is cheated. He's gone and I'll never have any answers. Why did he hate me so much? Did he know I wasn't truly his daughter? If so, why did he claim me as his child? Why would he let Malphas torture me? And then I'm suddenly concerned … where is Counselor Malphas? I guess none of these questions will get answered now.

I grab the letter and look it over but there's no mention of Malphas.

Fiona, did you … hear anything, a rumor, about another man … a man close to the King? I need to know if that man is still alive or if he's dead like the King…

Her owlish eyes zero in on me before her head tilts a bit in thought. *No. I didn't hear anything about another man. Your hawk friend didn't mention it. This man … he was important to you? He was in the castle?*

Blowing out a frustrated breath, I answer her, *Yes, he was … important but not in a good way. I just want … no, I need to know what happened to him.*

Fiona, the sweet and intelligent owl that she is, chirps in distress obviously seeing that this information means something to me but she's unable to provide it. *I can go back … find out from your friend? But, princess, I will say there was a lot of smoke in the air and the castle was damaged.*

Thinking wishful thoughts, I mentally say, *No. Rest, Fiona, I appreciate the thought and hopefully he's gone like the King.*

Frustrated, exhausted and now confused, I hunch forward in defeat. I'm overwhelmed. What do I do now? Do I go back to Laevaris? My people need me …

Strong arms wrap around me from my front and back holding me up and strengthening me. My mates. They must have felt my fatigue and darkening thoughts through the mate bond prompting them to comfort me.

"I think we've discovered all we can for today. We will leave now as my mate is exhausted and this is concerning news for us. Please accept our thanks for your help," Ragnar states firmly tucking me under his arm with Jorah on my other side. Tempest takes up my back protectively watching the room.

"Very well. I apologize I can't help you more, Solveig. Please accept our guest cabin to stay in tonight. I'll send you food and refreshments and you can leave in the morning if you wish."

Solveig, let me know if you need me to send a message for you. In return, I'd appreciate you telling Davinia to stop giving me dead mice. I prefer live mice. The little black ones are best. I'll stop by your window in a bit to see if you need me.

Surprised by the second offer, I agree to both parties. Then I say to Davi as we are being escorted to the cabin, "Fiona says she doesn't like dead mice for her meals. She prefers *alive,* little black mice and would be appreciative. Also can you provide me with some paper and ink?"

Davi's head whips around so fast to me you would think it could break right off. "What did you say?"

"I said—"

"No, I'm sorry. I heard you. I was just surprised. How did you—never mind. All of you keep surprising me. You will be good allies to have, and I will stay in contact in the future. Fiona, is that what you called her?"

I nod my head in response.

"Pretty name. I was just calling her Snow but I suppose Fiona fits her more." She affectionately pets Fiona's feathered belly. "I'll make sure her requests are fulfilled. Thank you and the desk within your cabin should have everything you need. Goodnight," she says waving us to a small cabin three houses down from the gathering hall.

Food arrives shortly after we clean ourselves up. Tempest crashes immediately in one room while Jorah, Ragnar and I all settle down in the large bed of the only other room. Everyone's exhausted including me.

I wake when its dark outside the window, only a few hours later based on the moon. *Why am I awake?* Then I hear the tapping on the window by the desk.

Fiona! I practically shout towards her. Her feathers ruffle a bit as I scurry over to open the window quietly letting her in so she can hop onto the desk.

Yes, princess. It is I! No need to shout! Do you have a message?

Sorry. Yes, here, I say attaching the rolled up letter in a leather case to a strap on her foot. *I need it to go to Galeport in the Kingdom of Beamus.* Then I project to her a mental picture of my friend and a picture of one of her many hideouts in the city. *If she's not there, then you can try the palace since she works there but … I'd prefer not.*

No issue. I will get it there. Owls have good eyesight. If she's in the city, I'll see her. Safe travels, princess, Fiona projects back before hopping out the window and soaring off in a streak of white.

CHAPTER
Twelve

SOLVEIG

It takes nearly three days for us to travel to Dolinmaar, mostly because of the weather and how exhausted Ragnar and Tempest are. We travel south and rest a bit before flying over the Hidden Fjord. Bless Valirr that the Essents restocked our supplies before we left, or our journey would take even longer. Crossing the Fjord is dangerous, weather is unpredictable even with Tempest trying to control it. Wind and rain attempts to pull us off course many times, and it's a damn blessing we have Tem to manipulate the weather allowing us to make it through without injury or getting lost. I can tell he's exhausted by the paleness and strain of his face when we land in the Kingdom of Cavaril.

From there, we travel across the land slowly towards Dolinmaar. My Drakoni companions have to stop and hunt frequently to regain their strength and energy. Something about being this far south is manipulating their energy and they're more fatigued by my observation. I too am starting to feel some strain but unlike them, I can sleep in Ragnar's clutches while we fly towards our destination. Jorah on the other hand seems to have enough energy for all of us, constantly chatting away and pointing out landmarks. He spouts off facts about this mysterious kingdom in a steady stream of commentary.

We arrive in the city of Dolinmaar in the morning on the third day of travel. Ragnar walks confidently down a Main Street in the city to a local inn and procures us a room to rest in. Given the early hour, the innkeeper only has one room available which we gratefully take. After eating breakfast that's sent to the room, we all fall asleep haphazardly throughout the room. It has a large bed and somehow we all fit with Tempest sleeping at the foot of the bed.

I wake up to Jorah and Ragnar talking quietly over my head. Stretching my arms and legs out, I hear a loud grunt then the sound of a body falling to the ground. *Oops! I forgot about Tempest down there!*

Tem's disheveled blonde head pops up a moment later over the end of the bed with a look of irritation on his face while Ragnar and Jorah start to laugh.

"Sorry, Tem! Honestly, I'm sorry!" I say holding my hands up apologetically before he loses his temper. "I forgot you were down there! Are you okay?"

Soft muttering about flailing princesses and uncomfortable beds can be heard in Drakonian before he says in an irritated voice, "Yeah. I'm fine … just not how I thought I'd wake up to you in the morning, Solveig."

Ragnar immediately gives off a growl of warning shutting Tempest up. I swat Ragnar's chest with the back of my hand to stop any further arguing and catching his attention. "He was just teasing, Ragi. What were you and Jorah discussing?"

Ragnar lets out a huff of air at my words and grabs the hand that I slapped his chest with before kissing the back of it gently. "Good morning, or should I say afternoon, my Maseeri. My mate-brother and I were discussing plans for the day. He has a map of the kingdom in that traveling library he carries around and has a few thoughts on where this other coven could be."

"What time is it? I still feel exhausted, but better," Tempest says in a sleepy voice sitting back on the end of the bed.

"I think it's past the mid-meal. I heard a servant outside the door talk about serving lunch a half hour ago," Ragnar responds.

"Wow. We slept for a while then. Time to get up! So, what's the plan?" I say popping out of bed before I'm tempted to stay in there with both my mates. Preferably without clothes. *Damn, not the time, Sol. Especially with Tempest here.*

Jorah peeks out of the room and asks a servant to bring up food left over from lunch. After everyone's dressed for the day and our bellies are filled, we discuss the next step. The plan is to split up to discover the location of the coven and with it-- Navelia.

Ragnar argues for a bit with me since he refuses to leave my side again for our search, and after a bit I acquiesce to him. He's a bit traumatized about losing me in the city last time so I guess I'll let him shadow me like a protective mother hen.

Jorah meanders off to the library to look at some maps of the city and see if they can tell him anything, while Tempest leaves for a tavern nearby. You'd be surprised with what information you can gain from bartenders and local gossips under the influence of alcohol.

Ragnar and I visit the local Main Street market to see if we can eavesdrop on conversations and pay off some venders to give up information. We also want to get a feel for the layout of the city in case we need a quick escape. The plan is to meet back up around dinner at the inn we are staying at.

Dolinmaar is a smaller capital city than Falal and even Marsael. But for what it lacks in size, it makes up for in beauty and bulk. The entire city is stone: all the buildings (mostly), the roads and ground, intricately carved stone structures set up on a stone base overlooking the water. There are big pillars and columns everywhere. It's pretty and the views are spectacular! But all this stone makes me feel a bit claustrophobic. I guess it just reminds me of a familiar dark cold dungeon room … *nope. Not going there right now, Sol. Be calm and know yourself.* I close my eyes trying to center myself while I bury those depressing thoughts of my past. *You are free of that part of your life. Batair is dead,* I remind myself. *Now, only if Malphas was rotting more than six feet under as well.*

Ragnar leans over with a concerned look and softly says, "Are you okay, little warrior?" before brushing my loose curls away from my neck and kissing me gently behind the ear (his favorite place).

"I'm fine. Just—all this stone makes me thinks of something else," I say with a shiver wrapping my arms around myself. "Come on let's check out another vender. I could really use some lavender soap. I'm sick of using that bar of mystery goop that Tempest gave us for cleaning with. It smells horrible!"

Ragnar chuckles and fake cringes before threading his fingers with mine and walking. "It is rather repulsive. I think he said that wolf pack harvested it from animal fat after hunting. Either way, I miss your lavender scent so let's start over there at that soap merchant."

We spend the next two hours buying a few things mostly so we can converse with the merchants and less because we need it. Although, Ragnar seems to be taking great pleasure in providing nice things for me. Must be his dragon side instinctively trying to provide for his mate. It's cute and—it's nice. For once, someone wants to take care of me.

Unfortunately, the only hint of gossip we can obtain is about a group of women who create elixirs of various sorts that have potential magical properties. It's also said that they tend to visit the market selling their wares on a certain day of the week. Specifically Fridays. Tomorrow.

We meet back for dinner at the inn and after eating retreat to our room to discuss our findings.

Unsurprisingly, Tempest returns drunk. "Ugh, I'm still sooo hungry! Can I have your extra bread, Solveig? Pretty, pretty please?" He says making puppy dog eyes at me and leaning slightly to the side. It was a bit of a challenge to get him up the stairs but Ragnar ended up supporting most his weight. I saved some bread from dinner hoping to have a snack later, but I suppose Tem needs it more than I do. Hopefully, it'll soak up some of that alcohol so we can actually talk.

"Fine. Here, take it." Shoving the piece of bread wrapped in a napkin at him, I take a seat in the chair by the small fireplace in the room. "So. Other than drinking way too much liquor did you actually find anything out?"

When I turn to look at him his eyes are closed and he's leaning against the bed while sitting on the floor.

"Tem!" Ragnar yells before gently kicking him back awake.

"What? Oh yeah the witches! I forgot!" He says rubbing a hand over his face. "Ugh, no I didn't really hear much. But…"

"This was a bad idea. He'd not exactly a reliable source of information right now." Jorah says rolling his eyes before he looks back down at the book in front of him.

"As I was saying…I did hear that there were some sightings of people down by the beach at night. Groups of people. No one could confirm if they were magic uses or Essents for that matter though." His eyes start to get sleepy again and he yawns before continuing. "People in the bar did say that you can use magic here, it's just not openly flaunted. There's no laws against it supposedly."

"Interesting. I think we should consider looking into those groups seen at the beach." Jorah says looking up at us. "I was able to find a map of the city and read about Essents a bit today. Some of the scholars there were very helpful! There was mention that Essents do prefer to be located by water and sometimes more natural structures. Something about it having more power and life force for their magic."

Ragnar nods approvingly at Jorah from his position leaning against the door, and I see Jorah sit up a bit straighter at the acknowledgement. It makes me chuckle a bit internally at their dynamic.

"I agree with my mate-brother. We should investigate this group's activity. However, we still don't really have a location." Ragnar voices while he runs a hand over the stubble on his jaw.

"Why don't we return to the market tomorrow and check out our one lead about the women that make those magical elixirs?" I say before noticing Tempest is already asleep again. "Then, if that doesn't give us any leads, we can stalk the beach tomorrow evening…since Tem isn't in any shape to do it tonight."

The next morning, we take our time at breakfast downstairs waiting till the street market opens. Tempest is in rough shape from yesterday's escapades and rather irritable. I decide to let his cousin update him about the plan today and avoid his surly attitude. Then as a group we all head over to the market.

I braided my hair back today or rather … Ragnar did. It's one of his favorite things to do, add a braid here or there in my hair. I also want to be prepared for a fight in case this woman is as dangerous as we were warned. I don pants and a tight shirt with my twin katanas strapped to my back making me feel more confident in today. Everyone rested well last night, and I can tell we're all ready for this to be over.

Somehow, I feel lighter. Stronger. More free since I found out my "father" is dead. It's like half a weight is lifted from my shoulders. Now, I just need to conquer the other half, and I'll be unstoppable. Already my nightmares and flashbacks have decreased significantly since finding my mates and leaving Laevaris. It also probably has to do with Ragnar guarding my dreams at night. *The sweet dragon cares for me. Protects me even when asleep. I think … no, I know—I love him.*

As if he could hear my thoughts (which he very may have—*oops*), he turns his head and looks intensely at me.

I thought it was obvious I love you, little warrior. My Maseeri. But if not … Ragnar states through mind speak before grabbing my upper arms and kissing me passionately in the middle of the street. People gawk a bit before flowing around us in a crowd.

I love you too, Ragi. You're mine and I'm so grateful that I have you in my life now. I reply kissing him back deeply while grabbing the front of his shirt.

A throat clearing brings us apart and back to the present. It makes us aware that we are still standing in the middle of a crowded street and I can't help but feel my face flush in embarrassment. Jorah and Tempest look at us with raised eyebrows while I bite my lip sheepishly for forgetting where we are. Ragnar looks smug as fuck.

"Come on. Selfish fucking dragons. It's my turn, Sol, to hold your hand," Jorah says grabbing my hand and tugging me down the street while Ragnar and Tempest follow us like bodyguards.

I notice a few new booths compared to yesterday while we walk but it's the large black and purple draped tent that draws my eye. Above it a sign reads: *Navi's Natural Elixirs.*

Perfect. I think. Then, I decide a little discretion is advised so I tap into my mind-speak rune and try something I haven't used in a while. I send a thought to everyone. *Well, look over there at the big black and purple tent boys. I don't think it can get any more obvious than that. Davi's sister's name was Nivelia, no?*

I see everyone in my group simultaneously stiffen up at me speaking to them. I probably surprised them all. Honestly, I surprise myself with how easy it is to communicate with multiple people at the same time. Then again—I'm standing pretty close to them which makes it easier. Distance tends to strain my powers.

Solveig? Wow—how amazing! I hear Tempest reply.

At nearly the same time, Jorah says, *Sol! Very good! You always had a good eye. And I like it when you speak to me mentally. I feel closer to you.* Jorah squeezes my hand when he says that.

Ragnar chimes in by saying, *Keep this mental connection open, little warrior, but guard against others. These Essence Wielders could have powers we don't fully understand.*

Okay, I agree, I say before relaying what Ragnar said and telling the others to be on guard and aware that I can hear them if they want to talk with me mentally.

"Let's go and follow my lead," I say walking towards the tent knowing they will follow. I mentally build a strong barrier around my mind while tethering open connections to all three men in my group. Just in case. Ragnar is right…I should be more careful with this mental ability.

We walk into the tent and it's like another world. It's dark and quiet with incense burning, making my nose twitch in discomfort. Ragnar and Tempest must be uncomfortable with the strong smell of frankincense filling the tent.

Fuck, that's gross. I hate that smell, Tempest mutters mentally to me making me snicker. I look over at Ragnar thinking he would be uncomfortable and I see the smoke pulling away from him like it's repelled.

Smoke and shadow rune. Remember? Ragnar says to me.

Oh! Right. Can you help a mate out then? I'm not very particular of this scent and Tempest is getting irritated too, I ask him.

Me too! Jorah says to me and Ragnar. I forgot I connected the two of them in conversation with me since we are all mates. Tempest is the only one who can communicate only to me.

Focusing back on the bigger issue, I see a young girl with black hair and nearly all white eyes sitting on a stool behind the table with various bottles displayed.

"May we help you?" the girl asks in a mature, full-bodied voice. It's disconcerting especially with her nearly all white eyes. *Creepy,* I think.

"Well, we are just looking. What kind of things do you have to offer?" I ask looking around at the table while the boys spread out behind me.

The young girl smirks and with a head tilt says, "Whatever you need, princess. Perhaps a tracking spell, fertility potion, or even …"

She looks down as if she's inspecting her nails like she's bored.

"A reversal spell? Hmm, say for a curse?"

Startled I look up from the bottles and see her smiling at me in a greedy way. It must unnerve my men too since the Drakoni start to emit a deep rumbling in their chests and Jorah places a hand on my back.

"You know who I am … how? I don't know you …" I say putting on my expressionless princess mask I perfected over the years.

"I know everything. I knew you were coming to find me. Don't play the idiot, besotted girl. How was my sister, hmm? Does she miss me? She thinks she's so perfect with her pristine community. Well, let me tell you … she's not as much of an angel as she lets on," the young girl states in a sneering voice. She looks only to be about twelve at most. There's no way she could be Davi's twin sister.

Ragnar stiffens and steps slowly in front of me effectively blocking my view, his eyes changing to his dragon form with a golden glow. Then I notice shadows wisping around his arms and legs. "Witch. Do you always glamour yourself into a younger, more bitter form of yourself or is this only for our amusement? Don't insult my mate."

Within the blink of an eye, the young girl changes into an older woman nearly identical to Davi except her hair is a longer and pulled harshly back into a bun on her head. This must be Navelia. The woman we've been looking for.

CHAPTER
Thirteen

SOLVEIG

King Ragnar, what a pleasure to see you again ..." Nivelia states in a mocking voice with a slight curtsy behind the table.

Confused by her statement on multiple accounts, I glare daggers at Ragnar's back in front of me and ask, *Um ... hello? What the fuck? King Ragnar? You have some explaining to do ... mate.* I state that last word angrily through mind speak. I can feel Ragnar's guilt through the mate bond so I know he was keeping it from me. Then I feel around his emotions and notice fear, determination and ... confusion.

I—I'm sorry, little mate. I can explain later. But—I'm not sure how she knows me or—what she means by that. I don't remember ever meeting her, Ragnar replies.

"I beg your pardon, I don't recall meeting you before ... but perhaps you took on a more—appealing appearance in the past?" Ragnar says in a cold expressionless voice.

I look around Ragnar's back to watch the encounter and see a slight twitch at the corner of her eye which is the only indication his words irritated her. Otherwise, she presents a cold and calm demeanor.

"Yes, well, I was rather young then. Beautiful. Black hair. More voluptuous most of which was natural. I just added some extra curves to my chest back then. I mean what man doesn't like full breasts?" she states sneering at Ragnar while he looks confused and staring in the distance as though he's trying to remember. "Your memory may have been a bit altered. I did have to put in quite the effort to lure and then contain you. You can thank me later. So, I'm assuming that plain woman behind you is your mate?" She waves her hand at me before looking disinterested again and taking a seat.

"*You* were the one to place the curse on our lands. You put me into my never-ending hibernation …" Ragnar says while she claps her hands slowly.

"Wow. I forgot how slow and unintelligent Drakoni are. And how meek you Elarians tend to be," Nivelia states condescendingly. "Do you always hide behind your mate?" Ragnar growls loudly in response and shadows enclose the room.

Stepping around Ragnar, I place a hand on his chest and say mentally, *Calm down. She's just a bitter old woman that was scorned remember? We need information and to not anger her—yet.*

"I am anything but meek. And you would know much more accurate information about the Drakoni and Elarians if you wouldn't have contributed to their destruction. I'm assuming you're Nivelia?" I ask to which she nods. "Yes, we did meet your sister Davi." She tenses imperceptibly. "She was very welcoming and respectful. And … insightful. She told us part of your history and how close you two were growing up. I believe she misses you … she said a deceitful man tore you apart …" I start to say as she stands up angrily and blue sparkling magic shoots between her raised hand up to her elbow.

"You know *nothing* about me. And Davi—she was always meddling in my life. Never believed I was as strong as her in power. She was always too concerned about others. We're better as we are—separate coven leaders. And that man—Gaargon—he loved me! He told me his whore of a wife was just an arranged marriage, that he didn't care for her other than the heir she would produce. I know he loved me … but yet he still betrayed me. He didn't stick to his promise and threw me away like trash once he got what he wanted," she says clenching her fist and diffusing the blue crackling power. Then she leans over and picks up a bottle on the table between us inspecting it. It has the symbol for poison on it and gives off an aura of—stay away.

"Well, he got what he wanted—his curse. But I got the last laugh," she says with an unhinged smile at us shaking the bottle in her hands back and forth. "Thallium is a lovely metal when mixed in a potion with my magic to inflict the maximum amount of pain slowly over months. Huh—no one including his perfect wife suspected the healing elixir he took after a battle wound was the actual thing that killed him."

Holy fucking shit. This woman is crazy. Remind me not to have a drink with her afterwards at the bar, I send to my group.

Damn. This is why I haven't found a woman yet. You all are freaking crazy when spurned, Tempest replies back to me.

Keep her talking, Sol. We need more information on the curse. She seems to talk more to another woman. Jorah wisely recommends.

Don't get any closer to her, little warrior. I'm barely holding on to my dragon. He wants to keep you far away from her. She could kill you with a touch of that power. Ragnar growls into my head.

Uhh … Solveig? Tem states mentally to me. *I don't know what Ragnar is saying but you'd best heed his words since he looks about three seconds from shifting. Drakoni males are extremely protective of their mates.*

His statement doesn't really warrant a response so I focus back on my actual conversation with Nivelia.

"Well … it sounds as though he may have deserved what he got. I mean, the men in that family are all fucking disrespectful assholes to women. I had to deal with the current king as my father," I say with a cringe trying to commiserate with her while she looks thoughtfully at me.

"Yes, I suppose you did, Princess Solveig. And—I hear he recently died. What a shame," Navi says sarcastically. "Word from my spies say it was a man who did the killing … the presumed dead Elarian King, while another says it was a human rebellion leader … who knows? Either way, I'm guessing you are here about the curse. I never truly thought it possible an Elarian survived." She tilts her head thoughtfully while intensely staring at me. "I'm surprised Batair kept you alive even *if* he thought you were his daughter … which can't be true given your strong Elarian features."

Shocked by what she just said, I stumble on my words before I'm able to reply by saying, "I was told King Batair might not be my true father. But I did grow up in the castle under his thumb. I never knew there were others like me until recently."

"Yes, I can tell your naivety is an issue," Nivelia says.

"We only know what we have. I knew nothing else."

"Well, as much as this is enlightening about your family. Why are you here?" She asks with a knowing look in her eyes.

"Tell us how to break the curse you placed. Many people are depending on this. *Please*. And—how is it you knew Ragnar? You met him before, but he doesn't remember you," I say with a determined voice sending up a prayer to Avilt, the God of knowledge, that she will impart the information we need.

"Ahh—you wish to return to Elaria and restore the Lost Lands? How noble of you to take up this task princess. I'm willing to help you break this curse …" she says with a slow drawn out pause making me lean forward just a bit and the men with me straighten up with intense focus.

"*If* …you trade something with me. Two things really. Simple," she states with a greedy smile and a snap of her fingers. "And as for how I know your Drakonian mate … why I was the one who coerced him back into his lair and placed him in his dream state. You're welcome by the way. Otherwise, there would have been no way to break the curse."

"Um, okay … vague. Can you tell us more … I'm willing to trade, but don't really have anything of significance to trade with," I say causing Ragnar to berate me mentally.

You have plenty. Remember these Essents use life force for their power. Do not make any deals without us first discussing. I'm serious, Solveig! Ragnar angrily tells me but I feel fear and concern through the mate bond. He's scared for me.

Okay. Sorry, this whole magic thing is new to me.

Let's just find out what she wants first. Then—group meeting, Jorah interjects. Tempest is silent in my head since he's not part of the mate bond and can't hear my mates' discussion.

"You have plenty to trade, but I suppose giving up a few years of your life is off the table?" she says with a smirk making Ragnar and Tempest growl and step forward. I can hear a distant rumble in the sky and smoke is starting to come out of Ragnar's nostrils. "I didn't think so … oh well. I want to know what it is you are carrying in your bag there, princess. I can feel magical signatures and objects in close proximity. And *you*—have something with you of importance."

Squinting at her in confusion, I pull my bag over my shoulder and open it looking inside. Most of it is bare necessities, but then I realize what she's referring to. My notebook.

Years ago, I met a woman similar in age to myself when I was swimming at Silver lake, back in Laevaris. Vidarr took me there after a rebellion mission for fun and to take my mind off the more stressful things in life. It's when I met Jicquara. Or Ara as I liked to abbreviate her name. She was friendly and we hit it off right away. I was a bit of a lonely teenager with my past and Vidarr was great but sometimes a girl just needs another woman to talk to. Vidarr had left me for a bit to hunt and he never even knew I made a new friend that day. When he returned, I went to introduce them as darkness approached but I turned around and she was gone. In her place was a small notebook. I hid it, unsure why other than the fact that she obviously didn't want to be seen, and I didn't open it until later that night. Inside, she wrote that she was glad she made a new friend and could use the companionship. She said she was lonely and lived far away but this notebook would allow us to communicate.

Confused those many years ago, I stared at it and flipped through its otherwise blank pages. Then shrugging and thinking I could just use it as a diary of sorts, I wrote—*I could use a friend too.* Like magic (which I suppose it was), I instantly got a reply back seeing cursive black script appear on the page. Her prior note faded as her new one appeared. It was indeed a magical notebook! Amazing really. From then on, we stayed in contact through notes and I learned more about her but mostly she was there to listen to me and my daily struggles. I wrote about most things—including my father and Counselor Malphas' mistreatments however, I didn't give her details. She wanted to travel and rescue me, but I strongly declined worried about what my father would do to her and also not wanting to abandon my people who were struggling in the kingdom. I deduced she lived further north of Falal or in the mountains since she always spoke of cold weather and snow, but otherwise she was rather secretive. All I knew was that she's not only my friend but also the keeper of many secrets.

Flipping the notebook open, I see no new messages today. It looks blank. *Good.*

"Do you mean, this?" I ask holding up the notebook which her gaze is intensely focused on.

She licks her lips hungrily and says, "Yes. I can't believe it! I've only heard of two or three in existence. Do you have the other one?"

Confusion radiates down the mate bond from Jorah and Ragnar immediately. While Tempest's face is scrunched up like he's about to ask a question.

"No. I don't know where the other one is located," I say honestly. I mean—really I don't know exactly where my friend is located.

Sol, I thought that was just your journal? Why is she so interested in it? Jorah asks confusedly.

Yes. What is that, little mate? It feels strange for an object but you've never mentioned it to me … Ragnar asks leaning forward.

Solveig? What's going on? Just give her the book and let's get out of here. Am I missing something? Tempest asks me through my mind-speak power.

"Ahh. Pity that. Well, I suppose it's not as valuable as I thought. But if you are willing to part with that *book* into my care and one other thing then I will help you break the curse. That is my deal," she says with her arms crossed.

"What's the other thing you want Nivelia?" Ragnar asks mimicking her with his arms crossed and an intimidating look on his face. Fuck if he looked at me that way I'd be drawing my weapons.

"Just something simple really … one of your dragon scales," she states dropping those words into an utterly silent tent. Both Drakonian males stiffen up in anger and alarm.

"And what would you do with one of those scales, *witch*?" Ragnar grits out offended and angry.

"Dragon scales are known to be packed full of power and life force. The number of spells I could cast with just one dragon scale … it could last me a whole month or more!" she says with a smile rubbing her hands together.

"*No!*" Ragnar yells out at the same time Tempest does as they step forward in sync. I quickly grasp his arm and Jorah grabs Tem as I see at least three other Essents step out from the shadows behind Nivelia holding hands.

"Just give us a moment to discuss? This seems to be a rather big decision," I say pulling my mate backwards out of the tent.

"You have an hour. Then we pack up our tent and the deal is off," Nivelia says before we step into the afternoon light and bustling street of Dolinmaar.

We all walk silently down the street and around a corner before I turn around and yell, "What the fuck was that Ragnar?! We need this deal! We could end this curse. Today! Fuck, let's just get it done. I'm willing to part with my notebook even though I'll be sad. I just need to write out a quick message to her. What's the deal with your scale?"

Instead of Ragnar answering, though, its Tempest.

"Dragon scales aren't given lightly. We can regrow them once removed but it takes time. Sometimes a month or less. But—that's not the issue. They are rare for a reason and that's because when one is removed we lose some of our life force. It can shorten our lifespan. We never know how much but it could be weeks or even months, possibly years. It's a bit unknown since many don't want to risk it and—giving that kind of power to someone … it's concerning. Especially someone as crazy at Nivelia," he states running a hand through his hair while he seems to be thinking. "It has to be me …"

"No, Tem. She asked for *my* scale. I won't let you do it," Ragnar says in response to Tempest. Me and Jorah look back and forth between them confused again.

"Okay, this sounds dangerous. Maybe we should find another way … Maybe one of us has something else she could want. Or we could offer her a favor …?" I say.

"No, you're right, mate. We need to finish this. Enough time has gone by and this curse needs to be reversed before we lose our chance. I'll give her one of my scales and she will do her part or I will destroy her," Ragi says slamming his fist into the palm of his other hand while smoke starts to seep out of his nostrils due to his angry state.

Tempest shakes his head back and forth. "No, Ragi. You can't. I'll give her my scale. You're mated and need those years for the future. You know why. You can't risk not being able to protect your mate, your future children, heirs … She can't be allowed to get her hands on a royal dragon scale especially a king!

I'm the best choice. She will just have to be satisfied with that or we walk."

"Oh. Yeah. Right. *The king ...*" I sarcastically say with emotions locked down tight and sealing up my thoughts like a vault before crossing my arms in irritation and hurt. *Why would he hide something like that. I thought he was just related somehow to the royal family. And what does that mean for us ... I mean King of the Drakoni ... pretty sure he needs a Drakonian heir and possibly a Drakonian wife ...*

"Yes. I'm sorry, Solveig. We can discuss this later. It's not important right now," Ragnar huffs out a frustrated (and still smoky) breath dropping his arms in defeat. "But—I suppose Tempest is right. Giving her my scale would give her too much power. It's already a risk giving her one at all. But for our people and yours, we have to risk it. Tempest, cousin ... I'm sorry. Are you sure?"

Tem nods his head in acceptance and determination lights his eyes. "Yes of course, Ragi. Let's just get it over with. It's worth it for the chance to see Elaria restored. I'll half shift and you can remove one from my leg or back." They do it quickly taking a blue iridescent scale from his left lower back. Tem grits his teeth in pain but otherwise seems fine afterwards.

"Okay so I understand why the witch—er—Essent—wants the scale but ... why does she want your diary, Sol?" Jorah asks me shifting his bag of books slightly on his shoulder. *Why he carries those everywhere I'll never understand. They must be heavy. But at least it does nice things to his back and arm muscles.* I contemplate running my heated eyes over his fit and lean frame secretly appreciating the way his muscles are defined in his arms. He smirks at me and his eyes heat up predicting my lustful thoughts and feeling my arousal through our connection.

Later, he whispers to me huskily in my head.

"Uh ... well ... you see." Then clearing my throat I gather my scrambled dirty thoughts and my dignity. "It's a magical notebook. It was given to me by a friend. I've been writing to her for *years*. It's a bit strange because I've only met her once but we're close. We just talk or I guess write to each other almost daily. The notebook allows us to directly write to each other instantly. Like this see …" I write out a note to her: *Are you well?.*

Everyone looks over my shoulder and we wait a few minutes with Tempest tapping his foot a bit in impatience before wincing at the wound on his back.

Yes. Worried about you though. What's going on? Ara replies in her scrolling handwriting.

"Wow. That's amazing! No wonder Nivelia wants this so bad. It's the second best thing to mind-speak. However, not as useful if you don't have the other notebook," Jorah says.

"I remember these books. They originated in my lands. They were created by the Drakoni. One day they disappeared. My sister's mentor created them into existence with her help. He had a rune for creating, as did my sister. She was an inventor," Ragnar says sadly and in a longing voice.

"I didn't know you had a sister, Ragi. I'm sorry," I say squeezing him in a hug and opening the mate bond a bit to send affection down our connection.

"Thanks, little warrior. Did you ask her how she got these books? She could be a thief!" Ragnar says dismayed.

"She's not a thief. But I did ask her and she told me to be patient. That she couldn't tell me or it would put her at risk. Now, give me a second to write her a note and say goodbye. Let her know our situation and that she shouldn't write back unless she wants a witch hunting her down."

I write out a quick explanation to Ara and a request … specifically a meeting point and a time, to which she agrees. I think we've gone long enough without a visit to each other. It should give her plenty of time to travel there since I don't know how she traveled before when I met her. But I suspect there's more than meets the eye when it comes to Ara.

CHAPTER
Fourteen

SOLVEIG

Two minutes before our hour is up, we enter back into the dark tent.

It looks different inside now though. Lanterns light the space and several chairs surround a small table which has tea and snacks set up.

Nivelia is sitting regally at the end of the table sipping on her tea and petting a large black cat. Three other Essents stand at her back with expressionless faces.

"Please sit. I'm pleased you decided to take me up on my offer. I wasn't a huge fan of placing that curse in the first place and thought about reversing it for a few years after but…it takes life force and energy that I didn't have at my disposal at the time. Plus—I lacked the motivation. Now, I will have both."

All of us walk in cautiously sitting in the open chairs in the room. Ragnar sits next to me closely on a loveseat. I don't think he or Jorah have taken their hands off me since we were in that alley. Both are acting very protective at the moment and seem tense.

"We've agreed to your requests however we have our own stipulations. I'll hand you the notebook first, then you give us what we need to reverse the curse before we give you the dragon scale. After that, we leave," I say tilting my chin up a bit and crossing my arms.

"You're smarter than I took you for princess but I would rather have the dragon scale first."

"No. You take this deal or we walk and figure out another way. That's final." Tempest says with a cool anger as he holds out his blue scale taunting her. Her eyes light up seeing it in front of her just as we planned in case she was reluctant to follow our stipulations. It's like dangling a carrot in front of a horse … they just can't resist. And—she's no different.

"Fine! Hand over the notebook and I'll start," Nivelia states with a huff and extends her hand making a grabby gesture. It's like a toddler looking for its toy.

I smooth a hand over the notebook that's been with me for almost four years before holding it out to her. She snatches it up and it's gone from sight before I can even say anything. Then she nods to a man behind her who places a small bowel in front of her on the table and a cup. The single cup is full of a smelly substance making my stomach churn.

The black cat stiffens up and she grabs the back of its neck harshly as she starts to chant some words. She then dumps the smelly substance into the bowel and it begins to bubble like it's boiling before turning black. The black cat looks me in the eye before projecting into my mind, *Thank you, princess,* in a deep male voice. Startled I focus on the cat just as she uses a sharp knife to slit its throat and hold its dripping bloody neck over the bowel.

I go to shout out and tears enter my eyes at realizing she just sacrificed that cat for our purposes. *Fuck, I didn't know.* Guilt hits me hard and Jorah places a firm hand on my shoulder.

Looking over at him, I see a look of horror on his face. Then he shakes his head and says to me mentally, *I know Sol, fuck, I know … just don't interrupt. Let's finish this since it's already done. It's horrible, sad and disgusting but—she says she needed life-force for the spell. Best to think of its sacrifice as help- ing many others.*

The blood and black bubbling substance in the bowl swirls together while she continues to chant before it dissipates into the air. Suddenly, I feel an overwhelming sense of rightness fall over my shoulders before it's gone.

"There it's done. Now you only have to complete it for the curse to be totally removed. Hand over the dragon scale," Nivelia says with a greedy smile but there's a slight tension across her brow as if that was move work than it appeared.

We all look at each other in confusion while Tempest reach- es out with the scale hesitantly. Just as she snatches it out of hand with a sound of triumph I shout, "Wait!"

Nivelia clutches the scale to her chest and runs her finger over it smiling while Tempest looks slightly nauseous watching.

"How do we know the curse is removed? And what did you mean *we* have to complete it? You left something out!" I say in a cold voice while internally I'm alarmed and worried.

"I didn't remove the curse, foolish girl. I said I would reverse it and I did. Now *you* have to remove it fully so your people can return to Elaria. I gave you a chance at it, that's all I did, by reversing it. It's impossible though…"

She starts to cackle like an evil witch, which is so cliche I would roll my eyes if I wasn't freaking out on the inside.

"The only way you can totally remove the curse is if a royal Drakonian male that is in line for the throne bonds with his fat- ed mate who happens to be the Elarian heir to the throne. Just being a princess to the Kingdom of Laevaris isn't enough. You need the Elarian royal heir. It's next to impossible given that your two people are nearly extinct, however you are one step there, seeing as you have King Ragnar here. It's up to you all to figure out how to find the Elarian heir to the throne and then get her or him to mate with King Ragnar," she says laughing, unaware

I'm supposedly the heir and we are already mated. "You also have to step foot in Elaria together before the curse lifts fully. You're welcome!" she says clapping her bloody hands like she fooled us. Then in flash of bright light we are all sitting in an empty tent alone. Nivelia and her minions are gone.

"Bitch! Why does everyone have to be so particular with their words when making a deal? I mean—what happened to honesty and integrity?" I mutter.

"Well looks like the final joke is on her though," Jorah states with a slow smile. "She obviously didn't know you are not only the future queen of Laevaris but also heir to the Elarian crown. And … Ragnar is supposedly a king which we still need to address." Ragnar nods his head thoughtfully in response. "Well then, we are all done here! So, all we will have to do is return to Elaria and this curse will lift. " He clasps his hands together and makes a silly gesture lifting them into the air.

"He's right. We lucked out or it truly was fated in every sense that you two met. We should travel back tomorrow," Tempest says with a relieved and far off look. " I can't believe we did it! Home …"

Smiling and feeling a sense of pride in myself and our group, I lean over and kiss Jorah. *Holy shit! We really did it! Thank you Patrov for our patience!* Then I look over at Ragnar as we all stand and leave the area. He's already staring at me with … reluctance and chagrin. *Oh yeah … King Ragnar. Someone still needs to explain themselves.*

"We are going to have a nice *long* talk tonight, mate. You have some explaining to do your majesty. Then we leave in the morning but—not for Elaria. We have something we need to handle first before heading home," I state in a determined voice.

The whole walk back to the inn is silent while everyone is lost in their own thoughts. While Ragnar's royal title is not necessarily going to change anything between us, it still upsets me that I found out like I did. I can't help but feel some self-doubt and insecurities rising to the surface.

I've always had issues trusting men given my past abuse at the hands of my father and his advisor. Is there anything else he didn't tell me? Could he have some prearranged engagement to a Drakonian female who would make a better mate than me? Can I give him what he needs as an Elarian woman? Then, there's the whole discussion of heirs…

CHAPTER
Fifteen

SOLVEIG

I'm sorry, little warrior. Keep your sharp katanas and daggers sheathed for now while I explain," Ragnar states in a rumbly deep voice once we settle into the room at our inn within the city of Dolinmaar.

The others in our group all went to clean up and give us some privacy before dinner since we are all sharing one room. We're going to discuss a plan for tomorrow once we meet up at dinner.

"Ragnar, you deliberately kept that from me. Why? I told you the first time we met and subsequently mated that I was a princess. You also know I have some … trust issues with men. So … why wouldn't you tell me?" I say feeling hurt and slightly angry. Maybe I could just stab him a little with my dagger. I mean … the dragon can heal rather fast or I could heal him after.

I think another part of why I'm hurt is that Tempest knew as well, of course he did! It also made me realize maybe I don't know Ragnar as well as I thought. He's more complex than I took him for. He's had centuries longer in life than I have. So what else don't I know about him?

Ragnar walks up and cups his hands around my face catching my attention before saying, "No, no—my Maseeri. I didn't deliberately keep it from you. I meant to mention it but … things just progressed quickly as it usually does when you meet a fated mate. Then, we were busy at the castle and you were injured, several times might I add, before getting kidnapped."

He huffs out a breath with a tired expression and runs his hand over his stubbled jaw.

"You knew I have royal blood, but I should have made it clear that I was next in line for the throne of the Drakoni. My father had died during the year before our people were massacred and I was new into my reign. My mother was killed during the war a year later. I also had an adopted sister as you know—but I couldn't find her or her body during the war. She must have died fighting. And afterwards— I was forced into a hibernation, a sleep that kept me dreaming but aware that I was missing out on the world and my surroundings."

He sighs sadly then continues.

"I also had several aunts and uncles as well as cousins including Tempest. It's sometimes hard to think about my family since we were all very close. The royal family, my family, were well respected and loved by our people. We interacted informally with our people unlike most monarchs. It wasn't as strict as the humans or Elarians were although there was a hierarchy. I'm not truly king anymore since my people are all gone so it's a moot point, you see? When I met you, I had just woken up from a sleep that lasted over a hundred years. To say I was a bit confused and disoriented would be an understatement. All I felt initially was instinct, the need to bond with my mate who I sensed—and to protect her. Everything else, like being king, was secondary. Honestly—still is. *You* are most important to me, Solveig. My Maseeri. We were meant to be and the Gods must have agreed. But regardless of fate, I've fallen in love with you. Your fighting spirit, your compassion for others and your fierce determination make me proud that I've earned not just a bond with you but your *love*. For once, the Gods were right and I'll thank them every day for you," Ragnar says sliding his hands down my arms lovingly while his heated gaze looks over my body. "Now, take off those clothes so I can show you how sorry I am."

"Very well. I suppose I can give you one chance to make it up to me." Giving him a half smile with a teasing glint in my blue eyes, I quickly shed my clothes hoping we have enough time before the rest of our group returns to the room.

"I can be a very attentive mate to you, demonstrating my apology and groveling on my knees…" Ragi slowly says in a serious voice as his eyes hungrily take in my naked body like it's his last meal "… as long as I get to do it between your thighs."

Not waiting for my response, he fists his shirt and pulls it over his head before dropping to his knees before me. It's a powerful moment seeing the King of the Drakoni kneel before me. It makes me feel he's worshipping me. Like I *am* the most important thing in his life.

My thoughts cut off when I feel his strong, callused hand grab my right thigh hoisting it over his shoulder before I feel an intense heat over my core. Ragnar breathes out a puff of steam onto my most sensitive area making me startle before looking up at me with hooded and golden reptilian eyes.

Then he breathes deeply in scenting my arousal and his long, shifted reptilian tongue licks straight up my center. Our mate bond throbs with intense emotions and arousal nearly making me come already but I somehow manage to reign in myself for a moment longer.

He's using his tongue to lick and taste me so deeply that when he hits that spot inside of me, my legs collapse as an explosive orgasm rocks through my body. I feel dissociated with my body for a moment before I return to reality and notice Ragnar must have carried me to the bed. He's laying with his chin propped on my pelvis watching me, smiling smugly. *Devious lit-*

tle reptile. But damn if I don't love his long when its shifted longer. Having a Drakonian male definitely has its benefits.

His smile gets wider and I know he heard some of my thoughts. I'm open like a book in more ways than one. Mental barriers down, legs wide open.

"Am I forgiven yet, little warrior?" He says with an earnest and yet knowing expression. His right hand squeezes around my left inner thigh.

"No! *Definitely*, not yet." I say in a rushed voice which only makes him look smugger. "Ugh… I mean… you should try again. *Harder.* "

"I was hoping you'd say that my Maseeri." He replies while crawling up my limp, post-orgasm body like a predator. "I'll do whatever I need to do in order to prove myself to you. For forgiveness's sake. Even if it is rather a *strain.* " He says that in a smirking voice. "If my little warrior likes it hard, then harder is what she'll get."

Without any warning other than his words, his already hard cock impales me fully to the hilt sliding easily inside given my recent orgasm. *Fuck, that feels so good. I think…no I know I'm going to come again. Too soon…*

Ragnar withdraws his cock slowly before thrusting it back in *hard,* just how I asked. It makes the bed creak ominously and a loud moan slips from between my lips probably notifying the whole inn what we're up to.

My Maseeri. Forgive me. Ragnar whispers in my head as he continues to fuck me hard into the mattress. The sounds of flesh slapping on flesh can be heard with the bed rocking.

All too soon though, I feel myself on a precipice of bliss trying to hold off.

Let go mate. Come for me. Ragnar's rough strained voice says mentally before I fall over that cliff into pure pleasure. Ragnar roughly grabs my hips and bruisingly pounds into me until my head nearly hits the wall at the top of the bed before he roars loudly and finds his own release.

After getting cleaned up, we spend time relaxing in each other's arms and talk of our past getting to know each other a bit more intimately. Its memorable as one of the best times I've experienced with Ragnar and I'll always cherish it. I've never had someone focus so much on knowing *me* as a person.

Eventually, we both realize it's getting late and head down to the common room for dinner with Tem and Jorah.

When I walk into the common room in a simple lavender dress with my hair down conversation pauses, making me feel awkward. I notice there isn't many women in the crowded inn or at the bar. Ragnar distracts me by tugging my hand with a soft growl and gives a few men around the room a dangerous look of warning before he pulls me over to our group at a large table in the back.

Jorah immediately jumps up from his chair at our approach and smiles hugely tugging my hand from Ragnar who again growls a bit possessively. Jorah ignores him and says to me, "You look gorgeous, Solveig. You always do. I missed you. Ragnar's stealing all your attention lately." He leans in to gently kiss my lips then tugs me down into his lap while I lightly laugh.

"He does tend to do that. I'll make it up to you tonight," I whisper in his ear making him smirk while his cheeks flush red and his hand on my hip tightens. Ragnar must notice my growing arousal before his head snaps over in our direction and he scoots his chair closer placing a warm hand on my thigh.

"I'd like that, Sol. For now though—let's get you fed," Jorah says.

"Okay. Let's calm the mate possessiveness for a second while I eat. And—I need my own chair. I'm not use to people fussing over me," I say standing up and sliding into the chair next to Jorah.

"Thank Valirr!" Tem says dramatically with an eyeroll. "If I have to watch this gooey love fest any longer and smell all this arousal at dinner, you're going to ruin my appetite." I can tell he's teasing but the slight strain in his eyes tells me he's actually sad … or jealous?

I silently mouth the word sorry to which he subtly nods back.

We eat roasted venison that the server brings over to us and some delicious mead that's local to the area before everyone sits back satisfied.

"So what's the plan, my *queen*?" Tempest says with a teasing smirk and crossed arms while leaning back in his chair. It looks precariously close to falling backwards with the way he's balancing it on two legs.

Ragnar kicks his leg out making Tempest fall backwards and we all roar with laughter while he sputters from the ground. From their interactions so far, I've noticed their relationship as cousins involves a lot of good natured ribbing. It's entertaining to say the least and makes me jealous I don't have a sibling or cousin. Several others in the common room chuckle at their antics before going back to their conversations.

"Idiot. Don't call her that here," Ragnar quietly says once Tem is back in his chair with a chagrined face.

"Sorry, Sol. So—what's the plan? You sounded like you aren't ready to return home yet," Tem says curiously.

"Well, we have other business before traveling to Elaria. We need to stop and meet with a contact of mine. She's important and we may need her support in the future if the rumors are true," I say leaning over the table while the others all squint at me.

"What rumors?" Jorah asks sipping at his tea which he asked for instead of mead. Honestly—the mead is a bit strong and I'm already feeling its effects … so … not the best choice tonight.

"The rumors that my father is dead and I'm now the rightful queen. I'm not sure who has taken the throne while I've been gone, but we'll find out. Also—this war with Jaarn. It's likely underway or just started. We need to be prepared. The first thing Captain Mavin taught me when we trained was, *keep your eyes on your enemies and your hands on your allies.* He explained that when you make an ally you should stay in contact and quietly tend those relationships. I think he was trying to prepare me for when I had to take down my father and Counselor Malphas. A contact of mine is in Beamus, and I need to see her. It should be quick and is on the way."

"Smart man this … Captain Mavin. I agree with his advice. We were taught similar things growing up as Drakonian royalty," Ragnar says keeping his focus on me.

"I thought the Kingdom of Beamus was hostile with Laevaris in the past? How would a contact you have there help you? Also, what do you mean *on the way*? I may not be the smartest in the group …" he says glancing at Jorah. "… but I know the Kingdom of Beamus is *not* on the way to Elaria!" Tem stares back at me while tapping a finger on the table obviously trying to figure out the politics of our warring kingdoms.

"They were hostile in the past but over the last ten years have been neutral. I also know they trade with Jaarn regularly so they definitely aren't an ally… yet. My contact will be able to provide us more insight and it'll make more sense how she can help us then," I say while Jorah pulls out a map from a bag I didn't see he had with him. I trace my finger over Dolinmaar and then over to the town of Jael which is in Beamus.

"We will meet her in Jael before traveling on to Sterling Outpost in the Kingdom of Gorva. We need to be quick though. I worry we will already be too late," I say anxiously looking up.

"And why are we rushing off to Sterling Outpost, my Maseeri?" Ragnar says with an assessing look on his face and a head tilt.

"I need to see Cadoc. One of my other mates. He needs me or … will need us. And, I can't let him down," I say staring directly back at Ragnar challenging him to deny me. But he doesn't deny me and instead smiles back at me.

"Very well, little warrior. I've been wanting to meet more of your mates and you are always right to seek them out. No explanation is needed but …" Ragnar says looking down at the map now and tracing a finger across Daelarias. "It will take a week maybe less if we fly hard to get there."

"Come on, Ragnar! We can do it in five days! You forget I have an affinity for air and a rune for weather. The air currents will be in our favor and if you want to bet … I think we can even make it in as little as four days from Jael," Tempest says with confidence.

Jorah claps me on the shoulder before rolling up his map and saying, "Then we are agreed! *Wow*. This is exciting! I can't believe I'm getting to travel to so many kingdoms all in one trip." Jorah looks so young and excited at that moment that sometimes I forget we are only nineteen-year-olds surrounded by two old (I mean really old) dragons that have seen the world.

"So it's planned. Let's get some rest and leave at dawn," I say distractedly.

We all head up to the room, but I notice Tempest parts from us and heads to a room directly across from ours. Seeing my questioning look he smirks and says, "They had a single room available tonight and seeing as you three are mated … I thought I'd give you some privacy. I mean—don't get me wrong … I'm willing to watch if you want …" He cuts off his joking when Ragnar walks over and smacks his shoulder. Then chuckling and rubbing his sore shoulder he disappears into his room.

"Come on, Solveig. I think your mates want some time with you before we have to deal with all the others vying for your attention," Jorah says grabbing my hand and pulling me into the room. Ragnar follows us and closes the door softly before leaning back on it.

Looking nervously between the two of them, I walk over and pour myself a small glass of aruvian liquor and taking a small sip to bolster my confidence. I haven't yet had intimate interactions with more than one mate at a time. Well… other than that one time with Vidarr and Cadoc. *How could I forget that?* Regardless, it's making me break out in a nervous sweat but also anticipation. *How will they both work together in the bedroom? I mean—they seem to be getting along.*

Jorah walks over to me and grabs the now empty glass from my shaking hand placing it on a nearby table. He shares a look with Ragnar over my shoulder who's still resting against the door burning me with his intense gaze. They look at each other for a second as though they share some internal conversation before Ragnar nods his head in agreement. *Wait a second … I thought they needed me to communicate mentally?!*

Stop, little warrior. Put away those figurative daggers of yours. We do need you to allow open mind-speak between us. We weren't speaking mentally just a silent communication between mate-brothers on what we want to do with you, Ragnar says from across the room while his eyes turn reptilian and a rumble starts in his chest.

Jorah leans in and kisses me softly where my neck meets my shoulder causing me to arch a bit and tilt my head to the side providing him more access. He greedily accepts my submission and slowly slides my dress off each shoulder. *When did he undo all the buttons on the back of my dress?* The dress slides down and pools at my feet. Jorah then kisses down my chest and his large gentle hands cup my breasts. He leans back a bit and his heated gaze takes in my nakedness.

"She's stunning, no? These breasts …" Jorah says to the room or Ragnar or himself … I'm not sure because he then slides his callused thumbs over my nipples distracting me. He pinches them gently, causing me to gasp and arousal to pool in between my thighs. *Fuck. Do it again.*

He must have heard my thoughts or felt my arousal through the mate bond because he pinches and licks my nipples with fervor slowly dropping to his knees. My hands instinctively slide into his hair while he next gazes at my wet pussy.

"Damn, Sol." He lifts one of my legs over his shoulder and crouching down a bit leans in licking from back to front. He pays extra attention to my clit as he sucks and licks it until it's swollen with need. Next, his fingers part my slit and run around the rim before two dip inside and curl before pumping back out. I can't help but buck my hips and push my core into his face more. "You're so responsive to my touch. I must be doing something right. You want me?" he states, looking up at me with heat and a touch of vulnerability.

Panting with arousal and wanting more, I moan, "Always. More … Jorah."

Jorah stands up quickly lifting me under my thighs and places me on the bed. I hear a small scuffle of feet in the room and am reminded that my Drakonian mate is watching. He's now standing a bit closer with his hands fisted at his sides and breathing heavily. His golden eyes are burning me with intensity as they shift between my naked chest and my needy wet pussy.

Jorah used my distraction to shed his own clothes and is now kneeling at the end of the bed. "Ragnar … you joining us or just into watching?" Jorah innocently asks while sliding his hands up my thighs and pushing my legs to the bed by my hips.

Come here, mate. I want to feel your hands and your mouth on me. Please, I say to Ragnar mentally making him groan and quickly discard his clothes before walking over. He positions himself near my head with his erect cock directly in front of me. *The things I can do with that …*

Ragnar leans over and kisses me using his long serpentine tongue to manipulate me into an unexpected orgasm as Jorah restarts his ministrations on my pussy. The combination of both of them touching me, worshiping me, makes me come faster than I ever have in the past. It's a heady sensation when you're with two mates at the same time and can feel their own emotions and arousal. It makes me confused what feelings are mine and which are theirs, but the general consensus is that everyone wants more … needs it. Our instincts and bodies want to fuck.

I turn my head toward Ragnar's protruding hardness when he leans back and wrap my entire hand around the thick base. Then I place my lips around the tip licking up his pre-cum that's sitting there and asking for acknowledgment. Sucking his cock down my throat, I make him growl and fist my breast roughly. Strangely it makes me feel a sense of accomplishment that I can make him become so unhinged.

Jorah uses Ragnar's distraction to shift himself between my legs and thrust his cock up into my soaking wet pussy. I gasp in surprise and arch my back unintentionally causing me to take Ragnar's cock all the way to the back of my throat. He fists my hair and holds me in place while I gag for a second before relaxing. They both take control of my body, before withdrawing and then roughly thrusting into me in sync. *I swear, these two are communicating mentally … without me! Fuuuuckk.*

Good, little mate. Taking my cock all the way back into your throat. You're going to swallow all my cum and lick me clean after, Ragnar growls into my head continuing to thrust his hips into my face and holding my hair in a firm grip while he uses me. I completely relax into his hold trusting him not to hurt me and finding it's easier and more arousing to relinquish control. *After I'm done, you're going to take my cock. You should know Drakonian males don't have a refractory period and can mate all night. Or don't you remember our first time together?*

My inner channel squeezes in response to his words turning me into molten heat. I'm too aroused and wet. Jorah moans loudly, not pausing in his firm even thrusts, then says, "Fuck, Ragnar. What did you just say to her? She nearly took my dick off with how tight she got."

He reaches up and swirls his thumb around my clit while thrusting into me hard.

"You liked that, Sol? Your pussy is so wet and tight I might never leave it. You're going to make me cum embarrassingly fast and I can't help it. Now … come with me," Jorah says as he squeezes my clit and tilts my hips up a bit with his other hand hitting that blessed spot inside me and making me shatter. I think I pass out for a second because Ragnar tugs my hair a bit to garner my focus before he grunts out his release into my throat.

I swallow quickly but can't nearly keep it all in. He pulls out and scoops up any extra cum before putting his fingers in my mouth.

Mine, Ragnar says to me.

Ours, Jorah adds into our connection.

Oops. Must have let my barrier down between everyone. I think I left my sanity back one or two orgasms ago, I contemplate but they must have heard my thoughts because they both chuckle.

I'm not done yet, my Maseeri. Turn over. I want to show your young human mate, how long Drakonian males can last, Ragnar says to me as Jorah pulls out of me and flops onto his side, propped up on an elbow. The look on Jorah's face is a mix of offended and curiosity.

I somehow manage to control my body and turn over onto my hands and wobbly knees while Ragnar shifts behind me. He tugs my hips up further and puts a firm hand on my back pushing my upper body down into the bed. I don't even have a second to brace myself before he slams his *still* hard cock into my cum filled pussy.

Ahh. Yeeesss. Ragi! I mentally shout while loud moans ring out through the room.

"*You. Are. Mine … Ours,*" Ragnar says to each pump of his hips while my body shifts forward in delicious friction against the sheets. "You will come again. On my cock this time. *Now.*"

As if his words caused it instead of his huge cock, I'm instantly thrown into an orgasm that continues for several minutes while he continues to thrust for a while and we both become coated in sweat. Then finally, he grunts and shouts out his release with a roar. We both collapse down next to Jorah in an exhausted heap of bodies.

"Fuck, that was hot. Literally and figuratively, of course," Jorah says running a hand over my hip. "I guess I can learn a few pointers from my mate-brothers on how to satisfy our mate." Both men share a smirk over my body which I don't mind, seeing as I'll benefit from his words in the long run.

"Our mate is insatiable and may need our attention more frequently," Ragnar says with a satisfied voice as he runs his hand through my hair tucking it behind an ear. All I can do is pant and lay there in a boneless body.

"My mates are going to kill me. But—damn—what a way to go ..." I say to myself out loud causing them both to laugh loudly and look at each other with *again* male satisfaction written all over their faces.

"Get some rest, little warrior. Tomorrow, we head closer to battle to find another of your mates," Ragnar says softly while I smile into the fading darkness of the room.

Cadoc ... I'm coming to you!

CHAPTER
Sixteen

CADOC

Fuck! I mentally scream as I kick over a heavy barrel full of swords. *This is a complete disaster. How could we be so unprepared? It's almost like someone sabotaged us!*

Eirik and I made it to Sterling Outpost four days ago. We arrived and it was already chaos everywhere. Supposedly, the captain in command of Sterling Outpost, Captain Garish, died last week of an unknown cause in his bed shortly after dinner.

His second in command suspects poison, but I guess I'll never truly know. The whole sneakiness and timing of it has Jaarn written all over it. The young lieutenant, Devin, who's been in charge sent word immediately to Harkaenforge our capital city for support. Little did he know, he needed to be preparing for a full scale battle. After a week of no word from our king, he assumed the role of captain and kept the place from falling apart. Or—tried to.

When I arrived here, I sensed a tension in the air. Rushing into the battlements, I yelled out orders and questions regarding the surrounding area. *Have the scouts seen any surrounding sol-*

diers? Who's in charge? Why are there so few men on the walls? The poor soldier I intercepted nearly pissed himself before I stormed off. I immediately sent out Eirik and six other scouts to the surrounding land for an update on where Jaarn is camped out.

The news was not good.

They are already here and we are unprepared. Eirik lost three men to their arrows before they had to retreat back to the outpost.

Where are the reinforcements I ordered sent? Did my father not get my message? He should have had time to send soldiers here ... I think while I run over different scenarios in my head, worrying for my father and king. *No—it's more likely the messenger was intercepted. Jaarn was prepared. Too prepared. And it doesn't help that the Kingdom of Laevaris is allied with them now.*

That first day was a whirlwind of dealing with the chain of command, preparing the battlements, and convincing everyone that war is coming. I think I only got two hours of sleep before they attacked.

The rafters in the outpost shake waking me up and disrupting dust in my room. I slept prepared in my fighting leathers so I quickly don the rest of my armor overtop and add my sword into its sheath before storming out.

Eirik nearly plows me over running towards me. "They are using some sort of toxic mix of explosive in a hard shell that they are slinging by catapult at our walls. The solution inside—it burns the skin ... bad. And it releases a toxic gas that you can't really breathe through. Fuck, Cad! We haven't even seen their special weapons yet!"

"Damn. Where *the fuck* are those reinforcements we asked for? Why isn't my father responding?!" I shout to him over the noise and booming of the walls.

We make it outside into chaos. Men are running around yelling and stocking up supplies while women and workers are being shuffled inside the main outpost. This won't do. I need organization. Control.

Placing my fingers in my mouth, I blow out a loud whistle catching everyone's attention. Silence reigns except for the occasional boom onto the walls followed by a few screams.

"You will all follow my orders explicitly or heed my second in command, Captain Eirik. I want all available soldiers on the walls and my archers prepped and ready to go in the courtyard. *Now*!" I yell with cold confidence and people rush to do my bidding.

Eirik takes off to the wall while I check on the archers in the courtyard. Lieutenant Winn stands at attention organizing the twenty archers we have then notices me and nods his head. "They're ready, General … er … I mean—your highness. You want them on the north wall?" Ignoring his nervous sputtering, I nod my head before answering. Even though I'm the crown prince of Gorva, I'm also the general and leader for the Gorvian army which is more important right now.

"It's General given our current situation. Now, split up on either side of the gate. I'm going to go take a look at the situation and if needed I'll form a group of mounted cavalry to clear the gate."

I stalk up the stairs to the battlements and find Eirik with a look of irritation on his face.

"They have too many men, Cad. We're fucked. Hope you can pull something out of your royal ass because we're going to need it. I sent out another rider for reinforcements when I scouted the other day. If we can just last the week, then we'll be okay," Eirik says quietly to me to avoid being overheard.

"Shit," I say looking over the surrounding army scattered out in front of our outpost and taking a quick head count. "We'll be lucky to last four-five days if that." I run a hand through my white hair that's a bit too long for my taste and is starting to hang into my eyes. "We have to make it. We have enough supplies. It's just men we're lacking. So as long as the walls hold …"

Just as I say that, a resounding boom fills the air and the battlements shake. Our gazes shoot to the left, and I see a cloud of dust and smoke from an explosive that hit the northwest corner of the walls. Screams follow the explosion and I see a soldier running away with severe burns covering his face and chest.

"I got this. Man the gate," Eirik says before he starts to jog along the wall towards the site of the explosion and the injured.

"Wait." I reach into my pocket and pull out a small rag handing it to him. "Don't breathe that shit in if you can help it." I take another out of my back pocket which I placed there earlier and tie it around my lower face. He mimics me and nods his head before turning. "Watch that catapult out there. They're probably reloading or there could be another one."

I tap one of the archers on the shoulder and order him to follow Eirik with a command to get that fucking catapult out of commission. Then I turn back to the gate just as the first group of soldiers approach. Sterling Outpost doesn't have a moat or channel of water for defense but it does sit on a hill and has a small ditch at the base of the wall making it more difficult to approach.

Soldiers from Jaarn pause at the ditch and our archers ready their arrows. I realize they aren't pausing due to hesitance in getting shot but rather they are waiting …

Several large Jaarnian steel harpoons are shot simultaneously at specific locations along the northern wall and another one is shot into our gate. Watching in horror I see them shoot deeply into the stone like butter before expanding out sharp barbs at the end. The front line Jaarnian soldiers all cheer and wave before the harpoons are pulled backwards by rope attached to men and horses. Stone scatters everywhere and our fortified wall develops huge holes in a matter of seconds. *Dear Faktirnor, save us. Those must be the weapons they were talking about.*

I snap out of my shock quickly ordering the archers to fire and Lieutenant Winn directs their shots towards the men pulling those harpoons. I yell orders for men to double up in areas of the damaged walls in preparation for those Jaarnian soldiers that are now crossing the ditch.

Feeling adrenaline pump through my veins at the thought of the upcoming fight, I grit my teeth as I race down the battlements and gather men for a mounted attack to defend our gate. The harpoon that hit the gate is still lodged there but hasn't been pulled yet. I'm assuming our archers are doing their job in keeping Jaarn from applying tension and destroying our gate.

Once I'm mounted on my horse, I pull my large broadsword and turn to the ten men I picked for this job. All of them seasoned warriors, most of whom I fought with as a young soldier at a similar battle here years ago. We won then and we will today. I'll make sure of it.

The large wooden gate groans as Jaarn applies pressure to the tethered harpoon. So—before they can destroy it—I yell out to open the gate once the tension releases and let us out. Signaling Lieutenant Winn, he nods and has several archers target the Jaarnian soldiers controlling the harpoon stuck in the gate. Once the tether on the harpoon relaxes, the gate slowly swings open and I call out to get the harpoon dislodged before I return. With the gate open and the portcullis raised by my order, we exit the outpost as a mounted group of soldiers ready to defend our territory.

We charge into battle in a mounted V formation hacking our way through Jaarnian soldiers and clearing the gate. Arrows fly over my head and take out some of the approaching enemy.

It almost feels good to stretch my arms and swing my sword. This is what I was trained for. Battle. Leading. Responsibility.

That last word sits heavy in my head and makes me realize this is life or death. I'm responsible for all those men, and I can't let them down. I'm also not just fighting for me and my kingdom but … for my mate. I have someone else to consider now.

Suddenly looking around when my sword doesn't meet another, I realize I'm surrounded by bodies and my enemies are giving me a wide birth. I've never been so deadly in battle, and I'm confused for a second. Yes, I'm one of the best fighters in Gorva but even this is more advanced than my usual skills.

"Damn, General! I've never seen anyone pull those moves! They couldn't even touch you. You were so fast and I didn't know you were so limber. You nearly bent over flat avoiding that last man's sword," Lieutenant Farrian shouts to me from his horse. He has a few scratches and a nasty cut to his forehead but otherwise appears fine with an awed look on his face.

"Come on let's get back in for a break before the next tide of soldiers." I turn and we ride back into the gate which now has one less harpoon in it. Somehow the wooden gate is still intact. Doing a mental count, I see all our men made it back with few injuries.

The gate closes and I dismount grabbing some water that a young boy hands me then dumping it over my sweaty face. There's fighting on the north and western walls but I don't see anyone other than our soldiers on the battlements which is good.

A strong hand clamps down on my shoulder making me tense before I turn. "You're faster, Prince Cadoc. I've never seen a better fighter out there. It was like you moved so fast their hits could never land. Almost like it was impossible. Magic even. You took out nearly twenty soldiers, General," Lieutenant Shane says to me with a proud smile. "Who trained you—because if I survive this battle—I want to practice with them!" It's quite the compliment coming from him. He's one of the oldest soldiers here and honestly should be a captain now but doesn't like to lead and has turned my father down several times. He helped trained me as a young soldier so his approval means the world to me.

"I—I'm not sure. I haven't trained with anyone new, mostly Eirik. It was disorienting out there. I'm not one hundred percent sure how I could move that fast. It was like something came over me … maybe adrenaline?" I say catching my breath in sudden realization.

Solveig. My mate. She—she has a rune for agility. Could it have boosted me somehow? But … I'm not Elarian.

113

Either way, I won't look a gift horse in the mouth. It probably saved our asses out there. *Fuck, I miss her.* I'm not sure if I'm imagining it for a moment, but it almost feels like she's slightly closer through the mate bond. *Now's not the time, Cad! Focus on the battle not the prize at the end...* Solveig is more than my prize. She's my future. But without winning this battle, I won't be around to embrace it.

We fight from the walls for another few hours before they retreat back out of range for the night. By our count, we only lost ten men today which I'll count as a success. Mostly though, our men were lost through arrows or explosions.

We held the walls and survived another day. Hopefully, tomorrow we can continue.

CHAPTER
Seventeen

SOLVEIG

Walking into the town of Jael was a bit like stepping back in time. The roads are a dirt and sand combination and there is a significant lack of stone in the structure of the place. It appears more basic than most places and lacks any color that's not a shade of brown, tan, or cream. I know it's not the biggest town in the Kingdom of Beamus, but I expected a bit … more.

Everything is made of a combination of clay like material with some wood scattered here or there. The buildings appear to be built into the surrounding hills and blended with the landscape around the town. It's soothing and calming in its own distinct way, I guess.

We arrive in the middle of the day when the central part of town is bustling with activity. Surprisingly, no one pays any attention to our small group walking through it. Farmers trade their goods, bakers yell out their daily specials, and trappers prowl around showcasing their recent hides.

I ignore all of that and head straight for a young boy that I see trading a horse in exchange for money. Luckily, Ragnar and the rest of my group don't question me as I veer towards the boy.

Just as the boy completes the exchange and is about to take off, I snag his sleeve and say, "Excuse me. Can you tell me where I may find a woman named Sia?" A flare of recognition enters the boy's eyes before it's gone and replaced with a stubborn look. "She has bright red hair and—"

"Look, lady. I don't know you," the boy interrupts me, speaking in a haughty voice before looking around at the men with me. "And—I don't know the rest of you. Here in town we protect our own and information ain't free. I don't know any woman named Sia. Best look for someone else to help you." The boy pulls out of my grip quickly and jogs away.

"Wait!" I yell but he's already walking away and doesn't respond to my shout. I pause for a second considering my options which are few since I don't know exactly where to find her in this town. I sought the boy out because he was dealing in horses and Sia loves horses. And, I just happened to be right.

I subtly tilt my head after the boy and tell the men individually through mind speak using my rune power, *Come on. The boy knows her. He could lead us to wherever she is at.*

All three men simultaneously nod their heads which must look strange to others given we never said anything out loud. I jog to catch up to the corner I saw the boy last turn at. Already far ahead of us, he takes a dirt path off the main part of town towards a large log cabin like structure set a few buildings back. It rests between wooden fencing, and I can see multiple horses in the field behind it.

The boy sees a group of kids his age and takes off into the field full of horses. Instead of following him, I enter the wooden building with the others following on my heels. There's an office in the front with a desk and another door propped open leading into the stables connected behind it. A scruffy older man with black and grey peppered hair looks up at our entrance.

116

"May I help you?" he asks in a guarded voice eyeing my weapons then looking over the hulking men behind me. "Are you looking to buy horses?"

"Greetings, sir. No we aren't looking for horses—" I start to say.

"Well, then you're in the wrong place. There's a sword-smith two streets down off the main street in town. Good day." He looks back down at his paperwork dismissing me.

Huh! Prickly people here, I think to myself.

Clearing my throat loudly to gain his attention again, I say, "We aren't looking for new weapons. I'm looking for a friend, a woman. She has bright red hair and goes by the name—Sia. And, before you act like you don't know who I'm talking about … just know that she's waiting for me. She's expecting us."

The older man looks intensely at me for a moment before he responds. "She's not here." I open my mouth to interrupt him but he holds a hand up cutting off my next words. "She left just a bit ago for lunch. More than likely, she's two ales deep at the Hilltop Tavern. It's one street over up some stairs off the main street."

"Thank you," I say but he's already ignoring me again signing papers on his desk.

Come on, men. I think we could all do with an ale or two as well. Hopefully, he wasn't lying, I tell the men as we leave and walk back towards the bustling main street in town.

"I'm starving! I could eat a whole dampkir by myself, maybe two!" Tempest says out loud making a few people glance over at him.

Ragnar attentively runs his hand over the bottom half of my braid before placing it on my lower back. He then says, "You *do* need to eat, my Maseeri. We will find your friend. I believe that man was telling the truth."

"Honestly, I could do with an ale too! This place is strange … I wonder how they make such structures here. Some of these buildings appear to use sand or clay and create a solid compound to form the walls …" Jorah says running his hand over the nearest building in contemplation. Then he clears his throat embarrassingly as he realizes we're all silent. "Sorry guys! Just a thought. Sol, you still haven't revealed *why* in fact we are meeting *this* friend." He moves his other hand to hold mine as we walk and see a set up stairs leading up.

I look up and see a sign saying: *Hilltop Tavern*. I glance over at Jorah and say, "I know. I just thought … we're so close to Beamus and I haven't seen her since we were just kids."

Jorah smiles and squeezes my hand before we all climb the stairs and enter the rustic tavern.

All noise cuts off at our entrance before quickly starting up again. The front of the tavern and one wall showcases windows with a nice view of the town. Jorah and Tempest walk over to the barkeep and order us ales as well as the current lunch special.

I look around trying to spot red hair and come up empty. But just as I'm starting to lose hope, I see a darker corner of the tavern with a table of concealed people all staring at me. Before I can fully think through my actions, I quickly walk over and stand before them. Ragnar and the guys follow a moment later voicing a few complaints that I should have waited for them.

One woman with a bandana covering her hair and an amused smirk sits with two burly men at the table. The men don't appear to be simple stableboys and I casually notice the other tavern occupants give their table a wide birth.

The two men have a hefty amount of blades attached to their bodies and expressionless looks on their faces. They're older than me and look as if they're assessing for threats, clueing me in that they're likely her guards. The woman, on the other hand, although dressed in simple garb with dirty brown leather pants and a loose cream shirt falling open haphazardly off one shoulder, is beautiful. Her demeanor appears relaxed and teasing, but I can tell it's actually confidence. The dirty bandana cover her hair reveals a single red curl falling in her face. A face … that I slightly recognize. Sia.

"Well look what the horses finally brought in … Solveig, I presume?" she says leaning forward and propping her head in her hand while staring at me. "It's been a long time, I almost didn't recognize you. And—you made me wait a whole extra day than your message! I nearly left. Lucky for you, Jael raises some of the best horses in Beamus and I tend to spend a lot of my time here. Sit."

Pulling up some chairs, we all crowd around her table while Ragnar stands behind me with a protective and suspicious look on his face.

"Sorry, Sia. *Damn,* it's been a long time. But you actually look a lot like how I remember you." I pause cautiously assessing her and hoping she's still the friend I remember. I suppose she wouldn't be here if she wasn't. "It was slower travel than I expected. It was also a bit tough to find you in this town. Everyone is pretty closed mouth but I figured you'd be somewhere near the horses."

"Yup. You remember well," she replies popping her "p" and smirking at me. "Now, tell me what was so urgent you interrupted my boring routine and made me travel here. I suppose I should thank you. Also—who are these sexy men you have with you?" Although her words include all the men, her gaze is only focused on Ragnar standing protectively behind me.

A flare of irritation and a green wave of jealousy flows through me unjustly. Ragnar most notice through our bond because his hand suddenly comes to rest on the nape of my neck and rubs soothing circles there.

No need to feel jealous, little warrior. You are mine and I am yours.

Love you, Ragi, I reply to him.

Jorah rests a hand on my forearm at our words and I relax from their contact.

You're mine too, Sol. I think your friend was just teasing … Jorah says to me through our mate bond trying to reassure me.

Tempest is leaning back in his chair with his arms crossed as though he's enjoying the show. I can tell he's trying to suppress

119

his amusement at her words and appear tough but the twitch at the corner of his mouth is a giveaway. Luckily, he can't feel my jealousy or hear our conversation.

Love you too, Jorah. I look back over at Sia and see he's right because she's full on smiling in a teasing sort of way. But, she also appears a bit confused with a head tilt. Her eyes track the hands of both my mates then look over at Tempest who's now chugging his ale that just arrived.

"Wow. Okay … so I suspected one of them was yours but," Sia clears her throat, then says, "now I'm not sure."

Taking a deep breath I pat the hand of my Drakonian mate and nudge Jorah saying, "These two are my mates. This here is Ragnar." Then I look over at my scholarly mate. "And this is Jorah."

Sia's eyebrows shoot up her forehead in surprise before she claps her hands in glee. "Damn, Sol. That's … *well done*. And … that one?" She looks over with a questioning gaze at the last man in my group.

"Oh, that's Tempest. Ragnar's cousin. *Not* one of my mates."

"Okay … awesome." She stares at Tem raising her eyebrows up and down before pulling the bandana off her hair and primping a bit. The two men next to her stiffen up, while Tempest smirks and leans forward on his elbows giving her a hooded look. "So, what do you mean you have mates? I thought that was just a shifter term and not part of our human physiology? I do know a pack of wolf shifters and some of the Mervians, the water nymphs, here in Beamus tend to have mates, but why do you? And, how do I get in on this multiple mates thing?"

One of the guards with Sia makes a growling noise in his throat and starts to finger a dagger in his hand catching her attention. "Oh, sorry, I forgot. These two stuffy men are the guards my father assigned to me, Riktus and Adar. Addy! Loosen up, they're friends." The man she nicknamed Addy, the one with the growl and dagger, immediately relaxes once her attention is off Tempest making me chuckle.

"I see you have your hands full too, Sia," I say before focusing back on our conversation. "I have mates … several, in fact. I've found out that I'm actually only part human and am more Elarian than anything else. They're a magical people who used to live in northern Daelarias particularly in the Elaritian Forest. It's a long story, but in the interest of time I'd like to discuss it later."

"Seriously? Sol, that's amazing! I always knew you were more than those idiot Laevarians said you were. They treated you so poorly," she says angrily scrunching her nose and pounding her fist on the table. "Elarian, though? I've never heard of them. But I honestly didn't pay enough attention to our magical species tutors since I was always sneaking out to ride." Her words cause the guard, Riktus, to snicker and she elbows him before looking back at me expectantly.

"We'll tell you more later but we're in a rush to leave tomorrow. I need to travel to Gorva in order to help one of my other mates. You should know … Laevaris and Gorva are likely at war now. And Jaarn is at the center of it." I say seeing her shocked expression before I delve into an explanation on how I overheard my father and Malphas scheming with the Jaarnian nobles. "It's all because of their greed for power and money. Jaarn is hoping to invade through Sterling Outpost and I fear they may have already started to attack, hence my rush." Then biting my lip, I say, "We also heard while we've been traveling that my father was killed …"

Sia's shocked gasp is loud in our secluded corner. "Fuck. This is all bad news. I'm sorry, Sol. But maybe it's a good thing if he's dead. I mean … your father was kind of an asshole." I can't help the laugh that slips out of my mouth at her words. She's always been bluntly honest which I appreciated.

"Thanks, and you're right. There was no love lost between us. It's just … now what? I'm not sure who is ruling in Laevaris and they just helped start a war with Gorva. It's a complete disaster which is why I wanted to meet up with you."

"I see … you're worried my kingdom will join Jaarn or Laevaris in this war against Gorva?" she replies with a calculated look on her face. It's easy to see how intelligent she is behind her teasing demeanor. Tapping her chin she pauses in thought while I somberly nod my head.

The men in my group all look between us with baffled expressions. So, of course it's Jorah who asks what they're all thinking. He raises a hand like he's in a classroom before saying, "Um, Sol? Perhaps I missed something but I'm confused as to why your friend here, excuse me—Sia—is the right person to consult with these political matters?"

I go to answer but it's the guard, Adar, who answers by saying, "It's because … young man, you're speaking to the crowned Princess Cassia and you—including your friend there," he nods his head disrespectfully towards Tempest who smirks but also raises an eyebrow in surprise, "--would do well to remember that by treating her with the respect she deserves."

The explanation is met with silence from my men while Sia and I share a secretive but pleased look to have flabbergasted all the men.

Keep your eyes on your enemies and your hands on your allies, Ragnar says through the mate bond with a proud look in my direction. I smile back and tilt my head up for a kiss. He leans down anticipating it before kissing me chastely which makes me pout. In response to my immature pouting, he smiles and tugs my braid.

I hear a cough come from someone at the table breaking up our moment before I see Sia's amused and watchful look.

"Well, now that the cat's out of the bag, so to speak, we can enjoy our time today. You'll tell me about what you've been up to the past few years that you didn't include in any of your letters, and I'll tell you about all the boring things my father makes me do. I'll plan to leave in the morning when you do.

Don't worry, Sol, I'll make sure my father understands we need to support Gorva or remain neutral in this war. That's what you want right?"

"Yeah, if you can. I don't want you to get in trouble …" At my words, the two guards burst out into laughter while Sia narrows her eyes and purses her lips in offense at their amusement. "Uhh-- well, if you can support Gorva that would be helpful but only if I can't stop the fighting first. We have to act quickly since I don't know what all is happening at the border yet."

Sia stands up quickly and comes around the table throwing her arm around my shoulders. "Don't worry, friend, trouble is my middle name back at the palace as these two goons know. Also, my father dotes on me. Now, tell me more about these mates of yours …" she says conspiratorially as we all walk out of the tavern. We spend the next few hours in an enjoyable haze of friendship, allowing me relax for the first time in a while.

CHAPTER
Eighteen

CADOC

nother day of defensive fighting comes and goes. On the third day of battle, we run out of luck.

I'm on the northern battlements overseeing the men fighting off harpoons and enemies scaling the wall when suddenly I'm knocked off my feet and an ear splitting boom sounds through the air. All I can hear for the next several minutes is ringing in my head.

Lifting my head off the ground and feeling for injuries, I can feel blood on my forehead or rather my eyebrow which must be split open from impacting with the stone underneath me. I look around and see a huge crater in the upper eastern wall.

Fuck! Eirik! He was over there pushing back a small siege before that explosion. I stumble a bit drawing my sword and racing toward the toxic cloud of dust and chemicals while raising the bandana around my neck to cover my lower face. I see Eirik sprawled on the floor of the courtyard below and realize he was thrown off the wall. He's subtly moving his hand so I know he's alive. *Thank Valirr!*

I want to head down there and help him but Jaarnian soldiers are already scaling the wall up into the opening they just created.

Shaking my head to clear the fuzziness of a probable concussion, I attack. Several men from the southern and northern walls back me up and help hold off the stream of soldiers trying to breach our walls. But—it's too much. We are too scattered and don't have enough men to counter their mass. I'm too slow…

A sword cuts through my left arm shooting blood everywhere and I stumble to my knee holding up my broad sword to block his next swipe. When I look around, I see my fellow men struggling as well and have a moment of self-doubt. Maybe I'm not enough. Maybe, I failed.

No. I have too much to live for now. I refuse to let these sneaky conniving back-stabbing Jaarnians to overrun my kingdom! With a burst of adrenaline and pulling some of that mysterious energy from my bond (which I've utilized over the past few days), I twist under his arm and around him sliding my sword along his abdomen. I manage to take out four more soldiers before I feel the fatigue of blood loss creeping in.

I see a streak of red out of the corner of my eye and go to duck behind a crenellation thinking it's some sort of flying projectile or explosive that the catapults are throwing. When nothing hits the wall, I peek out just as a deafening roar sounds and a shadow falls over the light on this side of the fortress.

Is that a … dragon?! I mentally stutter in shock.

A massive gleaming red dragon flies over the wall, soaring back around before it lets out a stream of molten fire, encasing the soldiers at the bottom of the outer wall, effectively killing a large number of our enemies in one impressive burst of power. My men on the walls slowly recover from their shock at our unexpected savior before disposing of the few soldiers that made it to the top of the wall.

The red dragon soars over us again and loops into the air before disappearing in a burst of fire and landing on the wall as a … *woman*?

What the hell is happening right now? I think I hit my head harder than I thought. I shake my head and rub my eyes before taking a deep breath and centering my thoughts.

The woman is gorgeous. Dark red hair cascades down her back while her body is encased in tight black fighting leathers. She's eye catching, dangerously beautiful and mysterious but … I feel nothing towards her. Not like I do for my mate. My Solveig.

Her golden eyes narrow and look around the area like a predator searching for its prey. One soldier approaches her cautiously with hands outstretched and she must say something to him because the next thing he does is point directly at me leaning against the battlements.

Her eyes intensely hone in on me as she marches my way. I try to straighten up and look confident but it probably comes off as a slouch given my weariness and blood loss. Though, I still manage to hold up my broadsword and halt her progress.

"Prince Cadoc?" she says in a gravelly voice. I nod my head in acknowledgment. "Is Solveig here?"

Before I can get any words out, my jaw falls open in shock and confusion like an idiot. *She knows Solveig? How does she know who I am?*

"Who are you? And how do you know me? Why are you here?" I ask her sternly once I gather my wits.

"Well, you look like you needed my help. So … you're welcome!" she says with a smirk while popping her hip out. "That soldier over there told me who was in charge. Now … *Where is Solveig*?" She drops all pretense of joking and anger leaks out into her last words making me take a step back. She's a bit intimidating and knowing she changes into a huge fucking dragon makes me second guess myself.

"She isn't here. How do you know her? And who are *you*?" I say in an expressionless voice shifting my stance.

Her facial expression quickly changes to one of concern as she bites her lower lip before answering. "Fuck. She was supposed to be here." Then she walks closer and tilts her head back a bit smelling the air. "Her scent is still a bit on you under all that blood and the acrid smoke of battle. Let me wrap that wound for you or you'll pass out before I have a chance to explain." She reaches out to grab my arm, and I hesitate with my sword. "Put your sword away and be a good boy or I'll tell your mate you haven't been taking good care of yourself."

Once again my shock makes me flounder like an idiot and my sword drops at her words. She takes the opening and pushes my sword to the side. Then she grabs my shirt and rips off a piece at the bottom before wrapping it tightly around my wound stemming the flow of blood.

"How did you know?" I ask her, confused that she knew I was Solveig's mate. No one here knew that secret other than Eirik. *Shit, Eirik! I need to check on him.*

"I can scent her on you. Us Drakoni can scent whether someone is mated or unmated. Also—she told me about you. Sit. Just for a minute," she says waving at the floor below a crenellation.

"Drakoni? She told you ... I'm confused. I've never met you before." Rubbing my temples, I try to gather my concussed thoughts.

"Yes, Drakoni. That's a story for another time, but we are essentially dragon shifters to you humans. You saw my dragon form just a moment ago," she says picking at the blood on one of her nails.

"We've never met but Solveig's told me about you. She's my friend, one of my only friends actually. It's strange ... but we're friends through letters. I've only actually met her once but we've written to each other for years. She ran into some trouble recently and told me to meet her here at this this time," she says looking up and around the area before her gaze hones in on me again. "She asked me to help you. Protect you that is ... and your kingdom.

She must really like you since she's never asked me to meet up before now. Not that I haven't tried before … she tends to be a bit too independent and reckless if you ask me. The stories I've heard …"

She chatters on fondly thinking of my mate.

"I'm Jicquara or Ara as your mate likes to call me," she says with a smile holding out her hand to shake.

"Wow. Okay … that's not what I was expecting. Well met, Ara," I say shaking her hand. "Thanks for helping. We—we were a bit in a bind there until you showed up."

"Yeah no shit! You guys are severely lacking men here from what I could see … unless you're hiding more in the outpost?" she says raising an eyebrow.

"No, I wish. Our messages went unanswered and reinforcements never came. We're just holding on *barely*. Their weapons are more advanced and we're sitting ducks here," I say sheathing my sword that was laying on the stone floor. "What did you mean Solveig ran into trouble? And she's supposed to come *here*? This is the worst place for her! She'll get herself killed!"

Ara again raises an eyebrow at me as she stands up and dusts herself off. Then her gaze focuses on my injured arm before she says, "Oh, really? Please … as if you weren't almost hacked to death just a moment ago? I think you underestimate our girl. She's fucking tough *and* a fighter. She can handle herself. She was supposed to meet me here and she warned of a possible battle but I wasn't expecting *this* when I showed up!"

She throws her hands up in frustration.

"I'm sure she was just delayed and will be here soon. She was dealing with a little witch issue … oops, sorry, an Essent Wielder, but she wasn't injured at the time."

Chagrined appropriately, I look down. She's right. Solveig is stronger than I sometimes give her credit for but … I just want to protect her. Keep her safe. Someone has to look out for that woman.

"You're right. About my mate anyways. However, I think I'm going to pass on understanding what you mean by witch or ascent wielder or whatever. I only just learned about magic and powers from Solveig. Too much information right now. Come on, I need to see the healer and get back out here. I also have to check on my best friend. He was thrown off the wall in the attack." I nod my head to the side and she follows me off the battlements towards the inner part of the outpost. Taking a right turn, we make it to the healers' office and infirmary.

We find Eirik towards the back of the room. He's still unconscious and per the healer he has a nasty head injury but seems to be stable. They are optimistic he will wake up soon. Otherwise, he lucked out with only a broken left wrist which they have already reset and placed in a cast.

I needed ten stitches for the wound on my arm before I was able to get back out on the battlements. Ara went off to grab some food before returning and meeting me. Now, she stands at my back munching on a leg of dampkir.

"So what do you think?" I say in an exhausted voice glancing at her from the corner of my eye and waving a hand at our enemy. I need to motivate the men since I can see them walking around with a slightly dazed and defeated look. They think we are a lost cause … that no one's coming. *They might be right.*

"Umm … argh … Urm noaught reeahlay a straughtogihzer," she mumbles around the food in her mouth. When I look at her fully with a raised eyebrow, she swallows her food and repeats, "Sorry, I'm not really a strategizer. I'm more of an inventor. I'm good at making things. Weapons included. It's my rune—creativity and innovation. That mixed with my elemental fire affinity is good for forging weapons as you can imagine. But I wasn't the war leader in my family. I tended to stay up in my lair most days tinkering around with my inventions. That doesn't mean—I don't know how to fight."

Then taking another bite she mumbles out, "You have a Drakoni at your disposal—use me."

The next two days is a blur of fighting, blood, and fire. Thank Faktirnor for Ara! She saved our asses more times than I could count. Every time it looked like they would break through our walls, she was there. But—they have so many soldiers and weapons.

My arms are sore and I'm dead on my feet tonight. The fighting has slowed down for now and Ara just went to get a few hours of sleep before switching watch with me.

She's sort of acting as a second in command while Eirik is down. It's strange since I just met her, but she has this powerful presence that the men respect, including me. It also helps that she put hope in the men's eyes—they feel more confident having a Drakoni defending them.

Once she sneaks up behind me and tells me to get some rest, it's the middle of the night and I'm barely functioning. I can't even remember the last time I rested. My arm is throbbing from the stitches in it and I'm sore just about everywhere from swinging my broadsword too much.

I sink instantly into a deep sleep once I fall into bed.

I wake up groggy and confused rubbing my face and trying to gather my thoughts. And when I look out my small window, it's still dark so I know I didn't get nearly enough sleep. *What woke me?*

A resounding *boom* rattles the room and causes some things to fall off the desk near my bed. I'm on my feet and securing my weapons in the next second. Then, I chug a quick glass of water before racing outside and see chaos. Utter chaos.

Two of the outer walls are literally on fire and smoke is filling the courtyard. Men are racing everywhere and several lay injured screaming. I can see Ara slowly sitting up from the ground rubbing her head so I race over to her first.

"What happened? Why didn't someone wake me!" I yell over the cacophony.

When I don't get an answer from Ara, I grab her shoulders to look at her more closely. She has a dazed look in her eyes and is blinking rapidly. *She must have hit her head hard. Shit.*

"Get to the healer. *Now!*" I grab her arm to lift her off the ground then gently nudge her towards the infirmary. She mutters out something in another language that I don't understand and honestly don't have the time to decipher.

As she stumbles away, I assess the situation. It's not looking good. The Eastern wall is in shambles and the northern wall has taken a good amount of damage. Our main gate is barely hanging on there. I can tell—this is it. We don't have enough men to defend that big of a hole in the eastern wall and protect our gate.

I scrounge together a contingent of battle hardened soldiers to accompany me in defending the eastern wall while I find Lieutenant Shane. Placing the older warrior in charge of defending the main gate and northern wall, I mount my horse and signal my men. While the sun starts to rise on a new day, we race to the eastern wall just as Jaarnian soldiers climb the ditch and approach the rubble where the wall once stood.

My broadsword cuts diagonally across the first soldier nearly slicing him in half before I move on to the next. I lose track of time as I hack and slash, thrust and slice. I can feel my arm start to fatigue. We are being pushed back towards the wall now even though in the beginning we gained ground all the way to the ditch surrounding the outpost. Knowing my fighting arm is getting too tired, I drop my broadsword and pull my short sword from my hip allowing me to get a bit closer to my enemy.

It's when I stumble back into the broken wall that I see it … a deadly and agile moving warrior cutting towards us through the throng of enemy soldiers. They're hooded so I can't tell who it is.

I'm distracted for only a second watching—wondering—if it's friend or foe before I see them look up.

Piercing sapphire blue eyes look directly into mine from across the distance. But … before I can mutter her name, I feel a slashing cut across my thigh forcing me to my knees.

CHAPTER
Nineteen

SOLVEIG

After seeing the destruction of Sterling Outpost from the sky, I'm panicking with anxiety. *My mate!*

Ragnar lands and shifts in a haze of smoke back to his two-legged form beside me. We race into battle before Tempest, carrying Jorah, even lands. I think Ragnar can feel my anxiety through the mate bond prompting him to not even question my next move.

As we flew in and saw how the Jaarnian soldiers were swarming the eastern wall, we decided to land and help spear in from the side hopefully giving Cadoc's soldiers some help in defending the crumbling wall. It may have been easier to just land in the Outpost, but Ragnar was concerned his dragon form would only break the wall further. His dragon form is *huge* and probably wouldn't fit well within their courtyard without squishing some of the men.

Plus—Ragnar is giving me a heady dose of battle lust through the mate bond. The need for blood is now flowing through us both. And—I want to fight. Sword to flesh.

I tuck my braid into the back of my tunic and pull my hood up over my head, casting my face in shadow. Sometimes it helps to be anonymous in a fight. No need to place a target on my back in case others realize who I am. I pull both my katanas from my back harness with finesse then charge into battle.

The enemy turns just as I approach with a surprised look. The first one falls easily beneath me with a simple slice across his neck. Nearly ten or is it twenty men later, I lose track of Ragnar in the fighting. I watched him from the corner of my eye take on three men at once in a dance of deadly grace. He fights so smoothly and lithely. His moves remind me of the twisting and curling of smoke that floats up from an extinguished candle. Smooth and confident. I'd never seen Ragnar fight in his two-legged form, but I'm glad I did. He's just as deadly as his dragon form. *But, where did he disappear to in this horde of soldiers?*

I parry the sword of the man in front of me before hearing a shift in the air behind me as a warning. Quickly arching one katana over my shoulder, I block the sword slicing towards my exposed back and twist around, keeping the two soldiers in my peripheral vision. Unfortunately when I twist, my hood falls and my long, dark brown braid swings around over my shoulder. Both soldiers' smirk and hoot out loud when they notice that they're fighting a woman. Simple-minded men think I'm easy prey just because I don't have a dick between my legs. *Poor idiots. Their tiny pea-sized brains can't comprehend a woman that's a warrior or better than them.* I'm a threat … a deadly one … and I'm done fooling around.

Ducking under their synchronized pitiful attempts at sword play, I smile and cut out their legs with my katanas. Then standing over them I stab down into their necks.

Suddenly, I'm hit with a strong ache in my chest. And like a beacon directing my gaze, I look over into Cadoc's brown eyes. I go to yell out to him but it's too late. The warrior in front of him charges in his moment of distraction and cuts him deeply on the thigh.

I'm already racing towards him hacking and slashing at anyone in my way. *Faster,* I think as my agility rune burns on my thigh giving me a boost of power. I make it just as the warrior raises his sword in a killing move before I thrust all the way through his chest from behind.

Cadoc is on his knees holding his thigh together and looking up at me with adoration and relief. "About damn time, mate."

"*Cadoc*!" I yell before I throw myself at him and embrace him in the middle of battle. Our mate bond thrums in response causing us both to sigh in pleasure from the contact.

Abruptly, he shoves me to the side and lifts his sword from the ground but it's in vain. Ragnar walks over with smoke blowing out his nostrils and his sword stuck through a man about to skewer me during my embrace with Cadoc.

"Little warrior … didn't I tell you to stay by me? That was our deal … if I knew you were going to race off and not watch your back, then I would have just incinerated all these useless men," Ragnar says with irritation and a look of reprimand. Then his eyes shift to their more reptilian form for a second before filling with heat. "You fight well, my Maseeri. I'm lucky indeed. We need to put that agility you displayed in battle to better use later tonight." Then Ragnar winks. He. Winks. *Fuck, that's sexy when he does that covered in blood and confidently holding a sword.*

"Who the *fuck* are you?" Cadoc says angrily attempting to stand but his right leg is nearly split open from that sword. I scramble to support him so we can walk back into Sterling Outpost.

Ragnar sheaths his sword after he glances around the fallen bodies surrounding the area. It looks like we won the fight and Jaarn has retreated back from the eastern wall.

"I'm her mate. Her soulfire. Her Makati. You must be Prince Cadoc," Ragnar says with his arms crossed and a smirk. "You're welcome by the way."

Cadoc squeezes me in tighter to his side like he could protect me. Unfortunately, he's leaning heavily on me and needs medical attention, now.

"You have another mate, Sol?" He sighs heavily and closes his eyes for a second before focusing on me as we turn and walk through the rubble into the courtyard of the outpost.

I sheepishly peer at him and reply, "Yes … Cadoc, this is Ragnar. My Drakonian mate. We are soul mates—sort of like fated mates—similar to how Kaeden and I are connected. Oh—and he's a king supposedly." I decide to throw in that last bit just to dig at Ragi for keeping it from me.

Cadoc stumbles a bit at my words and looks at Ragnar disbelievingly. "Another one? And a king at that? Damn, Sol. You sure do know how to pick them."

Once we make it inside the infirmary, I help ease Cadoc down onto a cot.

"Yeah, another one. Sorry. I think that makes up four mates—five, if Kaeden and I decide to complete the bond."

"No, no. I mean—another *Drakoni*. Your friend is here …" Cadoc says trailing off when a healer rushes over to stitch up his thigh.

"*W—What. Did. You. Say?*" Ragnar shouts suddenly full of tension. "*Where?*"

"Right here, big brother!" I hear a raspy voice say behind all of us. Everyone turns and all eyes fall on my friend Jicquara. It's been years since I saw her. She looks a bit worse for wear but still beautiful as ever. *Wait …did she say, big brother?*

Ragnar rushes over and embraces my friend picking her up into huge encompassing hug. Both cry out in joy with tears running down their faces as they talk in a flurry of Drakonian.

"Praise Valirr! You're alive. I can't believe it! Are you injured? What happened? Where have you been? Are you okay?" Ragnar mutters out question after question in their foreign language. Lucky for me I can understand with my mind-speak rune.

135

"I'm fine. Just a little head bump. I got here a few days before you, but I'm surprised you're traveling with my friend," Ara says in Drakonian holding Ragnar's shoulders before looking over at me and switching to the common language. "Well met, Sol! I've missed you! It's been too long but it feels like yesterday."

Ragnar turns and squints at me confused. "You two know each other? You know my mate?" Ragnar asks Ara.

"Mate!" she squeaks excitedly. "You didn't tell me my big brother was your mate Sol! Now we are sisters!" She dislodges Ragnar's embrace and scoops me up hugging me fiercely.

I laugh a bit before replying, "I didn't know! I swear! I think I forgot to mention Ragnar's name in all our writing to each other otherwise you'd probably have figured it out. So you're Drakoni then?" Ara nods to me with a smile. "Now, I understand how you traveled around quickly and how you had those magic notebooks. You helped make them didn't you? Ragnar told me his sister was an amazing inventor and creator of magical objects!"

"Yeah, I helped make them with my mentor. They were one of our creations before the war. I'll have to invent something different now that those nasty witches have one. But—I'm glad you're both here. I never thought I'd see another Drakoni again!"

Just as Ara finishes her statement, Tempest and Jorah walk in the door looking around for us. Both are a bit disheveled but uninjured. I totally lost track of them in my rush to rescue Cadoc.

Tempest locks eyes with Ara from across the room and he growls out a primal sound before stating loudly, *Mate,* just as Ara simultaneously tenses up and repeats, *Mate.* Scales shift down their arms and their locked eyes turn reptilian while the rest of us watch in confusion.

"Wait just a moment. Did you say *mate?* Jicquara? Tem?" Ragnar says with a hand in the air but it's no use.

Ara and Tempest cross the distance to each other in a flash and embrace in a tangle of limbs. They kiss wildly with teeth and tongue as I look on in fascination. Just as Tempest pulls off his shirt and reaches for Ara's, Ragnar steps in to try and break them apart. Tem growls loudly again while pulling Ara to his chest and saying in Drakonian, "*Mine!*"

I lean forward and pull Ragnar back before saying, "Remember when another male approached me? You got all growly and protective too. Let me try to get some sense into them. Clearly, they need to get a room." Then I walk cautiously to Jicquara and say, "You and your mate need to find a private room to complete the bond. Here is not the best. Too many people would see your mate."

Ara's head snaps over to me assessing in a predatory way. It's like she doesn't even recognize me anyone. Instinct is currently ruling her and Tempest's heads right now. But—I must have gotten through to her since she climbs up his waist wrapping her legs around him and whispering words into his ear. He smiles in a feral way before stalking off with her further into the Outpost with a single purpose in mind.

"*Fuck*," Ragnar says in shock, running a hand over his warrior braid running down the center of his scalp.

"Yeah, that about sums it up. It was like two animals about to mate," Cadoc says uncomfortably and a bit confusedly. "I'm assuming that other man … Tem, is Drakoni too? Damn … three dragons. What did you get me into, Sol?" The nervous healer is just about done stitching up his leg at this point, but it obviously took longer than usual since we all were watching that display of raw lust including everyone else in the infirmary.

"Ugh, honestly I don't know! I thought Ragnar was the only one left of his kind. This is crazy! I can't believe they're mates! Speaking of *mates* … Cadoc have you met Jorah before?" I nervously ask picking at some of the blood under my nails.

Jorah's head snaps up at his name, and I see the blush covering his face. Probably from seeing two Drakoni paw each other I public.

"No, we haven't met." Cadoc nods his head towards him in greeting. "I'm assuming you're one of the four—er—possibly

137

five? Mates that is? Solveig might have mentioned you and I think I saw your face a few times in the stables back in Falal."

"Well met, Prince Cadoc. You're correct on both accounts. Sol and I are mates ... so I believe that makes us mate-brothers, as Ragnar likes to call us. My father is the stable master at the castle so I was frequently working there. But usually you'll see me in the library or with the scholars. I'm not a fighter like all of you, but I suppose I should learn given all the trouble Solveig seems to attract."

"Ahh, yes. Solveig is a bit reckless. I'm sure one of us can help train you," Cadoc says, then as an afterthought tacks on, "Mate-brother. Also call me Cadoc. It seems a bit superfluous to use titles."

We all spend the next hour eating and talking while Cadoc rests in the infirmary before he falls asleep. I ask Jorah to sit with him and watch over him while Ragnar and I head out to the battlements.

CHAPTER
Twenty

SOLVEIG

Those huge harpoon-like weapons seem to be a major problem. We're going to need to address them if we want to finish this," I say with arms crossed overlooking the land in front of the northern wall. Several large chunks of stone are missing along the northern and eastern walls from those harpoons and the front gate is a mess. Luckily, they have a portcullis still intact.

But … that troublesome eastern wall has a gaping hole in it creating a massive target for invasion. I already ordered men to use what materials we have to try and fortify it.

"True. The catapults though are creating just as big of an issue with that strange toxic liquid exploding on impact," Ragnar replies mimicking my power pose unintentionally.

"You're both correct and they still have more men than us. Now what are we going to do about it?" A large burly warrior walks up to us with a curious expression. He's an older man but still in top fighting condition based on his physical shape and confident walk.

"I'm Lieuten—I mean—Captain Shane. I got a recent promotion yesterday since all the other Captains were either severely injured or dead," he says in an angry voice spitting on the ground. "Fucking greedy Jaarnians. I ain't never asked to be a Captain … I liked not having all the responsibility and instead I could just kill those bastards. But here we are … so … I can tell you all look like damn good warriors and saw you come in with the General. So, like I said before—what are we going to do about it?" He crosses his arms at the end and looks at us with a raised eyebrow.

Ragnar's gaze turns assessing and a bit predatory as he shifts behind me and wraps his arms around my waist before saying, "Mine."

I reach down and pat one of his hands on my waist soothingly. "Yes, I'm yours, Ragi. Now lower the possessive male dominance down a peg." Then I turn and look at Captain Shane before saying, "Ignore him. We were discussing taking out the harpoons and the catapults since they seem to be the biggest threat."

"Ahh—yes. The catapults are a bit easier to take out if we had that dragon woman back. She already took out two before. But—I haven't seen her since she was injured. As far as the harpoons … they are tougher to get rid of. They're made of Jaarnian steel and don't burn in the dragon fire as far as we can tell. The only way we've been stopping them is taking out the shooters."

"I see. Well, lucky for you—I have the biggest, baddest Drakonian male right here." I say shifting around until I'm facing Ragnar. Then I lean forward and run my fingers along his scalp causing him to rumble in pleasure at the touch.

"Uhh—erm—very good," Captain Shane stutters uncomfortably at our public display of affection while humorously his face turns a bright shade of red. "So he'll take out the catapults. What about the harpoons?"

"Ragi? Any thoughts?" I ask my mate while he continues to rumble and lean into my touch. His eyes crack open at my words and they are completely reptilian full of heat and promise.

"I have a lot of thoughts, little warrior. Dirty thoughts. But— I suppose that's not what you want to hear right now," he says in a sexy purr that rumbles through his chest. *Holy fuck! Now I'm aroused standing in the middle of a battle. Get a grip, Sol! Not the time …*

Yes, it is the time, Ragnar says into my mind while he leans down and kisses me hungrily. Captain Shane clears his throat loudly and looks away. We break apart for breath and smile at each other. *I'm going to finish this battle for you, little warrior. Then, I want you in my bed … beneath me. I want to mark you … to make sure all these males know you're mine.*

Yeeesss … Fuck yes. Let's finish this fast then, I reply squeezing my thighs together to prevent him from noticing how wet I am from his words.

"Tempest can use his air affinity to keep those harpoons from landing in the wall while we take out the men behind them," Ragnar says keeping his gaze on mine and running his hand down my long braid. He wraps that hand around my braid in a fist keeping me locked into his chest. Then he says to Shane, "You should take a team out and kill the enemy behind the weapons."

Ragnar tugs my braid a bit making me squint up at him in annoyance. But I can't pretend with my mate—he knows he's turning me on. He can scent my arousal. *Fucking tease.* I can act like him tugging on my hair and holding me in place like a dominant male is annoying, but he knows the truth. I secretly like it.

"Sounds good. If we had any more archers, we could take them out but unfortunately they all died with that last explosion on the eastern wall. I'll form a team now. When is your—Tempest—friend going to block those harpoons?" Shane asks looking between us.

141

"Whenever you are ready, my King …" Tempest strolls up to us right at that moment looking as smug as a child who got the last pastry. Ara is next to him with an arm around his waist.

"I'm going with Captain Shane," I say stepping away from Ragnar as Shane nods and takes the stairs down to gather a contingent of warriors.

I only make it a few steps when I'm pulled back by the tension on my braid. Looking back at Ragnar in disbelief, he smirks and reels me back in while I swat at his hand.

"Little warrior. I want you to stay up here on the battlements. It's going to be a mess down there, and I want to be able to see you," Ragnar says letting go of my braid. *Finally!*

"No. Nope. Not how I function, dragon boy … I *need* to fight. I need to feel like I'm in control of something or this isn't going to work," I firmly state with my arms crossed. "If you can go into battle, then so can I."

"She has a point, brother. Your mate is strong. You want an equal … then let her be one," Ara says smiling widely. "I'll be here as backup and watch over her from here. I also need to protect my mate's back. He's a bit distracted lately." She pinches Tempest on the ass causing him to squeak a bit in surprise which makes me choke out a laugh while Ragnar's eyes twinkle in amusement.

We break apart after that going our separate ways. I mentally focus on the mate bond to Jorah and then Cadoc. I want to see if they are okay and if Cadoc's awake yet before I leave. My tether to each of them is strong and they both feel well. Cadoc is still resting, and I can feel Jorah drifting off to sleep as well.

I approach Captain Shane and run through checking my weapons. Then I tuck my braid in and raise my hood again. Our group consists of ten men and me. I bend over to stretch and adjust my boot a bit before we let the gate opens.

Mine! Ragnar shouts into my head causing me to straighten up abruptly and look up into his golden reptilian gaze. *Do not bend over like that, mate! Or I will have to murder those soldiers staring at your perfect round ass.*

Okay, noted! I squeak into his mind. *Be safe.*

He nods his head in response then shifts into a cloud of smoke. A large black dragon appears in the sky a moment later which roars loudly causing the walls to shake and the men around me to duck a bit in fright.

"Holy Valirr and all the Gods of Daelarias! That dragon is *huge*! And—he's your boyfriend?" Captain Shane states looking up into the sky. "Bless you! You must be one tough woman."

"If you're done ogling my *boyfriend*, can we get on with the killing?" I say huffing out an annoyed breath but internally I'm shining with pride for my mate. All the other soldiers chuckle a bit and adjust their weapons. They look a bit more confident now knowing that the Drakonian male above us is on our side.

The gates start to open right then and Shane says, "Split into teams of three. *Girl*, you are with me. Let's see what you've got." And with those words we all race out, seeking our targets.

Some race across the field while Shane and I turn right along the wall. We make it pretty far across the way without anyone seeing us. We knew there was one of those harpoon weapons over in this direction, but it's hard to tell where, especially from down here.

I feel the air shift before I see it. A quick glint of metal and whoosh of air above us, draws us towards our target. Tempest must have changed the wind in the air because I'm nearly knocked over into an approaching enemy soldier. But it's worth it when I see the harpoon veer off just left of the outpost wall.

Shane dispatches three soldiers and I get a cut along my collarbone by the time I turn away from my distraction. I hear a roar in the distance and then a large explosion of fire.

No more injuries! Ragnar shouts angrily at me. And then I feel his healing strength flow through me stopping the blood from the cut on my upper chest.

143

After I dodge the man in front of me, I flip my katana around and slice across his stomach. As he falls forward over his injury, I bring my other sword around twirling to sever his head. It took only a second, but I don't have any time to waste. Two more men approach me but I'm focused now, in the mental space of a warrior. They barely take a step before they're dead. I see Shane ahead of me and race to catch up. *Damn he's fast for an old man.*

Together, we both step around a large boulder and a wall of brush, before we see it. The harpoon launcher! There's one resting in its mechanism on the edge of the bolder for stability and facing the outpost wall. Six men surround it for protection and one man takes aim.

Shane and I look at each other with a smile of anticipation before we rush them. We fight back to back taking out all six men in no time. The shooter attempts to fire while we are killing the last two men. A large gust of wind blows in suddenly making me stumble right into his legs. His harpoon swivels nearly ninety degrees on its holder and fires running through one of the remaining men and straight out the other side of him into a distant copse of trees. We hear a shout and then another large harpoon fires up into the sky. *Oops. That's like a two for one move.*

Shane disposes of the shooter as I gain my feet. "Did you see where the next harpoon is?" he asks breathing heavily.

"Yeah, that was either lucky or Faktirnor is smiling down on us today! Follow me ..." I say taking off in the direction of that misfired harpoon. Another large fire explosion shoots into the air closer to us this time and I know Ragnar was successful in taking out two catapults. The blood lust and pride running down the tether between us makes me jump into battle again with a shout of excitement.

There's again six men but the shooter was killed somehow by our stray harpoon. Its looks like the soldiers were attempting to load another steel harpoon into its holder when we interrupt them. We finish them efficiently but this time Shane takes a sword to his flank. It looks to be through the muscle fortunately and not hitting anything vital. We decide to head back after successfully sabotaging two harpoons and see to his injury.

We make it just inside the gate when I'm scooped up into a pair of arms. *Cadoc.* I mentally say, feeling his protective strong arms carry me further into the bailey.

"Damn it, Sol! I woke up and didn't know what was going on. I felt you get injured but I knew it wasn't bad. You're lucky I didn't race out there! Captain Shane—you have some explaining to do!" Cadoc yells angrily in an authoritative voice. I should feel offended that he has so little confidence in my fighting skills but at the same time I find it attractive that he cares and is so protective. *He was worried about me.*

Smiling to myself, I lean in and kiss his neck wrapping my arms around him. "I'm fine, Cadoc. We took out two harpoons! Let Shane see the healer, he took a sword to his side."

"Forgive me, General. You were recovering and since Captain Eirik wasn't awake yet either, I assumed command. We had a planned attack with the Drakonian male," Captain Shane states while standing at attention.

Cadoc sighs and runs a hand through his hair. "I'm sorry, Captain, you're right. At ease. Go get that side looked at by a healer, now. I'll take over." Shane nods and replies, "Yes sir!" before he limps off to the infirmary.

Jorah walks up and wraps his arms around me from behind. I knew he was approaching since our mate bond was humming in response to him getting closer. He whispers to me, "I missed you, Sol. I'm glad you are okay. You freaked us out for a moment there. I grabbed you some food and water. Come sit with me." He grabs my hand and tugs me towards a room just inside the outpost.

Cadoc walks with us and sits. I update him on our plans to which he nods in appreciation and then takes off to check on the other teams. I hear another explosion in the distance and then feel a surge of blood lust again from Ragnar. A loud roar shakes the outpost again nearly knocking over my cup of water with its vibrations. Jorah is chatting my ear off about the information he was able to gather about Jaarnian weapons while I stuff my face with beef stew.

Done. You best be ready for me, little mate. I expect a reward for taking out all those catapults, Ragnar sends through our mate bond making me choke on water. Jorah looks up alarmed and proceeds to pound on my back.

"Sorry. Got surprised. Ragnar is on his way back. He took out all the catapults," I tell Jorah with a smile. He pumps a fist in the air and gathers his stuff.

We rush outside to hear the men on the battlements cheering. Cadoc is standing in the courtyard with his arms crossed over his chest as the gate opens and Ragnar struts through in a cloud of swirling shadows and smoke. His shirt is torn in one spot but I don't see any blood so my anxiety lowers a bit.

"Fucking cocky Drakoni. Have to always steal the spotlight," I hear Cadoc say quietly to Ragnar but there's an underlying tone of relief in Cadoc's voice despite his words.

Ragnar smirks in response and goes to walk right past Cadoc, but at the last moment pats him on the back and says, "Mate-brother. You can thank me by letting me reap the reward while you clean up the mess."

Cadoc looks confused for a second then follows Ragnar's gaze over his shoulder towards me. He gets a look of irritation then and rolls his eyes. "Fine. *Mate-brother*—but just this once. And—I'm joining her bed later. Don't you say a word. You've had her for days, weeks! I need to see her too."

"Ahem … shouldn't I have a say in this?" I ask crossing my arms and looking down at my nails as if I'm disinterested. Internally though, I'm preening.

They both shout out a loud, "*No!*" before Cadoc stomps away like a child who lost his toy and Ragnar stalks me like an animal hunting his prey.

Jorah quickly says, "I'm going to go check on Tem. See you in the morning, Sol." He leans in to kiss me on the lips then looks at Ragnar and says, "I get her tomorrow night."

Ragnar doesn't respond since his intense focus is on getting me alone. His shadows consume the area around us and before I know it, he has me in a dark room against the door. His arms lock me in on either side of my head so I can't really see much of the rest of the room but I know we are in a private space now.

"Did you just move me here? In your shadows?" I ask in awe gazing up at his golden eyes. He leans down and kisses along my jaw before reaching my lips and licking their seam.

"Yes? I didn't want to waste any more time. I *need* you, little mate. I've waited long enough. I did your task. The fucking battle is over. I not only incinerated those catapults, but I pushed those soldiers back with my dragon fire until they were running away like the weak, scared humans they are. Now I want my reward and—you better deliver." His long serpentine tongue slips in between my lips and tangles with mine. He consumes me with the force of his kiss.

Our hands make quick work of stripping our weapons and clothing. Before I can do anything further I feel the grip of his hand in my hair. He softly unwinds my braid and wraps my loose curls around his hand before tugging me down. The mate bond pulses with need, with lust, with devotion.

Dropping to my knees, he doesn't need to tell me what he wants. I can feel it. His thoughts are mine right now and we feed off each other. His needs … my needs … it's an endless loop where I can't tell whose thoughts and wants are whose.

His huge cock rests against my lips before I open them fully and take his length in. I gaze up at him while he holds me in place with his fist in my hair. He fucks my mouth hard using me as he needs and I enjoy every moment of it since I can feel his satisfaction and content as he comes in my mouth. I swallow it all down like it's a tasty meal before he pulls me up and kisses me.

147

Fuck, little warrior. Such a good girl in the bedroom and a fierce naughty girl in battle. I preen from his words and lean into his touch while he places me gently on the bed and looks down at me. *I'm proud of you, Sol. You are a skilled warrior and a loyal mate. Now ... I have a task for you ...* he states while I gasp out loud. His still hard-as-a-rock cock thrusts abruptly into my wet pussy. We both moan in pleasure at the sensation.

Yeeesss! More! Anything for my mate, I say submissively.

You are going to ride my cock and show me how fierce you are. Mark me. Fuck me. Use me. I'm yours. He says fanning my desire and my affection for him.

I flip him over using a fighting maneuver I know which lands me on top. I successfully pin him to the bed and mentally confirm with him, *You're mine!*

We're still connected so I start to move over him pushing my breasts into his face as I ride him. He rumbles deep in his chest and his hands instinctively palm my breasts before squeezing them together and licking. I shake with my approaching orgasm and stop moving wanting to lengthen our time together as he licks my nipples that harden under his attention.

I'm reprimanded suddenly by his slap on my ass. My eyes fly open which I didn't know had closed, and I start to move again.

Good girl. Like that. Keep moving and find your release. I want my cum filling your womb, Ragnar says placing his hands on my hips to assist me in moving. Making sure I don't stop again.

I lean back on my hands, still riding him and finding a new angle which makes us both quiver in response. I arch my back and shout out screaming his name as I find my release while his cock is soaked in my slick of body fluids. He holds my hips firmly and pumps up into me one, twice, three times before he roars out—*mine*—and finds his own release. We stay locked together like that while we both catch our breath.

He pulls me down to his side before pulling his *still* erect cock out. A gush of cum and body fluids starts to leak out which he notices. He kneels between my legs and scoops up the fluid pushing it back into my core and making me moan since I'm so sensitive still.

I told you I want my cum inside you. You will keep it. Do not move from this spot. He orders me in a dominant voice. Then he surprises me by leaning down and licking me clean with his talented and long tongue. It forces me into *another* orgasm before I collapse back onto the bed in a post-release sleepiness. Again, he strangely collects his cum pushing it back inside my channel before closing my legs tightly together in a possessive move and snuggling up against my side.

We cuddle like that while affection runs between us through our bond. His hand runs patterns over my hip and traces along the scars on my body that Malphas placed there.

"I love you, Ragi. Thank you for helping me save my other mate, Cadoc. I truly feel as though I'm not alone anymore. You help make me stronger. You allow me to feel safe enough to submit to you. I—I trust you," I softly say into the darkness. It must be well into the night since there's no light peeking through the window. We've been in here for a few hours now.

I can feel him smile against my side before he nips me and sucks. He says into my mind, *Marking you.* Then once he finishes his artwork of bruising on my side he says, "I shouldn't have to say it but I will, you are my heart. My Maseeri. My one and only for the rest of time. I love you little warrior, and I'm proud that I have gained your trust. *Honored.* You can always trust me with your body, your mind and your heart. I will not let you down, *ever.* Now rest, for tomorrow brings a new day."

I turn over onto my side and snuggle up into his chest licking and sucking a spot there of my own which causes him to chuckle. *Rest*! He orders into my mind in amusement.

As I lay there in his arms and my eyes start to drift closed with contentedness, I sort through my own thoughts. I realize that since I've formed my mate bonds, I no longer feel alone. And since Ragnar has become a part of my life, I no longer have any nightmares. But most importantly of all—I realize that since

I started this journey, I'm stronger than I used to be. Mentally. Emotionally. I haven't thought of my past or Counselor Malphas in some time.

I feel pride. Righteousness. And strength. Maybe it's a feeling that is leaking through from my mate bonds, but I don't think so—I think it's mine. And damn does it feel good.

CHAPTER
Twenty-One

ZXIAN

We need to be careful. With Counselor Malphas gone, I don't see how we can refuse a direct order to stand down. I want the same thing you want, Val, but it's not looking like we are going to get that reward he promised us," a blonde-haired, middle-aged soldier states to Captain Valence. Based on his lapels, I would assume he's a lieutenant in the army. I've been hiding in the shadows of the woods using my camouflage rune for the past twenty minutes and this is the first word of information worthy of my time.

"Of course we need to be careful! Especially with that disgusting Elarian spy they sent with me. I still don't understand why they sent him. The fact that they let those slaves run loose in Laevaris again makes me sick," Captain Valence states quietly looking around with a sneer on his face. "Counselor Malphas isn't gone by the way ... he's simply gathering our allies. He's holed up in Ironstead over in the Kingdom of Jaarn. My contacts confirmed it. We need to bide our time here and per him—

create a bit of confusion. We can pretend we didn't understand orders or maybe …"

He taps his chin in thought.

"We could go against orders and lay the blame with someone else. Then the damage is done. No one will suspect us. That rebel scum sitting in the castle thinks I'm trustworthy just like Captain Mavin." Valence scoffs. "Captain Garr who's here in charge is a good fucking choice for our plans. He's loyal to Princess Solveig and sickeningly loyal to the kingdom. He acts like he's better than everyone else or some shit. Tomorrow let's set a trap and make sure Captain Garr is to blame for attacking the Gorvians regardless of orders. Come on Raeker let's head back and see where that sneaky Elarian has been."

The two traitors head back to the central outpost for the Laevarian army while I hang back and let my power disperse. Using my camouflage rune can be tiring, but out here in the woods, I can last a lot longer. It took us just over four days to make the journey from Falal to the southwestern border of the Kingdom of Laevaris. I suspected Captain Valence was dragging his feet a bit trying to delay us but now I know. He wants to undermine Vidarr and therefore my future queen, Solveig.

I'm going to have to somehow sabotage their traitorous setup, prevent this Captain Garr from taking the blame and make it back quickly to Falal to inform Vidarr of the traitor in his army. He also needs to know that tidbit of information about Malphas being in Ironstead.

I spend the rest of the night spying on Captain Garr and assessing if he's indeed loyal to my future queen. Nothing seems out of the ordinary so I decide in the sake of saving time, I'll have to trust that the enemy of my enemy is my ally.

I sneak into Captain Garr's private room in the officer's building during the middle of the night. He's a better soldier than I thought when he wakes with a dagger at my approach. I spend the next hour laying out all that's happened and what I heard. He's leery at first being that I'm Elarian, but his hatred of Captain Valence supersedes any prejudice I suppose. *Thank Valirr!*

The next day the Laevarian army is attacked at the border. At first glance it appears as if the Gorvian army is attacking us, but based on the information I acquired, we knew it was Valence's men in stolen uniforms. Captain Garr doesn't take the bait and attack across the border in retaliation after subduing the deceptive soldiers. He has trustworthy men surrounding the area as witnesses to the traitorous soldiers. We apprehend them and force them to admit to their orders from Captain Valence. While Captain Garr handles this, I watch the back of the Laevarian outpost. Captain Valence and his crony, Raeker, nervously attempt to flee the scene when they see our soldiers quickly surrounding the area.

It's almost too easy for me to render them unconscious with the handle of my axe to their heads. Cracking my neck side to side, I look around and continue dragging Captain Valence into the small prison at the outpost. The man is worse than scum and a poor fighter barely able to block any of my moves. Nothing disgusts me more than a traitor.

I anxiously have to wait another day before I'm finally able to leave the outpost in loyal hands. I give Valence a close up look at my fists as I try to get more information regarding the Kingdom of Jaarn to no avail, but it's my camouflage power that cracks his traitorous mouth. The man nearly pisses himself when I disappear into the room right before his eyes. Now I can leave. Captain Garr understands his orders and Valence is set for trial by army the next day. Under the cover of darkness, I begin the journey back to my King and my home.

CHAPTER
Twenty-Two

VIDARR

I t's taken a little over a week to clean up and organize the mess we made when I took over as regent for the Kingdom of Laevaris. And—I cannot *wait* for my mate, Solveig, to return and remove this mantle that currently weighs on my shoulders.

Thank Avilt for the help of my mate-brother, Kaeden, and priceless knowledge in ruling a kingdom that I received from King Lochlann. Without them, I would be lost in a sea of overwhelming tasks and uncertainty. It also helps to have the council we made shortly after our takeover:

Darritt, advisor on the ongoings in our capital city, Falal,

Zxian, Elarian ambassador,

Pia, network of spies in the kingdom,

Mavin, Captain of the castle guard and current general of Laevarian army,

Valance, Captain in Laevarian army, 2nd in command of the army to Captain Mavin,

Camaeron, Lieutenant and 2nd in command in the castle guard.

Each person on the council assists me in ruling in some way. And, through our regular meetings help me make decisions. Ultimately, I have the final say but it helps to appease the rebel in me when we make decisions as a whole. Leading a rebellion is a lot different than running an entire kingdom, but I'm trying my best.

Kaeden's standoffish behavior towards ruling with me is irritating too. Whenever, I ask him why he isn't regent with me he always says, "*Because I'm not truly Solveig's mate yet. She hasn't accepted me fully into a bond and rightfully so. I betrayed her trust, choosing to follow Elder Aren's orders and keeping secrets from my potential mate. Until I can prove myself to her and ask her forgiveness, I can't share that responsibility with you and take my place at your side.*"

Other than organizing who is handling what in the kingdom, we have been mostly repairing damage in the city, cleaning up bodies, and slowly fixing the castle but it's slow going. I also have been trying to sift through the various documents in the late King Batair's office. His prior steward pointed out a few things but I had to relieve the man of his position. He, simply put, couldn't be trusted.

Thinking of his office, I head towards it just as a messenger runs up. A boy sporting a few feathers stuck on his vest, must have come straight from the messenger loft that houses some of the late king's messenger birds on a section of the roof. I thank him after he hands me the letter before I enter the office and shut the door.

To the current Regent of the Kingdom of Laevaris,

News of your successful revolution has spread south into our great Kingdom of Beamus which is disconcerting to me as a ruler. It has come to my attention that the late King Batair has been removed from his negligent reign and you are now responsible for the consequences of his actions regarding the war against Gorva.

I have it on good authority that your rulership is temporary and the throne belongs to the rightful future Queen Solveig Andraevian. I have also been informed that this war your kingdom is partaking in is attempting to be absolved. The Kingdom of Beamus, therefore, will remain neutral in the war and not side with either party unless it becomes apparent that either you are not abdicating to the rightful queen when the time comes or that Jaarn has overtaken land outside of their designated borders. Please notify me when the impending coronation of the rightful heir is scheduled so we may attend.

Yours truly,

King Havik Tamar Rubarvian

Well, damn! I can't quite tell if the letter is a threat or a congratulations, whether they support me or not. Either way, I have no intention of keeping the throne for myself nor continuing the war with Gorva. Not if I can help it.

Rubbing my chest to diffuse the ache there, I think about my mate and *again* wish she was back with me. Setting the letter on the desk, I lean back in my chair and close my eyes in a moment of exhaustion and self-doubt.

I must have slept for a while, because the next thing I know I wake up to the head cook bringing me dinner after a knock on the door. It's still strange that these people serve *me*—a low-born commoner who was homeless for years. Until recently, I used to eat leftover scraps around the restaurant I helped at in the city, so these prepared meals are excessive. Regardless I finish the tasty meal quickly, I'll never let food go to waste. Not with my background.

Just as I finish and stand up, Kaeden bursts into the room with his wild brown hair flying around his face.

"Zxian just got back," Kaeden huffs out obviously having just run all the way up here. "He's in the stables right now and has important news. I guess he had to switch horses twice and ran through the past night."

I rush past Kaeden out the door with him close on my heels. We make it to the castle stables, and I see Sigurd the stable master talking with Zxian. He looks exhausted leaning against the stall door chugging some water but doesn't appear injured. I do notice the absence of Captain Valence.

Sigurd's deep voice echoes across the barn saying, "Don't worry about the horse, Zxian, she'll be fine. I'll make sure she gets extra attention tonight and some extra grain once she cools down. One of the boys here will walk her before we put her in the stall otherwise she could go lame."

"Thank you. She ran that last section making good time. I pushed her hard and worried about her," Zxian replies before leaning forward and rubbing the horse on her forelock. "Good girl, rest now."

I step up to them just as they notice us and look around to make sure no one else is here before I say, "Why the rush, Zxian? What's going on?"

"Vidarr. Kaeden. Well met, I'm glad to be back." He smirks which falls flat since I can see the exhaustion setting in further. "I—I rushed back to report everything I learned. Captain Valence is a traitor and is either dead now or removed from his position. I'm not sure, seeing as I left before his trial, but I would assume he was executed for his crimes. He was plotting with Counselor Malphas and betrayed our orders to avoid war with Gorva. I did what I could to expose him and prevent the rest of the Laevarian army from being killed." Zxian pauses while a huge yawn overtakes his face. "The southwest border of Laevaris should be secure now under Captain Garr and the fighting with Gorva paused. Now … my concern is that since Captain Valence was a traitor, could Captain Mavin also be one? He *was* the one that recommended his comrade …"

We all pause in thought at his words and I get a sinking in my gut that I may have yet another issue on my hands. I feel as though I'm running out of hands to deal with everything, and soon I'm going to drop something.

"There's no way," we hear Sigurd state into the silence of the barn. "Mavin is one of the good ones. I've known him to be loyal and fair once you gain his trust. And … Solveig … she is like a daughter to him. They spent a lot of time together. I think you should talk to him and give him the benefit of the doubt."

I share a glance with Kaeden seeing what he thinks. He somberly says, "I agree. I think we should first talk with him. He may be just as betrayed to learn about Valence."

Nodding my head in agreement, I go to speak when Zxian interrupts. "Also, I wanted to tell you … I overheard that Counselor Malphas is hiding at Ironstead. I'm guessing we haven't seen the last of him. Or the Jaarnian soldiers for that matter."

I can't help the anger that floods me whenever that cowardly, disgusting man is mentioned. Malphas is a dead man walking … or hiding. I'm going to have to deal with him eventually and I know my sunshine will want to be involved.

"Thank you, Zxian. Get some food and rest. One of the maids can show you to a guest room for the night. See me in the morning before you leave for the Elaritian forest, which I know you're wanting to get back to."

"You know me so well already Vidarr. I'll see you in the morning," Zxian replies putting a fist over his heart and bowing before heading towards the castle.

CHAPTER
Twenty-Three

SOLVEIG

I'm having the most sensual dream involving my mates when I wake up from myself having a sudden orgasm.

My eyes snap open and I can hear my loud panting breaths in the dark bedroom. The next thing I notice is that my hand is tangled in soft hair … between my legs. *What?*

I pull my hand back and prop myself up on my elbows, so I can see what's going on. Cadoc looks up at me with a devious (and smug) smile on his handsome face. It was his white, blonde hair that my hand was holding onto a second ago.

"Sorry, Sol. Did I wake you?" Cadoc whispers before kissing my inner thigh. "I just wanted my breakfast before starting the day."

Raising an eyebrow at his smug words, I ask, "And, was it as good for you as it was supposedly for me?"

"Mmm, yes. I want your pussy every morning, mate. But I'm nowhere near done with you yet. I've missed you too much and I wanted you awake for this next part."

"Next part?" I ask intrigued. It's then I notice he's completely naked as he crawls up my body.

He doesn't answer me and instead sucks my right nipple into his mouth swirling his tongue around it and making my back arch off the bed. Arousal and pleasure release through our bond making Cadoc moan against my breast. Without waiting any longer and obviously feeling how aroused I am, he thrusts his hard long cock inside me until his pelvis meets my hips.

"You don't know how much I missed you, Solveig." He thrusts slowly, deeply inside me drawing out his words. "I can't go that long without being with you. Now, you have to put up with me vying for your attention this morning."

I gasp as his cock hits a sensitive spot deep inside me causing my pussy to flutter. I can barely say a response as he slowly pumps all the way in and then back out. "I missed you too. Ohh … so much. Yes! Right there. Cadoc … faster."

Cadoc's thrusts get more frenzied and faster. His pelvis hits my hips so hard the bed starts to shake. When he reaches down and swirls his thumb over my clit, I fall apart feeling my pussy squeeze his cock for a what feels like a couple minutes as he continues to thrust rapidly. He shouts out my name and curses before falling forward and to my side.

As I get my post orgasmic thoughts back in order, I remember I went to bed with Ragnar but am waking up with Cadoc (*and* what a way to wake up too). I turn my head to the right in realization and see glowing golden reptilian eyes intensely focused on my face in the shadowed room. *Ohh fuck.*

If looks could burn, then I would be on fire. *Is he angry? Jealous?* Before I can ask Ragnar or apologize, Cadoc starts to laugh.

Cadoc is smiling and chuckling when he says, "Sorry about that, *mate-brother*. Did you like the show? Or was it helpful in giving you pointers? I can demonstrate again if you want … "

"Youngling, I could show you more *pointers* than you could ever comprehend in your small human brain," Ragnar scoffs and places a gentle hand onto my abdomen and caressing it. Then he snarls to Cadoc saying, "The only reason I didn't interrupt that arousing, although rather *brief,* show is because our mate seemed to be enjoying herself. Now lay back, watch and I might just let you participate if you keep your irritating mouth shut."

Cadoc's mouth comically shuts with a snap and his eyes track Ragnar's hand as it smoothes over my body leaving tingles in its wake. Heat starts to pool in-between my legs again and I try to wiggle getting his hand where I want it. Instead, Ragnar sits up and grabs my hips flipping me onto my hands and knees while Cadoc watches propping his head up with an elbow on the bed.

Ragnar lines himself up behind me and smoothes his hands over my hips causing me to push back a bit against his hardness. One of his hands reaches up and wraps in my hair tightly locking me in place, which he seems to enjoy. Then he says, "Stay, little warrior. You're going to follow orders now from your Drakonian mate and let your other mate watch." Ragnar's thick, long cock slides into my already wet channel easily. "Good, little mate. You're going to take all of me. There you go … I want you to feel full of my cock." When his entire length is pushed all the way into me, I'm panting for breath feeling so full with all of Cadoc's cum and Ragnar's cock that it's dizzying.

I can feel my back nearly bend backwards with my flexibility as Ragnar pulls my hair and thrusts into me from behind.

"Goddess Fallia! Holy *fuck*, Sol, I didn't know you could bend that far backwards." Cadoc curses in a soft voice making my hooded gaze look over at him. He's already starting to get hard and running a hand over his rising cock.

"I told you to stay quiet, mate-brother," Ragnar admonishes Cadoc in a deep growly voice. "Watch and learn."

Ragnar holds me in this position so tightly I can't move an inch. My upper body makes a backwards C-shape from Cadoc's point of view on the side. It feels amazing, giving up control to my mate, forcing me to just *feel,* and opening my mind … my desires to him. Our thoughts flow back and forth ramping up our sexual experience. Ragnar is a fast learner with this mate bond connection and how to use it effectively in the bedroom, which is something my other mates have yet to fully figure out. He pumps into me so hard and so wildly that I'm sure I will have bruising on my hips or may even have a few chunks of hair missing later. I look over my shoulder at him as he growls and thrusts hard to see his eyes glowing with his dragon possessively. He looks wild and his thoughts continue on a loop about mating and fucking me until I'm sated.

My pussy flutters a bit and I feel like I'm on the precipice of coming when Ragnar stops thrusting and just holds his cock inside me. I nearly sob in frustration and glare over my shoulder at my mate. It doesn't faze him though since he seems to be on a mission. One of his hands snakes around my belly and straightens my body out as he pulls back on my hair at the same time. Still inside of me, he leans back on his heels and sits me up on his lap facing Cadoc. Ragnar's knees spread apart a bit forcing my legs open and giving Cadoc a view of his dick sliding in and out of me.

Cadoc stares hungrily at me as he pumps his own cock watching us. Ragnar's hand releases my hair and starts to massage my scalp making me moan. He begins a repetitive slow thrusting into me building me up again.

"You can touch our mate now, brother," Ragnar says to Cadoc before he kisses my neck and scents my desire. "Give her release and see that it's my cock that helped her get there. Then maybe you will remember we can both bring her pleasure."

Cadoc hesitates for only a second at Ragnar's order before he scoots forward with his gaze intensely focused on Ragnar's dick disappearing into my spread open pussy. His hand reaches down and gently touches my engorged clit making me nearly cry out. *So fucking close … just move it a bit!*

Cadoc doesn't listen to my projected thoughts but smirks telling me that he heard them. Instead, two of his fingers slide up into the stretched opening of my pussy alongside Ragnar. It's so much pressure that I stop breathing from the stretch. Together they both push in and out and I start to breathe again after a minute, feeling more wetness and pleasure. Cadoc takes his soaking wet fingers then and runs them up … up … and *finally* rubs them in circles over my clit. I scream out my release loudly. My orgasm is almost painful in its intensity and Ragnar grunts with the force of it before I feel him fill me up. We collapse into a pile of sweat, body fluids and satisfaction. The mate bond feels supercharged right now with our connection growing between us.

CHAPTER
Twenty-Four

SOLVEIG

Sometime later after my morning sexual escapades and a group bathing experience, the three of us emerge into chaos.

"What's going on?" Cadoc yells into the loud and chaotic gathering hall of Sterling Outpost. "Are we under attack again? *Eirik*!" People are running in every direction and I see several women rushing with linens back into the hallway we emerged from. Large platters of food are being prepared and napkins are being arranged at place settings on the tables. It's strange. This place just barely survived a massive attack from its neighboring kingdom and now they are … hosting a party?

People pause at Cadoc's loud commanding voice echoing through the hall and his friend Eirik looks over his shoulder from across the way. He then gets a relieved look on his face and storms over to us.

"Thank Valirr! I was wondering when you'd leave your bed and help me handle this." Eirik says in a frustrated voice running a hand through his light brown hair before waving it around indicating the hall.

"What the hell are you talking about?" Cadoc angrily says grabbing the lapels of Eirik's coat and shaking him. "Are we under attack? Why didn't you wake me!"

"Easy, Cad! I just put on my nice clothes! No one is attacking … well at least not in that way," Eirik says removing Cadoc's hands from his coat and brushing invisible dust off himself. "I did come to *wake* you but I could tell through the door that you wouldn't appreciate me interrupting." His eyebrow raises at Cadoc and I feel my face heat in embarrassment. "Your father must have finally got our message, obviously too late, but he should be at the gate any minute and I hear he has quite an entourage of soldiers with supplies so prepare yourself."

"Shit. What took him so long, I wonder," Cadoc says worriedly to Eirik. Then realizing I was still standing next to him with Ragnar, he reaches for my hand. "Come on mate, time to meet my father. Let's go greet him."

"I'll go find our other mate-brother and my sister then meet you at the entrance," Ragnar states kissing my cheek and disappearing into the shadows with his magic.

Cadoc looks around confusedly at Ragnar's sudden shadowy disappearance before shrugging and tugging me towards the entrance of the outpost. Eirik still has a flabbergasted look on his face in the midst of Ragnar's magic but after a moment follows us. The entrance to the outpost isn't even close to being as large as the castle back in Falal but it is a decent size with a vaulted ceiling over the gathering hall leading to a large double door at the entrance. The doors are thrown open and Cadoc pulls me to stand next to him.

I look down into the small courtyard that's still a mess from the battle to see a large man riding through damaged gate followed by a sizable army. Only about ten men dismount their horses alongside the King while the rest of the army camps outside the gates due to the size.

The man, I mean king, stands up and I realize he's in full body gleaming gold armor with a large broadsword at his hip.

He also has pure white, close cropped hair and gold crown adorning his head. I look down at myself to see a clean but plain loose white shirt gaping open a little and tight brown pants. I forgot to put my katanas on my back but at least three daggers are strapped to my legs just in case. Overall, I look like an embarrassing excuse for a woman, nevertheless a lady or even a princess. *Fuck.*

I'm fidgeting with nerves as the King of Gorva looks up in our direction and starts to walk towards us. Cadoc is standing at attention with his feet together and a straight spine and shoulders back almost like he's being inspected in the army. I guess he did tell me at one point that he's their general.

Oh Valirr ... I—I shouldn't be standing next to him, I think self-consciously trying to step back and avoid his father's notice. *What if the Gorvian King is like my father ...* I can feel myself go pale at the thought and my anxiety escalates. But before I fall into a flashback or succumb to a panic attack, Cadoc reaches for my hand and squeezes it tightly then says through mind-speak, *Whatever you are thinking right now, stop. You are worthy to be by my side and I want you here. With me. I can tell you're trying to pull back but you deserve to be by my side. My mate. My love. And ... this outpost's savior. If it weren't for you we'd all be dead. You came and brought your friends which is why we were able to defeat Jaarn's attack.*

Cadoc's words make me pause. I suppose in a way ... I did help save them. I mean ... Jicquara wouldn't have come if I didn't ask her. And Ragnar definitely wouldn't be here. Tempest too. That's three Drakoni that I brought. And from what I heard last night before bed, Jorah has been nonstop researching the toxic liquid and explosives that they saw in battle providing valuable information to the captains here. I also forgot that I took out those men shooting the harpoons and defended the broken wall when Cadoc's men were falling back. Maybe I did deserve to be here.

At those thoughts, Cadoc sends a flood of affection and love through the mate bond making me look over at him. He's looking down at me with love in his eyes and it makes my eyes water in response.

I love you too, Cadoc.

Don't ever doubt that I want you by my side. I love you, Cadoc whispers into my mind.

I feel Jorah and Ragnar join my side through the mate bond.

A throat clears in front of us, breaking up Cadoc and I's intimate gaze. I see Cadoc's father standing there with a curious expression on his face.

The King leans in and surprises me when he embraces Cadoc lovingly. "Son," he says, "I'm so glad you're still in one piece. I came as soon as we could but we were delayed. I'll explain later."

"Father … I'm glad to still be alive as well and happy to see you. I was worried something happened when we didn't hear from you." They both step back with a hand on each other's shoulders. Then the King's gaze zeros in on me again. "Father, let me introduce you," Cadoc says clearing his throat but with a proud look on his face. "This is my mate, Princess Solveig Andraevian from the Kingdom of Laevaris and also heir to Elaria and the Lost Lands." Cadoc's father looks shocked then confused for a moment before is face settles into a calm mask I know well from my time in the royal courts. "And Solveig … this is my father, King Ignatius Desmond of Gorva."

I drop down immediately into a curtsey as best I can while wearing pants instead of a skirt. Keeping my head down and avoiding eye contact I say, "Well met your majesty. I'm sorry for my appearance. I—" I stutter and then pause when I feel a hand on my chin lifting.

Standing up fully, I look up into King Ignatius's friendly blue eyes which are the only thing in appearance that he doesn't share with his son. "I'm very pleased to meet you, Solveig. Although, I am confused as to why you are here amidst war. I also didn't realize you'd be such a unique beauty…" he says looking me over and causing me to blush. Cadoc nudges his father. "Yes, well. Mate, you say? I'm not sure what that means … which you'll need to explain to me. When I told you to attempt an alliance with their kingdom through marriage, I didn't realize you'd be so blessed with such a strong gorgeous woman. She reminds me of your mother when I first met her standing in the stables …"

"Father, please," Cadoc says with a look of nervousness my way and I realize what his father just said. "We can talk inside. And I've already heard that story about mother. How is mother? How's Xana? I miss my little sister," he says obviously trying to distract his father and pulling him inside the hall. While I stand there a bit confused, Cadoc looks back at me with an apology in his eyes.

Alliance? Was he lying to me before? Is he just with me for this alliance because his parents ordered him to? He just wanted the princess side of me … not the real me. My thoughts tumble around in my mind while my stomach drops. Looking at the ground, I follow Cadoc and his father into the hall. Jorah places his hand on my low back in reassurance like he can tell my mood is soured but I have my emotions and thoughts locked up tight right now from my mates. I just need a moment to process this … alone.

As we all walk over to take a seat at the table with the King, he greets Eirik with a familiar manly back slapping. Putting the King at the head of the table, the rest of us find a seat nearby before Cadoc says, "Father, let me introduce the others. This is King Ragnar of the Drakoni and Jorah both of whom are my mate-brothers with Solveig. They've both been essential in helping me through this war with Jaarn in different ways." Both of my other mates look up and greet the confused king who has the graciousness to hold his questions in. "Those two over there are Jicquara and Tempest, both Drakonian and newly mated to each other. They have also been essential in the fight against Jaarn."

It's suddenly very quiet in the hall and I don't have the mentality to help fill the silence. I still feel a bit off about the revelation that Cadoc's goal was to gain an alliance through me. *I fucking hate politics.*

"Well met, friends. I owe you all my deepest thanks for your sacrifice and hard work for the Kingdom of Gorva." King Ignatius bows his head to everyone and says, "King Ragnar … I've heard stories or what I thought legends … when I was a young boy from my father about you and the Drakoni. I'm pleased to meet you and happy to hear that his stories weren't the end. My son has been busy building alliances since he's been gone and from the sounds of it … it was needed. Now, can someone please explain what you mean by mates?" He looks around for an explanation.

Ragnar confidently answers him for everyone but instead of looking at the King, Ragnar stares at me with a question in his eyes. I know he wants me to open our mate bond back up. When I continue to stare at my lap, his hand slides over mine to hold it tightly. "I will explain for you since it is something that has obviously been forgotten by many except among shifters. Although, please call me Ragnar … Mates are a sacred thing to us Drakoni as well as other shifters and even Elarian, which your son's mate is. A mate bond can develop in one of two ways. It's either fated through an instant soul connection from our Gods and Goddesses of Daelarias *or* it is chosen. Many only have one mate in their lifetime but in some cases a person can have multiple mates. Especially if that person is powerful and needs those connections to ground them or for other reasons known only to the Gods."

Ragnar looks thoughtfully at our linked hands before continuing.

"Mates are special and should be revered. It's a connection that is deeper than human marriage and unbreakable. Mates can share emotions and in our case even thoughts if they *choose* to through the bond, connecting them more intimately than just physically. It is not just a connection of convenience or for political gain," Ragnar says with a look of disdain on his face towards Cadoc making me feel even more upset for some reason. "Once a mate accepts the other, they should devote themselves to their mate's wellbeing. Mate-brothers or sisters are what we call the other people bonded in that connection and whom we share that bonded with. It becomes like a tight knit family over time. Solveig is my mate, just as she is your son's, just she is Jorah's and supposedly Vidarr's. Therefore, we are all mate-brothers and I will do anything for them including telling them when I'm disappointed in them."

The King's intelligent gaze doesn't miss the tension in the room as he looks back and forth between Cadoc and Ragnar.

He speaks slowly after a thoughtful pause. "Thank you, Ragnar, for the explanation. I feel like I'm missing something here … but maybe in my old age I'm not as sharp as I used to be," he jokes but only Eirik awkwardly chuckles in the group. "So … Cadoc. You have a … mate connection with Solveig and she has several men that she's connected with?"

Cadoc swallows and nods flicking his nervous gaze over to me before looking back at his father.

"This could cause a bit of a problem for the succession and … heirs. Which we will need to discuss later and plan for. But I am very happy for you, son. Your mother and I have always wanted you to find love such as we have for each other. We just didn't think it would be possible when the rising war with Jaarn escalated and we needed your marriage to create an alliance for the kingdom. I'm glad you seem to have found both. I can tell the way you were looking at each other that you both care for each other deeply. Now … tell me what happened here and in Laevaris. I received a report that King Batair is either missing or dead yesterday on our way here."

Cadoc stands abruptly making everyone look over and the king to stop talking. "Excuse me, Father, but can I speak with Solveig for a quick moment in private? Eirik can fill in what happened here then I can tell you about my time in Laevaris when I get back," Cadoc asks before looking over at me with a pleading expression.

"Of course, son. Eirik move down here by your king and tell me of this battle."

Just as Eirik launches into a report of the battle. Cadoc reaches a hand down to me and pulls me out of the room while Ragnar glares accusingly at Cadoc. When I glance back to him, I surprisingly see Jorah with his arms crossed and an angry look on his face as well. My bookworm also seems to be offended for some reason. Double checking my emotions are locked up tight, I follow Cadoc into a small storage room before he shuts the door.

Cadoc is standing with his back to me and his hands on his hips hunched over in frustration. I'm not sure what to say but I've always been bluntly honest so I jump straight to the point by saying, "Did you only mate with me because your kingdom needed an alliance with Laevaris? Was it real at all for you?"

Cadoc's head snaps up and before I know what happened, I'm pressed against the wall with his hands braced on either side of my head. He's looking down at me with his jaw clenched tight then taking a deep breath says, "Shit. Sol, you have to know that's not entirely true. *Fuck.* Can you just open the mate bond again? I'm dying here not knowing how you feel even though I can see it on your face when your mask slips."

When I don't say or do anything, he sighs. "Fine. I'm sorry … It is true that I sought your father, King Batair, out for an alliance when I first traveled to Laevaris. It's also true that I was going to ask for an alliance through marriage to you if nothing else worked. We were worried for war with Jaarn and my parents told me it was past time for marriage anyways. Your father obviously denied me so it didn't matter. But, then I met you … I didn't even know you were the princess initially and I was interested in you. Once I knew you were not only beautiful, but smart and a deadly warrior in your own right, I knew I had to have you. It only made my parent's request easier … like an added benefit."

"So it just so happens to be a benefit that I'm a princess?" I say in a snarky voice which is unlike me before looking away. He grabs my chin with one hand and forces me to look at him.

"Yes it is a benefit because I've not only served my kingdom in doing my duty but I've also found the woman of my dreams. A woman I love and will spend the rest of my life protecting. A chosen mate. Sol, do you think the mate bond would have formed if I didn't truly love you or have a connection with? This isn't fake or for political gain. It's way deeper than that. Open the bond and tell me you can't feel the answer."

Damn it. He's right. How could I be so stupid. I open my mate bonds again and I'm flooded with emotions and thoughts. Narrowing it down to just Cadoc for the time being, I search his eyes and his emotions. And, mostly what I feel is. … love. So much love and pride for me it brings tears to my eyes.

"I'm sorry," I say with my lip quivering. "That was childish and stupid of me to doubt you. I guess these past couple days … or hell … weeks have been a lot."

"It's okay, Sol. This is still pretty new and honestly I should have told you sooner about the alliance thing. It wasn't consciously kept from you, I promise," Cadoc says before kissing me deeply. His hands run through my hair on the sides of my face before holding me still. He takes and continues to take my mouth in a passionate kiss then pauses placing his forehead against mine and breathing deeply.

"Let's go back out there. We need to figure out our next step," I whisper.

"I know. I just … like having you to myself for a second," Cadoc whispers back and then gives me a soft kiss on the lips before pulling me back out into the hall.

CHAPTER
Twenty-five

JORAH

You could have cut the tension in the gathering hall with a knife.

Finally, Cadoc decides to take Solveig from the room for an obviously much-needed explanation. I like to think before I react and in my opinion, Cadoc wasn't trying to keep anything from her. She obviously doesn't see the way his eyes follow her across the room. My mate-brother is devoted to her and not just because of a political alliance.

We spend time talking with King Ignatius getting him up to date on all the events that occurred here at Sterling Outpost followed by what happened back in Laevaris.

I'm finding I actually like the King. He's not only friendly to a low born stable worker like me, but he's also highly intelligent. He's a lot like Cadoc in many ways and it's obvious they're related in ways other than their hair color. They both appear to be the stern intimidating soldier type but underneath are actually quite caring towards their people and selfless in providing protection to those in need. The King and Cadoc are also rather sharp and thoughtfully listen before strategizing. It's easy to respect them both after spending time with them, and I feel blessed now to consider Cadoc, a prince no less, one of my mate-brothers.

Right as I finish explaining my research and findings about the toxic liquid that Jaarn uses in its explosives and how to counteract it, my mate and Cadoc return to the table holding hands. *Good.*

I'm surprised I find myself happy our shared mate connection is in harmony again and that I'm not feeling any jealousy at all towards my mate-brothers. I'll have to look through that book I obtained on magical species to see if sharing a mate negates any jealousy between everyone included in the bond. *Hmm, something to think about.*

"I'm assuming then that you will be leaving soon to get back to your kingdom, my dear," King Ignatius states with a soft look over at Solveig. "Your mates and my informants confirmed that your father was killed. My condolences … He was … Anyways, you'll want to get back and take a firm hand in sorting out the succession then."

Solveig's facial expression blanks and her 'princess mask' is firmly in place which she portrays around the nobility. In a chilly voice, she says, "Thank you, King Ignatius, but he will *not* be missed by me. Our relationship was … strained and that's putting it nicely. I do indeed want to get back as soon as possible but more so to check on my other mate and … Kaeden." She gazes off into the distance for a second before her mask cracks a tiny bit allowing a smile.

"Ahh, yes. Please call me Nate when it's just us family. My name and title can be cumbersome to say. From what your mate Ragnar tells me, being far away from your mates is an uncomfortable feeling." Sol nods her head before he continues and says to Cadoc. "I can handle anything further here, son. You should help your mate settle her kingdom first before returning home. Family comes first, and if this mate thing is truly deeper than marriage as you say, then Solveig is family. We can have a wedding at some point once things have settled down. However, the succession of our two countries will need to be discussed at some point given that you are both heirs. I'm guessing you'll have to figure out a schedule to visit somewhere periodically."

I hadn't thought much about how this relationship will work other than I'm the least qualified to be with her. Who will marry Solveig out of her mates? And … does it even matter really? I suppose when you compare it to the connection we feel, it's rather trivial. But I know it will never be me, a common born stable servant, that she would marry.

I love her and she loves me. It's more than enough. I slide my hand over hers under the table and she flips hers over squeezing mine.

You're right. I do love you, Jorah. And you are meant to be with me. Who else knows me and my past as much as you do? You're not only my love but one of my best friends, she says into my mind having easily heard my thoughts through the bond. Skin contact makes our thoughts flow so easily, and I can feel her affection making me smile like the infatuated teenage boy I used to be.

"Father, don't you think it's a bit too soon to discuss that? We have a war still going on and Solveig needs to handle the chaos in her kingdom. Marriage isn't important right now. What we have is stronger than that … it's hard to explain." Cadoc runs a frustrated hand through his hair while we all look back and forth between the King and his son. My gaze keeps straying to my mate next to me and her callused hand in mine.

Can I stay with you tonight, Sol? I ask her mentally while holding my breath in anticipation.

Of course. I'm yours whenever you need me, she replies turning her head and looking at me with her deep blue sapphire eyes.

Our conversation is abruptly stopped when Cadoc angrily smacks his hand against the table while continuing to talk to his father. He says, "I am *not* separating from Solveig again, Father. We won't live separate lives and meet up twice a year. I can't … I won't … We love each other …"

175

The King holds up a hand stopping him and says, "Stop, Cadoc. I'm sorry I even suggested it. I guess I wanted to know for sure. Your mother and I are still very much healthy and dare I say still capable of running our kingdom. There's time to hash out the succession for our country but … as General of our army you may need to pass the title to someone else after the current war. I'm assuming you won't be around enough to manage that. Just think about it, okay?"

Cadoc takes a deep breath and I see his shoulders drop when Solveig places a hand on his shoulder at her other side.

The King and Cadoc exchange a few more words before they both stand and lovingly embrace as only family can do.

"So, does that mean we are leaving tomorrow?" I hesitantly ask to everyone. They all look at me and then at Solveig.

"Yes. As long as Cadoc isn't needed here anymore. We should leave after breakfast early tomorrow," she states with confidence. Everyone seems to agree at the table.

"Well, if that's true then please excuse me and Solveig for the night," I quickly announce tugging Sol to her feet and hastily exiting towards the room I used last night before any of her other mates can stop us. I hear a few chuckles behind us. Cadoc shouldn't mind since he'll probably want to spend time with his father before we leave. But Ragnar …

Umm … Ragnar? I'm sorry about not including you … is this okay? I ask him through the mate bond while I lead Sol around a corner and open the door.

His chuckle echoes in my head before he says, *Don't apologize, mate-brother. I won't interfere … this time. I was thinking of doing the same thing. You just happened to beat me to it. Go pleasure our mate and tell her to keep her mind open so I can enjoy some of the night from a distance.* Then like a door shutting in my mind, he leaves me mentally. I need to learn that trick.

Paying more attention now to my surroundings, I see Solveig shyly smiling up at me. I close the door and grabbing her long brown braid start to unravel it.

"Finally, I get you alone for a minute!" I mutter making her chuckle.

Next, I nudge her towards the bed to sit down before kneeling in front of her and unlacing her boots. I make quick work of helping her get ready for bed before I strip myself of all clothing. Her hooded gaze takes me in hungrily and gives me a sliver of male satisfaction. Now, the only thing between us is her shirt and a tiny scrap of fabric that makes up her underwear.

She slides her hands over my shoulders as I reach one of mine to the exposed collar bone peeking out from the loose neckline of her shirt. Running my fingers over the bottom of her rune, I trace my way up the right side of her neck to her temple. Then I tuck some of her beautiful curling hair behind her delicate ear. As I trace the pointed tip, she lets out a wonton moan and leans forward pushing her chest towards me.

"Didn't any of my other mates tell you that's an erogenous zone for Elarians?" Sol whispers huskily. "You touch that and … I'm not going to be able to control myself around you." *Hm, must have missed that very important fact about Elarians. Good. Noted.*

"I don't ever want you controlled, Sol. You're very much free with me and in fact—I encourage you to act however you want. Also, I'd like to see if you have any other *special* areas on your body that could cause such a physical reaction. Perhaps, I should examine you … for research purposes of course? You know … because we don't have much documentation about Elarians as a whole. I'll catalog all my findings about your unique anatomy if you'll let me …"

"Yes, *yes!* I mean … I think that would be beneficial for multiple reasons." Solveig eagerly replies while her pupils dilate in anticipated desire. "What do you want me to do?"

I pause to lean in and kiss up the path my fingers just traced as she pants loudly into the silent room. Then I place a hand on her thigh sliding it up soft skin until I meet the junction of skin and fabric.

Just before I cross that barrier in between her legs, I whisper against her ear, "You're going to let me touch and explore every part of you and then let me see how wet you get from it." My tongue flicks out along the pointed shell of her ear before sucking it into my mouth. At the same time as her gasp, I slide two fingers under the edge of her underwear and feel how soaked she is.

"You're so sensitive and wet from just a small amount of contact to your ear," I state while running my fingers up and down her slit.

"*Please, Jorah.* Fuck me," she says in a pleading voice surprising me.

"So needy already? I'm not done yet exploring …" I reply before pushing two fingers into her wet pussy. Her head falls back in a moan and her body shudders. "You like that, I see." I plunge my fingers in and out a few times while she pants and looks at me with needy eyes.

I withdraw my fingers and quickly flip her shirt off her before laying her flat on the bed. Before I can even reach for the underwear, Solveig kicks them off with a sexy smirk.

I narrow my eyes playfully at her while I start to run my hands up her feet making her giggle like she used to when we were kids together. Then I softly move my hands up her graceful looking yet muscular calves. "Okay, so toes and feet, not a turn on," I state focusing on each area of her body which makes her smile at our sensual game. When I reach her thighs though, and spread her legs while sliding my hands up, her expression switches to sultry as she bites her lower lip.

"You're such a tease, Jorah."

Smirking back at her but also extremely aroused by my actions, I decide to prolong it by sliding my hands past her core and over her hips. Then, I lean in and snake my tongue around her navel as my hands clasp her waist just under her breasts. I feel her hands grasp my forearms trying to tug them up. Instead of complying, I say, "Okay, navel and stomach area are mildly titillating but not as impressive as prior findings."

When I feel her huff out a breath of frustration and she lets go of my arms, I slide my hands up and cup those luscious breasts before my mouth sucks one forcefully in. Her back arches off the bed and she lets out a cry of release. I can't stop my body at this point when it covers hers and my hardness slides up and down her core.

"*Fuck. You …*" she starts to say as she comes down from her orgasm.

"Shh, we'll get there, Sol. Oh, I nearly forgot. You need to make sure you leave the mate bond open with Ragnar. He …" I can't help but chuckle. "He doesn't want to miss anything." Her surprised look is adorable and I feel our mate bond open further making me moan when I'm flooded with desire from her. It just about makes me cum right there on her stomach. Thank Valirr that Ragnar had the forethought to block us from each other.

Gritting my teeth to give me strength in lasting a bit longer, I sit up against the headboard and ask her to sit on my lap. I've honestly wanted to try some new positions with my mate and maybe the new angle will be interesting especially since I have some thoughts on exploring. Solveig eagerly crawls into my lap straddling me. And before I can do anything, she sheathes my rock hard cock into her wet pussy all the way to the hilt.

"*Fuuuck! You …*" I stutter out closing my eyes in ecstasy.

"Shh Jorah, don't worry, we're getting there," she says with a smile in her husky voice throwing my words back at me.

She bounces a few times on me, and I can't help but react reflexively by thrusting my hips up into her. The sound of our bodies coming together with a slap is erotic. I'm getting pretty close to my limit as a man recently introduced into the world of sexual pleasure so I need to get Solveig closer to coming a second time.

One of the hands I have on her hip for support slowly snakes around to her back end and squeezes her ass. Feeling nothing but pleasure through the mate bond, I decide one more exploration of the night is in order. Her eyes close for a moment as she rides me seeking her release so before she opens her eyes again, I slowly slide one finger over her back opening and gently inside, timing it with my next thrust.

Her eyes snap open and those beautiful blue eyes widen in surprise. *Fuck. That's it.* I thrust my finger a few more times before adding a second digit in time with my hip thrusts. Her response is faster this time and explosive as she screams her release. The tightening of her pussy around my cock instantly makes me cum yelling out her name.

Afterwards, she melts forward onto my chest and I hold her while running a hand up and down her back. I smile into her hair before smugly saying, "I think I can safely confirm and mentally catalog your other erogenous zones now. However, I doubt I'll ever be able to distinguish whether that area if simply arousing to you or particularly Elarians since I never want to be with anyone else."

She leans back and looks at me with such a comical face that I can't help but laugh while she slaps my chest playfully.

"You heathen. I think you're corrupting me. And to think … you're my most innocent mate!"

"Hmm. I like that I surprise you in that regard. I don't want to bore you in the bedroom and let the others have all the fun. Did you like it?" I ask curiously.

She bites her lower lip *again* in uncertainty. Then with a shy look which she only gets in private with me, she says, "Yes, I thought it was obvious."

I lean in for a quick kiss and smooth her hair behind her ears before I say, "Good. Now, let me get you cleaned up and we should get some rest. I'm not looking forward to riding in dragon talons again tomorrow. Maybe I can ride with you on Ragnar?"

She chuckles in response with an unfocused look in her eyes before it clears. "Ragnar says after that show he'll gladly carry you tomorrow."

We both laugh and snuggle up to sleep. Soon after, I hear Solveig's breaths even out and feel through the mate bond the blankness of sleep. But before I can succumb to sleep, I hear the door softly open in the dark and a hulking presence enter before the door shuts. I tense up instinctively to defend my mate.

It's just me. Sleep, brother. Sleep, I hear Ragnar say in my mind as I plunge immediately into a peaceful slumber.

CHAPTER
Twenty-Six

SOLVEIG

I t takes us three days to make the journey from Sterling Outpost to Falal.

Tempest and Jicquara traveled with us for the first day so Tem could manipulate the weather over the Traverian mountain range and ease our passage into my kingdom. Supposedly weather is tricky passing through the mountains, so I was grateful for his rune power and how it'll allow me to make it home sooner back to Vidarr and Kaeden.

I'll miss my new sister and friend, but it's for the best that they return to the outpost and stay a few more days. I don't trust Jaarn. Especially given that Counselor Malphas is likely hiding in that kingdom somewhere. I don't think we've seen the last of them and I have an ominous feeling in my chest indicating I should be wary of what's coming next.

We also said goodbye to Eirik temporarily. Cadoc thought it best for him to manage the Gorvian army in his absence until a more permanent arrangement can be made. Plus, Cadoc doesn't need a guard since he has me and the others to watch his princely, well rounded ass. Eirik and King Ignatius will join us whenever things are more settled in Laevaris for my coronation.

I feel a rumble of warning from Ragnar's dragon between my legs just as we crest a cloud and see the capital city ahead. Jorah squeezes me tightly from behind. He has to be excited to be home too. I wish excitement was all I felt however, instead there's a sliver of uncertainty and insecurity. It makes me remember last night when I was sitting around the campfire after everyone else had fallen asleep.

"What's troubling you, my Maseeri? I can feel your tiredness but your mind is awake," Ragnar quietly says as he sits down beside me. He volunteered for first watch so I'm not surprised when he appears out of the shadows.

Sighing, I stare into the fire and answer him, "I—I'm anxious to see my mates, er—mate and ... Kaeden?" Then biting my lip in insecurity, I look down and search for words.

Ragnar reaches over and plucks my lip from my teeth. "Why are you anxious? Tell me so I can relieve you of this fear."

"What if their feelings have changed ... or diminished? What if they've moved on? Or, what if I don't feel as strongly for Kaeden-- enough to complete the bond?"

Ragnar's face scrunches up in a way I've never seen. Disbelief and confusion can be seen in his expression before he answers, "Bonded mates are forever, little warrior. He would never betray or insult you in that way. I honestly, don't even believe it's possible to 'move on' as you put it. But—I'm sure their feelings have changed ..." My gaze quickly snaps up to his with a question. "They're likely feeling more desperate, more restless, and needy for you than they were before. Being separated from a mate is painful and downright distracting. And, I'm sure the one that hasn't completed the bond fully will be ever more desperate. Both of them will likely scramble in their haste to embrace you. While I ... unfortunately ... will have to tolerate them stealing you from me for the next couple days."

His words bring a half smile to my face knowing how possessive and selfish he is with me even if he won't admit to it. I know he's

183

right though … at least about Vidarr. Vi is my rock. He's always helped me gain my independence and made me better. He can manage on his own but we've never been apart this long.

Kaeden on the other hand isn't even my mate yet … at least not fully. So, will he react differently to my return?

"Ragnar, can an incomplete mate bond sever through distance? Can … it weaken?" I ask trying to keep the insecurity from my voice again.

"You are asking this because of your other fated mate? The one you have yet to accept?" I nod my head in response. "That is different. Fate found you and hooked both of you in its snares. It connects you even without your choice or even without completing the bond." He sighs and looks into the fire before continuing. "Time and distance are harmful to a developing bond, it's true. It will eventually fade and dissolve in time especially if one person were to move on from the bond. It needs tending and trust."

Tears enter my eyes as I think about how I failed Kaeden by leaving him. I miss him and should have found him before I left. But … he withheld secrets with my grandfather. It hurt and I know it set us back a few steps in our developing relationship. Still … I think about his tortured, vulnerable eyes when I first saw him so close to death in that slave camp when we first met. We shared something that day. An acknowledgment of each other's darkness. I know Kaeden will never judge me for my past. I remember how he made me feel wanted after Malphas violated me. Then I think about his tall, warrior honed body moves as he walks through the forest. How he respects life and finds peace in nature just like I do. We share a great many things and I have an admiration for his loyalty to the Elarians. I just wish one day he has that same admiration for me.

"Do you think … that Kaeden will still want me? As a mate? That I still have a chance?" I ask turning towards Ragnar.

"Little warrior, he'd be a fool to let you go. You are worth waiting for, worth wanting, and worth loving. You're once in a lifetime for all of us. And, if you want me and your other mates to pound

that into this man's head, then we will. However, I feel like he will already know this."

I can't help but throw myself into Ragnar's arms and kiss him with abandon. Holy Gods and Goddesses. I don't know what I did to deserve him, but I intend to make sure he knows how appreciated he is.

I pull back from our kiss to hold his face in my hands and say, "I love you Ragi. Thank you for being … you." His unguarded smile and the affection flowing from the bond lets me know he understands before I'm finally able to rest.

I shake from my thoughts with a jolt as we land just west of Falal outside of the city walls. Things seem quiet right now in the city, but it's only just past dawn. Jorah quickly slides off the side of Ragnar's dragon form before reaching up to catch me from far below. Feeling a little reckless I spin my legs onto the same side and push off Ragnar's big body to drop through the air towards Jorah's waiting arms.

Jorah gets this look of horror when he sees my rapidly approaching body soaring at him. I can't help but laugh out loud at his expression just as I crash into him and we tumble to the ground in a tangle of limbs. There's an angry growl coming from behind me, but I ignore it and kiss Jorah while he dazedly looks up at me.

"You okay? Just thought I'd wake you up a bit!" I say standing up and reaching a hand down to him. He grabs it and stands to dust himself off.

He gives me a distrustful look in a teasing way as he mutters, "Reckless. Nothing's changed. Still acts like she's ten …"

I laugh again and look over to see a disgruntled Cadoc brushing himself off. His white, blonde hair has been cut short again just before we left Gorva, however he has a leaf sticking to the top. His shirt and overlying coat are rumpled and his pants show dust from where he must have been dropped to the ground by Ragnar.

185

"I can't *believe* you guys made me ride in his talons! I still don't understand why we all couldn't have rode together on his back … or better yet ride horseback!" Cadoc yells with an irritated look. Usually he's more on the stoic serious side so it's unusual to see him like this.

"Sorry, Cadoc," I say swaggering over to him with a hip sway and trying my best to distract him from his uncomfortable ride. I can't help but feel a bit giddy knowing I'm about to reunite with all my men! "You know we couldn't fit three on his back comfortably and horses would have taken too long to get back. Plus, Jorah already *did his time in the talons* as he likes to say. It was the best choice we had," I plead while he stretches his back.

Seeing that, I realize I'm also a bit stiff from the last day of traveling. Bending down to touch my toes, I grab the back of my calves and fold myself in half relaxing into the stretch. I hear Cadoc say, "I know. I know. You're right, but that really is unpleasant riding around like an egg inside a dragon's talons."

There we go. That's it. I think as I get that last muscle to relax in my legs.

"Yes, that *is* it, little warrior. You need to stretch more, especially while I'm watching," Ragnar says from behind me suddenly in his human form. His pelvis notches directly against my ass while I'm bent over and his hands tightly squeeze my hips holding me in place. A very large, very hard cock seems to be pushing against me and making me curse. *Fuck.*

There will be plenty of time for that later, I hear through the mate bond from Cadoc. When I start to lift my head up and stand from the stretch, I see my face at eye level with his hips. He must have moved closer while Ragnar fondled my ass. And there's no doubt Cadoc is aroused if the tenting of his pants is anything to go by. I clear my throat hoping to dispel my dirty thoughts and stand up. Jorah has moved closer too and is now standing to my left looking at me with heated emerald, green eyes.

Damn, Solveig. Don't tempt us with that agility right now. We have too much to do and are out in an open field! Save the flexibility for later. I'll make sure I stretch all your muscles out, one by one, if you'll let me, Jorah says through the bond mentally.

Before we left on this last leg of the journey, we decided to keep the mate bond open between all of us so we could communicate while flying in the air. It's nice being able to speak with all of them together and has definitely helped us grow closer as a unit these last couple days.

I agree brother. I want to see those legs stretched behind her head while she's laid out beneath our gazes like a meal I want to eat, Cadoc says to Jorah.

Ragnar just grunts out a response and grips me tighter before I bat his hands away and admonish all of them.

"Alright focus, boys. No more sexy mate talk. We need to get to the castle," I say out loud focusing on the two remaining towers in my vision. Then I rub at the ache in my chest that's been growing more intensely the closer I get to home. I search through the mate bond for Vidarr and can tell he's probably just waking up. Kaeden's tether is fainter but there, meaning I still have time. I can't read his emotions or feeling so I'm in the dark when it comes to him though. *Guess I'll just have to see him and ask him.*

CHAPTER
Twenty-Seven

MALPHAS

I absolutely *hate* waiting for these incompetent imbeciles to get their act together. It's torture knowing you can do everything better than someone else but at the same time knowing you need them. I'm only one man, and I'm smart enough to admit that I need the bodies and resources to get the results I want.

Careful planning and manipulation has gotten me this far, and I'll be damned if I let it all slip through my fingers because of a few idiots taking their time and a simple minded girl who plays like she's a princess. *One more week, Malphas …*

I had that *girl*, forgive me— *princess*—right where I wanted her before she messed it all up. Luckily, I'm a strategist and had a backup plan just in case. I thought it necessary given the unpredictable and drunken King Batair as well as the rising rebellion in Laevaris. It's unfortunate really, a shame, after all the careful grooming I put in with that woman since she was a naive fourteen year old. All the chess pieces were carefully moved around to get that betrothal into place but … all is not completely lost. The nobles and tradesmen still look to me for direction, mostly out of greed or from me holding something over their heads. But greed and blackmail can be hefty tools when used properly. No matter, I'll have what's due to me. The throne is mine and hopefully by the end of the week it'll be history in the books. The only place my betrothed will stay after that is underneath me begging for forgiveness while I force her to submit to me, *again.*

Jaarn has been an undercover ally of mine for decades unbeknownst to its King and Queen. My conniving sister just so happens to be married to the Jaarnian queen's brother, Phaelip Keven. He—like myself—yearns for the throne and subsequently the power which comes with it. We just happen to want different thrones but are willing to do anything to get them. Making us allies.

My sister and her husband have been planting seeds of distrust in the Jaarnian royal court for years. And finally with the death of King Batair, the Jaarnian King Armond Garish has decided to test and potentially grow its borders past the Travernian mountains.

Today, I finally get to leave the rocky, desolate Kingdom of Jaarn and leave for Laevaris after waiting for way too long. We have nearly a quarter or more of the Jaarnian army with us and one of the royal princes, granted there are *five* of them. Half of the Jaarnian army is still indisposed at Sterling Outpost so we're less in numbers than I'd like for taking back my proper place, but we'll make do. I heard through my spies that things aren't going well for Jaarn over at the border with Gorva, so I'm rushing to get this invasion started before they change their minds. Going to battle on two fronts is never a good idea, but it's their demise if they lose—not mine.

One week of traveling with these brainless soldiers and I'll have my castle, my status, my power, and my woman back. Soon, I won't need to hide. I've waited this long already so it should go quick.

As I ride towards my future, I drift off into pleasant memories of dark dungeons, sharp tools and a screaming sexy princess who thrashes under me.

CHAPTER
Twenty-Eight

SOLVEIG

Walking up to the city gates is an interesting experience. For the first in a long time, I see soldiers posted there monitoring any people coming and going. My prior father, or rather King Batair, neglected this kingdom and especially Falal for so long. I can barely remember a time when the city walls looked so inhabited. There's only a few soldiers I can see given the sun is just starting to rise. Many people who live outside the city travel here for trade or business early in the day.

I take notice that each person and wagon is fully inspected. I wonder who oversaw increasing the security around here since I left. *Maybe Captain Mavin? Dear Faktirnor, please let Mavin be well.* He was my mentor for so long when I felt like I had no one but Jorah in the castle. Sending up a prayer for him to the God of Strength, I hope he wasn't injured after Ragnar in his dragon form destroyed half the castle in a fit of rage. I worried that the King would punish the Captain for the whole event and subsequently my disappearance. Mavin was a mentor to me and although stern, he took the time to build my abused self-confidence through weaponry and sparring. It helped me feel more in control of my body and actions. It also made me into one hell of a warrior.

I remember his words back from when I was a scared girl of fourteen years old. He was telling me that I remind him of his own daughter, "*Strong. Resilient. Just remember, Princess, that we gain strength from the lessons we survive in life.*"

With King Batair's death and the war between Gorva and Jaarn, whoever's in charge must be taking extra precautions here in Laevaris. Changes in the monarchy always leave a kingdom vulnerable to attack and Falal is our most important city. If it's compromised, then the whole Kingdom of Laevaris potentially could fall.

Our group steps up next in the line to enter under the arched gates of the city. Ragnar and Cadoc are given a look of suspicion and assessed, but they walk through after showing the weapons on their hips and are given a stern warning about fighting in the city. Jorah's pulled to the side to let a guard look in his bag of books but is then waved through. I assume I won't be stopped either since I'm not carrying anything other than the katanas on my back. So it comes as a surprise when a man's hand is abruptly placed on my chest stopping me in my path.

I look up into leering eyes that peer down my loose shirt and don't recognize the nondescript soldier in front of me. His right hand slides down just shy of my breast as he says to me, "One moment." Then he looks over my shoulder at the other guards and says, "Hey guys. I think this one needs searched. Anyone want to help?" Rolling my eyes and then giving him a look of disgust, I look around him and see my mates still walking and assuming (like me) that I would just pass through quickly. I mean—I am the princess of Laevaris. You'd think I'd be able to walk into its capital city unaccosted.

Before the soldier can delay me further, I side my left hand up and grab his thumb pulling it towards his wrist and twisting it backwards. He cries out in surprise and pain falling to his knees in front of me and trying to relieve the pressure on his thumb. *Way too easy. But this asshole needs a lesson.*

His shout of alarm makes my mates pause and turn back towards me. Cadoc steps forward as if to interfere and save me, but Ragnar throws an arm out blocking his path before he calmly crosses his arms and waits.

Smiling to myself, I stretch my neck to the sides anticipating the upcoming rush of adrenaline that comes with fighting a man and showing him I'm not as weak as I look. I'm going to teach this perverted soldier a lesson in manners and respect towards women.

Two guards rush towards me and it all happens rather quickly. While I maintain my hold on the soldier in front of me who's pathetically begging to be released, I kick out with one boot and crunch an approaching guard's nose causing him to fall back holding his head. I can't help but glance over at my mates and meet Ragnar's heated gaze as he holds an angry Cadoc back before he mouths hurry up. Using my distraction, the other guard steps in closely and yanks my braid back. *Oh fuck no! Big mistake!* He puts an arm around my neck as my back hits his chest attempting to put me in a choke hold, however he doesn't see my right elbow swinging around and up into his temple. As he releases his hold on me, I duck under his arm and swing around punching him in the flank. *Sorry, you might be peeing blood in the morning.*

Tiring of this already, I then kick the kneeling soldier in front of me in the groin as I release the thumb hold, making him groan and fall backwards into the fetal position. The guard whose nose I broke rushes at me again but instead of bracing for impact like he expects, I crouch down at the last minute using my agility rune and swipe his legs out from under him. He falls flat onto his face in an embarrassing display and manages to damage his face further.

Two more guards look poised to approach but think better of it when they see my bloodthirsty smile in their direction.

They look at the three soldiers moaning on the ground and hold their hands up. In my peripheral vision, I see an amused smile on Ragnar's face, pride and relief shining through Cadoc's eyes but Jorah just shakes his head back and forth in exasperation. He's probably thinking again how reckless I tend to be. But he should be happy I didn't even pull any weapons out. I raise an eyebrow at him in response when I notice an injured guard on the ground at his feet and a heavy book in Jorah's hand.

I go to step over one of the injured guards and hear a voice call out from the street running parallel to the gate. "Well I'll be … It's about time you got back." Darritt, a friend and Vidarr's right hand man, shakes his head in reproach. But I know it's in a teasing manner given the happy smile on his face. He walks up and embraces me saying, "Well met, Sol. Glad to see you still in one piece. I was wondering if you still had those old skills of yours after being carried off by a dragon like some damsel in distress. But now that you've proven your point can you leave my soldiers alone?"

As he leans back to look me in the eye, I see my mates stiffen up and approach us. Ragnar's openly growling and staring at Darritt's hands on my shoulders. I chuckle and pat his hands before saying, "Well met, Darritt. I'm glad to see you too. Now, you might want to remove your hands from this damsel before you become dragon food in two seconds."

Darritt looks to the side and sees Ragnar's intensely possessive gaze and lifts his hands in a sign of mercy.

"Sorry, man. Just greeting an old friend. I'm Darritt. Blacksmith, sword smith, and now city councilman." He holds a hand out in greeting towards my Drakonian mate. "Also, I'm in charge of these buffoons here. Vi has me overseeing the city guard most days."

Ragnar stares at his hand and relaxes a fraction now that Darritt's not touching me. "Ragnar," he states coldly. And after a brief pause since Ragnar doesn't say anything else, Darritt drops his hand with a shrug.

"Darritt's a friend. Behave!" I say smacking the back of my hand to Ragnar's chest and give him a smile so he knows I'm not angry. "He's the dragon who carried me away that you mentioned. Darritt, do you remember Jorah? He worked in the castle stable and his father's Sigurd, the stablemaster. I think you worked with him before." Darritt still looks a bit shocked from my quick remark that Ragnar's a dragon and he can't help but side eye him as I talk. I notice a flash of fear enter his gaze and I can't help but feel as if I'm missing something other than the normal wariness that most give my drakonian mate. He processes my words before greeting Jorah warmly. "And this is Prince Cadoc of Gorva." Darritt's eyebrows hit his hairline for the second time.

Darritt goes to bow but Cadoc waves him off and says, "Well met. Any friend of Solveig's is a friend of mine. We should be going through."

"Yeah. Even though I'm glad to have caught you on your way through, you should get up there and see Vidarr, Solveig. He's going to faint when he sees you again. The man's been non-stop pining for you," Darritt says with a conspiratorial wink.

I'm sure I miss him just as much if not more. My attention drifts thinking about running my hands through Vidarr's dirty blonde hair while I climb his tattooed muscular body like a tree. I mentally trace those tattoos along his body as they scroll down the V-line of his hips all the way onto the base of his …

Ragnar clears his throat effectively breaking up my dirty thoughts and says, "Let's go."

Five minutes later, we're all riding a few spare horses toward the castle. Darritt had the guards loan us their horses that were staked at the gate as an apology for delaying us. I also whispered to Darritt about the one handsy soldier. He reassured me that he would *deal* with it.

I look around at Falal and am happy to see there's not much damage to its beautiful stone streets and characteristic lanterns that hang along the Main Street leading to the castle. A few buildings seem to be in the process of repair likely from the recent revolution but overall things look well handled in the city. People look genuinely happy too.

However, now that I'm looking, I see a lot of eyes on us. And as we continue down the street a small crowd starts to form in our wake. Whispers and pointed fingers are directed my way, but they don't seem malicious. In fact, several people call out greetings and shout, "Welcome back, Princess Solveig!"

I forgot my hood was down and my pointed ears on full display. I'm well known in our kingdom for my unique features which usually brings disdain but for some reason today people are much more accepting. I see a woman drop her basket and curtesy while another man bows across the street when I pass. Jorah pulls his horse up next to me with a soft smile and nudges me with an elbow.

"Looks like more than just Vidarr missed you," Cadoc says over his shoulder from in front of me riding next to Ragnar. "It appears your people have been awaiting their next queen."

It's hard to suppress the awed and surprised expression on my face as we continue through the slowly growing crowd of people. Never in my life have I felt accepted by the general people mostly because of my unique appearance and the resulting stares, however I guess it's fair to say many people were too scared of my supposed father to voice any opinions. It was more the nobility who openly ridiculed and shunned me.

I look deeper into the city as we ride and see some of the more impoverished. But, instead of begging and hiding amongst the shadows, they have food in their hands and are laughing. Many even wave in recognition including two kids that've carried messages for me in the past. I get a bit misty eyed waving back to them while seeing my people are happier and fed. They're getting the support they need *finally*. I'll have to thank whoever has been in charge in my absence for not forgetting the less fortunate.

CHAPTER
Twenty-Nine

VIDARR

Yawning loudly, I stretch my bulky arms over my head before getting out of bed. I was up late *again* trying to run through all the messages and invoices that circulate to me as the regent for the kingdom. Its why I'm so late to rise this morning, usually I'm up with dawn but as I peek out the window in this area of the castle, I can see the sun already up. I never thought I'd be doing paperwork and making decisions about an entire city nevertheless a whole kingdom. I'm a simple man. Punch people that get in your way. Steal what you need. Although, I never needed much and always had the bare minimum. The most complex I ever got as a man was becoming the Rebellion leader in Falal.

Ever since Solveig entered my life, things have grown in complexity. And I've come to realize that simple is boring. Complex is amazing—as long as Solveig is involved. Without her—it's horrible.

I get ready for the day which doesn't take much. Dressing in a simple black shirt rolled up at the forearms, donning pants and boots and running a hand through my messy blonde hair I'm done. I rub my chest at the growing ache in its center. *Damn this ache is horrible today.* It's by far the strongest it's been in the past week making me confused. *Maybe I should see Healer Thaemon today. I suppose all the stress from the piles of paperwork on my desk could be adding to my symptoms.*

Leaving my room lost in my thoughts, I distractedly walk towards the kitchen hoping to snag a quick breakfast and better yet a cup of karaf. Karaf is a glorious hot drink that can rouse most people into attentiveness even if they stayed up most of the night. I might have a small addiction to the stuff since taking on my new role here. The cook dotes on me by cooking three full meals a day since I'm regent now, so I suppose there's some perks to the job.

I go to turn the corner into the kitchen and hear several voices making me pause with my hand on the door. *There's no way …*

Filled with hopefulness, I push through and enter the castle's main kitchen to see the most beautiful sight in the past two weeks. I hungrily stare at a petite but lithe body full of curves in all the right places. Long, dark brown braided hair rests over her shoulder and piercing blue eyes lock onto mine from across the room.

Solveig's words cut off at the sight of me before she bites her lower lip holding in a choked sob. The soft sound of it breaks the hold over my body and I rush forward, encasing her in my arms. Scooping her up off the ground I step towards the nearest wall and pin her there with my mouth. I can't help but kiss her like I'm consuming my last meal. Even though technically, it's my first meal of the day. She tastes like honey and sweetness just how I remember and yet … better. So much better.

Pulling back a bit with my lips still brushing hers. I rest my forehead to hers and say, "*Fuck,* I missed you. You aren't allowed to leave my bed. *Ever.*" Then I kiss her again nipping her roughly on that plump lower lip she keeps biting. "Best breakfast ever."

She smiles against my lips and I feel a tear trickle from her eye. As I rub my thumb across its wet path she whispers, "I missed you too, Vi. But … I'm not in your bed, silly. Did you forget we're only in the kitchen?"

I grab her under the ass and wrap her legs around my waist before saying, "Oh, I'm well aware, sunshine. I was simply letting you know the new rules. You're forever staying in my bed. I'm tying you there so you can never leave me again. Then I'm stripping you bare and eating the rest of my breakfast. *I'm starving.*"

She squeezes her legs around me in response and I swear I can feel the dampness of her core against my waist even through our clothes. It's then I notice a loud growling in the room next to me before a hand shoots out onto the wall next to us and blocking my exit from the kitchen.

My eyes follow the arm connected to a huge growling man with black hair. It's shaved on the sides and a longer braid runs down the center of his scalp. It's interesting and unique in a fierce warrior-type way especially with the silvery tattoos running up his arms and around his neck. The neck tattoo almost looks like the sleeve of ink on my right arm except it's around his neck and is silver instead of black ink. "Little warrior … care to introduce us?" he says to Solveig but keeps his challenging stare aimed at me.

Instead of backing down which I'm sure this man is used to, I tighten my hold on Sol and stare back. She opens her mouth to respond but instead I quickly say, "Name's Vidarr Rikare. And you are?"

His growling cuts off and his intense gaze flicks back and forth between me and Sol. She smiles at him before raising an eyebrow as if to say, *Can you answer him now and be polite?*

His arm drops from the wall breaking the tension in the room and he says, "I'm Ragnar, your mate-brother. Solveig is my Maseeri and my mate. She's spoken highly of you," he says in a respectful manner while sneaking glances at Sol. "I'm sorry for my protectiveness. It has been quite the journey."

"I'd say it's nice to meet you Ragnar, but it's not since you're blocking our way. But don't worry, I get it. She's hard to let out of your sight." I reply with a snicker seeing that my sunshine already has him wrapped around her tiny finger. "We can address the whole mate-brother thing later on. Right now, I'm stealing our girl." I dexterously carry Solveig around the hulking man before he can block me again while Solveig starts to kiss her way up my neck showing me she's just as eager. Right before I make my escape, I smugly shout out, "Welcome back, Ca-*dick* and … I'm assuming another mate-brother I have yet to meet. It'll have to wait though!"

Solveig's laughter echoes down the hall as we leave her other men behind in the kitchen. I make it in record time back to my room and throw her on the bed. I feel like I black out for a few seconds because the next thing I know, I'm stripped bare holding a naked Sol down.

Her hooded gaze stares up at me with desire and I groan at how much I missed her. It's the best feeling in all of Daelarias to be skin to skin with her. It's also the first time in weeks that I'm completely pain fee. No ache in my chest at all and I realize what a fool I've been. It was the mate bond telling me the closer she got. Now that we're together it's completely settled.

You remember how to use that thing between your legs or are you just going to stare? Sol says to me through mind-speak and fully opens our connection. I nearly cum on her stomach at the amount of arousal and … love flowing into me. *Good god of love, I forgot how good this feels.*

Feel this, Sol says in response to my thoughts completely scrambling my mind as she grabs my cock and runs it through her wet slit. The breath in my chest stutters out of me and I moan while my head falls forward. *This woman is going to kill me.*

I take control from her and notch my cock at her opening before sliding in slowly, inch by inch. Now it's her turn to become mindless. I send her dirty, sexy arousing thoughts and intense feelings of love through our bond making her gasp loudly into the room.

Then I put her hands above her head and say, *Don't move those hands. It's your turn to feel my cock while I'm in control. You're going to feel every inch. I'm going to ruin this pussy for all those other fuckers.* Then I pull my cock out all the way before slamming into her. Hard. She may not walk straight after I'm done.

I slam my hips into her over and over while she whimpers begging to touch me and herself. The raw sound of skin slapping against sweaty skin can be heard as I continue to pound into her pussy. I'm close but I need to savor her body before it's back to reality. I let go of my bruising grip on her hips while I continue to thrust. Her breasts are so soft and supple while I palm them and feel the bounce in them with each thrust I make. Taking mercy on her, I reach out with one hand for a pillow and shove it under her ass. It tilts her hips up at just the right angle. *There.* Then I fuck her hard … once … twice … My sunshine screams out her release loudly as my cock rubs internally against that spot she loves. I only make it another three pumps before I find my own release with a roar of pleasure.

I collapse onto her but manage to hold myself over her chest with an elbow on the bed. Finding her rosy nipple near my mouth and lean in and suck it into my mouth surprising her. My slowly softening cock is still inside her but when her pussy squeezes after my oral ministrations it perks right up ready for round two.

"Fuck, this body …" I whisper licking her breast and reaching a hand between her legs while my cock softly thrusts in and out of her again.

"You just did … are … *fuck—ing*. Vi … stop or I'm going to come again," she huskily says before yelling out, "*Ahhh!*" Her second orgasm arches her back off the bed nearly bending her in half when I pushed a finger into her pussy alongside my cock.

201

I flip us so she straddling me on the bed and feel our combined body fluids leak between us. It's dirty and erotic and I love it. Love her.

The next hour (or maybe it's two) are vigorously spent in that room as I told her repeatedly that she's not leaving my bed and that pussy is getting ruined for anyone else. It wasn't easy … but luckily I'm the right man for *this* job.

CHAPTER
Thirty

SOLVEIG

B est. Welcome. Home. Ever.

Vidarr definitely wins some sort of award for his attentiveness. He could have been silent the whole time we were together since I got back, and I *still* would have known how much he missed me. Actions speak louder than words anyways—or at least in my opinion they do. Vi showed me time and again—and again—that he missed me. That he wants me with him and even better … that he loves me.

Our mate bond is near exploding with joy and fervent affection.

After a quick bath together, we get dressed and return to the responsibilities of rulership. We both leave his room holding hands and probably looking all starry-eyed.

Following my mate bonds, I find my other mates sitting in the castle library around a roaring fireplace sharing a bottle of Gorvian wine. I'm glad the library was one of the rooms still intact after Ragnar's dragon went berserk protecting me weeks ago.

From what I've seen since we got back to Falal, the castle seems to be already in repair with many walls rebuilt.

During our private time together, I told Vidarr how proud and thankful I am for how he's taken care of the kingdom in my absence. He's done amazingly well for someone not born into this life. Although, I shouldn't be surprised since Vidarr has always been a leader. Someone who inspires trust. It's just who he is.

With our entrance into the room, my other mates' laughter and conversation abruptly cuts off. All eyes zero in on us or rather *me.*

I notice my other mates all seem to have bathed and look more rested now making me instinctively feel pleased. Ragnar and Cadoc both appear to have shaved, given themselves haircuts and changed clothing. And—*damn* they look good. Jorah seems to be in his element here in the library but also looks more rested with the dirt from traveling washed away. He gives me a soft smile when he sees me, but it becomes more hesitant and self-conscious when his intelligent gaze takes in Vidarr standing next to me.

Clearing my throat which suddenly becomes clogged with nerves, I say, "Guys … this is Vidarr. My first mate." Squeezing his hand I look up at him and smile before looking back at the other three men. "Vi … you already know Cadoc. But these other two are Ragnar and Jorah. I know you met Ragnar in the kitchen, but you were a bit distracted at the time. Jorah worked in the stables and was hoping to train as a scholar here in the castle before we left, however I don't think you two ever crossed paths."

Vi greets Cadoc with a smirk before they both embrace with a manly pat on each other's back. I swear I hear Vi mutter something like "*Ca-dick*" before he steps back prompting Cadoc to teasingly punch Vi in the shoulder.

Then Vi looks to Jorah and walks over offering his hand. Jorah's eyes light up and his expression is so open that I feel my heart squeeze at their interaction. I can tell Jorah was nervous about this greeting for whatever reason.

They shake hands and Vi says, "Nice to meet you, Jorah. Your father is Sigurd, right?" Jorah nods his head with a questioning look before Vi continues. "He's a good man. He was part of the Rebellion when I was their leader. He helped us a lot with the information he passed on. I haven't had much time to talk with him since everything but he should join us for a meal sometime. No need to stand on formalities with a rebel as the regent."

"Yeah, he's my father. He also considers Solveig like a daughter to him," Jorah replies setting a book to the side. "I heard about you from Sol and I have to admit I was a bit nervous to meet you finally. You're one of the few who probably knows her almost as well as I do." Jorah looks at me quickly before focusing back on Vi. "Also, no offense but you're a bit intimidating." Vi chuckles and pats him on the arm while Jorah inspects Vi's many tattoos overlying his thick muscular arms.

"I'm not nearly as intimidating as Sol when she gets angry and defensive over something," Vi says teasingly before he tugs on my newly braided hair.

Huffing out a breath and glaring at Vi in pretend irritation, I then chuckle before saying, "Maybe if everyone would stop pulling my hair, I'd be less irritable all the time. I swear … I need to teach all my mates manners!"

Vi leans into me while taking up all my space and says huskily, "I thought you liked that I don't have any manners, sunshine. You enjoyed having a rebel in your bed just a moment ago. Don't go changing your tune now."

Fuck! I get a delicious curl in my center at his words and the memory of how he dominated me in the bedroom for the past few hours.

Up until now, I realize I had forgotten about my other dominant mate in the room who is apparently standing closer than before. Golden reptilian eyes burn a hole in the side of my face making *me* now nervous. I shove Vidarr back a step with both hands, creating some breathing room with all the male phero-mones floating around.

"So, this is the infamous first mate," Ragnar says in a deep growly voice gaining Vidarr's attention. "I am Solveig's soul bond. Her Makati. I've been eager to speak with you, Vidarr."

"Okay. I don't know exactly what that means but I'm assuming you're referring to a mate bond," Vi says standing up straight and crossing his arms over his chest in a closed off position. The next few seconds, which feel like minutes, are spent with the two of them staring into each other's eyes in a battle of male dominance.

Eventually, Ragnar subtly nods his head to Vi while maintaining eye contact, and they both simultaneously break apart. *Huh. I wonder what that was all about.* Whatever it was, they seem to have worked it out because the next few minutes they spend getting to know each other.

"So, Ragnar … tell me why your eyes looked strange a moment ago? I'm assuming it has to do with some sort of magic … you'll have to excuse me since the only experience I have with magic are the Elarians and Solveig," Vi says putting his arm over my shoulders as we rest back into the couch we're sitting on. "Here in Laevaris we haven't had much exposure."

"I am Drakonian, which means I can shift into my dragon form at will. Occasionally, my emotions get the better of me and my eyes will partially shift as my drakonian instincts take over. I was considered the drakonian ruler and king before my people were massacred in a senseless war with your kingdom. So far as we've discovered in our travels, only my adopted sister and cousin survived. They have recently mated together and will likely join us soon," Ragnar says leaning forward onto his elbows across from us in a chair. "Drakoni have their own power in a sense, other than shifting. We are all born with an elemental affinity that connects us to nature. A few are also gifted with a powerful unique rune like our mate. These are generally related to our connection with Elaria and its special magic."

"Wow, okay. So you're their king?" Vi says with surprise before looking at me and laughing. "Damn, sunshine. You have quite the harem here. A prince"—his gaze cuts to Cadoc who looks bored with Vi's antics and also subtly gives Vi a rude gesture before smirking—"a king, a scholar, and a … very handsome, dangerous rebellion-leader-turned-kingdom-Regent."

"Alright, Vi. I'm very well aware that I'm lucky and happen to have multiple powerful men in their own right connected with me." I interrupt his teasing tangent with an eyeroll before I continue saying in a more serious voice, "But—honestly—I would have chosen each of you even if you were homeless on the street. Your status means nothing to me but your support, your loyalty, your trust, and … your love … means everything to me. I just hope we can make this work. That … you all can come to some sort of … understanding."

Cadoc takes that moment to lean forward and puts a hand on my thigh in support. Squeezing my thigh he then says, "We love and trust you too, Sol. What this asshole should be saying is … he thinks we'll all make a good team. We'll keep you safe and protect you—together. Even if you don't really need us to. Some of us having powerful roles can benefit you in different ways. It will also create some challenges, especially with me being the heir to Gorvian throne, but we'll figure it out… together. Sort of like a family." Cadoc leans in and pushes an escaped piece of my hair behind my pointed ear before he kisses my cheek.

Vi squeezes my shoulders from my other side on the couch and says, "Yeah… what he said. You know we're just teasing each other, sunshine. These guys … even Ca-*dick*—oops— I mean *Cadoc* are all good men, and I'm glad to have them supporting you. Especially when I couldn't be there for you recently."

"Yeah, Sol. We'll work it out. I'm just glad you chose me too," Jorah says eagerly with a smile. "I may not be a king or someone with a title even, but I'll prove my worth to you. I can help you with the logistics of ruling the kingdom. Someone must do the accounting for the kingdom and maintain organization or you'll never keep up trade and finances. I did pay attention when you let me tag along with you as a kid during your tutor sessions."

"We are family now, little warrior. We will protect our own and work together once we learn each other's strengths and weaknesses," Ragnar says from in front of me. He then nods his head to each man respectfully before continuing. "My mate-brothers and I will form our own bond with time. You should keep our mental connection open between all of us so that we can communicate as needed like a flight of Drakoni would."

Vi raises his hand like he's a funny school boy but he's way too dangerous looking to be silly. He then asks, "Wait. So, we can all talk to each other now? That will be extremely useful and save a lot of time and messages. Also then I can keep track of you easily so you don't disappear again." He gives me a meaningful look before looking over at Ragnar. "What's a flight?"

Ragnar waves his hand in the air dismissively saying, "Sorry, it's simply a term Drakonian warriors used to describe their group of brothers in battle. We were able to mentally feel each other and predict their next actions as our bond grew over time. I suspect sharing our bond with our mate as well as the mindspeak will allow us to grow closer as a unit."

I agree, I say mentally opening up a square of communication with me at its center. Closing my eyes, I picture us standing in a densely wooded forest with them able to see me and each other as they surround me. *Is everyone here? Can you all hear me?*

I am present, little warrior. You are stunning, Ragnar replies heatedly.

Amazing, Sol! Count me in, Jorah says excitedly. *Also, I hear Ragnar.*

I'm with you, Solveig. And—I can hear the others. It's ... strange, Cadoc whispers in a serious voice.

I'm here, sunshine! Vi shouts mentally making everyone cringe a bit. *Sorry! I also can hear everyone. And it is strange ... I also feel like the dragon needs to keep it in his pants.* He chuckles and I mentally roll my eyes.

Ragnar however sends an erotic mental image of me spread out naked on the bed with him and Jorah tending to me. I physically blush in response and all the guys groan in response.

"Alright, that's enough," I say out loud standing quickly before they notice how turned on I'm getting. "Vi—you need to update all of us on what's been going on here after I left and then we'll tell you about our side of things."

Vi sits up straighter on the couch and adjusts himself in his pants before clearing his throat. Then in a serious voice, he proceeds to tell us all about the revolution, seizing the castle, the death of my father, and …

"Wait … *who* did you say killed my father?" I interrupt and ask in a detached cold voice.

Vi gets a look of panic and uncertainty on his face before he stands abruptly and grabs me by the shoulders. "Sunshine … I—I mean … I forgot to tell you. .. with everything … "

"Vi! Just tell me! Did you say … *King Lochlann?* As in my supposed real—um—birth father? He … he's alive?" I ask in a high pitched voice with wide eyes and a look of shock before I quickly conceal my emotions with my cold "princess" mask to hide the hurt. He kept this from me? Him and Kaeden … *oh fuck, Kaeden! Where is he?*

Everyone stiffens in the room and tension fills the air at my words and cold expression. They must be able to feel the hurt and betrayal through the bond. Ragnar and Cadoc instantly fill with anger in my defense. Jorah feels confused but supportive of me knowing how much I always wanted a father that accepted me as a child.

Vi starts to open his mouth in response with his hands in the air pleading. He's grasping for words and when he sees my expressionless face angrily says, "Don't do that, sunshine. Don't you close yourself off with that mask you put on for those fools in the past. I can see past it. Anyone who knows you well can.

And with this bond …" He hits a fist at his chest angrily but then deflates with a sad look. "… I can feel your hurt and sadness. It's unnecessary, Sol. I never meant to keep it from you. I swear. You know I've never lied to you … *ever*. I only just found out about him after you had left and then you were too far gone to tell you mentally. I should have said something earlier today but … *damn* I just missed you, okay? I wanted you and didn't even think about it."

He reaches a hand out to touch me gently and feeling his sincerity through the bond, I know he means every word. The tenseness of my shoulders and my cold mask fall immediately away with his touch. Then leaning into his chest he embraces me and rubs my back while I feel confusing tears enter my eyes. I'm not sure what I'm feeling now and I'm sure my mates are even more confused by my jumbled thoughts.

"So, I—I really have a father … King Lochlann?" I sniffle into Vi's chest and can feel his chin nod in reply. "What—what does he think about me? What did you tell him? Does he know who I am? Why did he kill my fath—I mean—King Batair?"

Vi pulls me back onto the couch and sits down before speaking. "Your grandfather, Aren, and the other Elarians with Kaeden rescued your father, Lochlann, from the slave camp. Ugh— Mortgaard— I think it was called. It all happened right around the time you were injured and I guess they returned shortly after. Then you disappeared so he never had a chance to meet you."

Vi sighs and rubs my back.

"I met him in the Elaritian forest. He looks like you, Sol … He's clearly your father. He's also very excited to meet you. I think he's truly happy to have found out he has a daughter. I told him how amazing you are and that I love you. That I'm your chosen mate. I'm not sure he knows that you have other mates yet. He knew Kaeden was your fated mate but that you two got into some sort of disagreement and haven't … ugh … solidified the bond yet. He acted like he was disappointed in Kaeden and honestly rather hard on him."

I don't know what to think about everything Vi has said. It's crazy! Also why would Lochlann care what happened between me and Kaeden. And—how did he find out? Kaeden must have said something. *Kaeden ...*

When I remain silent in thought, Vi says, "Your *real* father, Lochlann, had some bad history with Batair. I guess he wanted revenge. Lochlann holds Batair responsible for the death of your mother and the battles that occurred as well as his captivity. He also was upset that Batair kept you from him all these years." Vi then rubs a hand over his face tiredly. "It's best that you weren't there that day, Sol. Lochlann showed no mercy for Batair. He—he beheaded him and put him on a pike at the castle gates."

I nod my head silently and then with sudden weariness lean back into the couch and rest my head back in contemplation. So much has changed in such a short amount of time it's hard to process sometimes.

Four hands slowly make contact with me in support as I sit there. I'm just glad I have someone ... or rather multiple someones with me. I'm not alone, not anymore, and it makes it better.

CHAPTER
Thirty-One

SOLVEIG

Eventually, Vidarr catches me and my mates up on all the recent events since my departure. He was shocked when he learned about the curse on Elaria and worried when we discussed the battle at Sterling Outpost. It took a bit longer than I thought, and it definitely took much longer to explain my adventures to him. But overall, Vidarr listened and proved he's grown into the role that was thrusted upon him by asking pertinent questions throughout. He was always wild and reckless with me but I can see over the past few weeks he's grown more into his leadership role. Jorah added in comments with mine, making sure I didn't miss any important details. Cadoc also talked briefly with Vi mostly about the politics of an alliance with Gorva and ending the war between our countries.

It's growing late in the evening and we decide to discuss the war with Jaarn more tomorrow, preferably with this new council that Vidarr set up. A knock on the library door has us all ceasing conversation and looking up.

Liv pokes her curly blonde head into the room and looks around. Her gaze sees Vidarr but continues over the men and settles on me. Her facial expression instantly transforms into one of happiness and a beaming smile overtakes her heart shaped face.

I stand quickly and we rush towards each other obviously of the same mind. Embracing Liv is like finding your way after being lost. You hold on tightly and don't let go because you worry you won't find your way again. Her embrace projects comfort which is why she makes a great healer not just a friend. Liv is one of my best friends in the castle and close enough to me that I'd say she's like a sister if I ever knew what one would be like.

She steps back and inspects me head to toe while holding my shoulders so I can't escape her perusal. I can't help but laugh at her typical healer-like actions.

"Are you okay, Sol? Goodness! I prayed to Fallia nearly every day that she'd bring you back safely. I didn't know if you were dead or alive after that dragon attacked the castle," Liv says before leaning in and hugging me once more clearly relieved. "You look to be in one piece, but I never know with you … always getting hurt and scoffing it off as if it's nothing. I'll have to do an exam later just to make sure."

I step back from her embrace and say with amusement, "No need for an exam. I'm fine! Truly Liv! Good god I missed you too! How are you?"

"Oh, I'm fine!" She waves her hand dismissively in the air with a smile. "You know me. All work and no play. Healer Thaemon says I'll be done with my apprenticeship in another two months or maybe sooner! I can't wait! He says I've had more experience than most of the healers in training because of you …" She gets a sheepish look on her face and starts to apologize but I cut her off.

"Shh. Don't apologize. I'm glad all of it was good for something. You've worked tirelessly and deserve the recognition. We'll have to celebrate. So … no play huh? No special someone?"

She giggles and finally looks around at the four men closely paying attention to our conversation before she deviously says, "Oh, I don't know … I've been trying to get your attention for the past year…" She throws an arm around my back and squeezes my butt cheek with a wink to my mates. They all stiffen up in surprise, clearly unaware of Liv's preferences. "But, alas, I'm coming to realize it's a lost cause."

I roll my eyes at her antics and swat her hand away from my ass. Then I pinch her side and say, "Stop it or you'll make them all growly."

Liv's eyebrows shoot up before she replies, "*All* of them?" I blush and shrug my shoulders before nodding. "Well … I suppose I *have* moved on. Saraeh and I are officially together now. You remember? The pretty strawberry blonde who is apprenticing to the royal tailor?" I smile remembering their looks at each other when they first met in the hallways. "The woman sure does know how to dress. *And* undress." She wiggles her eyebrows up and down making me laugh out loud.

I then introduce her to my mates who appear more relaxed now knowing that she was only teasing.

"Oh! I forgot the whole reason I came back here. I was looking for you Vidarr … the cook says dinner is ready. I don't usually run errands but Tessia injured her ankle earlier and couldn't help out. I thought I'd just run and tell you so they didn't have to find someone else."

"Thank you, Liv! Want to join us?" Vi asks her.

"No thank you! I have a date with Saraeh in the city. You all have fun," Liv says hustling away. "And Sol—make sure you let me know if you need me. I'm glad you're okay."

"Thanks, Liv. You're the best! Say hi for me?" I yell out as she waves bye.

We all make it to the smaller dining hall which is already laid out for all of us just as my stomach grumbles loudly. I go to sit down but am startled by the doors being thrown open roughly causing a bang to echo in the room.

Kaeden comes storming into the room with a large travel bag thrown over his shoulder and several weapons attached to his body. He doesn't see me at the far end of the table as he stomps over to Vidarr like he's on a mission.

"I'm done! That's it … I can't wait anymore," Kaeden yells out stopping in front of Vidarr. "I'm going to find her. I gave you over a week—more than you made me promise—but now I'm leaving. Are you coming with me?"

I open my mouth excited to surprise him but Vi gives me a *look*. I know that look and it spells trouble. It's the look he gets before he causes trouble. Groaning internally to myself, I decide to keep my mouth shut for a moment and watch.

"Now wait just a minute, Kaeden … you don't even know where you're going. She could be anywhere! Plus—the woman is more trouble than she's worth. I mean her body is perfection personified but she's mouthy. Wild and reckless. You sure you want that? You could just move on …" Vi says spreading his hands in a questioning manner.

Kaeden's mouth drops open in disbelief before he sputters in anger. "What? You—you're not serious! She's your mate … and she's fated to me. How could you even suggest such a thing!"

Cadoc stands there with an assessing look on his face and a stance ready for defense due to Kaeden's outburst. Ragnar and Jorah are curiously looking back and forth at the banter with arms crossed leaning back in their chairs. I can tell Ragnar has rubbed off a bit on Jorah based on how they've been since we got back. Jorah's been more relaxed and involved in the ongoings around him instead of his face constantly in a book. But—I just can't sit back and let Vi tease Kaeden anymore. Not when he's clearly upset about me.

I clear my throat from across the room and table making both Vi and Kaeden look at me. Kaeden's intense amber gaze flicks quickly back to Vi annoyed at the interruption before it dawns on him. He turns back towards me dropping his pack and staring in shock.

"You're here. Solveig!" Kaeden whispers disbelievingly before he leaps over the entire table as only an Elarian could and lands gracefully in front of me. He grasps my shoulders and runs his hands over my arms up and down before settling them on my face. "You're really here! Bless Valirr! I've missed you." He goes to lean in and kiss me but stops himself and leans back. "I have so much to say …" Then he looks over my shoulder and angrily says to Vidarr, "You're an asshole! You didn't tell me she was here! How long have you known?"

I reach up and clasp his wrists pulling them away from my face and see his expression fall. But instead of walking away, I lean in and wrap my arms around his waist with tears quickly entering my eyes. My head only comes to his mid chest since he's so tall, but the height difference makes for good hugs.

"I missed you too, Kaeden. I'm glad you're well. No need to worry about me. And don't be angry—we only arrived today." I look up at him with imploring eyes. "Can we talk later? I'm starving. And, you look like you could use a minute too." I look over his tense body covered in weapons and his travel gear. He looks even better than when I last saw him if that's even possible.

Standing almost seven feet in height like most Elarian males, his muscular body is honed for battle. His once pale skin from the slave camp we found him in is now tanned from the outdoors and sun. His dark brown hair is longer than most men in the city reaching just past his shoulders and it's braided back on each side of his face.

He hesitantly smiles and nods in agreement. Then his gaze notices the others in the room making him pause. I grab a chair and sit next to Ragnar while Vi settles at the head of the table and Jorah is to Vidarr's right.

When Kaeden continues to stand there assessing the situation, I reach a hand out and tug him into the chair on my left.

"Kaeden, I—I want to introduce you to the others. You already know Vi is my mate." I hesitate while nervously twisting my hands in my lap. "Cadoc and I became mated before I left which I think we talked about potentially happening." I smile towards Cadoc who smirks back before I see Kaeden nod his head.

"Yes, you mentioned that you were considering him as a mate." Kaeden nods and reaches over to squeeze my hand. "We know each other and I suppose congratulations are in order then." Him and Cadoc clasp hands across the big table before settling back down.

"Ah—well you see—while I was gone …"

"*My* mate—*our* mate— is trying to say that she has two more mates in addition to Vidarr and Cadoc. This is nothing to be ashamed of, my Maseeri," Ragnar says in a deep voice interrupting me and likely trying to resolve my discomfort that he feels through the bond. He places his arm over the back my chair possessively while he talks. Unfortunately, it just makes me more uncomfortable because Kaeden seems to be taking it hard.

"Ahem … as I was trying to say before a certain overly-protective, Drakonian male interrupted me … this is Ragnar one of my mates and that is Jorah another of my mates. Jorah and I grew up together as children in the castle and have been best friends so I guess it's not too big of a surprise that I chose him as a mate." I shrug and sneak a peek at Kaeden's face which appears initially hurt before a blank expression overtakes it.

"Excuse me, I know I'm rather late to join but did you mention *Drakoni?*" Kaeden looks over at me confused and with a colder look than he's ever given me.

"Yes. Uhh, Ragnar is Drakonian. He's the one who saved me … you know when the castle was destroyed. He was a bit … protective and things may have gotten a bit out of hand …"

Then I remember how he wasn't around and was keeping secrets.

"… you know … *or* maybe you don't since you weren't there, *again*." That may have been a bit childish to throw that back in his face but I'm hurt by his cold looks after our separation. Ragnar's right. I shouldn't be nervous or scared to tell anyone about my mates.

Kaeden's face flushes red for a moment before he looks down and says, "I'm sorry Sol. This is a lot to take in. You left with one mate and came back with three more. I—I'm worried I'm too late. That you might not want me now… and it hurts."

"I know, we can talk later," I reply running a hand through my hair and taking a deep breath, centering myself.

"So, you're Drakonian? I—wow—I remember from before the war. I was a young soldier when I last saw a Drakoni flying over Elaria and I'm glad you were not all decimated completely. Too many were lost in that senseless war of greed."

"Thank you, I'm glad to be alive too and to have a chance with my Maseeri," Ragnar replies looking at me affectionately. "There are two of my kind that we know are also still alive—my sister and her mate."

Our dinner is served and we all eat ravenously. Our conversations must have worked up our appetites.

"So, Kaeden … I can't wait to sit down and discuss Elarian culture with you. There's so much knowledge that's been lost over the years and the lack of documentation is appalling," Jorah eagerly says after everyone is finishing their meals. "Now that I know you, I can finally have access to a source of information …"

Kaeden gets an amused look on his face at Jorah's rambling which occurs whenever there's anything involving knowledge and books. "I'd be pleased to pass on any knowledge I have … especially to a potential mate-brother," Kaeden says in a serious voice while glancing at me covertly.

I take that as my cue to address the rising tension between Kaeden and I. Leaning to the right, I kiss Ragnar on the cheek preparing to stand which he anticipates through the mate bond. He grabs my chin forcefully and gives me a passionate open mouthed kiss before saying, "If you harm her in anyway—including your words—I'll know about it, and I'll make you wish you never survived that slave camp. She's my everything. My soul fire. And if she's harmed… I'll burn the world with you in it. So think over your words and actions while in my—our—mate's presence." Ragnar stares intensely into Kaeden's eyes. "I'm only allowing you to be alone with her because she wishes it and because you're a *potential* mate-brother."

"Alright, why don't you men open some of that Gorvian wine we have in the cellar? I'm sure Cadoc would appreciate some of it. Kaeden and I are going to have a much needed talk," I say walking to the other side of the table. I kiss Vidarr and Jorah softly goodnight trying to not make anyone uncomfortable but Cadoc—surprisingly— has other ideas.

"Sounds good, Sol. Just…don't forget about me." He tugs the hair at the base of my head making me tilt up towards him before he kisses me deeply. It must go on for a bit because someone jostles his shoulder and he nips my bottom lip before smiling. "You're mine tomorrow. Don't go too easy on him … he has some work to do," Cadoc whispers that last part in my ear before stepping back and slapping me *hard* on the ass.

I squint back at him before I grab Kaeden's hand and lead him out into the hallway.

A moment later Ragnar's voice is sent through all our shared mental connection. *Little warrior, don't forget to keep the bond open. We all want to know what's going on.* I roll my eyes mentally to him and hear chuckles from my other mates.

Kaeden and I walk in silence down the hall holding hands before finally entering my new rooms. My old rooms were destroyed when Ragnar's dragon went berserk but also they supposedly assigned me the queen's chambers based on my new soon-to-be status.

CHAPTER
Thirty-Two

KAEDEN

Walking into the prior Laevarian Queen's suite is a bit surreal and I can tell it's bringing up mixed emotions in Solveig as well if the look on her face is anything to go by. She seems … lost. Vulnerable. Nervous. Sad. This is the first time since the night I spent talking in her bedroom with her that I'm seeing the unfiltered and raw facial expression of my little mate.

I'm sure it's strange entering and sleeping in your mother's old bedroom but surely this couldn't be the first time she's been back in here.

"Solveig?" I softly ask her. She doesn't respond in fact she seems completely lost in her thoughts and likely memories. "Sol? Little mate, are you okay?" When she doesn't respond and a tear slips down her cheek, I decide I've had enough. Picking her up is easy since she's light as a feather compared to my bulky size.

I place her gently on the end of the bed and kneel before her on the ground. Searching her eyes I finally see her awareness returning. "Solveig … let me in, little mate. Tell me what you're thinking."

She blinks a few times staring into my eyes before a soft tilting of her lips appears on her face. "Why does everyone always want to know my thoughts?" she says blowing a piece of unruly brown hair out of her eyes.

"Maybe because we all care about you. Well, I'm assuming those men out there do even though I don't know them well. Now we just need to make sure you care about yourself too. Your thoughts and opinions matter, Sol," I say holding her hands before gently kissing the back of them. "I—I truly am sorry for my actions before you left. I want you to know that I'll never pick someone else over you or keep secrets from you. I suppose I kept our mission to save the remaining slave camps from you because firstly I thought I was protecting you and knew you'd want to go even though you were recovering from an injury. I didn't trust you enough to know your own capabilities and your own body. And secondly, I think I was so used to following orders from the Elarian elders and my commanding officers in the Elarian army that I forgot they don't take precedence anymore. *You do*."

Solveig leans in and our faces are at eye level with her sitting even though I'm kneeling in front of her. She rubs a callused thumb over my bottom lip and affectionately says, "I think I know that already Kaeden. In here." She places her other hand on her chest. "I forgive you. It's hard for me to trust given my past. Men have tried to manipulate and control me since I was a child. It'll take me time to get over my own issues and sometimes I forget that you have your own. You were a slave for many years and before that a soldier. You've taken orders most of your life but no longer. We both can find freedom in our bond by telling our truths and making our own decisions."

I can't help but feel a weight lifting off my shoulders knowing that she forgives me and we're building something here … understanding. I realize suddenly that I need to lay it all out there so nothing comes between us. Taking a deep breath I say,

"There's more I need you to hear …" Her face fills with anxiety but I continue despite not really wanting to. "When I got back to the Elaritian Forest after freeing the remaining Elarians, I went straight to see you. It was late in the evening but I snuck up to your window. You had a man with you in your bed … which I now realize was Ragnar. But at the time, I was angry and felt betrayed. I ran off when I should have confronted you."

Solveig squeezes my hands and says, "I'm sorry, Kaeden! I can't imagine what you must have felt like—no— I know you must have been upset. I would have too. But—I would never betray any of you. You need to know … I think I have found them all. You—you're the last one. I can feel it deep in my chest and the mate markings on my chest are nearly complete."

Feeling relief, I suddenly feel guilt that I made her feel the need to reassure me that she has no more mates after me. She shouldn't feel ashamed or that it's her fault. Our Goddess Fallia decides who our family and mates will be in the end.

"I won't lie and say I'm sorry to hear that because it honestly makes me relieved. It's already hard enough to get you alone and I worry what if … I'm not the one. The last mate you need?"

I take a deep breath centering myself, and then I get up sitting next to her on the bed.

"I—I lost someone in that slave camp when I was imprisoned there. I wasn't sure at the time if she was my mate … we were first friends and then quickly became lovers for a few years before she died. She was human and not a warrior but she had her own strengths. Sometimes I think of her. But, I now know that my feelings for her weren't the same as ours. Our connection is soul deep—everlasting. If I met her outside of that slave camp, I probably would have never even looked her way. It was a relationship of comfort and basic needs but we did share affection which was lacking in that dark place. I'll always remember her and think affectionately on our time together, but I was able to move on after a time. If—if something ever happened to you, Sol … if you somehow died … I—I don't think I'd survive. I would follow you, with my only regret being that I should have spent every second of every day with you. Fuck everything else."

"Kaeden. I feel the same. I can't let you go. In fact, if you leave … I'm going to follow you. So, you'd best stay with me." Solveig embraces me throwing her arms around my waist and running her fingers up and down my spine making me relax. "I'm sorry for your loss. I owe her for giving you a reason to live in that horrible place."

"Thank you. Now, tell me why you acted so strange when we got in here. Were you just nervous to be alone with me?"

She looks confused for a second before she realizes what I'm referring to and says, "No, no. Nothing like that. I—I was thinking about my mother. I haven't been in these rooms since she died." She takes a deep shuttering breath. "I miss her. She—she was a good woman, but I always resented that she left me. I know it's stupid since no one can control death. But—she left me with him, alone. I think my mother knew he was rotten and yet we never left … Maybe she'd still be alive if she had been stronger and not so scared all the time."

I start tucking hair behind her ear and loosening her braid preferring her hair loose. Then I soothingly run my hands over her head in comfort before replying, "Perhaps. But it's hard to judge not knowing all the facts back then. She likely wasn't as mentally strong as you, little mate. And, honestly, you wouldn't be the woman you are today if she was. Our experiences and relationships mold us into a version of ourself. Without them, we'd all be the same. It's why the Gods and Goddesses gave us our free will. Even with this fated mate bond, you still have a choice."

I lean in to kiss her but hold back just over her lips giving her the choice—the control—which is something we both didn't have a lot of in the past couple years. It's in that brief moment that I flick my eyes up and see a blur of movement.

CHAPTER
Thirty-Three

KAEDEN

Following my Elarian instincts, I shift her body to the right throwing her off the end of the bed just as a man throws a dagger where her chest was.

It ends up impaling my left upper arm with a sharp burning pain. *Fuck!* I can barely move my left arm from the excruciating pain the dagger elicits and I'm hit with a wave of fatigue making me move slower than normal. The man—assassin—moves quickly holding a short sword out and charging towards Solveig who has already blocked his path and has her own dagger palmed in her hand. Her katanas are nowhere to be seen but I'm glad my fierce little mate is always prepared for battle.

She blocks a thrust of his short sword at the last minute with her steel dagger and I swear I can see sparks fly from the intense impact. Their movements are a blur and Solveig is clearly the better fighter. Her agility rune must be blazing in power given the speed and acrobatic moves she's using. The assassin's breaths are coming rapidly and I see the moment he makes an error. He glances past Solveig's shoulder and she lashes up with her dagger into an exposed spot. He cries out in pain but holds her off. That's when I notice what distracted him. Another assassin snuck in through a secret passage and has a cross bolt aimed at my future mate!

Grabbing the dagger in my arm and not giving a fuck if it hit a major blood vessel or not, I pull it out and throw it towards the assassin with the cross bolt hitting him dead center in the eye. But it's a second too late as I hear the twang of the bolt being released.

Lucky for me I'm a paranoid warrior and would never risk that thing hitting my Solveig from the moment I saw it. I grit my teeth at the amount of power I'm using when the bolt hits a wooden barrier formed from the furniture in the room. My nature rune usually only works on living entities or plants but if I expend a large amount of power I can sometimes manipulate objects made from nature. The burning from the rune on my left thigh extinguishes abruptly as my power runs out. It was difficult, but I figured draining myself of power was worth it … for her.

I collapse back onto the bed in dizziness and fatigue, while I hear the sounds of Solveig using her fists against flesh. When I only hear one person breathing in the now silent room, I squint open my eye and see Solveig checking that both are dead. She's covered in splattered blood from her fight and angry, but I think uninjured.

Next thing I remember is Solveig shaking me awake. *Must have drained myself more than I thought.* She's saying something to me but I'm having trouble focusing. I focus harder when I see her waving around the dagger that impaled me.

"Is this what injured you? Kaeden! Pay attention! Did it come in contact with you?" Solveig anxiously says to me. "Are you injured anywhere else? Why are you—how did you do that with the wooden furniture?" She asks worriedly before chucking the dagger across the room as if it burned her. Probably did since that thing stings worse than any I've ever felt before.

"No other injuries … ju—just my arm. Hurts pretty bad. I—I'm also very tired. Drained. Used a lot of power and energy with my nature manipulation."

"*Fuck!* That dagger was made of Avralite. It drains our—Elarian—energy. It's some sort of crystal that's from caves near the coast of Beamus," Solveig says in a distracted and concerned voice. I vaguely remember hearing about it but can't understand how she would know. I glance over at the dagger she threw and notice it's a smooth clear crystal with a green tinge to it. *Strange.* "I—I've had something similar used on me before," she says lifting her shirt and showing me a puckered pink scar from a knife on her abdomen. *Dear Valirr! Elarians shouldn't scar like that especially with the healing rune that she has.* "You'll need sun and rest from the effects of it. But as long as it's not in contact anymore, you should be ok…I think." She bites her lip again looking anxious.

I put a hand on hers that's resting over my wound before I ask in a deadly voice. "Who did that to you? Was it your father—I mean—King Batair … or was it that dead-man-walking, Malphas?"

She stares down at my wound avoiding eye contact as she holds a cloth to it. "Counselor Malphas did. He—he tortured me for years. He's a very depraved man and I'm only recently coming to realize that none of it was my fault. You and I—we both share a dark past. One of pain and abuse and captivity. He just started mine from a younger age."

"*Fuck*, little mate. I'm going to kill him once I find him."

"You aren't going anywhere right now. You saved me twice. *Twice!*" she shouts and her eyes fill with determination. "Now I'm going to heal you and—Ragnar said mates can share energy so … maybe we have enough of a connection …"

Her hand makes skin to skin contact with my arm before I can protest. The pain is literally siphoned from my body into her hand and I relax back into the bed. I look over to see the wound closing before my eyes in wonder just as a groan slips between her lips. I take in her fierce expression and see blood start to soak the left arm of her shirt. *Selfless little mate. I really need to complete the bond with her so I can know what in Daelarias she is thinking!*

My thoughts cut off and I moan in pleasure from the feeling flowing into my body. It's a sudden rush of power and ... *sunshine* ... yes pure sunshine that I feel twisting throughout. It's addicting and I feel myself immediately growing hard in my pants. It's a strange feeling to go from utter fatigue to instant lust and energy. She must have pushed energy into me and *damn* did it work. But, I think it worked a bit differently than she thought because she's suddenly straddling my hips and rolling her core along my hard length.

I grab her hips and stand pulling her legs around my waist. I quickly make the few steps to the ensuite bathroom getting away from the two dead assassins in the room and wanting to clean Solveig up a bit. Even through my lust filled haze, I feel the urge to tend that wound on her arm from healing me.

She's kissing me with little nips that make me struggle to control my own urges until she's tended to. I place her firm ass down on the table next to the washbowl for cleaning up trying to push her away a bit and grab a clean rag. But when she latches onto a soft spot behind my ear sucking hard and marking me before licking along the shell of my pointed ear, I completely lose it.

An Elarian male only has so much control. I wanted our first time together to be gentle and sensual—slow—but that's not going to happen now. Her shirt falls apart in my hands when I rip it from the hem upwards before I even know what I'm doing. I then lean in and kiss a trail down her neck to her collarbone. Sliding the rest of the shirt off her arms, I look over the wound she got from healing me and notice it's already starting to knit back together. *Fucking good. That's good ...*

I kiss and lick a line over the healing area as the sneaky woman grabs my shirt from the back pulling it over my head in a quick move. Now that I know she's not in pain or bleeding, I feel a frantic need to see all of my future mate bared to me and mark her—just like she did to me. I lean down and pull her boots and pants off. She tilts her hips up helping me remove them eagerly. She already has my belt loosened with those nimble fingers so I kick my pants the rest of the way down my legs and stand before her.

Good Goddess Yasmil! She's stunning. Perfect lithe body of a warrior and yet curvy in the places that a man wants to hold. Her chest is full … way fuller and lush than I thought. How she manages to do the moves she does with those beauties in the way … I guess I'll just have to find out.

She stares back at me with those heated sapphire blue eyes and I nearly embarrass myself. I somehow manage to rasp out a warning, "Don't give me that look little mate or I'll mark your skin with my cum instead of putting it where I want it most." She bites her lower lip in response reminding me that I want to mark her skin with my mouth instead of my cum. "Spread those golden thighs for me. Let me see what I've waited for. *Fuck,* Solveig.*" She does as she's told for once and spreads her legs, letting me look my fill.

My cock was already hard for her but now is almost painful as it grows further slapping my stomach in its eagerness to impale her wetness. Elarian males are well endowed like any muscular warrior, but it's a jesting rumor among them that when Elarian male's mate with their chosen or fated, their members seem to grow even larger to ensure full pleasure of their partners. I just don't know how much more my dick can do at this point but then again I've never been with my fated mate.

My hands find her luscious breasts and palm them running my thumbs over her nipples. Plucking their rosy tips, Solveig arches her back and moans trying to rub against me for more contact.

"Kaeden. I need you. *Please,*" she says through her moans while I work her with my hands. Trailing my nose and up her neck and into her dark brown hair, I inhaler her scent of lavender and freshness. Nature and pure sunshine. Then I lick along the pointed tip of her ear and she goes crazy with want cursing up a storm and begging me. Her hand finds my long cock and starts to pump up and down.

I can't help but rock my hips into her grip as I find a good spot for me to mark her. *I need a place where all those other fuckers can see it. They had their time with her to do it. Now it's mine.* I scrape my teeth along the left side of her neck before biting and sucking the soft skin into my mouth hoping it bruises a bit and lasts long enough for her other mates to see. I know—a bit childish—but too bad.

My fingers trail up her inner thigh and find her core. It's like a furnace in its heat but yet dripping wet.

"Solveig, little mate … you're soaking. Let's see if we can help you a bit …" I say slipping a finger inside her easily and pushing my thumb against her clit. She bucks into my hand and bends backwards with her legs wrapped around my waist. *Ohh damn. I forgot about her agility rune. That could make things interesting.*

"Take your hand off my cock, little mate, and put them both on the table. Yes … that's it. Now arch your back more and push those full breasts into my mouth." She follows instructions perfectly as her back makes a C-shape and I suck her right nipple into my mouth. One of my hands palms and holds her ass off the table allowing me more control while my other hand pushes two more fingers into her. It only takes five pumps of my fingers and a firm push of my thumb on her clit before she screams her release and more wetness coats my hand.

Her arms give out but I already have her in my hold against my chest while she comes down from her climax.

"Kaeden, I—"

"Shh, you're a responsive little one and needy too. Well, we aren't done yet. I'm not done yet …" I thrust my hard as a rock cock up between us making her gasp. "You and I … we have something we need to finish together. Tell me yes. Tell me you want me before I go any further."

"Yes, fuck yes. I want you, Kaeden. You saved me and I'm meant to be yours. I'm sure of us. But more importantly … I have feelings for you."

Not needing any more of a consent than that, I flip her around in my arms and put her kneeling upright on the table in front of me. There's a mirror resting against the wall in front of us and it makes for an erotic view of what's coming next.

I push her thighs apart wider and somehow perfectly my cock lines up at the level her pussy. She feels me behind her rubbing there and her hands slap on the wall next to the mirror while her blue eyes watch everything with heat.

I grab her hips tightly and in one move thrust up through her slick channel into her core. I have to stop for a second and gain control because it feels better than anything I've ever felt. Prior lovers pale in comparison to this.

I slide one hand to her lower back and brace her before I start thoroughly fucking her pussy. It's hard, rough, and wild. And Sol, she takes it all pushing back into me. At some point my hand finds her hair and pulls her body back into me so her back lays against my chest while I thrust. I can tell I'm close to coming because I get a sensation of my cock expanding un-willingly, so maybe the rumors are true regarding Elarian males and their mates. Solveig squirms in discomfort or pleasure—I'm unsure—but at this point she's going to take it because I'm too close to coming.

I need her to come again too so maybe an angle change would help. Sliding my right hand around her hip and thigh where that agility rune is located I get an idea. My hand pushes her right thigh and leg up straight in the air against my chest and her torso. She gasps with the new sensations and I continue to thrust forcefully making her take it all.

She reaches up with her hands and pulls my hair at the scalp inflicting a bit of pain as she cums hard on my cock. I push up into her one more time before letting go and feeling my cum mark her inner walls.

I set her leg down and turn her to straddle me before sinking to the floor in a puddle of contentedness. *Mine! My Solveig. She's so beautiful.* I kiss her shoulder and run my hand over the soft skin of her back enjoying this intimate moment with her.

"Kaeden, I—that was…I mean …" she stutters, looking utterly wrecked in the best way with her hair a mess and a few bruises from our lovemaking on her body. The marking I put on her neck especially looks like a masterpiece with deep purple bruising around it. Somehow it's not healing as fast as the wound did on her arm. *Good.*

"Yeah, it was … beyond anything …" I reply but she suddenly clutches her chest and promptly passes out in my arms. I get an intense burning in my chest but can't focus on it much since something's wrong with my little mate.

I hear a loud roar that rattles the walls concerning me but I try to focus on what's most important. *Why did she faint?* I lay her down flat and put a towel under her head while running my hands over her body. *Maybe I was too rough. Fuck! Did she eat enough? Maybe she used too much energy healing me?*

"Solveig! Little mate? Can you hear me?" I gently shake her without any response. "Wake up!" Again. No response but she's breathing easily so that's good. I decide maybe some cold water could help and get up to the washbasin reaching for a rag. As I look up, I see myself in the mirror we fucked against. A large tattoo sits on my left chest in a black ink design. It's a dagger with the hilt at the bottom and the tip pointing up, transforming into a growing oak tree set on a background of the sun. *Holy Valirr! A mate marking!*

I scramble to get a cloth and wet it in the cold water eager to wake her and share in my joy. I turn around to do so but am knocked backwards into the mirror by a hulking man. No wait—not a man.

"You fucking disgusting excuse for an Elarian. You dare to harm *my mate!*" I hear Ragnar growl loudly into my face while he grips my shoulders. Large black talons pierce my skin and black scales cover his arms up to his neck. There's swirling silver tattoos covering most of his body. "What did you do to her? I felt her pleasure and then pain ... then nothing!"

I reach up and grab his scaled wrists pulling his talons from my skin as I say, "*Our* mate."

"What?" he asks with a snarl. His reptilian eyes are completely gold and focused on my chest.

"I said ... *our* mate." I tap my chest over the mate marking. "And she's fine ... I think. I was trying to wake her up. One second we were good and then she fainted. Seems like it happened right when we got our mate markings."

Ragnar listens intently and stares me directly in the eye like a predator watches his prey. I decide fighting for dominance with the biggest predator in Daelarias is a bad idea and therefore, I lower my eyes to the side after a few seconds. He grunts in acknowledgment of my explanation or perhaps submission.

We both turn then and I notice her three other mates surrounding her. One of them pulled a clean shirt over her and she's now sitting in the lap of ... Jorah—I believe his name is. He's smoothing her hair back from her face and she seems to be starting to stir awake. Relief floods my body and that's when I feel a strange sensation.

Solveig's eyes flutter and when they open we all startle in shock. Her eyes were always a piercing sapphire blue but now they ... *glow.* They literally are glowing blue orbs full of power and they're locked on me.

Her face lights up and she smiles at me while her lips form the word *mate.* That strange sensation in my chest—it's Solveig! Or rather her emotions and feelings. She feels ... happy, confused, oh shit—now worried ... anxious ...

I drop to my knees and get closer putting a hand on her bare thigh and squeezing. Then I send love and joy through our bond making her tear up.

"Kaeden! You—you're happy? We're mates!" she says then her eyes squint and she looks down as she pulls the shirt away from her body. She frowns down at the large mate marking on her chest and I feel through the mate bond … trepidation?

"I'm very happy, little mate. I've waited forever to be able to connect with you like this. What are you concerned about?" I ask hesitantly while inherently knowing she's in a vulnerable state after developing a mate bond. She also just fainted. "You passed out on me. That's why everyone rushed in to your rescue."

"I—I feel strange. The mate marking feels strange … it's beautiful though. Complete and whole," she says dazedly staring at the tattoo.

"Did you eat enough today, Sol? Maybe I should send a messenger to get Liv in the city," Jorah says worriedly.

"You didn't sleep enough and are probably tired," Cadoc says but then looks around and says candidly, "Anyone want to tell me why there are two dead men in the other room? I mean—I don't remember our mating to be that violent. Maybe this is an Elarian ritual?"

Solveig bites her lip trying to hold back a laugh but one slips out anyways and she says, "Cadoc, did you just make a joke? I'm shocked!" We all chuckle and Vidarr pushes him on the shoulder teasingly. "But, no. I don't know any Elarian rituals anyways. We were talking and then Kaeden shoved me to the side taking a dagger in his arm meant for me. He saved me from being stabbed in the back. While I fought off the assassin, another slipped in through a secret passage and tried to use a crossbow bolt on me. Again Kaeden saved me but by using his nature rune. We haven't had a chance to see who they are yet since their faces were covered and well … we got busy."

"Sure … you two got *busy*," Vidarr says in a teasing voice while raising his eyebrows suggestively up and down. "Let's just say I want to *get busy* every day then." She chuckles and smacks him on the arm weakly while sneaking a shy glance towards me. It makes me smile regardless of the situation.

I feel Ragnar place a (now human) hand on my shoulder making me stiffen up preparing for an attack again. But instead he says in a calm voice, "I need to apologize, Kaeden. I shouldn't have attacked you. You've proven you can protect our mate by your actions and her words. Forgive me, mate-brother?"

Shocked and honestly a bit touched to be included in the prestigious group now, I reply, "Of course. I would have reacted the same … mate-brother."

Jorah clears his throat loudly interrupting our strange truce or I guess—brotherly bonding? He then softly says, "Am I the only one who's going to address the obvious and more concerning thing in the room?" Everyone silences and looks to him while Sol gets a confused look on her face. "Solveig, your eyes are glowing … still blue … but it's obviously something magically related."

Solveig gets up and peers into a broken part of the mirror I was shoved into. Her eyes are still glowing and I notice she stumbles a bit on her way there. Ragnar grabs her elbow for support before he says, "It's from the bond. She has all her mates now if we go by the marking on her chest."

Solveig whips around and nearly crashes to the ground in her haste to stare at her Drakonian mate. She anxiously asks, "What do you mean, Ragi?"

"You've completed all of your bonds and seem to have all your runes. You are coming into your full power, little warrior. Not that you need it since you are strong and fierce without it." He purrs into her neck running his hands down to her ass. *Touchy fucker.*

I just completed my mate bond with Sol and he's already got his hands all over her. I will admit I'm feeling a bit possessive at the moment. Solveig looks up at me and reaches to grab my hand since she must feel my emotions through our new bond. All I feel from her right now is internal conflict and fear.

"We'll figure it out, little mate," I say trying to reassure her.

"I—I feel different too. Is that the power you're talking about Ragi? Will my eyes go back to normal? I feel like there's a storm inside of me … like if it doesn't release I'll explode." Her words start to concern me and must scare the others because they all start talking at once.

"*Quiet!*" Ragnar shouts and astonishingly everyone listens including Sol. "From what I remember, when an Elarian comes into their full power they can release it through using their runes or through sharing with their mates." He nuzzles into her neck again making a weird as fuck rumbling noise. "I would prefer you share. Skin contact is best. Think of it like how you use your healing power … a transfer of energy. Sex works too. Either way, I can take it little warrior. Your eyes should go back to normal and you'll feel more … *relaxed* afterwards."

I snort in disbelief and amusement, but he appears rather serious. I see Vidarr raise his hand which looks silly on such a muscular and tattooed man. He says, "I volunteer as well for this *transfer of energy.*" He cracks his knuckles then. "I could use a little power anyways, sunshine. Give it to me."

We all laugh including Solveig who now feels less anxious. She wiggles out of Ragnar's possessive hold and runs to Vidarr. Jumping in the air recklessly, he catches her as she wraps her legs around him in a maneuver that looks effortless and kisses him quickly. Their love is easy to see in the way they interact with each other. It comes from years of knowing each other's mannerisms. I hope to one day get there with my mate, and now I have a chance.

CHAPTER
Thirty-Four

SOLVEIG

It was easier than I thought. Transferring my built up power to others was like second nature. It flowed into my mates similar to diverting water built up behind a dam. Sort of like a release once I made contact and … let go.

It's a *damn* good thing I have five mates now. It took the better part of an hour to release all that pent up energy and by the time I was done, I was exhausted. *Too bad it was so late and we had dead assassins to clean up or I would have found my release in another way.* I grumble to myself as I do my morning ablutions.

I ended up kissing and making out with each of my men *equally* to ensure no one felt left out by my power transfer. By the end, I felt sexually frustrated but too tired to do anything further. Shortly after, we all fell into bed together.

Smiling to myself, I look into the mirror one last time and see my blue eyes back to their normal light. I braid my dark brown hair tucking my pointed ears under a part of my hair still uncomfortable with people staring at them. Old habits die hard. I know the Elarians are now in a sense accepted but I still can't erase the feeling of disgust and disappointment I'd see in my father's eyes.

I don my weapons strapping on my harness with my twin katanas on my back since I need to feel capable to take on the day. I'm sure it's going to be full of challenges since there's so many things that need to be done. Vidarr and my other mates already went down to breakfast, and he recommended we call a meeting shortly after to discuss the war with Jaarn.

I turn to leave the room when I hear a rustle of feathers and a soft chirp near the open window. My eyes quickly follow the sound as I fill with anticipation. I see a large gray goshawk perched in the window pane staring intently at me as I feel my nature rune on my wrist tingle with intensity.

Tapping into the power associated with my nature rune I project excitedly into his mind, *Tyr! My friend! I missed you fiercely!* I jog over to him and run my hand affectionately over his under feathers.

Ah, Solveig! Finally! My mate and I have been looking everywhere for you! I suppose Allira was correct. She told me we should return here and wait for your arrival. She was just checking on our nearly grown eyas.

I'm sorry, Tyr. But I'm glad to be reunited again. I would like to meet your family and of course see Allira again. Do you want to join me for breakfast? I'll sneak you some eggs ... I project to Tyr with an image of him flopped over with a full belly and wings spread out.

Yes! Say no more. I don't wish to part with you yet. I also need to meet your mates other than the handsy painted one, Tyr states while he jumps onto my leather harness that overlays my shoulder. His feathers ruffle in irritation as he brings up his dislike for Vidarr.

I chuckle and start walking out of the bedroom door into the hallway. *Vidarr just likes to tease. And those are tattoos on his skin similar to my runes, not paint. Please try to not bite him again.*

I make no promises if he treats me like an eyas! I am older than him in our years and he should learn respect. I bite my lip trying not to chuckle at Tyr's disgruntlement. I'll have to warn Vi that he's likely to get a nip on the fingers if he feeds Tyr.

Our banter is cut off when I step into the small dining hall seeing a table set for eight. My mates are all sitting and their conversation stops as I enter. *Why do they all look nervous suddenly?*

"Ah, I see you've reunited with Tyr. Come here, friend …" Vi says leaning forward with some bacon in his hand trying to feed him.

Tyr shoots quickly from my shoulder and grasps the bacon in his talons before flying in a loop and perching on the back of my chair. I take a seat as I hear Vidarr mutter, "*Fuck.* Damn ungrateful bird cut my fingers."

I look up and see a gash on Vidarr's hand that's bleeding and although I'm slightly amused at their rivalry with each other I also don't like to see my mate hurt.

Tyr… that wasn't very nice! I look up over my shoulder at him perched there eating his spoils.

He looks slightly reproached but says, *I thought he was going to tease me and take it away at the last minute. I may have been a bit hasty in my judgement.*

"Tyr says he's sorry, Vi," I state poking Tyr in the stomach. "Want me to heal it?"

"No thanks, sunshine. It's just a teensy tiny scratch anyways. He's losing his vicious touch in his old age," Vi smirks but I can see he's leery of my hawk friend in the way he leans away slightly. *Hah! He's always been a bit of a baby when it comes to any predator type animal.*

"Wow, Solveig! May I?" Jorah asks reaching out to touch Tyr from the chair next to me. "I've never gotten so close to a hawk … I always forget how well you can interact with animals."

I tell Tyr to behave and then nod to Jorah. "He likes his belly rubbed even though he tries to deny it."

Jorah starts softly rubbing Tyr's white feathered stomach as he feeds him a piece of his eggs. Tyr makes a pleased chirping noise and I can tell Jorah will be his favorite of my mates.

Kaeden clears his throat and catches my gaze. Raising an eyebrow at him, I start eating my delicious breakfast of eggs, bacon and an apple pastry that is perfection personified. I glance towards the door to the kitchen and see the cook peeking in. I smile and put my hands together like I'm praying so she knows how grateful I am. She remembered that I *love* pastries and made sure to put one on my plate which I notice isn't on anyone else's. I forgot how delicious her cooking and baking is. Her smile is smug before she disappears behind the door again.

"Little mate, we have something we need to tell you …" Kaeden starts to say making me look up from my plate again. "It's about your father …" Tilting my head as I look at him and then the others, I realize why they're all so nervous.

"It appears we're late … maybe next time, Kaeden, you could give us more of a warning?" I look over to see my grandfather who gives Kaeden an irritated look.

I start to smile warmly at my grandfather when I notice the intimidating male standing next to him. He's looking intensely at me with emerald, green eyes. Assessing. Judging.

The new mystery man stands tensely next to my grandfather almost as if he's holding himself back from storming over to me. He has a regal presence but a warrior's body which is confirmed by the scars on his arms. He's also tall, taller than my grandfather but then most Elarian males are. His pointed ears are easily seen through his dark brown hair that's pulled half way back by two braids on the sides of his face. There's just something about him that's familiar …

Before I can ponder too much on that, I see my grandfather open his arms for an embrace so I slide my chair back abruptly making Tyr flutter his wings and hop onto Jorah's chair instead. I make the few steps to hug my grandfather and sink into his comforting embrace.

"Ah, granddaughter! I missed you. I'm so glad you've returned safely. You … feel different. Your aura is filled with power. I can sense it." Elder Aren steps back and looks me over. "I saw a vision that you'd met your mates but it was unclear. Which ones are the lucky men?" He steps to my side with an arm around my shoulders and looks questioningly over all my mates. I remember my grandfather telling me of his magical rune for sight. He gets snippets of the future, but they're sometimes unreliable as events can change and he never knows when he'll get his next vision.

"I missed you as well. I am different … better even. Our journey was successful which I'll have to tell you about soon," I excitedly say thinking about my interaction with the witches, I mean Essents. "And yes, these are my mates. We've completed the bond and my mate markings are complete. I—I came into my power last night. It—it was a lot but luckily Ragnar knew what it meant."

"All of these men are your mates, granddaughter?" he says with bulging eyes.

"Well … yes?" I say nervously biting my lip. Now unsure if I've displeased him in some way. I'm embarrassed to say that I really want the approval of my grandfather. It's important to me and probably has to do with my abuse as a child.

My grandfather blows a harsh breath out before he smiles down at me and smooths my hair over my head. "I'm sorry, Solveig, for my shock. You caught me off guard for a moment. You must be very powerful indeed to have so many mates." He taps a finger on his lips before saying, "I've never known an Elarian with so many mates. The most reported in our history was three. So it comes as a shock but it's not a bad thing, dear. It's actually quite good, in fact. It will symbolize to our people just how strong you are."

Relief suddenly hits me that he's not in fact disappointed. But my relief is short lived when he next speaks.

"Now, before he beheads me in his irritation and impatience. Let me introduce my son, King Lochlann of Elaria." My panicked eyes flick over to the man next to my grandfather who's already staring intensely at me. "He's your true father, Solveig.

He's been anxiously awaiting your arrival even more than the rest of us." Aren then looks between us at the continued silence. "Lochlann, greet your daughter."

Lochlann moves his hand subtly, and I immediately drop to my knees before him, bowing my head. I stay bowing down submissively just like my other father, King Batair, preferred and try not to flinch at the upcoming blow. I don't know this new father, but he's obviously important to the Elarians and also to my grandfather who's the only family I now have, so I want his approval. It's a reflex really. Years of being trained and tortured into submission by Batair and Counselor Malphas have me doing things against my innate nature.

I must have been distracted because I suddenly realize my mates are all standing and Ragnar is growling in displeasure at my anxious emotions that must be flooding our bond. I take a second and block my emotions off from the mate bonds so I can focus on this new threat.

I glance up and see a look on his face that is similar to the disappointed one I'd see in Batair's eyes but then it quickly changes to one of intense anger. I actually *do* flinch this time when his body moves but instead of striking me in anger, he kneels before me and grasps my hands in his large ones.

"Please …" Lochlann's voice cracks with emotion before he continues, "Please never kneel before me, daughter. I—I don't know what that conceited man ever taught you but you are never to kneel for anyone. I know he hurt you but please … it's insulting to me as your father to see you flinch away. I would harm myself before I'd hurt you, Solveig. May—may I embrace you?"

I look into his eyes and see nothing but sincerity shining back at me, so I nod my head. He eagerly throws his arms around me and tightly squeezes me. We both lose our balance and in this position and tumble to the ground forcing a chuckle out of me at the ridiculousness of the situation.

After sitting up on the ground, he runs a hand over his face in nervousness and says, "Sorry about that. I've dreamed of the day I'd have a child. I still can't believe it! I'm so proud. You're somehow even more than I expected and let me inform you … I already had high expectations after speaking with your mate Vidarr." I spare a glance over at Vi who's smirking at me but still looks a bit on edge.

I huff in disbelieve tucking some of my hair behind my ear that fell out of my braid. "There's no way you're proud of me. I just met you and you don't even know me," I say wrapping my arms around myself defensively. "How could you not be … disappointed. I saw the look in your eyes." I stand up brushing myself off and see his confused look before he stands as well.

"I could never be disappointed you," Lochlann says slowly and earnestly. Then he runs a hand along his jaw as he says, "The look you might have seen in my eyes was probably because I'm disappointed in myself. I failed you as a father. You and your mother were left with that evil man. Fucking coward, Batair. I should have tried harder to escape. I just wish I knew of you…" He clenches his fists in obvious anger. "I know he hurt you. Him and that other man … Malphas. Your mate inferred such and I can tell in the way you flinch in my presence."

I can't help but feel embarrassed at his words but also slightly hopeful. *Maybe he will be different. I should give him a chance. My old father would have never hugged me nevertheless gotten down on the ground at my level.*

"Batair has paid for his sins, perhaps not enough, but it's done. Malphas will get what's coming to him and I just hope one day you'll trust me enough to tell me some of it."

I take a deep breath and smile at Lochlann. Then I reach out and tug his hand so we're standing in front of my mates. Squeezing his hand, I say, "I'm willing to try … to be a daughter to you. And to get to know you." The joy brought on by my words is easily seen in his radiant smile and he throws an arm around my shoulders in response. "Let me introduce you to the few men I trust the most—my mates."

Lochlann's friendly smile and carefree posture disappear when I mention mates and he takes on a more intimidating stance. He hesitantly says, "Alright."

"Well, from what you've already told me, I know that you know Vidarr."

Lochlann smiles and embraces Vi as he steps forward. They do a side embrace and pat each other's back.

"Vi and I have known each other for years. He saved me one night in the city and initiated me into the Rebellion. He also taught me how to fight in the streets using just my hands or a well-placed dagger. I used to sneak out weekly to practice in the city's underground street fights. Vi always treated me as if he knew I could be better, stronger. He—he helped build my self-confidence up from the bottom and never tried to cage me. I'm proud to call him my first chosen mate." My affectionate gaze locks onto Vidarr who is looking at me with so much love I'm scared to open the mate bond back up but I do. I'm flooded with all their emotions. The other men are a mix of curiosity to longing to pride. But Vidarr is all love and need.

"Damn, sunshine, you're going to make me cry," Vi says leaning forward to kiss my cheek and irritatingly tug on my braid that's resting on my shoulder. I slap his hand away but can't contain my smile as he says, "Love you, Sol."

Lochlann is smiling widely at our interaction and I think I even see my grandfather's lips tilt up a bit at the corners. He was always leery of Vidarr given Vi's plebeian and rebellious background.

"And, you also know Kaeden, I believe?" Lochlann nods. "He is one of my fated mates and we only recently …"

I awkwardly clear my throat as my face fills with heat.

"… completed the mate bond last night." *Great, nice job, Solveig. Way to bring up having sex with a man in front of your father who you just met!*

Luckily, my father ignores the reference to mating last night so I continue. "Kaeden and I met when I helped Grandfather liberate the Stillgate slave camp. He—he and I … well we had some catching up to do since I disappeared for a while. But our bond is growing." I smile at Kaeden reaching out and squeezing his hand which he looks pleased about. Lochlann seems to hesitate for a second but then smiling he reaches out and shakes Kaeden's hand who looks surprised at the acceptance. *Well, that's strange. I'll have to ask Kaeden about it later.*

"Congratulations on your mate bond, Kaeden," Lochlann says. "I'm proud of you and happy for you both."

"Okay … This here is Cadoc—erm—Prince Cadoc. My second chosen mate. He is the heir to the Kingdom of Gorva and the general of their army." Lochlann nods his head in greeting and places a fist over his heart which Elarians do as a greeting of respect. "He has sort of been a bit of a shadow to me in the past when he arrived at the castle. Always watching my back and wanting to protect me." I smirk at Cadoc and he walks over to put his hands on my shoulders, standing behind me just like my shadow. "He fought for me and helped to rid the world of two of my tormentors. Cadoc may be a royal but he's a loyal soldier first and foremost. Not just defending his kingdom but also guarding me."

Cadoc gives my shoulders a quick squeeze of affection before whispering in my ear, "Don't forget I'm finding you later and I'll definitely watch your back, sweetheart, as I pound into you from behind." *Oh, fuck,* I mentally curse and my traitorous face likely blushes red in response. *Damn him and his dirty words for making me aroused in front of my father.*

Lochlann clears his throat and shifts his gaze away. My mates all have a smirk on their faces and likely felt the flood of heat take over my emotions. I elbow Cadoc in the stomach in reproach forcing him to step back as I gain my composure again.

"This is Jorah … He's my childhood best friend and now chosen mate. We met as kids playing in the castle when I was around eight. I used to be a great warrior while Jorah was always the fire breathing dragon that I had to slay." I chuckle while Ragnar snorts in amusement from the side. "His father is the stable master here and his mother is a maid." I look over at my smart and youngest mate who hesitantly smiles back at me. "He's not a fighter like my other mates but he still defends me in his own way." I think back on that day he stood up to Malphas as a young teenager and took a whip to the chest that was meant for me. "He prefers outthinking others and knowledge above all else. Jorah was vital to us locating those slave camps and also along my recent journey."

Lochlann again places a hand to his chest and nods his head while Jorah shyly smiles back and mimics the gesture.

"And lastly, this is Ragnar. King Ragnar and supposedly heir to the Drakonian throne," I state just as Ragi walks over and wraps an arm around my waist possessively. "He's my other fated mate … or … soul mate?" I say scratching the side of my neck as I try to explain while Ragnar says, *My Maseeri,* as if that explains everything. "It's harder to explain our meeting …" I say to my father while looking at Ragnar for help.

"Our souls called us together. She was called to my lair and woke me from my forced hibernation," Ragnar slowly explains. "I'd dreamt of her for months not knowing who she was to me but was unable to wake until she entered my cave."

"You dreamt of me? Why didn't I know about this?" I ask with a raised eyebrow.

Ragnar shrugs innocently and says, "You never asked. They are also rather personal and for our ears only." He leans in and softly says, "I can tell you about them later." I then get a burst of arousal though the mate bond from him and have to pinch his side in retribution so I can focus.

"Ragnar is the one who saved me from fath—I mean—Batair and Malphas. He's also the reason the castle looks the way it is now. He's possessive and sometimes a bit too intense," I say with a directed look at him. "But, we have a deep connection together and even though he's sometimes a bit too domineering …

he does respects me and demonstrates in a million different ways that he loves me."

Lochlann and my grandfather look shocked for a moment with their mouths comically hanging open before they recover and huge smiles overtake their faces. They both bow deeply at the waist with their fists over their hearts. Meanwhile, Ragnar watches stoically and strokes a thumb along the skin of waist under my shirt.

"I'm honored to meet you, King Ragnar," my grandfather says. "I met you once in your dragon form many years ago and therefore didn't recognize you. I—I'm sorry for the loss of your family."

Ragnar mutters a *thank you* before my father interrupts.

"I'm happy that the Drakoni survived the war. It brings me hope that our future can be great again and our past strength as a kingdom restored," Lochlann says to Ragnar. "But, regardless of your royal Drakonian status … you're one lucky man to somehow win my daughter's affection. Fated bond or not. Don't abuse your power or status with my daughter or our people will have issues."

I'm shocked at Lochlann's protective words and yet feel a warmth grow in my chest that he'd take on a dragon for me. I've never had family defend and protect me before. Even my mother when she was alive didn't truly defend me with my father.

Ragnar doesn't seem insulted or put off by Lochlann's words surprisingly for one so brash. "I could *never* harm my Maseeri. She's my soul fire and I'll die protecting her to my last breath before following her into the next life."

I smile affectionately up at Ragnar at his statement and send him an inferno of heat and love through our bond causing him to rumble in response and pull me more tightly to his chest.

Once all the introductions are finished, everyone relaxes back into their seats and breakfast is finished. One obstacle tackled, now on to the bigger one. War.

CHAPTER
Thirty-Five

SOLVEIG

E veryone gathers in a larger meeting room one floor up
after breakfast ends. I finished my karaf during breakfast
but definitely need a second cup to keep me focused on
today.

I start to take a seat to the right of the table head but Vidarr
grabs my hand tugging me up and kissing me. I'm distracted for
a second which he takes advantage of and shoves me into the
chair at the end of the large rectangular table.

"I'm not the one in charge anymore, sunshine. *You* are. I
never wanted the role and I'm glad to pass it to you." Vidarr
smiles smugly down at me then he turns and takes the seat I
was about to take. My other mates all take a seat nearest to me
with Ragnar on my left and Vidarr on my right. Jorah sits next
to Ragnar while Cadoc sits next to Vidarr. Kaeden ends up sitting by Jorah after looking a bit nervous while the other council
members filter in. Lochlann takes a seat by Kaeden and I'm happy to see Zxian appear next to him. He nods and bends at the
waist with his palm over his heart in greeting.

Next, Darritt and an elderly woman whom I've met before enter and sit across from the Elarians. I believe her name is … Pia? She was part of the Rebellion in the past and I'd seen her at some of their secret meetings. Darritt gives me a subtle nod with a nervous look in his eyes. I suppose this is a bit overwhelming to go from sword smith to council member in a week.

Lastly, soldiers filter in through the door. Captain Mavin enters looking around and at seeing me hastens around the table and drops to one knee bowing his head.

"Your majesty, Queen Solveig, I am relieved to hear of your safe return," Captain Mavin says in a serious voice. "I pledge my sword and my life to defending the Kingdom of Laevaris and with it you, my sworn and rightful queen. Please accept my vow as Captain of the guard and General of the Laevarian army to uphold honor and loyalty in this position."

Mavin continues to stay bowed before me not making eye contact. So, I reach forward and place a hand on his head then say, "Thank you, Mavin. I accept your vow and accept your position as General of the Laevarian army. I missed you and please stand so I can greet you properly!"

I tug him up as he stands and then embrace him tightly. He eventually loosens up to pat me gently on the back. The corner of his lips tilt up in the closest thing Mavin does to a smile.

Clasping his hands affectionately I then say gently, "However, I'd like to focus your duties specifically to the army and relieve you as Captain of the guard." Mavin sucks in a breath and he tenses up. "I want you to train and build up our army more without having to worry about castle security as well. To be honest, I'm surprised this wasn't done long ago." Mavin tilts his head and nods as he rubs a hand over the scruff on his chin. "I want one of my mates, Kaeden, to take over the position of Captain of the guard. He used to be in the army and it would be good to have him also integrate some of the Elarians in our ranks. Perhaps in the castle first."

Kaeden looks up at my words with surprise written on his face. I look back with a sheepish look since I didn't exactly discuss this with him yet and feel bad I'm springing it on him in a group setting.

"I think that's an exceptional idea your majesty. Kaeden is a good warrior and with his skills he could protect you better than I could," Mavin says thoughtfully. "It would also help the Laevarians see that the Elarians are supporting your position in more than just marriage … er … mating. I look forward to working with him closely."

"Kaeden? What do you think?" I ask hesitantly. He still looks a bit shocked but now I can feel some of his emotions trickling through the bond. Happiness. Determination. Pride.

"I am honored, my mate. It would give me joy to protect you in such a position. I won't fail you." Kaeden says in a solemn voice and soft eyes towards me. He's pleased with my choice which makes the mate bond thrum with happiness.

"Good choice, daughter. Kaeden will serve you well in that capacity and it is good to have your mates close while also giving them to freedom to use their skills," my father says approvingly with a regal nod.

"Solveig—excuse me—Queen Solveig … if I may introduce the other soldiers with me?" Mavin says after that's resolved. "You remember Camaeron?" The blonde handsome guard nods at me with a smirk of recognition and a wink. He's someone I've sparred with many times and shared an ale or two with afterwards. "He has been promoted to Lieutenant and is now my second in command given Valence's betrayal. I also believe you know Lanief. He has also been promoted to Lieutenant and will be below Camaeron in the hierarchy."

Lanief is a giant of a man standing taller than everyone other than the Elarians. He smiles at me in recognition as well since I've broken his nose several times in the sparing ring and we've formed a bit of a rivalry.

"Oh yes. I know those two troublemakers. I'm not surprised they've been promoted through the ranks since they're both good fighters and loyal to the kingdom." Camaeron and Lanief both walk over and drop to their knees before me, bowing and stating their pledges.

After I accept their vows and they return to their seats with prideful looks on their faces, I clear my throat and say, "Alright, I think now that introductions and such are done let's discuss why we're here. Vi?"

"Well after Zxian helped deal with Captain Valence's subterfuge at the border, we've managed to come to a standstill against Gorva at the Laevarian border," Vi says smoothing out the map laid out in the center of the table.

Cadoc interjects before Vidarr can speak further saying, "I don't think we've really had time to discuss it yet, Vidarr, but my father King Ignatius has called a truce at the Laevarian border and I've sent missives to our outposts to only defend if attacked. He's aware of the situation since we left Sterling Outpost, but we should send a messenger to update him further so that he can call off our army at the border and focus on Jaarn." Pausing, Cadoc runs a hand over his cropped hair while staring at the map. "We just didn't know the situation yet in Falal so we were cautiously optimistic." Then Cadoc points to the Laevarian outposts along his border, "You can call back your army from these areas and move them to the Jaarnian borders. I'm not sure how many soldiers you have in each location but those borders along the mountains can be tricky with men slipping through unseen."

"This is good news," Captain Mavin says leaning in over the map. "I'll send a messenger to Captain Garr at the Gorvian border to release half our troops and send them to the Jaarn borders." He gets a concerned look on his face for a second before saying, "We have about half our army there and the other half is spread between Falal and the borders with Jaarn as well as Avaria."

"So basically, we barely have any soldiers along the Jaarnian border then?" Jorah deduces writing in a notebook he has in his lap.

"We need to send as many soldiers as we can in Falal to the Jaarnian border immediately," I say growing concerned by the minute.

"My daughter is right," King Lochlann says looking over the room. "Captain Mavin you should send a man to prepare your army to leave. They may have already penetrated your borders. I'll prepare the Elarians to assist and nothing will get through the Elarian Forest north of Falal."

Captain Mavin nods and looks to me for approval. I wave a hand impatiently and nod. Mavin leans down whispering in Lanief's ear before the latter quickly exits the meeting room.

"What about the Kingdom of Beamus? Avaria? Are they to be considered threats to our backside while we face Jaarn?" Ragnar states in a deep voice looking at me.

I feel uncertain in my new role for the first time as everyone's expectant gazes fall on me. I've never had to make these types of decisions required to run a kingdom much less a war. Even though my tutors made sure I knew all the ins and outs of kingdom politics, I'm horribly out of date since my disappearance and unaware of the current status of our alliances.

Ragnar and Vi's hands land on my thighs simultaneously upon feeling my anxiety and insecurity escalate. It helps bring me back to the present and realize I'm not alone in these problems. I have my mates and now … a council to advise me.

"I did receive a message from Beamus … It was from King Havik." Vi says as I gather my thoughts. "He stated that their kingdom is going to stay neutral in the war and also that he wasn't pleased to have me as the Regent to Laevaris. As a king, I don't think he likes the idea of a rebellion leader overthrowing a king and taking control. But he did mention Solveig as the rightful heir. I'm assuming they will step in if they feel that we are losing the war and Jaarn is conquering new land."

251

"We don't need to worry about Beamus attacking us from behind," I state confidently thinking about my friend Princess Cassia. She'll make sure I don't have to worry about my borders with her. I get a few doubtful and curious looks from the council but they seem to accept my word.

"If I may, your majesty—" the elderly woman, Pia, who has been silent and observant so far asks.

"Please, call me Solveig," I interject. "Especially when in this chamber or in private. Vidarr obviously trusts you, and therefore I do too. I would appreciate any counsel you can add."

"Yes, well … thank you … Solveig," Pia says with approval shining in her gaze. "I was chosen for this position by your handsome man there"—she nods to Vidarr who winks at her—"for my network of spies which are now at your disposal. There has been word that Avaria will be busy dealing with a small unrest in its southern aspect. Supposedly, the royal couple will be busy dealing with a territorial war between the Essents there. My spies report that there is no activity of the Avarian army preparing for war."

"We will just have to hope that is the case since we don't necessarily have men to spare for their border," Captain Mavin says. "I can send a message to their border though and ask for an update on activities there." He looks up to me clearly seeking my thoughts.

Tapping my fingers on the table in thought, I say, "I—I wonder if I can use my nature rune to ask a friend for scouting some of our borders. It would save us waiting on messengers." *Tyr could use the exercise too. Maybe his mate would help as well …*

Zxian smiles at me proudly before saying, "That's brilliant. It would save a lot of time and it's also more reliable than interpreting messages or trusting others who may not be loyal."

Vidarr groans and says, "You're thinking of that pesky hawk?" I smile and nod. "Well, I guess he does come in handy. Where did he go anyways?"

"He wanted to check on his mate and eyas but said he'll return shortly. I'll have him check our borders with his mate."

"Using your powers could be the tipping point we need to win this war with Jaarn," Kaeden says obviously thinking about his own powers related to his nature rune. "We need to use everything at our disposal."

"Very good. Kaeden is correct," Lochlann says as he leans over the map pointing at the various gaps in the Traverian mountain range. "Now, daughter, you should plan for various scenarios on where they could attack. Best to be—"

My father is interrupted by my grandfather storming into the room suddenly with five large Elarian warriors behind him. The doors to the meeting room hit the wall and we all look up at him expectantly.

"They're already coming through the mountains!" Elder Aren states loudly. "I've had a vision of them sneaking like the cowards they are through the gap just north of Millsteele camp." We all look up in surprise and concern as he says, "Jaarn is coming and they're bringing war."

Feeling a sliver of anticipation at the upcoming fight and then firm determination to defend my people, I straighten my spine and say in a fierce voice, "We'll be ready. Laevarians and Elarians together. Now as for this plan…"

CHAPTER
Thirty-Six

SOLVEIG

We spend the next hour after my grandfather's enlightening vision on various scenarios and how to defend our kingdom. My grandfather has a rune for the sight and when he gets a vision it tends to be pretty accurate but we never know which path that our choices will follow. Based on what he told us, we figure we probably have a few days before they will exit the forest and enter the plains surrounding Falal.

After a passionate goodbye kiss, I send Ragnar to Sterling Outpost to get his sister and Tempest then meet us at the battlefield. He is hesitant to go and repeatedly told me to stay with his mate-brothers. *He's still upset about my kidnapping with his cousin Tempest. Overprotective dragons must be my thing.*

Jorah has been writing out missives to the other rulers of the surrounding kingdoms and also is looking into his research regarding defense against Jaarn's weapons. Meaning, he's disappeared into the castle library. He has plans to travel into the city tomorrow to talk with a local blacksmith about Jaarnian steel.

Kaeden threw himself into his new duties as Captain the guard. The Elarians who are training to be my personal guard including Kelda, a fierce warrior woman with a double sided blade that she wields expertly, are with him in a meeting. The plan is that they're in charge of defending the city walls as a last line of defense. They'll also oversee herding any Laevarians into the city walls who might not feel safe with the upcoming battle. Kelda argued that they should be at my side, but we just don't have enough men (or women) right now due to King Batair spreading our army out. Plus—I have my mates at my side and am an experienced warrior in my own right which Kaeden argued. His confidence in my other mates and my own skills must be growing which makes me feel unreasonably pleased.

That leaves me with Vidarr and Cadoc. We plan to head out with the last part of our army tomorrow morning. Captain Mavin left with Lieutenant Lanief last night taking the majority of the army here in Falal that they were able to prepare in such a short time. The rest will travel with us including any supplies.

My father and Zxian with the rest of the Elarians are preparing for the fight and will flank the Jaarnian army from the north. Elarians are best suited to battle in the forest anyways so it should be the best plan.

While Vidarr and Cadoc get all the supplies loaded for the morning and make sure the remaining men are ready, I decide to tackle some of my neglected duties since my disappearance with Ragnar. I check with the cook and everything seems to be running smoothly with travel portions set up to go with us in the morning. I check with the remaining nobles in the castle that they've sent all their men to our aid but honestly, there's not many left since my "father" King Batair was beheaded. Next, I head to the infirmary and it's a bit chaotic with servants and healers running everywhere.

"No, no, no. Do *not* put that there, child!" Healer Thaemon yells at a young boy who I've seen helping here in the past. "The bandages go in the cabinet to the right and agh—"As the boy runs to follow instructions of moving the misplaced bandages, he slips on the floor and the whole basket is upended. Thaemon throws his hands up in frustration and his glasses slide down his nose towards his large white mustache. Rolls of gauze and cloth fly up in the air before bouncing on the ground and unrolling. "*Liv!*"

"I'll help with this Healer Thaemon. You can continue on with your preparations," I say kneeling down and starting to roll up the bandages. The boy who slipped looks distraught and on the cusp of tears.

"Ah, Princess Solveig!" Healer Thaemon says sliding his glasses back up his nose. "Thank you, child. I suppose you *do* know where everything goes down here after all your time here. We will be ready by tomorrow to accept any injured soldiers. Just send them our way if needed but I'll also have one or two healers near the city walls for smaller injuries if that is acceptable."

"Yes, thank you for assisting us," I reply.

"Of course! I am a healer and will never turn away patients. I'll leave you to it." Thaemon states thoughtfully then hesitates and says, "I think the recent turn of events for Laevaris is good, Princess. I just thought you should know. I never did like your father … it was only a matter of time before his liver went into failure given the amount of wine that man consumed. As a professional, I don't appreciate laziness and neglect. Organization and dedication are the way to success. I believe you will do better for us, child."

As Thaemon walks away barking out orders to others, I look over to the boy who's staring in awe at me. "What's your name?" I ask him softly while rolling gauze.

"Um … I—I'm Charles, your Royal Highness," he nervously says. "I'm sorry I'm so clumsy. I don't think I'll make a good healer … I'm always dropping things and misplacing them. Are you really the princess?"

I chuckle a bit at the mix of reverence and nervousness in his expression. "Well met, Charles. You can call me Solveig if we aren't in front of others … and yes I am the princess." I quickly finish the bandages and slide the basket to the side when he nearly topples it in his haste to place the last one. Then I stand and offer him my hand which he takes. He smiles shyly at me as I say, "You don't have to be a healer you know? Healer Thaemon is tough but he's not harsh. Just expects a lot. What are your strengths?"

"Well … I am good at reading. Mother says I'm well above the other kids in school for my age. I just turned ten and have finished most of the books they gave us! I'm also fast and a good runner as long as I'm paying attention," he says blushing.

I hold in a chuckle not wanting to embarrass the poor kid. I think he may be better suited under Jorah's tutelage than here in the infirmary. *Maybe a page for the castle?* "I have an idea and I'll speak with Healer Thaemon, but it'll have to wait until after this battle. Plus—they'll need you down here fetching supplies." We take the basket of rolled bandages and put them away in the appropriate place, and I explain the general layout to him so he doesn't get in trouble again.

"Thank you, Princess Solveig! You'll really put in a word for me?"

"Yes. I'm glad we got to meet. Now, I need to check on a few more places before tomorrow. Be careful," I say ruffling his hair and walking out of the infirmary.

The last stop I make for the night before resting my aching feet is the stables. I want to see Sigurd before I leave and haven't had a chance for one of his characteristic all-encompassing hugs. The smell of leather and hay will always make me think of him and safety. Sigurd isn't just the stable master. He's the closest thing to a father figure I had growing up. Not many people would comfort a princess that's ostracized by her father, but Sigurd was never ashamed of being there for me. He treated me as one of his own, like his son Jorah. It probably helped that me and Jorah were always together.

I enter the castle stables and see him carefully brushing down a large black horse. The sight nearly makes me tear up but instead I chuckle and shake my head. The horse bends his arched neck around to Sigurd's back while he's turned and grabs a hoof pick from his back pocket sneakily.

What sort of trouble are you starting you crazy steed? I project mentally to the beautiful black horse.

His ears perk forward towards me and he snorts. *The stable master needs to learn some of us are more intelligent than others and he should treat me with respect.* He arrogantly states before flinging the hoof pick into a nearby stall. *He didn't give me any extra oats last night and I'm grumpy.* He follows his words with a hoof stomp.

When the hoof pick hits the wall, Sigurd looks up and around trying to place the noise then flicks a hand at the horses front leg telling him to settle.

"Alright, Sindari stop fidgeting and let me finish. You don't want to look a mess when Sol needs you." Sigurd leans down and places the brush into a container before reaching back for the missing hoof pick that's supposed to be in his back pocket. He reaches around for a while patting his pants before he narrows his eyes at Sindari in accusation. "You little shit! You threw my hoof pick again didn't you?"

I can't help the laugh that spills out of me at his words. Sigurd straightens up and looks back at the stable entrance where I'm leaning against the wall watching. Sigurd gets a huge smile on his face and turns with his arms wide. I run over to him and fall into his comforting embrace. His large arms engulf my small frame and I breathe in the scent of leather and hay with a sigh.

"I missed you, Sol," Sigurd says, "So, how long were you watching that interaction? Hm?"

"Long enough to see all the good parts. I missed you too," I reply before I step back. Then I reach out and scratch Sindari on his forelock. "So this pesky pony has been testing you, huh?"

Not a pony, Solveig, Sindari projects to me mentally as my nature rune tingles on my wrist with the use of my powers. *Also, where is my greeting? Did you not miss me too?*

I'm sorry, my noble steed. Of course I missed you. I'll need your speed and prowess tomorrow.

Sindari arches his neck in a show of strength. *I'll be ready … but maybe some oats would help tonight?*

I roll my eyes at his manipulative antics while Sigurd says, "Yes. Sindari is one of the more difficult inhabitants here and he's a bad influence on some of the colts. I can't help but feel like they're all plotting against me." I chuckle and now he rolls his eyes. "Fine. I know I'm being a bit dramatic but maybe you can have a word with him?"

"He's just grumpy because you didn't give him oats last night. But I'll still have a *word* with him," I say giving Sindari a scornful look. "How have you been? Any issues in the stables?"

"I'm doing well, Sol." Sigurd reaches up and rubs a hand along my upper arm. "Thank you for asking about me. We are doing ok but a bit low on those oats your horse is requesting. I need to get supplies but things have been a bit unstable here since you left. Any idea on who's going to handle trade?" I shake my head in denial and get that sliver of self-doubt that I'm ready to take the crown. "No problem. We'll deal with it after. You're going to do fine, Sol. But you need to be careful tomorrow. I worry about you."

"I'll be careful. I can take care of myself, you know. Always have," I say while I run the toe of my boot through the dirt floor. "Has Jorah stopped by since we've been back?" I ask anxiously peeking up to gauge his expression.

Sigurd smirks and leans back against the nearest stall crossing his arms. "Yes. He has. I wonder why you're asking …" He raises a challenging eyebrow and says, "He may have mentioned that you two are … together? Like a couple. Is that smart, Sol?"

My face falls at his words thinking I'm once again not good enough. Another father that sees me as a disappointment. He probably wants Jorah to marry some sweet woman in the city who will stay home and give him a house full of babies. He must see my expression because he gets a regretful look in his eyes and stands back up grabbing my arms.

"I didn't mean it that way, sweetheart. It's just…you're a princess, set to take the throne. And Jorah … well … we're common born. Our family is traced back to be hard workers in several trades but there's not a drop of royal blood in us. You need a strong *royal* consort at your side. Not that my Jorah isn't good enough or that you aren't good enough for him."

I sigh and run a hand over my face. Then, I realize Jorah didn't tell his father everything. Normally I would've let Jorah have this conversation but tomorrow is so uncertain. Deciding to just take the reins, I say, "We're mates, Sigurd. Not just in a relationship. I chose him as one of my mates. For Elarians it's forever, a bond, deeper than marriage. I love him and he'll always be good enough regardless of who his parents are." Then avoiding eye contact with him, I say, "If we're going to judge people based on their parents, then I'm definitely not good enough for him. I'll try, though."

Sigurd looks shocked for a moment then tilts his head and says, "*One* of your … mates?"

"Ugh—yeah. I have five mates," I say before nervously rambling, "My grandfather says that powerful Elarians tend to be polyamorous with multiple mate bonds. I mean … I know five is a lot but I'm not sorry. They make me feel whole, including Jorah. It just sort of happened. It's not like I planned …"

Sigurd leans in and hugs me cutting off my words. He sets his chin on the top of my head and says, "It's … *unusual* but times are changing. Magic has now returned to the kingdom and the Elarians aren't hiding away. You are changing things, Sol. And … well I'd like to meet these men soon." He leans back and smiles at me with a teasing light in his eyes. "I need to make sure they're good enough for my little dragon slayer. Now, let's get this grumpy horse back in his stall and if he's good I'll scrounge up some oats."

Little does he know that now … I'm a dragon tamer. I smirk to myself.

Sindari yinnys and quickly trots into his open stall standing perfectly still and looking like he's on his best behavior.

"See? Looks like it's true …" I say smiling. "The way to a man's *or horse's* heart is through his stomach."

CHAPTER
Thirty-Seven

SOLVEIG

That night, Cadoc and Vidarr fell into bed with me exhausted. Sadly, not much happened other than some fervent hands and cuddling. *Not that I wasn't interested.* But Cadoc quickly fell asleep snuggling his face into my hair while my rebel mate looked unimpressed at my excessive yawning and sleepy-eyes. We both decided sleep was necessary tonight and that we'd just have to restart this after dealing with Jaarn. I thought of seeking out some pleasure from Jorah when Vidarr denied me, but I know Jorah once he gets his head in a book. Besides, he told me he'd say goodbye to me in the morning before we left. It was as good as a dismissal from a scholar as any. I wasn't offended in the least it's just… Jorah. He's just focused and I understand that.

I'm still tired when I wake up but Cadoc slaps my pantless ass as I bend over to get dressed making me yelp. *Cocky prince. Payback is coming for you later.* I squint my eyes over at him letting him see the retribution in my eyes. He gives me this innocent look and backs out of the room heading to breakfast. *Well, at least I'm slightly more awake now. I just need a cup or two of karaf before the day starts.*

Vidarr is smirking at my wakeup call and instead of teasing me, he leans in to kiss me chastely on the cheek which is out of character for him since he's always the jokester.

"See you at breakfast, sunshine," he says before strutting from the room covered head to toe in weapons looking like the dangerous rebel I know he is.

I sigh appreciatively watching him leave and checking out his muscular behind. His tattoos only add to the whole dangerous vibe he's giving off and it makes me feel heated thinking about those muscular arms holding me down under his dominance seeking pleasure. He must have felt my interest through the mate bond because just before the door shuts, he stops suddenly and peeks back. A piece of dirty blonde hair falls into one blue-gray eye as his gaze fills with heat and he softly says, "Later."

Fuck, my mates are sexy. I finish getting ready strapping on my harness with my twin katanas and then attaching several small daggers and weapons to my body.

By the time I make it to breakfast, Jorah and Cadoc are done while Vi is stuffing his face on his second helpings.

"Be careful today, Sol. If you need me for anything, send a messenger to the city. I'll be on Silver street where that blacksmith, Tavian, is located. I'm just going to grab a few notebooks and then head out," Jorah says giving me a kiss and squeezes my waist affectionately before he turns to Cadoc and Vi. They all shake hands and he says, "Take care of our mate, brothers."

"Good luck, Jorah. Send over that counteractive mixture to Kaeden for that nasty toxic liquid Jaarn likes to add in their catapults," Cadoc says to him, clearly thinking about those explosives that hit the walls of Sterling Outpost.

"Where is Kaeden, anyways?" Vidarr asks making me realize I didn't see him last night.

I close my eyes and feel for our mate bond then pull on that tether to Kaeden realizing he's … close. *Where are you?* I ask mentally.

"I'm here, little mate. Sorry! I already ate." Kaeden walks in the door with his dark brown hair wild around his shoulders and fully decked out in a mix of armor and leather. He looks like a strong Elarian warrior. It's … a good look on him I think feeling my core clench in arousal. A long wooden bow is hanging over his shoulder with a quiver full of arrows. He also has a sword hanging at his hip and a dagger on his belt. A half smile shows up on his face as he senses my attraction to him. "Come here." He hooks a finger at me, beckoning.

I instinctually walk over and look up expectantly. His hands reach up and hold my cheeks before he leans in and kisses me. His tongue parts my lips and he tastes of mint with something citrusy. I moan into the kiss and my hand slides over his chest seeking out those muscles he's worked so hard on building up but unfortunately I can't get through all the clothing. He cups a hand around one of my ass cheeks and squeezes as he kisses me deeper. Eventually, we break apart gasping for air and remember what we were supposed to be doing.

"I could feel your arousal, little mate, and I couldn't help myself. But now's not the time. I need to get the city organized and head to the gate." He tucks a piece of my hair that escaped my braid behind my pointed ear. He grazes his finger over the tip of it and I full body shiver in response. "Be safe and I'll see you soon. Keep our mate bond open so I know what's going on out there."

"I will. Take care, mate," I reply as his gaze becomes more heated with the word *mate*. Then, he huffs out a frustrated breath before turning and storming out of the room. I see Kelda in the hallway who nods respectfully at me.

I pull on the power of my mind-speak rune that snakes up my neck to my temple seeking out Kelda's mind. *Watch his back for me. If I lose him … just make sure he's careful.*

Kelda holds my gaze and replies mentally, *Of course, my Queen. I swear it. Be careful yourself and call on me if you want me to join you.*

I nod and put a fist over my heart which she takes as good-bye before hastening after my mate.

I then sit and eat a fast breakfast but most importantly I drink down a full mug of karaf. Moaning in pleasure from the dark bitter drink. I get a bit more energy.

"I'll meet you two in the stables," Cadoc says before heading off and speaking to a guard in the hall.

Vi sits back and drinks his karaf before standing a few minutes later. He then says with an excited look in eyes, "Come on, sunshine. You ready for our most epic mission yet?"

"Oh I'm ready," I say linking my arm with his as we head out. "I just hope you can keep up, city boy. But don't worry, I'll stitch you back up if you get any *teensy tiny* cuts just like I did last time. Maybe we should get you some kevlar or something like Kaeden before we leave."

Scoffing like he's offended he puts a hand over his chest dramatically before he says, "How dare you bring up my past injuries. And—it was a tiny cut. I only allowed you to sew a few stitches in it to make you feel better. I know how you like to be in control." He nudges me and I smile which breaks into a yawn. "I think you'll need to keep up with me given how poorly you slept last night. I bet I'll have ten men down to your one."

We continue to rib and tease one another all the way to the stable but underneath our words we can both feel it's a front for our nerves. We're both tense and just trying to not show it. *Denial is a good defense.*

Cadoc is already standing with his horse ready to go as Vidarr is handed his reins by Sigurd.

"I'll have Sindari ready in a moment, Sol," Sigurd mentions before wandering back into the stables. Everyone is mounted and ready. Waiting on me.

Just as Sigurd leads Sindari out, Darritt runs up to me with a distressed look on his face.

CHAPTER
Thirty-Eight

SOLVEIG

Darritt is breathing heavily when he reaches me. Bending over at the waist, he rests his hands on his thighs as he says, "I'm glad I caught you before you left …" He stands and looks around. "Looks like everyone is all set to go. You might want to send them all ahead of you … I ran into your mate, Jorah, and he said he needed to talk with you urgently."

Confused, I tilt my head and ask, "But—I thought he'd already left for the city to talk to that blacksmith?"

Darritt looks flustered for a moment before his expression hardens in a manner I've never seen on his face. "I don't know why!" He throws his hands up in frustration. "He just told me it will take a while and that you needed to come and speak with him. Said that it was important to winning the war or something."

I give Vidarr and Cadoc a concerned look. They both look confused before shrugging their shoulders. They're already mounted and everyone is starting to get antsy to get moving.

There's over a hundred people waiting to leave spilling out the castle gates.

Turning my eyes back to Darritt, I say, "Alright, I'm coming. Wait a second and I'll go with you." Then I step closer to Vi and Cadoc saying softly, "You guys go ahead of me. I don't want to hold everyone up, and I can ride pretty fast on Sindari to catch up. It sounds like this is important to Jorah …"

"I don't like leaving you by yourself. No one is watching your back," Cadoc says directly. "Maybe we should all just wait."

"No, we don't know exactly when Jaarn will finish coming through those mountains and can't spare the time. Large groups like this move slower. It'll be easy for me to catch up."

"Sunshine, he's right. You shouldn't be alone. You're too important and this is strange, even for Jorah," Vi says rubbing a hand over the scruff on his jaw. "Why didn't he just say something earlier?"

"I don't know but we can't afford to lose any advantage and if Jorah found something important out then I need to know. Maybe he just discovered something after breakfast and didn't get a chance until now to tell me," I reply feeling antsy to get moving. "I'll have Darritt with me and Jorah in the castle. Plus Kaeden isn't far at the city gates. So I'm not really alone."

They both nod and then Cadoc says, "Very well. You're right. Come on Vidarr let's get this entourage moving."

"See you soon, sunshine. Be safe," Vi says then leans down and tugs my braid before quickly turning his horse away. I narrow my eyes at him and can see his smirk from down here.

The group as a whole slowly filter out of the castle grounds into Falal. I turn to Darritt who is pacing a bit anxiously, making me frown.

"You okay, Darritt?" I ask placing a hand on his shoulder. He turns to me and his expression clears. He then notices everyone is gone. "Should we go? Where is Jorah?"

"Yes, yes. Sorry, Sol!" he says gently grabbing my elbow to guide me into the castle. "I was just distracted for a moment. I'm a bit worried about my mother out in Tillian, that's all. You remember her? She doesn't live far from the mountains and where Jaarn is invading."

"Oh shit! I'm sorry Darritt! I completely forgot," I say feeling badly. "Maybe we can spare a soldier to check on her?"

"No, it's fine. She's a tough woman," Darritt says then tugs me a bit faster down the hall. "Come on."

I haven't been paying attention to where he's dragging me at first and when I notice we're in an empty kitchen I get confused. "Jorah is supposed to be in the kitchen? No one's here, Darritt …"

He chuckles nervously and says, "I'll take you right to him in a second but I noticed you were yawning a lot and figured you could use the extra boost first." He hands me a steaming cup of karaf and I greedily grab the mug taking a sip. It tastes a bit more bitter than I usually make it but it's still hot and so good.

"Thank you, Darritt! I really did need this." I drink half the mug and go to set it down but he stops me. "Shouldn't we be going? I need to hurry."

"Just bring it with you for now and finish it." He nods towards the door. "I'll return the mug after you talk with him."

Shrugging and taking a few more sips of the energizing black drink, I follow him. He doesn't lead me very far, in fact, we only go over three more rooms to an office that some of the counselors used in the past.

Darritt stops in front of the door and nods towards it avoiding eye contact. "Good luck," he says before grabbing the now empty mug from me and walking away. *Poor man, he must really be worried.* He's probably distracted with thoughts of his family again. I see him turn the corner heading likely into the city to help Kaeden on defending Falal.

As I lean forward to open the door, I stumble a bit and get a weird, flushed feeling throughout my body. My chest aches a bit after, but I try to shake it off and open the door rushing inside to see my mate.

It's dark in the room making the hairs on the back of my neck stand up in warning. Just as the door swings shut with a *snick*, my eyes slowly start to adjust to the dim interior.

"Jorah? Wha—what is going on?" I ask.

My eyes adjust quickly to the darkness and see a man move up behind me blocking the door. I go to turn around and stumble a bit in dizziness. He's tall and lean and definitely not my gentle mate. I shift my stance sensing a threat from this man who chuckles darkly.

It's his voice that I recognize first before my gaze zeroes in on his face. He tucks a piece of loose hair behind my ear and pets my neck making me flinch away and run into the wall.

"Tsk, tsk, princess. Once again I'm disappointed in you." Counselor Malphas walks closer boxing me in against the wall while I pale in realization that I was betrayed. "You always weren't the brightest. Too trusting. Too naive." While my vision swims with blurriness intermittently, he places a hand tightly around my throat. "And too wild. Never following orders. You've ruined a lot of my plans, girl. And I intend to make you pay in return."

I'm suddenly drawn inside myself to that place I hate. A graveyard of memories and trauma sit before me, and I can't get out. I can't move or break my paralysis. Panic sets in and nothing I do makes sense. My body betrays me and forgets all my training with Captain Mavin. All my strength and fight that I've worked so hard for—gone. Instead, I stand under his control shaking in fear like that little fourteen year old he started terrorizing. Manipulating. Training. Punishing. It's disgusting to think about and I feel the sharp pain of shame in my chest. *You're weak, Sol.* A submissive pitiful waste of space.

I have one rational thought as he drags me across the room and throws me on the desk. I should … tell my mates— I'm sorry. Let them know something. What happened to me …

I feel for my connection to them in my chest and … come up blank. There's a numbness there. It's not empty per se, but it's numb and difficult to grab. I can't read their emotions and definitely can't communicate with them. I—I'm on my own. Betrayed. Alone. *Stupid.*

Malphas is chuckling as he sees the realization on my face that my mate bond is blocked somehow. He's tied my hands above my head and removed my weapons while I was distracted. Then he quickly rips my shirt down the back.

"I see you're finally understanding your situation princess. I gave a special concoction to your friend so we don't have to deal with those pesky men you're whoring yourself out to. Jaarn has a great many magical poisons at their disposal." He pets me down my spine making me shiver and brace for what I know is coming. "Now, lay still like a good girl while I tarnish your perfect skin. I've been dreaming of making you bleed again."

His hands disappear from my back and I hear a soft unrolling of something weighted hit the ground. *Fuck. Fuck. Fuck …* I can't get my body to move due to this paralyzing dizziness and the numbness of my panic attack.

"Arrrgh!" I can't control the garbled scream that slips out at the first lashing of a whip across my back. I've grown too soft in my time away. Spoiled by my mates. *Fuck, I miss them. Did I lose my connection with them forever?* "I hate you. You sick, cock-sucking—"

Whop—eesh. The whip whistles through the air before landing on my back again and all words are lost as I bit my lip so hard it bleeds. *I'll be fucking damned if I let another scream out for him. The man gets off on this.*

"Ahh. Music to my ears. I love punishing you princess. Didn't you know?" Malphas says. "This isn't nearly enough to pay you back for the mess you made of my plans. I spent years grooming you and planning my rise in power before you blew it all up with your temper tantrum. Only Valirr knows how you managed to find a dragon to save you. I only had one more day before our marriage."

Whop—eesh. Whop—eesh. Whop—eesh. I grit my teeth and manage to hold onto my consciousness but the pain…the pain is unbearable. I've forgotten how to lock it away and fall into peaceful numbness. It's like I've felt too many emotions and lived too much now, that I can't let go. I just hope my mates can't feel anything because this is excruciating. *They'd probably be ashamed of my weakness. I didn't even fight.*

"You're going to submit to me, Solveig," Malphas states in a malicious voice. *Whop—eesh.* "You're going to beg to serve me. Beg for punishment. Beg for me to fuck you." *Whop—eesh.* "You're going to tell everyone in this kingdom that you made a mistake. That we're getting married and our marriage is tomorrow. You're going to hand over the crown and get on your knees in front of everyone or …" *Whop—eesh.* "I kill you and all those men that follow you around. I have a whole army at my disposal to kill them if you don't comply."

As black spots fill my vision and blood floods my mouth, I suck in a sharp breath at his words. More concerned with my mates than myself. But they're stronger than me … they'll have each other out there to watch their backs.

"Fu—fuck you, Malphas. I'll never beg you for shit!" I try to yell but it comes out more as a croak. Thank goodness I have a high pain tolerance after years of torture at his hands.

"Tsk, tsk. That's where you're wrong princess." He leans over my bloody back and slides a hand under my chest cupping my right breast. "Don't forget I've marked you here, Solveig. You're mine. It's *my* initial under this perky breast." Feeling an even ickier sensation at his touch than the harsh lash of a whip, I try to lean away but my body doesn't respond more than a twitch. He eventually withdraws his hand, but suddenly I feel him clasp something around my neck. A sinking feeling takes over my body and then heaviness. Fatigue. It reminds me of … *no! Fuck no!*

Malphas caresses my neck which now has a bejeweled collar around it as he says, "Much better. What? No thank you?" He chuckles. "I thought you liked wearing collars I place upon you. Especially one holding such beautiful crystals on it. Can you feel its effects, princess?" He grabs up the whip again. "You remember avralite? I had it specially made for you upon my return. I'm going to bedeck you in these crystals after our marriage knowing they'll keep you more compliant."

Whop—eesh. Whop—eesh.

"Submit like the good girl I've taught you to be," Malphas coldly says. *Whop—eesh.* "We can stop now and make an announcement. End the war. Save all those people…it all depends on you. You don't want to be responsible for all those senseless lives lost, do you?" He pauses and I have a moment of self-doubt that maybe I should just give in. Why is my life more important than others? If I can spare them this war it could save hundreds of lives. He must sense my hesitance as he continues, "Jaarn will stand down if you just agree to my terms. Or—don't and I'll kill your men and anyone you care about. I'm sure my assassins have already killed them by now. They were waiting for them in several locations. So easy … Darritt helped make sure we knew all their plans. Where they'd be at. When they'd be there. It's disappointing really that you all fell into my plans so easily."

I suck in a harsh breath full of worry. I was on the edge of losing consciousness after that last lash but his words … they spark something deep inside me. Like a fire, it grows exponentially catching more things ablaze inside me as he rambles his evil threats. My focus narrows down to that thing growing inside me from his threats. It's anger … anger and power. Something about him threatening my mates must have triggered it.

My energy is still super low from the avralite and probably from the blood loss that's pooling around me. And, who knows that else that poisoned drink did to me.

Slowly, my rune for healing on my upper back starts to heal the damage as its laid. It's bizarre … usually the avralite blocks my powers somewhat, but I can feel my healing rune working as this feeling builds in my chest. Then I remember … *stupid Solveig* … I have more than one power! And, I don't have to use the mate bond to communicate.

Concentrating is hard and I can see Malphas from the corner of my drooping eye getting frustrated.

"*Fuck you,*" I grit out in defiance then buckle down on mentally concentrating towards my mates.

Jaarn and Malphas have sent assassins after each of you! Watch your backs … I project using my mind-speak rune that burns on my neck. It's weaker but I think I connected with them.

Where are you?! Vidarr yells back.

Why haven't you caught up with us yet? Cadoc angrily yells. *We're approaching the forest soon. What assassins?*

Already dealt with mine! Jorah replies sounding pained. *Thank Valirr I was with that blacksmith, Tavian. He saved my ass.*

I'm in the middle of dealing … agh … with it, Kaeden huffs through the connection before he cuts off.

Why can't I feel you through the bond, sunshine? Vi asks.

I try to reach Ragnar but he must still be too far and I'm too weak from the avralite.

Whop—eesh. Whop—eesh. Whop—eesh.

I unintentionally drop the connection from the lashings. *Focus, Sol.* I need to use that anger and that power I can feel growing. I'm not sure where it's coming from but it almost feels like it's feeding my runes.

I'm pulled from my internal assessment when rough hands grab my waist and flip me over on the desk. I can't help the scream of pain when my back hits the wood unexpectedly. My wrists twist in their binds over my head. Malphas backhands me across the face splitting my lip as he says, "Pay attention, Solveig. I don't have the time for your resistance. Submit. To. Me. Now."

I get an overwhelming flood of power making me feel like I'll explode if I don't find a release. My back heals quickly and when I look up I see Malphas stumble away from me in shock.

"Wh—what is wrong with you? Your eyes …" he whispers in horror.

I instantly know that my eyes must be glowing blue. Remembering the other night, I know it's from a buildup of power since completing my mate bonds. It must be enough to over-power the avralite since my back is almost completely healed.

Using my agility rune that starts to tingle on my right thigh, I tighten my abdomen bringing my legs up and flip backwards over the desk. Then I quickly twist my hands in a way that dislocates my thumbs and slide them out of their bindings. Resetting my thumbs with grunt, I look to the right and see one of my discarded daggers near the desk and launch myself towards it grabbing it just as Malphas' angry face appears. He tries to choke me with both hands in his signature move. The avralite cuts into my skin and hurts like hell under his hands, but he didn't see the dagger yet. I slash at his arms wildly trying to get him off me.

"Fucking stubborn *whore*," he curses and stumbles back trying to stem the bleeding from his wounds. Then with a malicious smirk he grabs the whip and cracks it at me as I attempt to stand up against the wall. I'm weak and still a bit dizzy from that magical poison combined with the avralite, but I manage to get up just as the whip flies at me. I throw up the dagger in defense and the whip winds around the blade. Malphas pulls back on the whip expecting me to fall over with it, so I push the dagger away and somersault forward in rush. It takes him by surprise and using my agility rune it all happens within seconds. My speed is something not many can contend with given my power. In my somersault towards Malphas, I deftly grab my katanas on the floor and as I come up from my maneuver I slice them across his chest diagonally in an X.

He falls backwards with a cry of pain landing on his back. I stumble forward feeling my energy and power draining by the second. Victoriously, I stand over him with my katanas against his neck for once at *my* mercy.

"*Tsk, tsk*, Malphas. Such bad words coming from a *gentle-man*. Very disappointing," I say mockingly. Then I smoothly carve a curving letter on his collarbone with one of the katanas as the other one holds him in place. He sucks in a pained breath glaring daggers at me.

"I see defiance in your stare, counselor. You're supposed to be … hm … how do you say it?" I ask lifting an eyebrow. "Oh, yes … that's right … *silent, respectful … compliant.*" Chuckling, I continue mocking him with his own words that he's spat at me for years. "Now, you have my mark on your collarbone for everyone to see who is in control of you." Angrily, I think about the markings on my body both inside and out.

"You're nothing. Just a spoiled, stupid, disappointing little princess on a power kick," Malphas says spittle flying from his lips which are pinched in pain regardless of his words. "You're not strong enough to do it."

Using the last drop of my power, I feel the flare of my agility rune provide me with the speed to deeply slice one of my katanas across his throat just as the last words pass his lips. Blood spouts quickly out of his pulsating blood vessels onto the floor which I kneel down in. He gurgles and chokes on his own blood as I whisper, "You could never follow orders. Enjoy your punishment, Malphas. Now you're *silent.* Forever. Looks like this *whore* is stronger than you thought. So you can go fuck yourself."

CHAPTER
Thirty-Nine

KAEDEN

Kelda and I just walked the entire city wall which took most of the morning. Thankfully, it was strong and intact without any damage from the prior revolution that occurred. We'll lock the gates down once the last few stragglers make it in. Currently, the city guards are herding everyone in.

"It's a good plan of defense," Kelda says standing next to me off to the side of the main city gate.

She's standing with her hands clasped behind her back watching people hurry through as soldiers inspect everyone. Now that we have a plan, all the soldiers have been informed and are following their orders. I feel like I have nothing to do but wait. It's making me fidget and a tendril of unease is making me pace.

"You shouldn't be so stressed."

I look over at her stopping my pacing and say, "I know." Sighing, I run my hand through my shoulder length hair. "It's just I hate the waiting. I'm more of an attack first type of warrior. Not wait around and defend."

She chuckles. "Trust me I know. All Elarian warriors feel the same way. We handle the problem before it becomes a problem." Kelda nudges my shoulder with hers and says, "Why don't you go rest for a bit in the officer's room? We all need to keep up our energy for when it's needed which could be soon. I'll manage everything while you take a break."

Nodding my head and with nothing else to do, I agree. I walk through the halls within the city wall and head for the officer's room that's separated from the soldier's bunk house. They have a small living quarters here for the city guard in case they're here overnight.

I lay down on the small bed in the private room and succumb to my fatigue. I didn't sleep much last night being away from my mate and working on the city's defense plan so I am rather tired.

My rest doesn't last long before I hear a creak in the wood outside my door. It's dark in here and rather quiet right now since everyone is out doing their tasks. *Maybe Kelda is coming to get me?*

I lay still and see the door softly open before closing. My eyes are already adjusted to the darkness so I see the cloaked figure assessing the room. Pretending to still be asleep, I slide my hand under my pillow and grab a Jaarnian steel dagger that Vidarr had gifted me. My other weapons are across the room laying on the table.

A glint of silver is the only other warning I get before the man stabs downward towards my torso. I roll away onto the floor by his boots at the same time his dagger slices into the mattress. I don't waste a second in sinking my own dagger into his right calf making him curse and stumble backwards trying to twist away from me. I grab his other ankle so he can't escape and then I throw myself on top of him trying to wrestle for control. He's strong despite his injury and manages to flip me on my back slamming my head into the floor several times. I wrap my legs around him in an attempt to wrangle him off me when suddenly I'm distracted by a voice in my head.

Jaarn and Malphas have sent assassins after each of you! Watch your backs … My mate's voice rings in my mind. That's when I realize I haven't felt anything from our mate bond. She used her mind-speak ability instead.

As I wrestle with the assassin on the floor, I go to respond mentally when I get a sharp pain in my side. *I'm in the middle of dealing … agh … with it.*

I cut off the connection quickly when I realize I've been stabbed. Luckily his dagger missed everything important on my side but still hurts and there's blood everywhere. Just as I get the assassin in a head lock, the door bursts open and another one rushes in! *Well, that's just perfect. Where in Laevaris are all of my soldiers?*

The second assassin sees his partner on the verge of losing consciousness and rushes at me. *Fucking enough!* I think as I siphon power from my nature rune. It burns and tingles in response to my need. The vines growing on the city wall just outside the room break through the slitted window and magically grow wrapping around the second assassin's arms and then legs. They wrap him up like a spider trapping prey in its web. Looking down at the first assassin, I realize he's already lost consciousness and drop him. The other assassin is struggling in his binds so I quickly approach him and slam the hilt of my dagger into his temple making him go limp.

Kelda turns the corner with her sword drawn and gapes looking into my room.

"Everything handled here, Kaeden? Or … do you need assistance." I see three more soldiers at her back in the hallway. "I thought I told you to rest … I swear your mate and all of you attract trouble."

"I *was* resting! Fuck!" Standing up, I send my magically grown vines back to their place outside. "Can two of you restrain these men and take them to the dungeon. We'll have to question them later." As the other soldiers rush to follow my orders, I grab Kelda's arm and whisper, "I'm fine but took a shallow wound to the side. Can you bind it for me?"

Kelda's critical gaze runs over me spotting the bleeding wound. She forcefully pushes me to sit on the bed as the room clears of everyone else. Then she reaches under the bed and pulls out a healer's kit before saying, "We do have a healer or two on the city walls if you want me to grab them." She cleans the wound which stings a bit but is nothing I can't handle. Compared to lashings I took as a slave in the past, this is like a scratch.

"No. It's not worth their time. We heal fast and I can tell it's a minor injury."

"You're right. Looks like it just went through skin and a bit of muscle here. I'll wrap it tightly but if it keeps bleeding then we'll have to put a stitch in it," Kelda says finishing her task with focused determination.

As we leave the room and head back up the wall, I can't help but think—why? Why would they send assassins for me? Did they send them after everyone? My mate?

My anxiety spikes in concern for my mate but then I realize I didn't feel anything from the mate bond. Maybe she blocked it?

Solveig? I try sending mentally through the connection she used earlier but it's no use. There's no response. Just blankness. The only way I can mentally talk with her is through our mate bond unless she initiates communication through her mind-speak rune. *Please! Are you okay?*

I make the decision to check on her myself but then remember she left with Vidarr and Cadoc. I was walking the castle wall when they left so didn't get to see them. I'll just have to trust that they can look after her and wait on her to unblock the mate bond. *Stubborn woman! She just can't stay out of trouble.*

CHAPTER
Forty

SOLVEIG

I exit that blood splattered room of horrors exhausted both physically and emotionally after my encounter with Malphas. But surprisingly, deep down inside myself I feel satisfaction. Relief. Justice.

Vengeance has been served after years of suffering. And each step I take away from that room, my self-worth grows. *I fought back. I conquered my fear. I'm strong. I won.*

A smile overtakes my face from my self-reflection. And as I step out into the castle courtyard, I see a servant gaping at me in shock and growing horror before they scream and run away yelling for others. *Hm, I must really look a sight.* I look down to see what the issue is and notice I'm covered head to toe in blood while probably smiling like a lunatic. My shirt is a bit of a mess but mostly intact in the front. I put my leather harness back on which holds everything together in the back and keeps my katanas safely sheathed. *I guess smiling and being blood covered is a bit intimidating to the help.* I'm just too exhausted to make it back to my room and change. Plus I'm worried about my mates.

I try to focus on the mate bonds and can feel a tiny tickle of them at the edge of my connection. The magical poison that numbed my mate bonds must be starting to fade so all I have to do is wait. I make it to the stables knowing I need Sindari to make it quickly back to Vidarr and Cadoc's side.

Sigurd sees me and drops the saddle he was carrying. He runs over to me and pulls me into his embrace.

"Wh—what happened, Sol?" he croaks out in concern for me. "I thought—well I didn't really know what you ended up doing. I would have helped you!" He steps back and looks me over for injuries seeing the exhaustion in my eyes and the torn shirt on my back.

"I'm all healed now, Sigurd. It's over. He's gone," I say closing my eyes and leaning my forehead against his chest in relief.

"Who, Sol? Who?" Sigurd shakes me in panic making me snap my eyes back open. *Oh fuck! He thinks I was talking about Jorah since I was going to meet up with him.*

"No. No! I'm sorry. Not Jorah. He wasn't there," I say looking around and noticing a few stable boys looking our way. I pull Sigurd over into a stall in the corner for privacy. "I have to be quick but you need to know … Malphas is dead. I killed him." I straighten up and look Sigurd dead in the eye. "Darritt betrayed me. He led me right to Malphas. Jorah wasn't there."

Sigurd nearly falls over in relief and rests a hand against the wall while one runs over his face. "Thank Valirr! Jorah is—is okay?"

"Well, I assume so. He wasn't there. I need to get going. I need to catch up to Vidarr and Cadoc." Anxiety fills me at the thought of Malphas mentioning assassins. Then with a deadly serious look at Sigurd, I say, "Don't trust Darritt. If you see him grab some soldiers and apprehend him. I need you here and managing the castle until Jorah returns from the city. Maybe send a messenger for Jorah? To check on him? He did speak to me that he was okay but I'm having trouble with my mate bond connections since Darritt also poisoned me with some sort of magical potion."

281

"Shit. I'll send for him and don't worry about Darritt. If I see him, I'll handle him myself." Sigurd gets a dangerous expression on his face that I've learned in the past people take seriously. He then whistles loudly and Sindari trots up to me tossing his mane. "He wouldn't let me close his stall door. He must have known you'd need him in a rush."

I scratch Sin behind his ear before turning and hugging Sigurd. "Keep Jorah safe and hold down the castle for me?"

Sigurd smirks and nods as I run a few steps before swinging up and mounting Sindari. I can't mind speak with Sindari yet since I'm nearly tapped out of power right now but luckily he understands my haste. He takes off running through the city as I rest a bit soaking up the sun.

We reach the main city gate in no time and I slide off Sin's back marching toward the officer's barracks. A few men gape at me and bow at the waist in deference, but no one speaks. *If I knew covering myself in blood was this effective in keeping people away, I would have done it a lot sooner.* I mentally joke with myself still feeling a bit unhinged after my encounter in the castle. *Where is Kaeden?*

Instead of seeing Kaeden, I nearly run smack dab into Kelda as she orders all the soldiers back to their posts at the gate.

"My queen! What happened?" Kelda says placing a palm over her heart and bowing. She runs her eyes over my body inspecting.

I wave a hand in the air dismissively before saying, "Nothing. Just a bit of justice served. I wanted to check on Kaeden but I'm in a bit of a rush."

"Yes, I thought you'd be with your mate consorts Vidarr and Cadoc. We are about to close the city gates so you need to leave now," she says looking concerned at my appearance. "Kaeden is somewhere on the wall. He's directing the inspection of each gate as its secured. It may be a bit before he's back here. He—"

"Is he okay?" I interrupt. "I need to leave, now. I don't have enough time to wait but need to know ..."

"He was attacked by two assassins which we now have chained in the dungeon for questioning. He obtained a small wound to the side but is otherwise fine." Kelda says as I sag in relief. "What's going on, my queen?"

"Please Kelda, call me Solveig. Tell him I was here … that I was given something…poisoned with a potion that blocks the mate bond for a time. I think it's starting to fade but he'll have to wait to communicate with me. Darritt is a traitor and cannot be trusted. Make sure everyone knows. If you see him, I want him captured and locked up. Do not take any orders from him and keep your eyes out for him causing trouble."

Kelda's face hardens in anger and she spits on the ground before saying, "He'll be found, however it'll be hard not to serve him the justice he deserves for his betrayal." She pets a hand over her sword at her side. "I'll spread the word. Be careful, Solveig."

I nod and turn back to Sindari who's kneeling on a front left leg for me to mount easier. "Thanks, Sin. I might take a tiny nap as you race. We need to head northwest towards my mates."

Tangling my hands in Sindari's mane and laying over his neck, he stands then races out of the main gate. I hear the gears turning behind me signaling its closure just as Kelda mentioned.

CHAPTER
Forty-One

VIDARR

We arrive at the Laevarian army camp just before dinner and things seem to be well in hand. Captain Mavin greets me and Cadoc while the soldiers we brought disperse into camp getting set up. A small contingent unloads the supplies we brought which will be useful for an army this size.

"Any issues?" Captain Mavin asks me as he looks over all the activity. "We haven't seen Jaarn yet but I have several scouts that should be back tonight. We had an Elarian soldier notify us about an hour ago that they're almost in position to the north of us."

"No issues so far," I respond handing my horse off to a boy that asks to take him. "Sounds like things are falling together. I'm glad Jaarn hasn't made it past here yet."

Mavin hums in his throat in agreement. "It is good that we were able to make camp in the forest. It wouldn't have been as ideal to have to battle in the open plains while they had the advantage of trees to hide behind. Also, the Elarians are better within the forest. Where's Princess Solveig?"

Cadoc speaks up handing his horse off as well, "I guess we did have one issue. Solveig was delayed in leaving the castle since Jorah had something urgent to inform her about. She was supposed to catch up to us outside the city but never did." Cadoc squints suspiciously. "I think something happened. She spoke to us using her mind-speak a little bit ago and I can't feel her through the mate bond."

"Me either," I say rubbing my chest nervously. "She promised she wouldn't block the mate bond and would leave herself open to us. Also, I'm confused by what she said…"

"What did she say?" Mavin looks at each of us.

"She said—Jaarn and Malphas have sent assassins after each of us. It was weird," I say.

"Yes. She specifically said *Malphas*," Cadoc says rubbing his chin. "Why would she say that … unless …"

"*Fuck!*" I shout kicking over a crate in my anger. "You think he was there?"

Captain Mavin calmly interrupts, "Maybe it was the urgent message that Jorah wanted to relay to her. Jorah or even Pia could have gotten a message from our spy network in the kingdom. We shouldn't jump to conclusions yet." Mavin looks over at us and I feel a bit embarrassed by my outburst. "In the meantime, we need to place extra guards on you two. If there's a target on your back, then we need someone to watch it."

"I don't need a babysitter," Cadoc says with an affronted look on his face. "I have my mate-brother *and* I am the General of the Gorvian army!"

"No guards during the day, but maybe it would be smart to put some outside our tent at night while we sleep. Even the best fighter can be vulnerable in his sleep." I say placing a hand on Cadoc's back who loses some of his tension before he nods in acceptance.

"Good. I have them setting you up in the center of camp. Rest up, you'll likely need it tomorrow," Mavin states. "In the meantime, we'll just have to wait for Princess Solveig to either open her … uh … bond with you or show up here. She's tough and a fighter. I've trained her well enough to deal with any situation. Have a little faith in your mate." He nods his head before walking away and yelling out orders to some of the soldiers unloading.

Cadoc and I share a large tent in the middle of the army which feels a bit too obvious to me. Shouldn't we blend in more with the rest of the soldiers? However, I know Mavin put us here for more layers of protection and in addition for Solveig's protection since she'll be sharing a tent with us. *Whenever she gets here.* Mavin is right … I'll just have to trust my sunshine. I usually do, but something about this situation has me on edge and my protective instincts are going berserk not knowing where she is.

We eat a quiet dinner and fall into our cots once we notice the two guards outside our tent. I wake up seeing the darkness of the tent and hear Cadoc's heavy breaths of sleep. It must be the middle of the night since I feel like I got a few hours at least but am confused as to what woke me.

Then I hear it … a soft thud outside the tent.

As a prior rebel and spending most of my life living in the poorer part of the city, I'm very familiar with the sound of a dead body hitting the ground. *Shit!* I don't waist a second as a roll out of bed quietly grabbing my dagger and tapping Cadoc on the shoulder. He immediately wakes in silence as a trained soldier should. I put a finger over my mouth and then point to the front of the tent. Cadoc nods and reaches over to grab his sword.

We don't have to wait long before the tent flap is pulled aside and four men sneak inside. I see two more cloaked men standing outside and our two guards dead at their feet. I don't have time to ponder how they made it past all those soldiers since they start rushing at us with swords raised.

Cadoc hefts his large sword up blocking the first and swings it down catching the second assassin's blade with expertise. A third assassin attacks me and I manage to dodge his thrust before I slash his left thigh and turn looking for the fourth man. He's standing near the tent opening holding a crossbow aimed at my chest. There's no way he's going to miss at such a short distance and I feel my heart thudding in my chest. *Ahh, fuck it!* Just as I decide to charge at him while the other man is recovering, I blur of fur tackles the fourth assassin and the crossbow bolt releases. It shoots wide missing its mark and going through the back of the tent.

My eyes must be deceived because it's impossible what I see in front of me. A snarl followed by a harsh crackle sound and then tearing of skin can be heard before I focus on the large catchki brutally attacking the assassin with the crossbow. As the large cat like predator tears into his stomach, I turn away with a queasiness and deflect the assassin who I cut previously. Grunting and metal clashing can be heard from the other side of the tent but I have to focus on my own adversary. He has a long narrow sword out and thrusts towards me in an agile move, but he's not fast enough. I've been sparring Solveig for years now and she's ten times faster than this man. So instead of taking a sword to the gut, I twist and curve out of its path before twirling to his side and stabbing up into his flank. I pull another dagger from my hip and lay it across his throat before ending his miserable life.

Skkriiiipp. Skkkkrrriiip. Soft yet harsh crackles sound from in front of me. I notice Cadoc backing up towards the back of the tent and two dead men at his feet. He has a scratch on his face but otherwise appears unharmed.

Skkriiiipp. My gaze tracks over to the source of the noise and I see the catchki prowling towards me with its pointed ears perked up on its head. Its head tilts at a questioning angle and I realize I recognize this one.

Its shiny fur is sleek and mostly black with a gray and few brown stripes intermixed. I shuffle a bit nervously, not wanting to get a leg bitten off by this gorgeous creature if it startles. I also don't want to have to fight something that clearly saved my life and is possibly friends with Solveig.

I lower my sword nervously so it knows I'm not threatening it and Cadoc hisses at me from my side, "What are you doing? That thing is nearly the size of a small pony. And did you see it tear into that man's stomach? *Fuck.*"

When my sword is lowered, it approaches with its head lowered and piercing eyes locked onto mine. *This is for you, sunshine. I'm trying to make friends with your friends.* I nearly piss my pants when the large catchki makes that crackling noise and then rubs its huge head against my chest. I curls around me and rubs itself along my side and I huff out a breath of relief.

Cadoc laughs a bit under his breath and lowers his sword watching this strange interaction. Then, he nods towards his cot where there's another large catchki cleaning its sharply clawed paws off. It's watching us intently especially at each place the black catchki is touching me.

"What about that one?" Cadoc whispers, "You think it will eat us?"

The shiny black striped catchki that's scenting me looms up in front of me at its words and licks me across the face.

"Ugh!" I say trying to distance myself. It huffs a few times almost like it's chuckling before it tilts its head in a humanoid way towards the other catchki and they take off through a cut out hole in the side of the tent.

Cadoc and I both release a breath of relief simultaneously before we collapse on the ground surrounded by four dead assassins. That's how Captain Mavin found us.

"What in the name of Faktirnor happened here?" Mavin yells at us before shouting out orders to several soldiers with him who scramble to do a sweep of the camp. A few men start to dispose of the bodies.

"Assassins. Just like Solveig said," Cadoc says running a hand over his face managing to smear more blood across it from the cut on his cheek. He winces a bit obviously forgetting about the injury.

Mavin nods and takes it all in with a calm calculated demeanor before saying, "I thought I heard a noise outside my tent but not enough to arouse suspicion. I was just woken up by one of my soldiers …" Mavin says bowing his head. "I'm sorry. I've failed you both. I should have pushed you to accept more guards."

"Mavin, this is not your fault. We were being difficult and its done," I say trying to reassure him. "This is war. We don't need you to hold our hands." Cadoc grunts in agreement while he starts cleaning his sword off using his already bloody sheets.

Captain Mavin takes a deep breath before he looks at us and his entire body tenses up. He then says, "One of our scouts just got back. It was why I was woken up. The other two scouts are likely dead based on what the last one told me." Mavin paces a bit and crosses his arms. "He spotted Jaarnian soldiers. They're through the pass and moving fast. He said they nearly caught him and weren't far behind him. I've already spread the word to prepare for battle and you should too."

I look over at Cadoc and to see him watching me. Then he nods before turning to check all his weapons. *This is it. Time to show these Jaarnian fuckers why they don't want to live here.* I roll my shoulders back in a stretch and notice Mavin has already left. Sounds of soldiers waking up and camp being disbanded can be heard now. I decide to follow Cadoc's lead and begin checking all my weapons. *I just wish Sol was with me, watching my back, like in the past. Fuck, I miss her.*

I decide to try one more time to feel the mate bond and instead of a blankness and there's a flicker of surprise down the bond. *Yes!* However, when I try to hold onto the connection and speak to her it's difficult to hold onto. Almost like it's slippery and I can't quite get it to stay still for me.

I still try though and say, *Solveig? Sunshine?*
No response.
Where is she? Maybe I should go back…

Cadoc and I finish preparing for battle and head out of our damaged tent. A brief war meeting takes place in Mavin's tent with all the officers before we separate to different quadrants about one hundred soldiers each. There should be more of the Laevarian army coming up from the Laevarian-Gorvian border but we have yet to see or hear from them.

I end up staying with Cadoc under his leadership after it was decided that I have no experience in the army and am too reckless to be leading a quadrant. Grudgingly, I have to agree with Cadoc and Mavin. I don't really want the responsibility anyways and am used to fighting my battles in the shadows or undercover in the narrow alleys of Falal.

We march out to our positions less than an hour from the mountain pass, laying in wait within the forest. Mavin received word during our march that the Elarians are in position north of us and have spotted Jaarn. They've killed off several scouts heading north. The bad news is that there's more soldiers than we thought …

CHAPTER

Forty-Two

SOLVEIG

It took much longer to catch up to the Laevarian army than I thought, but it wasn't Sindari's fault. He probably would have made the run in a couple hours knowing how fast he is. It was me… I fell into a deep healing sleep shortly after leaving Falal and supposedly—per Sindari—I nearly fell off his back three times in my sleep. He ended up having to walk and slow his stride in order to keep me settled in place.

When I wake, it's nearly dark but I feel relatively restored from my sleep and exposure to the sun and outdoors.

Good, you're awake! Sindari projects into my mind. *I thought I'd have to shake you off my back to wake you.*

Ha. Ha. Ha. You better not, I reply squinting my eyes in warning even though he can't see my expression from his back. *How close are we?*

We just entered the forest but I haven't seen your two-legged friends yet. I did however see your feathered friend, Tyr.

Oh! That's good! Thank you, Sin.

I concentrate on using my nature and animal power and feel a responding tingle on the rune of my wrist. My body feels full of power again, thank Valirr! Focusing my mind on the surrounding forest, I search for any animal psyche in the area. I can sense Tyr's essence close by on a branch but there's also another one close or … several.

Just as my mind connects with his, he projects to me, *Morning, Solveig … or should I say—evening? You slept for much of the sun's movement. I followed you from above after you left the city.*

I look up and to the right sensing Tyr before spotting him through the dimming light. *Thank you for checking on me. Weren't you going to scout some of the Laevarian border?*

I did, my friend. I checked the Gorvian border which is quiet now before returning to you. My mate is checking along the western border while two of my eyas are checking the eastern border, Tyr says with pride. *I wanted to return to you with speed since you need someone at your side. Someone more equipped for battle than this bumbling hoof-toed creature. I can speak with Allira as my mate and she says the two-legged men from the mountains are already through and challenging your clutch of two-legged men. She says to hurry.*

Sindari snorts his annoyance at Tyr's insult before saying, *Just because I have hooves instead of talons doesn't mean I'm not dangerous in battle. I've stomped many an enemy beneath me.*

I tune out their banter and focus on Tyr's other words … *fuck!* They're already fighting! It started faster than I thought and at night no less. I just hope they had warning and that the Elarian contingent is in place.

As I'm distracted with my thoughts, Sindari continues his trot through the forest. A blur of brown comes from my right and then a blur of gray from my left in the trees. Stiffening up in alarm, I focus on my surroundings and feel the rune burn on my wrist. It's the presence of several animals that I'm feeling. Not men, thank Valirr.

Sindari stops suddenly and I look around his large head to see two reflective red eyes. A long sleek, black bodied catchki prowls forward with ears perked and head down. Its long razor sharp teeth can be seen in the growing darkness as its tail whips back and forth.

Vabira, the alpha female of the catchki, cautiously approaches me on Sindari who stands stock still. I can feel his body tremble in anxiety at the large pony-sized predator approaching.

I met Vabira a while ago while traveling in the Elaritian Forest with my grandfather and we made a friendly alliance of sorts. She was pleased to find someone that was able to communicate and allowed us passage. I look her over and can't help but appreciate her graceful beauty. Her fur coat is black with intermixing stripes ranging from brown to gray-blue. I see movement behind her and notice two of her mates, Euri and Tiguar.

Greetings Vabira, I state formally. *You are far from your normal grounds …*

Solveig, well met, she replies. *You can tell your hooved friend he doesn't need to fear us. Let us walk and speak.* I relay this to Sindari who cautiously starts walking again knowing we need to join the army, fast. *I saw your mates …*

What? Who? I say to Vabira with confusion. *When?*

A raspy crackle comes out of her jaw similar to scratching a bristled brush on a dry surface. Her mates also make the crackling noise and I realize they're chuckling at me.

Patience, my friend. I will explain … Vabira says looking up at me and walking along side. *You remember my mates?* I nod in greeting and look over at each who tilt their head at me in a rather humanoid manner. *Well, I was in the area which I will explain when I scented your mates. I decided to seek them out hoping you were with them. But, lo and behold … there were several men under cover of darkness entering their shelter. We decided based on their scents that they were a threat.*

I realize that she's describing assassins most likely. *Are they okay? Did they get injured?*

Patience. We intervened and enjoyed the hunt, Vabira states while licking a long black tongue around her sharp incisors

293

hanging out of her muzzle. *Your mates are alive with minimal injuries. I personally scented the one with the beautiful stripes on his skin.*

I relax in relief and gratefulness that she was there. Then I chuckle realizing she's talking about Vidarr who is covered in tattoos. I bet he nearly wet himself having her rubbing all over him. He's such a baby when it came to the catchki. *Thank you, Vabira. I owe you and your mates if that is the case.*

Vabira gives me a haughty side eyed look before saying, *You are welcome. But our help comes with a reason. We need you. Alive. Me and my mates have traveled to this area of the forest near the mountains due to a concern. My cousin is alpha of a clan of catchki in the mountains and she contacted me with concerns of two legged men invading their territory. Building those torture shelters in the base of the mountain, cutting down trees, and leaving trash near their dens. I traveled here to meet with her and provide assistance when we noticed the large war grouping in the mountain pass. We picked off several men ourselves but there are too many and we would like to join you in ridding them of the territory.*

Shocked, I stare at her for a few seconds processing her words. I never knew there was more than one clan of catchki but I suppose it makes sense. And, it's beneficial to us in the war. We could potentially end this war in one battle. That is if I ever make it to them. *Wait … you said … you need me? Alive? Why me?*

Ah, you are a smart and observant for a two-legged but I suppose it's the Elarian in you, Vabira says. *I did mention that. We need you to help communicate with us and tell your men not to attack us, however there is also a second reason …*

Okay, that makes sense, I reply. *And the second reason?*

We need you to break the curse, Vabira says quietly in my mind.

Wha—what curse? I quickly reply. *You mean the one on Elaria?* She nods her large cat like head. *What does that have to do with you?*

Many do not realize but we have … changed in the time since it was placed. We were always secluded so not many know or re-member, Vabira says vaguely. *It's becoming harder and harder to remember with each year that passes.*

Remember … what? I ask tilting my head to watch her.

That we had a two-legged form like yours, she says in response.

I'm speechless for a moment before I consider what she's saying. *You … all the catchki … are shifters?*

If you mean, we could change back and forth from fur to two legged form then yes. We are shifters. But we are stuck in our fur since the curse was placed. Many have forgotten our more delicate form and I worry soon it won't even be possible. May not ever be possible.

Well, I suppose there's only one way to know, I say seriously. *I will gladly help you and the others. I believe I already have what is necessary to lift the curse. Help us survive the battle and we can focus on the curse next.*

Vabira gives me a cat like smile showcasing all those wicked-ly sharp teeth in her jaw and making me cringe a bit in response. *You have a deal, Solveig.*

Vabira and I hash out some ideas for the battle and pick up speed now that we are in agreement. The sounds of battle are just ahead so I unsheathe my katanas and take a deep breath. *Now, where would my mates be? Where should I be?*

I focus internally for a moment seeking out my mates and feel a flimsy barrier between me and them. It feels as though it's thin and cracking and must be somehow related to the poison that has faded from my system, so I decide to push against it with my mind. It easily dissolves and I'm inundated with my mates' emotions. *Finally! I missed this so much.* Their warm and comforting presence is back but there are several who are feeling worried.

I focus on Vidarr and Cadoc's mate bonds and follow the tether linking us. It looks as though we're losing the battle. There's nearly three or four men to our one and we're vastly outnumbered. Our men are good fighters but they're put up against larger numbers with better weapons.

Vabira stays by my side with one of her mates. The other one having been sent to gather the nearby catchki clan. Tyr flies down at that moment. *Cak-cak. Cak-cak.* His talons gouge out a man's eyes and face as he attempted to approach me with his raised blade.

Leave some for me to fight, my friend, I project to Tyr who chuckles in a blood thirsty manner within my mind.

Three Jaarnian soldiers approach me with weapons raised. One aiming a crossbow at me. He doesn't have time to release it before Vabira pounces on him and rips into his throat. I engage the other two and smile as the savage part of me takes over enjoying the fight.

Block. Block. Swipe. Block. Cross. Twist and thrust. Enlisting the power from my agility rune, I speedily engage in the dance of combat. It's a beautiful thing to be able to counter strikes and attack in response faster than your opponent. Within five moves, I take out one of the men. Sindari flicks a leg out kicking the other in the leg and throwing his balance off which I take advantage of. He dies of a katana through his throat and looks at me with a shocked expression, but I barely spare him a thought since I've already moved on to the next man. Vabira and her mate are already clearing most of my path with a few soldiers leaking through to fight me. The Laevarian soldiers see me coming and do a double take looking me and my entourage of animals over with shocked and awed faces. Many mutter, *magic* or *unnatural.* But several nod their heads in deference and yell, *Our Queen is here!* I want to say something to my mates through our connection and let them know I'm here but I'm also scared I'll distract them in battle which can be deadly.

I still can't see my mates through the endless soldiers and fighting. There's bodies and blood everywhere. Fighting is intense, and as I see many Laevarian soldiers fall, I decide to just join the battle here and assist my men. I assist so many that are outnumbered and fall into a bloody daze of violence that after a while I fail to realize many of our men are retreating, and there are no more Jaarnian soldiers in front of me other than the ones on the ground. A few men are running away looking over their shoulders with fear.

Blowing out a deep breath of air, I crouch down and clean my katanas off on the nearest body. Vabira and her mate step in closer guarding my sides. At some point in the fight, I dismounted Sindari since soldiers pressed in too tight to battle on horseback and it was unsafe for him. Now that things have settled, I feel his nose nudge my back, and I lean into him in comfort. Fatigue fills me as the blood lust dissipates, and I trudge back towards where the Laevarian soldiers disappeared to.

Where are my mates? I think as I march into what must be the Laevarian army camp.

CHAPTER
Forty-Three

SOLVEIG

Changing my facial expression into my princess mask, I walk into their camp and present only a blank cold expression that the Laevarians have come to expect from a royal.

However instead of the usual deference with underlying animosity a reigning heir would get, many of the soldiers are instead whispering and nodding their heads with … awe and curiosity. Vabira and her mates flank me as I approach and many soldiers back up cautiously avoiding their sharp teeth and claws.

That's Princess Solveig…

She fought alongside the catchki!

No, idiot, she's now the Queen … I don't know why she's here. Most royals stay up in their castles and don't bother to dirty their hands.

She's a good warrior and saved my ass on the battlefield.

The princess uses magic! I saw her moving faster than it's humanly possible. Look at how she's tamed those animals!

Do you think she can work magic and win us the war?

We need all the advantages we can get since we're outnumbered.

I sparred with the princess many times in the past. She deserves some respect. Anyone who can fight like her has my loyalty.

Did you hear she has dragons as allies as well? Why didn't they show up?

The whispers and gossip continue as I walk amongst the soldiers heading for the central tent being set up. I recognize a few men and greet them with a nod telling them they fought well. Some of the moral is a bit low, I can tell. Soldiers such as these don't like to retreat. They're trained to push through no matter the cost, but Mavin doesn't like to waste unnecessary life which I'm grateful for. Retreating can come off as weak even though sometimes it's more to regroup and plan.

I make it closer to the tent and feel my mate bonds throb in response. Cadoc and Vidarr rush towards me in a frenzy and suddenly I'm squished in between the two of them in an embrace. *I missed this … I missed them.* The mate bond settles and thrums with happiness at finding they are unharmed. Cadoc looks me over critically while Vidarr cups my face and places kisses on my cheeks. I see a few soldiers staring at our open display of affection with curious looks so I tug both my mates' hands into the tent.

"I'm so glad you both are okay!" I say smiling at them. "I'm sorry I was delayed. I'll tell you all about it but for now I think we should focus on the current battle plan."

"Damn, Sol. You had me so worried and panicked," Cadoc says intensely looking into my eyes with reproach. "You aren't to leave my side! Why didn't you find us? Why didn't you tell us what's going on through the bond?"

"Sunshine, you look and feel exhausted," Vi says running a hand down my spine. "I'm just glad you're okay and that we can feel you again through the mate bond. Don't ever shut us out again like that!"

"You promised you'd leave the bond open so we could all communicate!" Cadoc angrily says crossing his arms.

"I know! I'm sorry but things didn't go as planned and—"

"Princess Solveig, I'm glad you made it. It's been a rough day." Captain Mavin walks over to us in the tent and interrupts. "We need to discuss the plan for their next attack."

Turning to Cadoc and Vi, I give them a pleading look and softly say, "Later, I promise I'll explain later." They look at each other and then back at me. I send a feeling of affection through the mate bond and they both blow out breaths before nodding in acceptance.

"Captain Mavin, update me on what's going on …" I say with a nod.

He clears his throat and tilts his head to a map laid out on a table in the center of the tent. "Well, we had four quadrants for the last attack and the Elarians to the north." He points to each area as he speaks where the men were assigned. "Unfortunately, Jaarn arrived with more men than we expected and the Elarians were under significant pressure preventing them from aiding any other areas in the battle with their powers. Your arrival with your …friends"—Mavin cautiously looks over at a sitting Vabira who's licking her paw by the tent flap—"helped us in our retreat. So thank you. Do you happen to know where your consort, King Ragnar, is?"

Shaking my head back and forth, I worriedly say, "No. He's not close enough yet but I can tell he's heading this direction. He's still too far to communicate with." There's a commotion near the tent flap and in walks Yaeril, an Elarian warrior who's also a friend skilled in weapon accuracy and climbing. I smile over at him in greeting which he places a hand over his heart in return before I turn back to Mavin. "Have you heard anything from the other portion of our army that should be coming from the Gorvian border?"

Mavin blows out a frustrated breath and hits his fist on the makeshift table before saying, "No. Damn it. There's been no messages from them. We should plan to hold off Jaarn for another day to give them time to get here. Once we have our full army, we can rid these foreigners from our kingdom."

"Do you think Jaarn will attack again tonight or wait until morning?" I ask Mavin curiously since he's the most experienced in the group.

Instead, Cadoc replies, "If I had to guess, they'll attack tonight. They're sneaky and I've seen it before at Sterling Outpost … they don't wait long and prefer attacking at unpredictable times."

"I agree." Mavin nods respectfully at my mate. "If it were me, I would attack tonight or sooner. We need to be ready. I've already set up a heavy perimeter and guard detail. I can send out some scouts to monitor their camp while our soldiers get food and as much rest as they can."

"Save the scouts, Captain," I say looking at Vabira and quickly communicating with her while one of her mates slips out the tent. "Our catchki allies will monitor our enemies and inform me of any activity. They're better at this and can hide in the trees. Let our men rest while they can."

Mavin looks impressed and nods in agreement. We then spend the next hour coming up with a plan in case the second half of our army doesn't show up.

"Yaeril, well met," I say walking to his side. "How are things to the north?"

"My future queen, Solveig, I'm happy to see you again," Yaeril says with a smile. "The Elarians are warriors and the forest is our home. You should have no concerns about Jaarn penetrating our defenses. We were simply surprised a bit by their extra men who spilled through a smaller pass north of the main one. It took some of our focus off the main battle and therefore we weren't as available to your soldiers in their time of need. Your father sends his regards."

"Yes, well—that explains it. It seems Jaarn sent much of their army to invade us. I wasn't aware they had more men coming through another pass but it makes sense. We're outnumbered until we have the rest of our army so we'll have to make do," Captain Mavin says staring at the map.

Yaeril nods and they speak for a few minutes before he takes off to get food and return to the Elarian camp.

Vidarr grabs my elbow and says to Captain Mavin, "If that's everything, we're going to eat and rest until the next battle." Captain Mavin looks up distractedly and waves us away. The poor man looks older than his years right now and I'm glad we previously discussed that he would have more help going forward after dealing with the war.

Vi pulls me from the tent with Cadoc close behind me. He leads me to a small tent off to the right and Vabira settles in front of it with a relaxed pose.

Rest with your mates. I will guard you, friend, Vabira says.

Thank you. Let me know if the enemy army seems to be mobilizing.

Once the tent flap closes behind us three, Cadoc reaches forward and starts to pull off my weapons one by one while Vi pushes me down onto a low set cot and starts removing my boots.

"Wha—" I start to say.

"Shh, sunshine," Vi says with a closed off expression, but I can feel an underlying emotion through the mate bond. It takes me a moment to understand what it is I'm feeling when I suddenly realize it's … fear and concern. "Let us take care of you. *Please.*"

"We need to do this, Sol," Cadoc whispers as well, now unbuttoning my shirt and grabbing a wet cloth from a bowl on the side of the tent. "I couldn't focus on the fight due to my concern for you. Nearly lost my head a few times. I need to look you over."

I'm filled with love and comfort just seeing how much they care about me. I can still feel their pain and worry at my disappearance. "I love you both," I say sending my own emotions of love through our mate bonds causing them to relax a bit.

Once they have me in my undergarments, they start cleaning my skin from all the grime of travel and blood of my opponents. "Here … I can do that," I say trying to grab the rag from their hands. I'm feeling myself become heated by their wandering hands and teasing. *Wrong time and wrong place, Sol.*

Once I'm clean, Vi hands me a bowl with stew and a travel biscuit that I eat in record time. They both settle next to me and eat as well. We sit in silence for a bit just enjoying each other's proximity. After they finish eating, Vi and Cadoc strip and freshen up causing unwanted heat to pool between my legs in response. I can't help but appreciate their strong muscular bodies as they wipe away the dirt from the day.

Excitement fills me when Vi's tattooed torso leans in close over me to pull the blankets off the cot and pile them on the ground. He smirks at me while his lips graze my neck before he quickly leans back and turns around. *Fucking tease.* Vi and Cadoc both chuckle as if they heard me. Well—perhaps they did. *Oops.*

"Why are you throwing all our blankets on the ground?" I ask with an eyebrow raised.

"Well, sunshine, I assumed you wanted both your mates to rest close to you," Vi says laying down on his side facing me within the pile of blankets. I look down at the small cot I'm sitting on and realize there's no way more than one person could fit on it nevertheless three.

Cadoc tugs me up and scoops me into his firm hold before he lays me next to Vidarr and says, "We want to hold you for a bit. And—you owe us an explanation." He then lays down on his side facing me and boxes me in. I can't help but reach for both their hands and maintain skin contact with my mates.

"You're right. I always want my mates next to me. Okay, where to start …" I say nervously biting my lip and looking at the tent ceiling. "Well, Darritt led me inside the castle and we stopped in the kitchen. I thought it strange at first but he said he wanted to make me a cup of karaf … since I was tired. It was a bit bitter but I drank it as he led me to an office with promises that Jorah was inside. I felt rather dizzy when I entered the dark room and it took me a bit to realize our mate bonds were blocked. You see … Darritt betrayed us. He poisoned me with a magical concoction. It made me dizzy and weaker and so I couldn't talk with you through our bond …"

"*Fuck,*" Vidarr curses running a hand through his hair. "Darritt …" Vi's face looks utterly devastated. Him and Darritt have been friends for years and were always close so I know this news must be especially hard for him to accept.

"I knew something was suspicious … I'm assuming it wasn't Jorah in the room?" Cadoc says angrily with his fists clenching.

"Yeah. Darritt must have taken off and it wasn't Jorah looking for me … it was Counselor Malphas," I say while Vi and Cadoc share looks of shock and horror. "He was waiting and timed his attack perfectly with the poison Darritt had just given me." Closing my eyes, I think about him ripping my shirt and tying me down. Feeling that helplessness. Terror. Weakness. "I'm embarrassed to say I froze up in panic. I—I didn't fight back … not nearly enough at first. I'm sorry …" Cadoc and Vi both place hands on me comfortingly but remain silent as I work through my thoughts.

"He—he took his time trying to break me. He wanted me to submit to him under the plan that I would still marry him and he'd take the throne. He threatened all of you and informed me about the assassins. I realized that even though the mate bond was blocked by the poison, my rune powers weren't. So I sent you all a warning as soon as I could. I was weak but able to get through to you. Thank Valirr! He used avralite on me then in another attempt to make me more compliant when I started to fight back. It weakened my power more which is why my words cut off."

I take a deep breath centering myself before continuing.

"He thought he won … nearly had too. But in the end, I showed him my strength formed after years of weakness. He thought he broke me, weakened me, but really all he did was train me to endure and find my inner strength." Vi and Cadoc's hands squeeze mine in support. "He—he's dead now. Finally."

I don't realize I'm crying until Cadoc starts kissing my tears away and says, "My warrior mate. So strong. So beautiful." He punctuates each sentence with a kiss. "I'm proud of you."

Vi turns my hand over and kisses each callus on my hand as he says, "You always were better than me. A better fighter. A better person." He looks up with a dangerous look but inside the mate bond … I feel sorrow, pride and … guilt? "I would have kept him alive … he would have suffered for days under my blade. But you were always better. I wish I was there with you— for your vengeance. I would have savored *his* punishment. But mostly, I wish … I was one who ended his miserable life." Then he smirks and says, "Go ahead and call me a jealous asshole."

"*Jealous asshole*," I say giving him a small smile and wiping my tears away. "You always have to compete with me. Trying to take my kills or fight my fights. This one was for *me* though."

CHAPTER
Forty-Four

SOLVEIG

We spent the rest of our time snuggling in the blankets and resting too tired to do much else. I felt like I had just fallen asleep before I was woken by a voice.

They're coming. Vabira's strong voice rings through my waking consciousness. I groggily try to roll over into a warm firm chest hoping to sleep more, but instead I get a scratchy wet tongue licking up my cheek and forcing me to bolt awake. *Wake up, my friend. Rouse your army. My scouts report your enemies are preparing for battle.* Vabira's large black head moves into my face.

Thank you, Vabira. Will you stand guard will I get ready?

Of course. The mountain catchki clan are already prepared for battle and will help you filter the enemy back into the pass per our plan once the battle starts. Vabira states prowling back outside the tent entrance.

I focus my power using my mind-speak rune to latch onto Captain Mavin's mind. He has a strong mental barrier but I'm able to gently nudge him so he can open up himself.

My catchki scouts report that Jaarn is mobilizing and preparing for the next battle. We need to get the soldiers ready now. Also the catchki in the mountain are ready for our plan.

Solveig? Captain Mavin asks in response. *I'll never get used to this ... I'm up and I'll rouse the men. Thank you. See you in five.*

I cut off our connection and look to my sleeping mates. Cadoc's muscular toned stomach takes my attention for a moment and I can't help but run a hand over each ridge of his abdomen. *Damn. Wish I had more time to explore this ...* Cadoc's eyes snap open as my hand pauses above his waistline. One of his hands grabs mine and pushes it below the waist band of his pants and wraps my hand around his large and hard erection. We both moan in response.

"Now ... now ... You wouldn't leave a mate out, would you?" Vidarr's teasing voice cuts into our moment startling me to remove my hand from Cadoc's pants like a child caught with their hand in a cookie jar. Cadoc laughs and adjusts himself a bit before standing.

Vidarr smiles at me and pulls me down over top of him. He grabs my hips and pulls my core flush with his hardness. "*Vidarr,*" I state in an admonishing voice.

"*Fine!*" Vi says with a pout before rolling out from under me and standing.

"We need to get ready. Jaarn's army is readying for attack," I say quickly dressing. "I already notified Captain Mavin. So we need to get into position." We can hear sounds of men quietly preparing now and the camp being readied.

Cadoc dresses and arms himself swiftly then picks up my weapon harness and helps me put my katanas in place. Vidarr smiles at us chewing on a piece of travel jerky. Once we have everything, we head out into the organized chaos of an army prepping for battle.

I mentally call Sindari who trots over to me. Cadoc and Vidarr's horses are already saddled and ready at the tie line for the army's horses. We see Mavin shouting orders and mounting his own horse nearby. He nods to us and sees all the other leading officers ready as well. Our plan was already established at the last meeting so we all head out to our respective places with our quadrants.

After much deliberation, it was decided I should fight alongside Captain Mavin since I can communicate with everyone and pass along messages mentally to coordinate our army. It just didn't make sense for me to stay with Vi and Cadoc no matter what they said. Eventually, they did agree as long as the bond is open. Plus—we are hoping Ragnar arrives soon and can join me.

Mavin and I ride through the soldiers of our quadrant once we are in position in the central aspect of our army. Several men nod in respect but keep a wide berth between us. I'm not sure if it's because I'm their future queen or if it's the pony sized, catchki prowling next to me.

We don't have to wait long before the first enemy soldiers are seen. Our archers hidden in the trees wait for the signal from Mavin before releasing their strings. Next, shields go up and our men rush forward. Jaarn has many weapons in their arsenal and I'm glad we insisted on shields for everyone. Several crossbow bolts are released and embedded in those shields while those soldiers fall over from the harsh impact.

Once the initial release of those deadly weapons is over, catchki pour from the trees attacking with our men. Sindari races forward quivering with excitement.

Cak-cak. Cak-cak. Cak-cak. Tyr's call rings out through the forest before he dives into the face of man coming at me.

Thanks, friend. Keep an eye on our backs, I mentally project to him but don't have the time to wait for a response as I engage in battle.

Throwing a dagger into the eye of a man to my right, I nudge Sindari forward before the dead man falls over, plucking the dagger out of him. I only have so many and hate to waste them. It gets thrown immediately again and I fail to retrieve it this time when another man attacks from Sindari's flank. I block his thrusting sword with a flick of my katana then kick my boot into his cheek. He curses and pulls a dagger while he recovers. He swipes his sword across my leg and shoves his dagger up hoping to catch me distracted. He doesn't realize I've been fighting since I was fourteen and his moves are basic. They're also rather slow when I utilize my agility rune.

The cut on my lower leg stings a bit but I can tell it's minor. Besides my healing rune is already pulling power to attend the area. I flick my second katana down at the man's wrist which is holding the dagger and cut straight through his wrist like its butter. My katanas are wickedly sharp and this man just learned how well I tend my weapons. He screams out in pain dropping his sword and falling to the ground cradling his severed wrist.

I sense two men approaching from behind me, and as they move closer I decide I may need to dismount to fight a bit more nimbly. One man swipes his sword forward hoping to take out Sindari's leg while the other thrusts up. I quickly backflip off Sindari's back using my power to speed my maneuver and land one of my boots on the man's sword who's trying to harm Sindari. His sword falls to the ground under my feet as I simultaneously block the other soldier's thrust. They both look shocked at how fast I took control of them. I start sparring rapidly with the man who attempted to skewer me before I twirl and efficiently slice his throat open. The other man subsequently got a sword to the gut. But just as I'm pulling my katana from his belly, I feel a jolt of pain in my left thigh forcing a grunt from my lips.

Something hit me with such force from behind that I fall forward into the ground face first. I can't stop the scream of pain that releases from me when I impact the ground. Shakily I reach down to probe my leg and see what hit me. A large metal bolt is running straight through my left thigh and oozing blood. Luckily it's not bleeding severely since it's lodged in there pretty snug, but when I hit the ground it pushed on the bolt shoving it backwards so the tip is closer to the skin.

I think I hear my mates yelling things through the bond at me, but I'm lost in a haze of pain for a moment unable to understand or reply to them.

I roll to my side in pain, ignoring the chaos going on in my head and try to gain back focus. I'm in the middle of a battle ground and there's men screaming everywhere with swords clashing around me. But as I compartmentalize my pain learned from years of abuse at the hands of Counselor Malphas, I snap back into awareness.

There's a loud roaring above which vibrates the ground I'm laying on. Then I smell it … fire. Burning flesh. Ashes. And next, I hear the screams of pain.

Ragnar? I mentally send through the mate bond connecting immediately with him. Unfortunately, he's filled with so much rage and anger that he can barely form a coherent thought nevertheless words. But I feel him approaching.

I look around and see the area cleared of men. Or—at least one's who are alive. Several men are running away from me and in another second I understand why.

A large thick cloud of smoke and shadow drops in front of me and unfurls into a beast of a man. Ragnar stomps towards me in all his raging glory. He's shirtless showcasing his silver runes and wearing black pants with at least ten sharp weapons attached to his body. His black hair is similar to how I last styled it. Shaved on the sides with an intricate warrior braid down the center of his scalp. But his eyes … they're glowing golden orbs of wrath staring straight at me.

Ragnar? I mentally ask again. *You look … damn good. I missed you, mate.*

Little warrior, who harmed you? he mentally roars while his teeth are clenched so tight in anger I worry he may lose one. *I will bathe in his blood … roll in his ashes before tearing his limbs from his body…*

I clear my throat at how inappropriately aroused I get from his words. *Wait…* I think on his words and chuckle before groaning in pain from the movement in my leg. *I think your torture is out of order.* Then I pant a bit in pain and keep rambling since it might help distract me. *You should first—tear his limbs. Then bathe. And lastly burn him before your territorial rolling.*

Do not mock me, my Maseeri! Ragnar grits out but I see a tiny flicker of his lips twitching in amusement before he looks angry and serious again. *I missed you. Let me tend to you,* Ragnar says kneeling down next to me on the ground and smoothing my hair gently back from my sweaty face.

"I guess I can let you …" I say out loud losing my focus.

He pushes a hand to the center of my chest forcing me to lay back as he assesses my leg.

"… just this once."

"You will lay still while I heal you. It is killing me to see and feel you in pain and your other mates are panicking," he says sending me comfort through our bond. Ripping my pants open further, he then probes around the bolt making me flinch. "I need to remove this metal arrow. It's hit a blood vessel and I'll need to focus my healing immediately on the area once it's removed. First though, I'm going to use my fire to melt the end off or the barbs will tear your muscles when I pull."

Fuck, this is going to hurt. Badly. Taking a deep breath, I nod my head when ready.

You are very brave, little warrior, Ragnar says looking me in the eye. Then he reaches a hand and wraps it around the back of the bolt. I feel a tiny bit of heat through the metal but next it's a slight shift in the bolt as he pinches off the end of it. *One second to let it cool before I pull it.*

I take another deep breath and dig my hands into the dirt nearby bracing myself. Without warning, Ragnar pulls the tapered bolt from the front of my thigh. My mouth opens in a scream of agony but I manage to hold onto consciousness.

Solveig! What happened? Cadoc yells through the bond angrily.

Where are you?! I feel your pain, Vidarr shouts anxiously finally getting through to me as I hold onto my bonds for comfort.

It's hard for a moment to respond and when I do it's more of a pathetic whimper from the pain. *Bolt. To. The. Leg,* I quietly grunt out.

Ragnar is silent as he works his healing power through our mate bond. I'm lucky he's the one to find me since he's the only one of my mates able to heal me. He once told me weeks ago that Drakonian mates can heal one another and it's a special blessing they share through their mate bond. They can also share energy when running low.

Fucking what did you just say? Vi mentally yells making me cringe. *I'm coming to you…just hold on.*

Solveig, stay awake. Stay with us mentally so we can find you … I'm a bit in a bind so I'll cover for Vidarr to slip away … Cadoc says grunting mentally in exertion.

No. I'll come to you soon. Hold the line. It's more important! I reply feeling tired but the pain is significantly improved. *Ragnar is here. He found me and is healing me.*

Oh, thank Faktirnor, because we're losing ground over here, Cadoc says as I feel a small injury to his left arm through the bond.

Alright. Don't worry, sunshine. I'll watch Ca-dick's back.

I *feel* more than hear Cadoc's grunt of annoyance in response to Vidarr's teasing words.

My body goes lax as Ragnar finishes his healing and sits back on his feet. He looks more tired but smiles affectionately at me. I sit up and scramble into his lap wrapping my arms around his neck and kissing him. His hands smooth over my back and tug my long braid so he can maintain control of our affection.

"Thank you, Ragi," I say before placing a hand on his shirtless chest and pushing a small amount of energy into him. He's likely to need it more than me. "Now, we need to get going and finish this war."

His fatigue fades at bit at my transfer of energy and he gives me a reproachful look. I can feel he doesn't like taking anything from me since he's always trying to provide selflessly to me.

"You are riding with me. I'll finish this war," Ragnar says staring directly into my eyes before he smirks cockily. "That is … if my sister and Tempest haven't already …"

I smirk back and stand up. "I can't wait …"

Ragnar magically disappears into swirling smoke and in his place is a large, fierce black dragon with his characteristic silver tattoos. He puffs a bit of warm smoke through his nostrils that instantly flows over my body. Waving a hand to waft the smoke away from my eyes, I walk forward and run a hand over his scaled snout causing him to rumble in pleasure. His shoulder drops and his leg stretches out allowing me to climb up and mount behind his large, ridged spine.

He takes off immediately to the sky avoiding branches on his way up thankfully. I mentally focus on Captain Mavin searching for him. Once I locate him not far from us, I open communication and say, *Mavin … I was injured but am better now. Ragnar and I are above you. Pull the men back to our line of defense and we can "remove" some of the enemy.*

Solveig! Thank Faktirnor! I was worried, Mavin replies. *We're losing ground and men. It's too hard to retreat since we're scattered. I think Jaarn has penetrated our defenses to the south. Cadoc's men are barely holding on …*

Just as he finished, we hear a roar from the north and see a large cloud of smoke and fire rise into the sky. *That's Tempest and my sister.* Ragnar says to me proudly. I can see a flash of red in the sky and rain clouds being pulled near there.

Since the north seems to be doing well, we decide to head towards the south and fix the broken defenses there. A few minutes later, I see a sight for sore eyes.

Mavin! Our soldiers from the south are here! I yell excitedly through the connection I kept open.

Good, he grunts out. *Fix that mess down there and then help Prince Cadoc. We're managing fine at my quadrant now that your catchki have been assisting.*

I close our connection and mentally nudge Ragnar towards our men. I've never met the Captain leading the other half of our army so I can't form a connection. Ragnar lands nearby and I hop off telling him to wait. Many of the Laevarian soldiers are shouting and pointing in fright seeing a legend in their midst.

Running towards them, I see a large man on a horse ride over. He pulls his sword making Ragnar roar in warning before he gets a determined expression on his face. I'm guessing this is the man I'm looking for.

"Captain! Hold your weapon unless you want to anger my mate." I shout holding my hands up. His horse slows to a stop ten feet from me but he doesn't sheathe his sword. "We don't have time … in about a minute Jaarnian soldiers are going to spill from that tree line."

"Who. Are. You?" Captain Garr calmly yells.

"Princess Solveig Andraevian heir to the Laevarian throne and future queen of Elaria. Now, heed my words since I've already spoken with Captain Mavin," I say getting frustrated and antsy. "My mate and I will clear some of the soldiers then I'll leave the rest to you. Head towards the central part of the forest coming up from the south. I need to assist the next quadrant. We're outnumbered but now that you've arrived we can end this war."

He gets a shocked and then thoughtful expression on his face before saying, "Forgive me, princess. You—you don't exactly look …" He hesitates and then shaking his head continues, "We'll follow your lead and clear out the vermin in your footsteps." Then with a nod, he turns his horse around and start yelling out orders to his men. They start mobilizing and steadily march towards the tree line.

Running, I leap onto Ragnar's waiting leg and he flings me into the air somehow causing me to land with a grunt on his back. *If I had landed one inch forward, I would have gotten a sharp ridge to my*—I say scolding Ragnar for throwing me around. He just chuckles in a raspy deep voice.

I share my thoughts with Ragnar on using his fire to both peripheral regions so that the Jaarnian soldiers funnel between the dragon fire towards our awaiting army. He readily agrees and carefully lights the forest on fire in a line on both sides of the Jaarnian army. I worry about the forest spreading the fire, but Ragnar reassures me that he can control his flames from spreading any further. The enemy soldiers predictably start running into our trap and meet an army prepared for battle.

Now that I feel Captain Garr has the south well in hand, I ask Ragnar, *Lets head towards Cadoc and Vidarr. I can feel their fatigue and injuries.*

As you wish, my Maseeri. I will follow the bond to my mate-brothers, Ragnar replies flying slightly more north of us into the southeastern aspect of the battle.

We both feel them just ahead but can't see as much given the thicker tree coverage. Ragnar dives carefully down and lands in a puff of smoke catching me simultaneously from the air.

"Show off," I mutter as he smugly looks at me. We take off running and I hear the *schnick* of metal as he unsheathes his sword. Pulling my katanas at the same time, I smile over at him with a blood thirsty look.

The next few minutes we spend piling up bodies around us as we make progress towards my mates. I feel the mate bond thrum from our closer proximity before I see them. I see Cadoc stumble in clear exhaustion just as two men go in at once for a fatal blow. I panic unnecessarily as Ragnar throws a dagger into one of their necks and Cadoc blocks the other's sword.

Ragnar immediately traverses to Cadoc's side and defends his back while he finishes his current opponent. Meanwhile, I set my eyes on Vidarr knowing Cadoc is safe.

Vidarr is handling himself well against two men, but I can't tell if he's injured given his appearance. The man looks like pure danger and lethal sin with his blood covered, tattooed skin while he skillfully battles with his dual swords. Focusing down our mate bond, I can tell most of his injuries are superficial but his energy is depleting.

I slip under the guard of one of the men he's battling and cut open the soldier's calf as I place my back against Vidarr's. I can feel his amusement and fond thoughts at my position through our bond. In the past, we always liked to spar back to back against groups of adversaries and have even practiced a few acrobatic moves from this position when fighting. Sending him thoughts of one of those moves, he thrusts his sword forward into his opponent bending at the waist and holding his position. I move in tandem with him and bend backwards over his spine as I kick out my boot and knock my opponent's sword away. Then I spring forward with a twist to the side as my braid circles around in the air and I decapitate the soldier in front of me with my katana.

"Thank Valirr you didn't perform that move with me, Solveig, or I'd be lacking a head as well …" Cadoc says off to the side watching us. Ragnar is crouched down cleaning his sword on a body in front of him but still watching me intensely with … heat in his eyes.

Panting for breath, I reply with a teasing tilt of my lips, "Don't worry you'd have the more important one still."

No one says anything for a second before they all bust out into laughter. I hear a few Laevarian soldiers chuckle as well nearby.

"Looks like we're under control here for the moment," Vidarr says looking around as he places an arm across my shoulders. I scout the area as well and see only our soldiers nearby. Sounds of battle still rage to the north and south of us.

"Ragnar …" I say hesitating.

"I'll go. But you have to promise to stay with your mates," Ragnar says in a no nonsense tone. "This war will be finished when I see you next, little warrior."

"I promise." As I reply, Ragnar shifts into his dragon form and takes off into the sky.

I reach out to Cadoc and push some of my healing power into him. A few cuts and bruises are pulled into me while Cadoc stands up a bit straighter showing less exhaustion than a moment ago. I plop down for a moment on a nearby log and rest while my healing rune burns on my back. The cuts and bruises are gone a few minutes later but I'm exhausted again. Cadoc and Vidarr's horses are nearby so we mount and head further north into the next quadrant of our army. The Laevarian soldiers join us ready to end this.

Roaring and fire fill the sky as our Drakoni finish the battle. We make it to the next section of our army just as they gain control.

Your enemies are retreating through the pass. Well … at least what is left of them, Ragnar says to me through the bond in a satisfied voice. *Should I collapse it onto them? Or, I could simply burn them to ashes as they bottleneck themselves in there …*

Smiling, I relay his words to my mates and out loud to our soldiers before I reply, *No. Let them run. I'll have the catchki enjoy their entails. My friend Vabira promised me they would guard the pass afterwards.*

I see another flash of fire and then an another fierce roar. It's not Ragnar now. That one belonged to his sister, my friend Ara. I send relief and gratefulness to my mates through the bond who respond with affection.

At some point in finishing off any Jaarnian stragglers, I find Sindari and rest my tired legs as I ride back with my mates. We make it back to the location of our prior camp and are awarded with cheers from the soldiers already there. Several catchki are resting and licking wounds while men are starting to set up more tents and campfires. I can tell tonight will be a night of rest and celebration for Laevaris.

When I dismount Sindari, I'm swept up into large arms causing me to tense up in defense before I realize who's embracing me.

"You did it, Solveig. I'm so proud of you … my Queen," Captain Mavin says with a tired smile. His eyes are shining with pride as he gazes down at me and I suddenly feel a lump forming in my throat. I can't remember Mavin ever hugging me before… It's usually a firm pat on the back from the stern captain. So, this feels especially profound.

"*We* did it," I say squeezing him back. "I'm glad you made it through." Then I notice blood soaking his shirt and leaking onto my hands behind his back. Before he can protest, I pulls the hem of his shirt up his back a little and see a small stab wound. Likely from a light sword but it seems to have most gone through the muscle there. I put my hand over the wound without thinking and draw on my power. I have some left and push my healing power into him. He grunts in surprise and then looks at me with awe.

"Praise Valirr! You healed me!" Mavin says twisting his back to test his wound a bit. "Thank you. Looks like I'll live to see another day."

"Of course, Mavin. I'll always heal you," I say while nervously patting him on the shoulder. "You—you're important to me … not just as my general, you know? But, like a growly, stern father-like figure. Or maybe uncle?" I scratch my head a bit in thought on how our relationship is.

He chuckles with a twinkle in his eye. "Growly, huh? I guess I can see that. If you had to deal with all these exasperating young recruits all the time, you would be *growly* too!" He shakes his head, pats my shoulder like he usually does and walks off to get some rest.

I take a step to head towards my mates and can't help but wince a bit at the wound in the side of my back from healing Mavin. Cadoc sees my wince of pain and steps forward swooping me up into his arms and carrying me towards a tent that's just being raised.

"You healed him didn't you?" Cadoc whispers into my ear. I tiredly nod my head into his chest. "Can you take any energy from me? Let me help you?"

I think about his question for a moment. I don't know why I didn't think to do that before. He may not be able to heal me like my Drakonian mate, but technically Cadoc and any of my other mates should be able to give me some energy.

"I'll be fine, Cad," I say as he lays me down on some blankets. "I'm just tired and I can feel it slowly knitting back together. Some food and water would be good though…"

"Fine. I can do that. But I'm not leaving you unprotected until someone else is here and you promised Ragnar."

I huff out a breath in response while he reaches around me and unbuckles my weapon harness. He slowly removes everything and then removes my boots which allows me to rest back easier.

Vabira and her mates peek their heads in our tent and Cadoc nearly falls over in fright. He finds his composure quickly though while Vabira makes her raspy crackling noise in amusement.

Solveig. All the living, two-legged enemies are within the pass leaving our lands. I still have a few of my clan scouting the areas and my cousin assures me her clan will guard the pass.

Thank you, Vabira. Laevaris owes the catchki a great debt. You are welcome anywhere in Laevaris and I will spread the word of our alliance together so you may roam freely in our kingdom.

She bows her large cat like head in acknowledgement before saying, *I only require the last part of our deal.*

I remember, I say looking her over and wondering what she'd look like in her human form.

Good, make sure you keep it that way, Vabira says sashaying her graceful body out of the tent. *I'll meet you in Elaria then.*

CHAPTER
Forty-Five

SOLVEIG

"What was that all about?" Cadoc curiously asks after Vabira leaves.

"She was just saying goodbye and reminding me of promises made."

He grunts in response and pulls his shirt over his head drawing my hungry eyes down his perfectly sculpted chest to a tapered waist. *Holy fuck …*

Cadoc looks over his shoulder at me with a smug look. But we're interrupted when we hear cheering outside the tent from the soldiers. He sticks his head out and yells in alarm from nearly hitting his head with Vidarr's as he tries to enter.

"The dragons have arrived! Looks like the army is grateful to have them on our side. Don't know why we didn't get as loud of a reception," Vidarr says looking around the tent and noticing Cadoc's missing shirt. "Hmm … I want to be included in this man feast for you, sunshine. Are we celebrating?" Vi whips his shirt off and somehow manages to give me a look that's both teasing and innocent at the same time.

I laugh and even Cadoc can't hold in his amused chuckle before saying, "Now that you're here, I'm going to grab some food and water. Stay here with her, *Vi-daft.*"

Cadoc goes to step out of the tent but Vidarr grabs his arm and raises an eyebrow while I try to smother a laugh. "Did you just—try to make a joke?" Vi says smiling while Cadoc looks … embarrassed? "Vi-*daft* … huh … not the best insult. Mine is still better … *Ca-dick.*" A huff of a suppressed chuckle slips past my lips as Vi pushes Cadoc out of the tent laughing. They may insult each other verbally, but I can feel their amusement and brotherly camaraderie through the bond which makes a warm feeling grow inside of me. It's a feeling like I'm home. With them—*my mates.*

A soldier coughs outside our tent before Vidarr grabs a water jug and bowl from him. We spend the next few minutes cleaning ourselves of blood and dirt. Cadoc joins us with bowls of stew recently off the fire and we all sit down in silence recharging. I'm able to borrow an extra shirt from Vidarr that he brought in his bag so I probably look ridiculous sitting in an oversized shirt but I'm too tired to care. It's clean and that's all that matters. I just wish Jorah's comforting presence was here to brush my tangled hair out and that Kaeden was here to hold me. After we finish our meal, Ragnar impatiently enters the tent and stalks over to me.

He picks me right up and plops me back on his lap before planting his face in the hair behind my ear and scenting me. I realize he's all clean now and in new clothes smelling like smoke and the outdoors.

"Sorry it took me a while to get back to you, my mate," Ragnar softly says nuzzling my neck now. "I needed to hunt and eat after expending all that energy. My sister and Tempest are resting now but can join us later."

I can feel the burning gazes of Cadoc and Vidarr sitting across from us. Ragnar's hands grip my hips sitting on his lap, and I feel his hardness grow underneath me. Wetness pools immediately between my legs in response and I realize I'm suddenly hungry for something different now.

Reflexively, my legs part a tiny amount as his hands clench the material of the shirt resting at my hips. The hem line of my shirt rides up just enough to expose some of my arousal to my other mates. I'm naked underneath since I have no fresh underwear after leaving my bag back in Falal in my haste to travel here. Cadoc and Vidarr's eyes immediately lower to the area and heat enters their eyes as the sexual tension in the room escalates.

I can hear Ragnar sniff the air next to me as a rumbling starts in his chest. I can feel the vibrations of it all the way from my back laying against him to my pussy.

"I can scent your arousal, my Maseeri," Ragnar growls out as he slides his hands from my hips to the inside of my thighs. "You are needing your mates." He tightens his grip on my inner thighs and pulling back spreads my legs further and exposes me more to my mates' perusal.

"Ah … *fuck.* Sunshine. You're so beautiful," Vi says running a hand through his messy hair on top before stripping his remaining clothes quickly. "Lay back against your dragon and let me make you feel good."

Ragnar is moving his thumbs in small circles at the tops of my inner thighs and driving me insane at this point.

"Stunning, exotic, and sexy … " Cadoc whispers kneeling in front of me. "Let us see all of you."

"I agree with my mate-brothers. Let us see all of our beautiful mate." Ragnar says sliding his hands up my body and pulling the loose shirt over my head. Ragnar slides me down a bit off his lap so I'm leaning backwards on his chest while he holds my legs apart. All my mates look at one another as some unspoken conversation occurs that I'm not privy too. *My mates are ganging up on me… Well, I suppose it's for a good cause. No objection here.*

I don't have time to voice a question before Vidarr's mouth is licking up my slit and his flat tongue lands directly on my clit. My body arches back pushing my hips forward but Ragnar holds firm. Cadoc's hands are wandering over my body reverently and end up cupping my heavy breasts. He leans in and sucks the nearest nipple into his mouth and I cry out in pleasure finding release so quickly.

As I lay there in Ragnar's hold after my surprisingly rapid orgasm, I notice one of Ragnar's hands has reached between us and released his engorged cock from his pants. It's standing tall and firm against my back so I reach backwards trying to help him, but he snaps, "No touching, not yet. You will do as we say while we bring you pleasure, mate." He pauses but Vidarr and Cadoc don't relinquish their focus on my body. "You scared me today and as a Drakonian warrior who doesn't fear anything, it was disconcerting to realize the one thing that could bring me to my knees. Losing you … it would literally kill me. So, I ask you to lay there and let us worship this body now. Grateful that we are together for another turning of the sun."

I turn my head and see the sincerity in his eyes. Ragnar was *scared* today when I was laying there bleeding on the ground. I kiss him passionately and moan into his mouth when Vidarr forces his tongue into my wet pussy. Cadoc tweaks my nipple for attention making me gasp before he picks me up off Ragnar as our lips break apart.

Cadoc lifts me easily in his hands as if I'm light as a leaf before he falls backwards and slowly impales me on his hard and slightly curved cock.

"*Oh*, Sol. *Bless Fallia*! You feel so good," Cadoc says groaning while I take his cock into my pussy all the way until our hips meet. "Ride me, my fierce warrior."

I eagerly follow orders *this* time. Heavy breathing and skin hitting skin are the only sounds in our tent for a while.

Opening my eyes which must have closed for a moment, I see Ragnar's massive cock in my line of sight. He gives me a predatory smile before he says in a commanding raspy voice, "You're doing well. Now open those lips and suck my cock while you ride my mate-brother." I again gladly follow orders taking his cock in my mouth. Ragnar takes control and slides a hand through my hair holding me still once he's fully seated in my throat. My eyes tear up and I'm get close to the edge of coming on Cadoc before Ragi withdraws from my throat and I gasp in some air. Him and Cadoc slow down and time they're thrusting together making me frustrated … *I'm so close!*

I've got you, sunshine. I once told you that I'd claim this ass … I hear Vidarr's heavily aroused voice in my mind as I feel his probing fingers slide from my wet pussy to an area of my privates that's never been fully claimed. Initially, I tense up but when he only inserts one slick finger, I moan and push back. Jorah's explored this area before with his fingers but I've never had more. I've also never been with three men at once… intimately. Vi reaches his other hand forward and pinches my clit throwing me into an explosion of pleasure. I orgasm so hard, I nearly collapse but Ragnar's hold on my hair keeps me up.

Vidarr doesn't let up though and pushes two fingers inside my ass while Cadoc slowly thrusts in and out of me. Ragnar eases up on my mouth a bit since I'm breathing so heavily and says, "Easy, mate. Relax back into it. Trust your mates to take care of you."

I take a deep breath and relax. Vidarr is palming one cheek and spreading me open. I feel his cock now against my ass before he says, "Give me a second, Cad …"

In my haze of pleasure, I see Cadoc nod below me before I feel him pull all the way out of me. His teeth grit and he says, "Hurry, I'm close. She feels too damn good."

Then I feel Vidarr enter my dripping wet pussy from behind before he pulls out again and rests it against my ass. His tip pushes in slightly and I stiffen up before forcing myself to relax and push back. It helps and once he's further inside of me, I start to feel the pleasure.

Vidarr must feel it too because he mutters into my head, *Fuck. Fuck. Fuck. Better than I ever imagined. Always wanted to claim this ass. That's it, sunshine … knew you'd like it.*

Ragnar and Cadoc groan as well as the mate bond connection between us floods open and my pleasure is released through them. Cadoc pushes his cock back inside my pussy and I start to pant at the fullness. Vidarr takes control gripping my hips and alternating his movement with Cadoc. Ragnar is growling now watching them dominate my body and I can feel his need through our bond. Now, that the initial shock has resolved and I've adjusted to the fullness I feel my third release building. Ragnar thrusts his needy cock back into my mouth on my next gasp but holds me still using my hair gently. He lets Vidarr's movements create friction between us.

Cadoc is the first to find his release below me and yells out my name reverently before licking and sucking a nipple into his mouth. Vidarr must feel me on the edge of that blissful cliff because he reaches around and rubs a callused thumb on my clit pushing me off into a forceful orgasm that makes me clench around him. I scream my release and probably would've woken half the camp if not for Ragnar's huge cock between my lips. The vibration, though, of my release sets him off and he fills my mouth with his cum. I try my best to swallow most of it down.

Vidarr thrusts … two … three more times before he shouts out my name and slumps forward over my back. Once his cock softens, he withdraws and rolls to the side. We all lay sprawled out on the blankets finding our breaths in silence while I listen to their combined heavy breathing in peaceful contentedness.

I look around at each of my mates and see their eyes closed with relaxed facial expressions that I've only seen present when asleep. Smiling softly down at them as I lean on my elbows from across Cadoc's body, I can feel each one of them touching me somewhere making our mate bond hum in happiness. My mates must be truly exhausted from today. I can't help but feel smug though, when I think on how *I* brought them all pleasure. At. The. Same. Time. Normally, feelings of inadequacy and past insecurities would rise at moments like this which Malphas ingrained into me.

"You're a whore, princess. A dirty disrespectful whore …"

But instead of feeling that insecurity and having self-deprecating thoughts, I feel confident and strong. These men were brought to their knees to pleasure me. It wasn't a moment of just lust but love. They weren't there to humiliate or forcibly dominate me. It was an act of our love and reassurance that I'm still alive after my nearly fatal injury.

A yawn slips out of my lips and my eyes droop, closing against my will. My last thought before sleep is … *damn, I love my mates. I'll never have to be alone ever again or handle my past by myself.* It's in that moment of self-reflection that I feel something dark and tight in my chest release just before I relax into sleep.

CHAPTER
Forty-Six

SOLVEIG

O ver a week later, I stand side by side with my mates in the Elaritian Forest. We used some of that time to clean up and mourn the dead. Then travel back to Falal with our army and handle the multitude of issues involving the ruling of an entire kingdom. I also spent nearly an entire day spending time with my absent mates from the battle, Jorah, and Kaeden. They were dismayed to have been left behind but eager to let me make it up to them.

Jorah, through his research, was able to create a mixture of dry materials to counter the explosive toxic liquid that Jaarn uses in its projectiles. Even though Jaarn never reached our capital city, it was decided by the counsel and myself that we should coat the city walls and castle wall in Jorah's dry mixture. This way if they ever attack again, their explosives will be rendered useless on contact. We're lucky they couldn't use catapults or any explosives in the forest given the difficult location of the battle. If we fought at the city walls, I'm sure it would have been different. Jorah was also able to replicate the strength of some of their weapons in working with his friend Tavian, a local blacksmith. So, he felt his time was well spent and I had to agree. If Jaarn comes for us again, we'll be ready.

Kaeden, on the other hand, was extremely agitated and restless within our city walls being away from me. He practically tackled me in his eagerness to hold me when I arrived in Falal. His wound from the assassins was mostly healed, but I still let a trickle of my healing power flow into him even though he admonished me afterwards. But once I told him I needed him in top condition for that night, his argument magically disappeared.

After our reunion and handling the affairs of the kingdom, I was quietly coronated Queen of Laevaris the very next day with the council members as witness. Liv, Marion, Isa, and Sigurd as well as several other servants and soldiers gathered to be present in support. My mates all stood beside me and were recorded as ruling consorts even though in truth being mates is a far more important position. Each of my mates was given a position of power in the kingdom with their own responsibilities to help me in my rule. We didn't want to wait any longer on the coronation given all the recent events and since our kingdom is still in a period of rebirth. The castle and parts of the city are still being rebuilt but its people are flourishing! I've also totally restructured many of the ruling nobility in the kingdom, sick of their political under dealings. Our hope is to have a celebration for the coronation and our kingdom's rebirth at a future time and invite all the surrounding kingdoms. Well—all except for Jaarn.

"Are you ready, granddaughter?" Elder Aren says with a soft smile walking up to me which brings me back to my current surroundings. "I think our people are getting restless being so close to Elaria."

"I'm ready and excited …" I say before looking around at the crowd of Elarians all waiting to travel the last leg of our journey. "Where's my father?"

"Right here, Solveig," King Lochlann says stepping through a few people that bow at the waist placing a fist over their hearts in deference. "Everyone is excited and hopeful. I just hope this is truly the end."

My father stands tall and strong now after having built up his muscles through hard work after his years in the Mortgaard slave camp. He has a royal presence that the other Elarians instinctively recognize by backing away and showing their deference. His dark brown, shoulder-length hair is braided back half way in the traditional Elarian warrior style. Our features are so similar from our pointed ears, dark brown hair, sharp facial structure, and lean bodies that it's nearly impossible to mistake our familial relation. However when his intense green eyes turn to look at me, it reminds me of the one feature we don't share and instead makes me think of Mother.

I can feel the anxiety of the upcoming day hit me suddenly and the pressure that goes with it. *What if the curse doesn't lift when we step in Elaria. What if that Essent lied to us? What if I'm not who they say I am?*

My thoughts spiral into a near panic attack when I get a slight whiff of lavender in the forest air. It brings my anxiety to a standstill as I'm reminded again of my mother. It was a scent that I always associated with her since she had these lavender bushes just below her window that I could always smell in her presence. Her frequent mantra suddenly pops into my mind, *Be calm and know yourself.*

I take a deep breath and center myself. My anxiety and self-doubt slowly disappear as I chant the words. I feel Jorah squeeze my hand and affection pours through my mate bonds.

"It's not the end, Father," I reply to him after a brief pause and a smile. "It's the beginning … Come on, I'm done waiting."

A few hours later, we ride through the forest and come upon the edge of Elaria. There's an invisible barrier and a sickening feeling of doom surrounding the place. But as I focus closing my eyes, underneath it all, I feel… power and energy. Elaria is our center for power and necessary to our future as a people and to the Drakoni even though they are few.

Ragnar and I dismount our horses and walk hand in hand toward the barrier. The Elarian scouts stand near it with a green tinge to their faces and clenched jaws in discomfort. A feeling of sickness and death fills me but when I clasp hands with my Drakonian mate, it's relieved some. I can't see a barrier physically but I can *feel* it just like the other Elarians here. My other mates stay mounted on their horses looking around confused and clearly unaffected by the curse's aura of doom. Instead, they appear as if they're unsure why they're here. Kaeden is obviously feeling similar to his fellow Elarians but gives me a look of trust and love that imparts me with some of his strength.

I look to Ragnar who nods his head and squeezes my hand in support. We walk through the barrier, and I feel like I might lose the battle not to regurgitate my breakfast. It's *that* uncomfortable. Ragnar's determined and serious face doesn't give an inkling to what he's feeling, but it takes only a few more steps before I notice a change.

A stone path can be felt under my booted feet leading away through the trees and the sound of rushing water ahead. Similar to when my ears pop from the release of pressure as I fly into the sky on Ragnar's back, the barrier drops with a release of the discomfort and my body fills with a feeling of contentedness. Of *home*.

Blinking my eyes in surprise and trying to clear the sudden tears in them, I look over at the rapture in Ragnar's expression. His smile is the most uninhibited one I've ever seen except for the time right after we mated. It involves nearly his entire face and he lets out a loud laugh of pleasure.

All the Elarians behind us suddenly cheer in joy. Some falling to their knees openly sobbing in happiness while others are jumping up and down or seeking the affections of their own mates. My other mates join us and we all embrace one another in joy and relief that our hardships were not in vain.

"That was the strangest feeling I've ever had …" Vidarr says into our small group.

"What do you mean?" I ask with confusion.

Instead of Vidarr replying, Jorah interrupts in his an inquisitive voice, "He means…it felt like we didn't know why we were here. It was like an unreasonable confusion. An unattainable understanding. I knew there was a reason but couldn't remember and it just slipped away every time I tried to figure it out.

"I also felt like we should turn around and leave. Like … we should head the other direction." Cadoc interjects.

"It was the curse. It affects you differently since you aren't Elarian or Drakoni," Ragnar says throwing his arms around Cadoc and Jorah and surprising us all in his open display of brotherly affection and joy. He's never this relaxed and happy so it's a strange change in his demeanor but not a bad one.

"Yeah, it was uncomfortable and sickening for the rest of us," Kaeden says threading one of his hands with mine and smiling at me in pride. "Come on let's go. I need see my homeland again. It's been too long. And tonight … we're bathing under the magically imbued warm waters of the Kevaril Waterfall."

I don't have much time to ask him what he's talking about before I'm pulled forward down the stone path towards Elaria. My father and grandfather join us smiling happily.

"I knew you could find a way, granddaughter," Elder Aren says smiling fondly at me before closing his eyes and stepping further ahead as if he could walk this path blindfolded.

"I'm proud of you. I should have never had any doubt. You're our salvation and hope, Solveig," my father states reaching over and squeezing my shoulder in affection. "It's been an honor getting to know you and I know your mother is proud too. You will make a great Elarian queen one day. I just need to show you our way …" When I look away from his happy face and proud gaze, my jaw drops in amazement. "Welcome home, daughter."

King Lochlann walks away into Elaria through the crowd of Elarians all congratulating him and including him in their talk of celebrating.

My eyes take in a beautiful white sandstone castle standing adjacent to a massive waterfall falling from between two rocky cliffs in front of a small mountain. The water is crystal clear and … steaming? It ends up pooling into a large reflective lake before the distant part of it trickles into a tributary that must lead to a river. The surrounding land is vibrant and luscious in growth with trees interposed in the city and surrounding the entire area. The city is mix of treehouses, log structures and dwellings made up of a similar stone as the castle though its lighter gray in color. All of them blend naturally into the surrounding outdoors into a beautiful and peaceful place. Small Riverstone paths are laid out branching from the main road and lined with flowers in various places. It's almost unnatural how there's so much color in the center of the forest. Various colored flowers give the city a clean and attractive look against the nearby stone and I spot a flower that has become my favorite over the past month.

I reach down to pick one of the pretty dark purple flowers, but it unfurls before I can reach it. *A temptress flower!* I remember the name fondly from my time near Ragnar's lair. Magically blooming in front of my hand, the flower gives off a soft smell like a lilac and I decide to not tamper with such beauty. As I stand and start to walk a bit further, my footsteps or that little flower must magically set off a domino effect as all the flowers along the main street in Elaria bloom suddenly.

I look over at Ragnar in surprise and he simply smiles at me.

"Wow. So beautiful …" Vidarr says tucking one of the flowers into my hair. "It looks like Elaria is welcoming you home, sunshine."

CHAPTER
Forty-Seven

KAEDEN

Returning home to Elaria after so long is a surreal experience, it looks untouched and just as I remembered minus the bustling Elarians on its streets. It's a bit eerie seeing a perfectly kept but empty city. I think I'm still in a state of shock and disbelief that *my* mate is the one to have broken the curse and is responsible for our *now* promising future. I can't help but walk with pride knowing Solveig is my mate and hopefully the future mother of my children someday.

Although, I need to discuss and plan with my mate-brothers a formal bonding ceremony. It's an important and sacred ceremony for an Elarian and some of the older Elarians may not acknowledge our bond without it. Times are changing though given the recent war and rebirth of our people, but I still want to honor my mate with the traditional rite.

We've all just finished a simple meal consisting of agari fruit, bread, and a vegetable soup in the formal dining room of the castle. I missed the agari fruit's sweetness and the burst of energy that comes with its juice since it's only found growing in the

333

trees surrounding Elaria. Many Elarians harvest it and use the leather like outer skin for clothing and accessories since it comes in several shades of vibrant blue. It reminds me of Solveig's sapphire eyes.

As if she can feel my gaze, her attention focuses on me from across the table and I feel her foot slide up the inside of my leg making the corner of my mouth tilt up. She smiles at me while continuing to trail her foot up in a teasing manner but given the distance can't quite make it past my knee.

What are you thinking about, Kae? Solveig asks me through our bond. She's started shortening my name over the past week since we reunited and at first I wasn't sure about it. But now, I like the fondness and familiarity it gives off when she says it. If anyone else were to say it though, I'd have to say I'd hate it.

Just thinking about you and your stunning eyes. I reply and see her eyes take on a softer look.

Everyone is chatting now that our mid-day meal is over, and King Lochlann is telling a story to anyone who will listen. No one is aware of our silent communication but I see my mate-brothers occasionally looking over at Sol. She opens her mouth to say something but startles at an interruption near the door.

A beautiful tall, dark skinned woman with long silvery hair enters. She's wearing a thin simple sheath dress that hangs to her knees and looks hastily thrown on, but it's her powerful and strong aura that makes you take notice of her. Her golden eyes zero in on my mate and she prowls towards her with a graceful yet dangerous stride. My instincts tell me that this woman is dangerous even without a weapon.

Two men flank her and have unusual appearances with disheveled simple clothing. As the group approaches Solveig, I push my chair back and stand readying to defend my mate if needed. My mate-brothers must sense the predator in the room as well since they're all standing except for Jorah who appears intrigued rather than alarmed with a contemplative look on his face.

Just as I reach Solveig's side, my mate stands slowly and shifts the weight of her stance as a true warrior would in preparation of a fight. Cadoc and Ragnar step forward in front of our mate defensively while Sol mutters under her breath, "Damn overbearing, protective mates."

Everyone is surprised though when the exotic woman, instead of attacking, crouches down half way and leans forward onto her spread fingertips of one hand before nodding her head in what appears to be a greeting of respect.

Solveig tilts her head in confusion before nodding back. She then shoves Ragnar and Cadoc out of her way and stares the woman down with a bewildered look.

"Do I know you?" she asks the woman. "No … I would remember someone like you …"

The dark skinned woman stands and starts to laugh while the lean warriors behind her share a look and chuckle with her. Seems as if we're all part of some inside joke that I can't for the life of me understand.

Elder Aren is suddenly at our side and smiling widely. He nods his head respectfully then says to the newcomer, "Welcome. The hunt was long but the bounty is plentiful. It has been a long time since I've seen you, Vabira Graystripe."

The woman nods back and says in a scratchy deep voice, "Thank you, Elder. The bounty is truly plentiful. All because of your grand-kit." Vabira then turns her gaze on Solveig and I see recognition in my mate's eyes. "I shouldn't be surprised you remember me or the catchki's formal greeting, Aren. It is strange to be back in this two-legged form."

"*Vabira?*" Solveig softly says in shock as she looks Vabira up and down with amazement. "You shifted! It worked …" Before Vabira can respond, Solveig throws herself at the woman and wraps her in hug.

Vabira lets out a deep purring and returns the embrace while she rubs her face along the top of my mate's head. Ragnar's chest starts to rumble as well at their familiarity but in one of warning. I guess the shifters are a bit threatened by each other.

"Yes, you kept your promise to me so I came to see you," Vabira rasps with a crackling sound as she steps back. "Calm your Drakonian mate, little one. I suppose he doesn't like me scenting you, even if it's only as a mother would her kittchkins." Solveig steps back into Ragnar's chest as he wraps his arms around her and rubs his own face in her neck. Shifters can be very territorial when it comes to their mates.

"Of course I would keep my promise!" Sol says with affront then looks around at Vabira's mates. "You all look just as dangerous and yet beautiful in a lethal way as you do in your shifted form. Are these your mates?"

Vabira waves her hand and the men flanking her step forward puffing their chests out and standing straight. She wraps a hand around each man's upper arm possessively before saying, "Yes, you remember Euri and Tiguar?"

"The hunt was long but the bounty is plentiful, princess. I'm glad to see our dreams come to fruition," the one was light brown hair and serious eyes states.

"I'm glad to see you again, Solveig. Maybe you could come see our kittchkins soon," the other man named Tiguar with black hair says with an earnest and friendly smile. "They're nearly ready to leave our den."

Solveig greets both with a smile and says, "I would love to! I've never seen Catchki … kittchkins. Is your other mate with them?"

"Yes, Gaergi typically cares for and guards the kits while Euri and Tiguar are my warrior mates," Vabira says fondly. "You are welcome to visit our den anytime, though I will warn you to only wear clothing you aren't fond of since it will likely get torn. The kittchkins are still unruly and have poor control over their claws." Tiguar rolls his eyes and nods his head in agreement.

"Well met, Vabira Graystripe." King Lochlann walks up and nods his head in respect while she crouches down and balances forward on her fingertips again in greeting.

"King Lochlann, well met," Vabira replies, standing up again. "I remember you as a boy and I'm happy to see you back in Elaria safely. The bounty is plentiful and you must be proud of your kit."

"Where is your den and catchki clan located now?" Lochlann asks. "It has been a long time since I've visited and I'm sure over the years it has changed."

"Yes. We *were* located in the forest between the human city of Falal and Elaria, but I'm moving our clan deeper into the forest to reside just east of Elaria if that is acceptable to you. Now that the curse is lifted, our fertility should increase and we'd like to be closer to the healing waters of Lake Prosper to the east."

King Lochlann nods thoughtfully and runs his thumb over his chin before saying, "I accept and think those lands will suite you well. It will help trade between our people for you to be located closer to Elaria."

Eventually, Vabira and her mates take their leave excited to begin the relocation of their Catchki clan while we all separate seeking out some rest before the evening celebration. Elaria will be busy tonight given our home-coming. Many are planning a feast and bringing out vintage wines that were stored in the cellars beneath the city.

I wave to Elder Aren and King Lochlann before they leave indicating I'd like to speak with them. Mentally, I ask my mate-brothers to stay for a moment and speak with me privately away from our mate.

"Are you coming, Kae?" Solveig asks me tugging on my arm. "I don't know where I'm going in this castle and haven't a clue on where our room will be."

I look over her delicate and beautiful face that is lined with exhaustion before I tuck a piece of hair behind her pointed ear. Then as she shivers at my touch I smile and say, "I need to speak with your father and my mate-brothers briefly before joining you. You should rest since you must be tired after everything that's happened." She opens her mouth to refute me but all that comes out is a yawn nearly splitting her face in two. "Kelda can show you where the royal wing of the castle is located. I'd suggest taking the Queen's suite since it's the biggest second to your father's." Then I lean in and whisper in her ear, "It's also likely to have the biggest bed, little mate, and I for one would like to see you spread naked for your mates in it later."

Her face flushes red at my crass words, but I can see the heat and interest in her eyes. "Fine. As long as you all promise to find me after you're done with your secret meeting. Don't think I didn't notice your silent communication with each other just a moment ago. But … I am rather tired and a nap sounds wonderful. Where can I go to get a bath?"

Kelda and the rest of my mate's personal guard step forward when I flick a gaze at them. Then I say, "There is a public bath chamber and steam room underground below the castle but each room in the royal wing has its own bathroom. The natural magic of Elaria allows for free use of water in the hand basins and the bath tubs. Its already preheated as it comes from the Kevaril waterfall next to the castle."

Solveig looks pleased and excited as I describe one of the wondrous perks of living in Elaria.

I then look over at Kelda and say, "Can you take my mate to the queen's suite?" She nods with a fist over her heart before leaving with my mate in tow whom I quickly kiss on the cheek. Her other mates also lean in for quick signs of affection before turning to me with questioning looks.

"I hope it's okay that I suggested the queen's suite for us?" I ask King Lochlann directly once the door to the dining hall closes leaving only our small group here.

He smiles and nods approvingly at me before saying, "Yes. It is a good choice. It hasn't been used in a long time and is large enough for all of you. I'd suggest the suite I've been in but I would have to move all my prior possessions assuming they're all still in the same location."

"No. I think the queen's rooms will be plenty. Thank you, your majesty."

"Call me Lochlann, please. You are all my daughter's mates which makes you my son. Now ... why did you wish to speak with us?"

"Kaeden, are you worried about something? Something with Solveig?" Jorah asks me hesitantly tucking a notebook under his arm and focusing on me.

"No," I reply then hesitate trying to think of how I can explain this to my mate-brothers. "We need to plan a formal mate bonding ceremony for Solveig."

CHAPTER
Forty-Eight

SOLVEIG

After enjoying one of the best baths of my life, I fell into the large bed in the queen's chamber immediately. I must have fallen asleep right away since I don't remember anything afterwards.

Waking up feeling rested, I sit up and rub my eyes before looking around at the space. It's beautiful in an airy and elegant way. Whites, blues, gold, and soft greens make up the rich fabrics and decor in the queen's chambers. I didn't have a chance to really explore and take it all in when I came in here since I was so exhausted but now I avidly let my eyes wander around the room. Somehow, it's not even dusty after nearly a century of abandonment. *Must be magical…* I get up and peek out the glass doors leading to a balcony, noticing it's approaching sunset soon so I must have slept for several hours. But that's not what has me immobilized in awe when I look outside.

My balcony overlooks and nearly touches the steamy mist coming off the large waterfall that's in front of it. It's a miraculous and stupefying view. I push the balcony doors open and step out into the mist breathing deeply and feeling replenished. It's loud … the tumbling water down into the lake below.

I want to share the view with my mates and see their expressions of awe as well. That's when I realize they weren't here when I woke. In fact, as I walk back inside I notice the other half of the bed is undisturbed, so they mustn't have joined me. I close my eyes to try and focus on the bonds, but before I can concentrate a knock comes at the door.

"Come in!" I yell planting my hands on my hips in frustration that my mates didn't join me like they promised.

A young Elarian woman enters looking a bit apprehensive at my expression. She's pretty and by appearances likely similar in age to myself but I know looks can be deceiving in the Elarians. She has wavy blonde hair to her shoulders that falls forward over her pointed ears as she curtseys and bows her head.

I wave a hand for her to stand and say more pleasantly, "Sorry, I didn't mean to sound so upset with you. No need to be so formal outside of the public eye." She smiles and looks up at me more relaxed now. "Please call me Solveig. What's your name?"

"Pelia, my lady. I'm very happy and excited to meet you. We are second cousins."

A genuine smile overtakes my face at meeting another lost family member. Stepping forward, I reach and clasp her hand. "Well met then, cousin." Then I look around and ask, "Do you happen to know where my mates are?"

She gets a look in her eye with a small secret smile overtaking her face before she says, "I do. Its why I'm here …"

"Well, don't keep me in suspense!" I say laughing and throwing my hands up.

"I'm here to help you get ready. I brought a dress for you to wear too," Pelia says herding me towards the bathroom where she starts to run a bath sprinkling lavender in it.

"Get ready for what?" I ask confused but quickly jumping in the warm water. I'll never turn down a steaming hot bath here.

341

"For your mate bonding ceremony, my lady!" She giggles covering her mouth. "I figured they didn't tell you … Ha! *Men*!" She smiles and blows some hair out of her face.

"But … I'm already bonded to all five of them," I sit up in the water higher and show her my chest. "See? I have a completed mate marking here."

She eagerly inspects it and then sighs dreamily. "Beautiful, my lady—I mean—cousin. I can't wait until I find my mate … they say it's a connection that goes soul deep and makes you feel so content and complete its beyond words." She finishes washing my hair and then rubs some oil into it making it shine.

"Yes. It's like feeling at home snuggled in a warm embrace when you're with them. Although, sometimes it can be a bit invasive when you don't want them sorting through all your emotions," I say with a huff but still softly smiling. "So, now, why are we having this ceremony? And why did no one inform me earlier?"

"I feel like I'll always want to share all my thoughts and emotions with my mate but I guess you have a point," she replies to the first half of my words. "Mate bonding ceremonies are tradition. The Elders in the past didn't always acknowledge a mate bond unless the ceremony was performed before or if it was fated. But … these are different times and we couldn't even get into Elaria … so allowances were made. Your mate, Kaeden, has been planning everything for hours! I think your mates wanted it to be a surprise for tonight but came to realization that you'd need to get ready and know what to say for the rite."

I step out of the bath and dry while she rubs a lavender scented lotion on my skin. She gives me a beautiful pair of white lacy underwear before revealing the dress.

It's gorgeous with a sleek and sexy style that will likely hug all my curves. The long and formal length is interrupted with a high slit up the right side. It's a dark sapphire color matching my eyes but has clear shimmering beads along the long sleeves that nearly fall off the edges of my shoulders making my neck appear long and graceful. It has a sweetheart neckline and the beading extends from the sleeves to the top of the gown before fading out. Overall, it has a stunning effect and blends sexy with elegant in a way that I approve of. I just wonder who picked it and where it came from.

As if she read my mind Pelia reverently says, "I picked it with the King's approval from the royal wardrobe. It was … made for a queen but never used. It looked to be about your size although the hem may be just a bit long and the bust a bit tight but I think we can make it work."

"I love it. Thank you, cousin," I say running my hand over the silky material. "You have good taste."

She smirks. "I do. Don't I? Now, come on get in …" She picks the dress up and holds it up allowing me to step in while she pulls the sleeves up my arms. I didn't realize the back is mostly bare except for a small crystal embellished chain running from shoulder to shoulder to hold the sleeves in place.

It is a bit snug in my chest but I suppose it only enhances my cleavage which my mates will definitely enjoy. The hem of the dress is only an inch or so too long so it seems to still work fine.

Pelia doesn't let me admire the dress fully before she pushes me into a chair and starts working on styling my hair. She creates this twisting braided effect on the sides of my head that join in the back with half my hair curling down my spine. It's by far my favorite look and she smiles at me when I compliment her skill. The last touch she adds are a few perfectly bloomed temptress flowers in my hair giving off their unique scent and adding a slightly exotic look to my overall appearance. The effect is beautiful and I hope my mates like it because we hear a knock at the door preventing us from fussing any further.

I step into the slippers Pelia found in my size and approach the door. My father stands on the other side and when he sees me his entire face looks shocked and pale before it transforms quickly into proud smile with affection in his eyes.

"You look so similar to your mother when I met her …" he says wiping his eyes as if there's dust in them. "I'm sorry. You look radiant, daughter. Your mates are blessed men and I intend to make sure they are aware of it."

I smile back at him and pat his arm. "Don't be too hard on them. I *do* want to keep them. Now, tell me what all this is about?"

He steps into the room and dismisses Pelia who I smile and thank before she leaves. "I have something first before we go to your mates." He pulls a wooden box from under his arm that I didn't notice and sets it on the table. Then opening it up slowly reveals a simple, delicate silver crown. There are only three small clear crystals on it which make it more special in its simplicity. "This crown is your birthright. The Elarian Queen's crown. I want you to wear it tonight even though you are still a princess here and my heir."

I wipe my suddenly sweaty hands on the sides of my dress and hope I don't ruin it. This feels like an important moment when my father places the crown on my head with a slight tremor. It rests nestled in my hair like Pelia knew about its arrival. Once it's in place, I get a resounding feeling of power hum through my veins. It's a connection to the land that takes my breath away in its depth.

"You are likely feeling the power of Elaria," my father says in a deeply serious voice. "With this connection, comes a responsibility to the land and its people. Many look to us as rulers of Elaria to protect our power. But I already know you would do so even without your royal blood. You may find your powers come easier to you on demand, that you don't have to focus your will as much, and that many will understand your command subconsciously. Its force will get easier with time and now that Elaria knows you, you don't have to be wearing the crown to siphon power if needed. Now, come. Let's not make your mates wait any longer."

Taking a deep breath to adjust to the new mantle placed invisibly on my shoulders, I hug my father. "I'll try to do my best and not disappoint you, father." He smiles at me and then turns to the door tucking my hand in his right elbow.

"I know you won't Solveig. You could never disappoint me, child," my father replies. "You'll be a better ruler than me. I can tell. Just keep that wild protective spirit you have and our people will thrive in your care someday."

"Thank you. But you're right … we should get going," I say with a chuckle and opening my mate bond connection fully. "I can feel Ragnar's impatience and Kaeden's insecurity that things aren't going to plan. Jorah's curious and wanting to document the ceremony while Vidarr is anxious to come to me. Cadoc is … huh … relaxed, happy, and confident." I tilt my head in thought at my last mate's emotions as I walk towards the ceremony with my father.

He chuckles at their descriptions then says, "Prince Cadoc's likely been through so many ceremonies as a royal in his kingdom that this is the only one he's actually enjoying. You've chosen well for yourself, daughter. I like them all even Kaeden. I doubted him in your absence but he's proving me wrong. He really has gone to extra lengths today to make it special for you."

Feeling touched by Kaeden's thoughtfulness in planning everything, I send him feelings of love and affection down the bond. I can feel his responding surprise and then love. "They're more than I could have ever hoped for. I can't wait to see what's next."

CHAPTER
Forty-Nine

SOLVEIG

Y ou do need to know a certain phrase for the ceremony, Solveig," my father says turning to me before a closed door. He slowly tells me the phrase to memorize and has me repeat it. Then, he tucks my hand into his elbow again and the doors open in front of us. Before I know what's happening, he's walking me outside into a luscious garden filled with temptress flowers and surrounding candles. Elarians are seated interspersed with nature in the garden or in the trees and everyone is smiling. I see several nods and a few palms overlying their chests in respect. I notice the catchki to the right—some in two legged form and some in their shifted forms. And to the left, I spot Tempest smiling at me. I haven't been able to speak with him much and I miss our casual banter. I don't see Ara next to him as we walk making me confused. He must see my questioning expression since he flicks his eyes towards the lake which has a raised deck connected off the castle's outdoor patio, and I see her standing on one side wearing a crimson gown that blends prettily with the sunset in the background.

My excited gaze then takes in the other occupants on the deck. My grandfather stands in glowing white, formal robes at the end of the deck which does look impressive especially since he has two glowing orbs of fire hovering in the air next to him and giving off a soft glow that only adds to the magic atmosphere of tonight. I look to the right of the deck and see *them* … my mates. Their appearance distracts me so thoroughly that I trip over the hem of my gown. Lucky for me, my father smoothly catches me and continues to lead me forward as if nothing happened.

My mates are all in similar outfits consisting of Elarian formalwear with a touch of their own unique flare. They're each wearing form fitting black pants with black boots. As my heated gaze travels up their muscular legs, I hungrily take in their bare chests proudly displaying their mate markings on the left upper side. Rich black leather harnesses strap around their chests to their right shoulder which has an overlying piece of shoulder armor and connects with a draping cape down their back.

Ragnar's is all black fading into a dark gray ombre effect while Vidarr's is a slate gray color throughout. Cadoc chose blue matching my dress and Jorah a dark brown. Lastly, I see Kaeden step forward as I approach. His cape is a hunter green with gold along the edges in a swirling leaf design matching his rune tattoo for nature. They look regal and imposing as a group together but the combined effect on me is alluring. I'm drawn to them as though compelled by a spell. They're too attractive for their own good and I can see several women in the surrounding garden eyeing them appreciatively. Not that my men acknowledge them.

I'm led to stand next to Ara on the deck and my grandfather smiles at me with approval.

"Welcome, granddaughter," Elder Aren says projecting his voice to everyone which is easy given the nearby lake. Everyone falls silent and my grandfather turns to Lochlann. "When you're ready …"

My father untangles my hand from his arm and turns to me saying in a formal voice, "May your mates be worthy and provide you with a fulfilling life of love. I approve of these men." His voice echoes across the area before he leans in and kisses my forehead. As he goes to stand behind my grandfather overseeing the ceremony, I see him wink and then hear my grandfather again.

"These men are deemed worthy of a mate bond with our treasured Princess Solveig, heir to Elaria. A mate bond, connecting the soul and inner magic of each person's entity, is not a trivial thing. It should be tended and honored with reverence and delicacy. Take this to heart … mates are forever. There is no one else for you going forward," Elder Aren says with all seriousness. "If there is anyone who contests these men as worthy of our princess, may they step forward in challenge now."

I jolt in surprise at his words. I wasn't privy to all the inner workings of the ceremony and definitely wasn't aware that other Elarians could challenge our bond. I look over at my five mates standing across from me and see determination and warning in their stances. They're fierce to watch as they seem ready to take on all of Daelarias … for *me*. Its humbling.

When no one speaks, Elder Aren continues the ceremony. "Please step forward and announce your status, name and commitment as we bind you together." My grandfather reaches for my left wrist and holds it in place in front of him. He then twines a glowing thin string in a spiral around my left middle finger.

"*I,* Ragnar Destraavi, King of the Drakoni and fated soulmate of Solveig present myself for our mate bond." Ragnar smiles proudly down at me while my grandfather twines the other end of the glowing string on my finger to his left middle finger. "As the power wills my soul, may I forever be connected to your light."

I stand there for a moment in awe as the string around our fingers glows to a nearly blinding level then realize I'm supposed to respond. "As the power wills my soul, may I forever be connected to your light." On my last words, the string seems to sink into my skin leaving a shimmery golden tattoo that's a mirror image of the one on Ragnar's finger. He leans in and kisses me to the cheers of the Elarian people before stepping back with a smile.

This process continues for each of my mates and marking each one of my fingers of the left hand as my grandfather twines a new magical string on me each time. The last one to complete the ceremony with me is Kaeden.

"*I*, Kaeden Vailspire, prior warrior in the Elarian army of Light, Captain of the guard for Laevaris and fated mate of Solveig present myself for our mate bond." Kaeden's smile is so big and full of joy it could fill the sky above us. Once my thumb is twined with his in the glowing string, he continues. "As the power wills my soul, may I forever be connected to your light."

I repeat the phrase and as soon as the strand dissolves magically into our skin, I jump into his arms kissing him animatedly. Everyone hollers and whistles in appreciation while I hear Vidarr tease, "Why didn't we all get that kind of kiss? I feel cheated …"

I break away from Kaeden's lips and smile while I see Cadoc smack Vi on the back of his head. Kaeden slides me down his body slowly and his eyes fill with heat.

"Finally official now, *mate*," Kaeden whispers in a sexy deep voice as his hand trails over the exposed skin of my low back.

I don't get to respond since my grandfather clears his throat loudly and says, "In celebration of their mate bond, please enjoy a small feast on the patio." Everyone cheers again and disperses towards the food. Grandfather leans in and says to me, "Sorry it's not a grander affair but we had limited time and resources given the situation. I just hope you—"

"It's perfect! I couldn't have imagined a better ceremony." I lean over and kiss his cheek. "I don't need grand. I just need my family. Thank you." He kisses the back of my hand and nods before wandering off into the Elarians celebrating.

My father approaches next and embraces me. "Congratulations, daughter. You were perfect. And—I suppose they did well too. Enjoy the night!" He pats each of my mates on the shoulder before he too disappears in the crowd of well-wishers.

Two feminine arms wrap around me from behind and I hear Ara's voice.

"I'm so happy for you, sister. Now I guess it truly is official! Be careful with my brother … he tends to get moody most days and overly protective but I guess you already know that." Ara kisses me on the temple and then her gaze sharply whips to the side. She growls out in a voice, "I have to go break a few Elarian women's fingers … be back later."

Before I can respond, she practically flies over to Tempest who's surrounded by several woman and I chuckle when I see her bend one of their hands backwards off his arm. I hear Vidarr laugh in my ear as he leans down and rests his chin on my shoulder from behind me. He's clearly watching the spectacle of Tempest and Ara like I am.

My emotions suddenly turn melancholy for a moment as my thoughts drift to my past. I feel a flash of self-doubt at whether I'm worthy of my men. *Maybe, I'm too damaged … too dark for them. There's so many other … untainted options for a mate out there.* I think to myself as I see all the pretty Elarian women in the garden. Stepping further onto the deck, I look over the water searching for the feeling of contentedness and peace that I had a moment before.

I feel them approach before I see them. My mates all surround me in a comforting presence and our mate bond thrums in response to our proximity.

Obviously aware of my turbulent emotions, Ragnar asks mentally, *Why are you feeling upset and sad, little warrior? Are you having regrets?*

No. Nothing of the sort. It's just … I say mentally hesitating. I can feel all of my mates listening in and curious as to my response. *I was having a moment of insecurity in myself. I'm full of shadows and dark thoughts. You don't think someone else ... someone less damaged ... would be a better choice for you? How can I make all of you happy ...*

My mates are filled with various emotions through our tethered connection after my words.

Ragnar considers me for a moment before he grabs my left hand lacing our fingers together.

Then he confidently says out loud, "Happy endings usually start with sorrow. The start of something doesn't really matter since it's in the past and the finish is only a trophy of your accomplishment. But it's the grit and determination of a warrior—a survivor—to keep going that will keep the outcome of our success alive. Happiness is yours, little warrior. You just have to hold onto it because I've already found it ... with you."

His words make me softly smile up at him in gratefulness while inside I feel a glow of warmth. He's right ... I am a survivor and I'm stronger for it. I just have to hold onto the happiness and not let go.

Vidarr grabs my attention next when he tugs on the end of my hair and pulls me into his all-encompassing embrace.

He whispers to me in his sexy voice, "I'll be your shadows, sunshine, if you can be my light. Sometimes I have dark thoughts too. The past is a hard medicine to swallow. Rise above the shadows and keep that beautiful face in the sun." He tilts my chin up before leaning down and nipping me on the lower lip. He kisses me so passionately I nearly forget what we were talking about.

Cadoc, my stern and fiercely protective mate, pushes Vi back with a hand to his chest as he says to Vidarr, "Careful, I see Vabira heading your way ..."

"Where?" Vidarr pulls away and looks frantically over his shoulder while Cadoc chuckles into my neck. He's clearly fooling Vi since there's no catchki near us and its common knowledge that Vidarr isn't a fan of the large predator woman scenting herself all over him.

While Vi is distracted, Cadoc boxes me up against the deck railing and kisses up my neck before he says, "I don't want anyone else but you, Solveig. I want all parts of you … your past, your trauma, your deep inner thoughts, and your happiness. I want our future, don't doubt it. I love you."

"I love you—all of you. And—I want that too," I reply, kissing him and running my hands over his perfectly formed chest muscles. One of his hands finds the slit in my dress and slides his callused fingers up my thigh in a teasing manner making me wish for privacy with my mates. *Now!*

"I'm with you, Sol, no matter what kind of trouble you get into or how reckless you are." Jorah interjects my wayward thoughts from next to me. "You were my friend first before becoming my mate and I'll always be there if you need me to hold you in the dark. Love you."

Jorah's hand somehow joins Cadoc's along my inner thigh and I feel my core clench in anticipation. I open my hooded eyes not sure when they closed, and I see Kaeden watching their hands slide up my leg with his own desire shining back at me.

"You're evil … every one of you! Maybe it's not such a chore to be tied to all of you," I say in a teasing manner, "if you take care of me later."

That silences them all quickly and they crowd around me as our bond fills with sensual thoughts and desire. I gaze back at each of them and feel a peace come over me again.

Dropping my taunting tone of voice, I speak in a deeply emotional voice stating, "I'm not sure where I'll end up, but I *do* know I'll be starting it with all of you. I love you. Now, let's leave this party and start our own … back in my room."

We're all smiling as we silently slip away into the shadows.

ACKNOWLEDGMENTS

I want to thank YOU, and all of my readers, for taking the time to join Solveig on her venture of self-discovery, love, and justice. She's truly one of those characters that inspires me as a woman to be stronger and has latched onto my thoughts indefinitely. Hopefully, she will do the same for you. All the men in this story contributed in some way changing Solveig into the strong woman she becomes, and I think each one individually brought something important to the table in regards to Solveig's inner growth. I've met and had the honor of working with several women with a traumatic past, and I'm deeply inspired by their strength. As Marilyn Monroe said, "Strong women don't have attitudes, we have standards." No woman should feel like she doesn't have a voice in her future, her body or how she is treated as a person.

Special thanks to my biggest supporter and best friend, who never made me feel stupid or self-conscious for writing and doing something I enjoy. Even though it involved fantasy, romance and polyamory, she still cheered me on and listened while I excitedly told her about each step in my process of becoming an author. She gave me some of my confidence to finally publish. Love you, bestie!

Last but definitely not least, to my crazy and amazing boys (who I hope don't read this for obvious reasons) and my husband Chris who let me pursue a dream of mine in writing even though there were certainly more lucrative jobs out there for someone with my education. I love you guys.

Please look for my next series going forward and I'll try to do even BETTER for all of you as a writer!

STALK ME!

ABOUT THE AUTHOR

J.L.Cres is an author of romantic fantasy, paranormal romance, and reverse harem romances. In her stories you'll find strong, kick-a** female lead characters with sometimes several love interests.

She lives in Ohio with her husband, three sons, goldendoodle Freya, way too many barn cats, a horse named Chance, a goat named Noah, chickens, guineas, ducks and the random rabbit that ends up stuck in their pool. She's a lover of reading, wine, coffee and dry sarcasm. When she isn't writing, she's usually toting her children to sports or school or you'll find her using her medical background to treat her boys' frequent rough-housing injuries.

Made in the USA
Monee, IL
10 September 2024